Elisa[...] [...]g car[...] [...]egan when she finished third in Harlequin [...] [...]ou Can Write contest in 2013 and she hasn't looked back. She teaches Primary school but would rather write full time because, unlike five-year-olds, her characters generally do what she tells them. She spends most of her spare time reading and is a pro at cooking one-handed while holding a book.

She lives in Cheshire because the car broke down there in 1999 and she never left.

elisabethhobbes.co.uk

twitter.com/ElisabethHobbes
facebook.com/ElisabethHobbes

DAUGHTER OF THE SEA

ELISABETH J. HOBBES

One More Chapter
a division of HarperCollins*Publishers* Ltd
1 London Bridge Street
London SE1 9GF
www.harpercollins.co.uk

HarperCollins*Publishers*
1st Floor, Watermarque Building, Ringsend Road
Dublin 4, Ireland

This paperback edition 2021
1
First published in Great Britain in ebook format
by HarperCollins*Publishers* 2021

A catalogue record of this book
is available from the British Library

ISBN: 978-0-00-840015-6

Printed and bound in the UK using 100% Renewable Electricity
by CPI Group (UK) Ltd

For Stanley: top puppy who sat by my feet while I finished this book – a short life but an excellent one. And for Missy, who joined us as a foster pup during edits and is now a permanent member of the family.

Chapter One

Effie Cropton was not a religious woman, but when she saw the wicker basket tossed atop the waves, the first thing that popped into her mind was the story of the infant Moses in the bulrushes. She was so surprised at the image springing to mind that when she heard the cry of an infant, she assumed it was her imagination and dismissed it, turning her attention back to gathering toothed-wrack and dulse from the rocks that jutted out along the tideline.

When she heard the thin, despairing wail for a second time she looked up, searching for a gull, but none circled above her in the steel-grey sky.

As the cry came for the third time, she could not mistake it for anything other than a human child.

The beach was deserted. The shortest day of the year was the coldest day by a long stretch too. Only Effie had ventured onto the shore.

The basket that now pitched alarmingly up and down, disappearing behind foaming crests, was the only possible source of the voice. Effie did not pause to wonder why a lone infant might be bobbing along the coast, but pulled off her shawl and bonnet, kicked away her sturdy clogs and waded out into the sea.

The ink-black water was as cold as you would expect for Yorkshire on Midwinter's Day when the shadows were at their shortest and the weak sun barely managed to fight its way through the clouds to offer meagre comfort. The first few steps over the shingle were unpleasant, but as the sea reached Effie's knees, the cold grew biting. She gasped aloud as the painful iciness stabbed her flesh and numbed her limbs.

She almost turned back, but the basket had floated closer to the jagged black rocks and the cry came once again, high and urgent. She persevered, pushing her way further out. The surging tide felt as thick as treacle, dragging at her skirts and petticoats. Her feet were bare – she would not waste a pair of stockings on a seaweed-gathering errand – and their soles scraped against rocks and periwinkles, leaving deep scratches. Now Effie appreciated the cold water. The soreness would come later when she had feeling in her feet once more, but for now she was grateful for the numbness.

The turning tide threatened to pull the basket further out to sea, catching it in eddies and tossing it to and fro out of Effie's reach with a vicious playfulness that made her think of a cat toying with a sprat on the harbour wall. She was waist deep before she succeeded in grabbing the edge and closing her stiff fingers around the handle. She fought to make her way back to the shore against the strong current, struggling as her sodden petticoats wrapped around her legs and conspired with the waves to drag her under. Panting and teeth rattling with cold, she staggered out of the water. She gave a cry of triumph and relief and crouched by her discarded shawl and clogs where the shingle became sand, well out of reach of the waves, to examine her salvage.

The basket was shallow and wide, and on closer inspection looked more like a cross between a nest and a raft rather than anything that could be used for carrying groceries from market.

It did, however, contain a baby.

A girl.

The child looked no more than three or four months old. She looked well fed, with wrinkled rolls of fat on her legs and arms, but her skin had a sullen grey sheen to it. She stared up at Effie with dark-brown eyes edged with flecks that were green like the sea trapped in a rock pool. Her pupils were too large and black, giving the impression they belonged to a face more ancient than centuries. The hairs on the back of Effie's neck began to prickle as she looked into the old eyes.

The baby was snuggled in a fur that was the exact same colour as the deep-brown down on her head. When Effie pulled the folds from around the child it was the softest thing she had ever touched. As Effie drew the furs back, the girl screwed her face up and began to cry: a high, angry wail that showed no sign of stopping. As well she might do, given her situation. She was naked beneath the wrapping, with not even a napkin to cover her modesty. It was a wonder she had not frozen to death, as Effie now realised she herself was in danger of doing if she did not get out of her sodden skirts.

Effie picked the baby up, fur and all, and held her close, bundling the soft pelt around her. The baby began screaming in earnest, but as Effie hugged her tight the tone changed to one of desperation and she began rooting at Effie's blouse. The cry was of hunger, not fear.

Effie's son Jack was five months old and the sound of the

girl's keening, coupled with the warm nuzzling face that butted against her breast, caused Effie's milk to gather in a hot rush. Effie ignored the cold wind that was sinking below her flesh and deep into her bones. She pulled her shawl around her shoulders, unbuttoned her blouse and guided the small mouth to her nipple. The baby latched on with a strength that bordered on painful and sucked with a determination far beyond that which Jack had ever demonstrated. The small brown head looked pale and delicate nestled in the depths of the red woollen shawl.

'You're starving, aren't you, chick,' Effie murmured.

While the child nursed, Effie walked to the edge of the shingle, searching the sea for any indication of the child's origin. The baby could not have sprung from nowhere, but the sea was empty. No pleasure boats would be making trips along the coast from Whitby at this time of year and, even if they had been, even the most inattentive nursemaid would have noticed her charge fall overboard long before the craft headed as far down the coast as Allendale Head. Besides, what child would be taken out for an excursion dressed in such an unusual manner even on the balmiest summer afternoon, never mind the very middle of winter?

Out beyond the safety of Whitby Harbour, shipwrecks weren't uncommon, especially in winter. If the baby had been on board a ship, her mother might have had no time to gather clothes before the waves claimed the vessel. The child might have been thrown hastily into the basket in an attempt to save her.

A prickle ran the length of Effie's spine and she did her best to dismiss the thought. Her husband, John, had left Whitby on the cargo ship *Serenity* that morning, heading for Norwegian ports. He would be gone a little under two months, and until

4

he returned safely to land Effie would not rest easy. There was no evidence of a shipwreck and it would be unlikely that one small basket could withstand the waves when nothing else had come safely to shore.

All the same, someone had placed the child in the basket deliberately, perhaps for safety, and most likely in haste. A sea fret was beginning to rise, veiling the water with grey, drifting into shore where it would become mist. Effie would find no answers staring at the disappearing waves and in the meantime both she and the child would be in danger of catching ill from cold. It would not do to stay too long on the beach. She eased the child off her breast, ignoring the plaintive cries for more milk. Jack would be waiting to nurse when she returned to collect him from her grandmother and she did not want to deny him his supper.

Effie wrapped the girl in the fur and bound her securely across her front with the shawl. She looped her basket of seaweed over one arm and tucked the child beneath the other. With a final glance at the sea, she walked determinedly along the shingle with the mystery still snagging at her mind like a torn fingernail.

The wind grew stronger. Effie's legs and feet became twin pillars of ice as she struggled over the shingle with her skirt and petticoats clinging to them. She was breathing heavily by the time she reached the top of the steps cut into the cliff. She sat for a moment on the gently sloping grass to rest her feet and scanned the sea again. The waves were grey and surging. Heavily laden clouds had darkened the sky in the distance. Her eye caught a distant flash on the horizon of something silver, but it was gone before she had properly noticed it.

She was still sitting on the damp grass, rubbing feeling back into her stinging feet, when a familiar voice hailed her.

'Good afternoon, Mrs Cropton.'

Walter Danby was walking along the cliff path as he did most days at this time, swinging a stick and whistling to himself. He ambled over and pulled his brown felt hat from his head, smoothing his unruly blond waves down. He gave Effie a smile that was, in truth, a little too warm for a young unmarried man to give to a young married woman, but they had known each other for years so Effie excused the overfamiliarity.

Walter lived in Allendale Hall which stood high on the cliffs set back in grounds behind the village. His father was a partner in the alum works a mile inland which employed most of the villagers who weren't in sea-based occupations. Effie's late mother had been a schoolteacher's daughter and her late father had been a senior clerk in a bank. As such Mrs Danby had shown an interest in Effie.

At least until she had disgraced herself in the eyes of the village that already saw her as an outsider.

She clambered to her feet, clutching the baby, and returned Walter's smile warmly. Sometimes, when he wasn't being too serious, she wished Walter had finished his studies at Owens College in Manchester in enough time to have asked for her hand before she took up with John Cropton, but she kept those thoughts hidden even deeper inside herself.

'How is young Jack today?' Walter asked, craning his head to look at the baby nestled against Effie's breast. 'Is he going to be a handsome fellow like his father?'

A flicker of desire made Effie's stomach ripple. John was very handsome, with a warm, open face, sandy hair bleached blonder by the sun and a brawny physique developed over years of physical work. He had been seen as a catch among the fishing families in the village, and Effie being the one to snare him hadn't helped her make friends with the young women.

'I hope so, but this isn't Jack.' Effie drew her shawl back to reveal the small head. The baby looked pinker now she was warm and fed and her silken hair had dried to match the colour of the seal pelt exactly.

Walter looked at Effie properly and gaped, reaching out a hand before drawing it hastily back.

'You're soaking wet!'

She explained how she had come upon the child and Walter frowned.

'Wading into the sea, of all places, on a whim! You put yourself at risk and it's hardly the conduct of a respectable woman.'

'You sound as old as your father, talking about respectable women,' Effie said haughtily, returning Walter's frown. Walter looked slightly injured and Effie felt a small pang of remorse. Walter was more forgiving than any man she knew, even though her habit of wandering alone along the shore to quieten her mind confused him. Walter's preferred method of relaxing was to lose himself in a scientific treatise in a comfortable armchair.

'It wasn't a whim, as it proved,' Effie continued. 'If I hadn't gone in, who knows what would have befallen the poor chick. There was no one else around to help.'

'Which is even greater reason why you shouldn't have risked your life,' Walter said, frowning again, though this time Effie suspected it was born of alarm not disapproval. He lectured her out of concern for her safety.

She put her hand lightly on the sleeve of his riding coat.

'Walter, please. Not now.'

He tailed off and looked down at her hand, his pale cheeks

colouring slightly at the overfamiliar touch. She straightened her bonnet and gave him a smile.

'Walter, I know you mean well but I'm cold and need to collect Jack from my grandmother's cottage. I can't stop here talking all afternoon in the hope I'll dry off and this poor mite needs to be inside.'

Walter looked contrite.

'Of course. I'm so sorry, I wasn't thinking. You must be half frozen to death.'

He shrugged off his heavy jacket, leaving him standing only in waistcoat and shirt. He held it out it to Effie with a keen nod.

'You'll freeze as you walk home,' she said.

'Not as much as you will. Please let me make amends for keeping you standing here so long.'

'Thank you. What a dear friend you are.'

'Indeed.' Walter draped the coat around her shoulders and tucked it about her as best he could. The effect of shielding her from the worst of the wind was instantaneous. Effie folded the shawl back around the baby's head, glad of the thick tweed to ward off the wind.

'What else can I do to help you?' Walter asked. 'Shall I ride to Whitby and see if the poorhouse will take the girl? They are always willing to take foundlings.'

He meant well but Effie clutched the child tighter, baulking at the thought of surrendering the child to the stern superintendents who ran the stark-walled institution.

'I'll take her home with me until someone comes to claim her.'

'In that case, tomorrow I'll ride to Whitby and bring news if anyone has lost a child.' He walked on with a lingering smile back at Effie that she returned.

Effie wasn't a witch, though when she had arrived in the hamlet of Allendale Head, some of the older villagers had whispered that, given who her grandmother was, she might one day show talents that had not yet emerged.

Effie, then aged fourteen and newly orphaned, had no time for such talk and did not even dignify such superstitious gossip with a response. A gaggle of village children was gathered round Alice Millbourne's door to whisper and dare each other to knock. Effie shooed them away briskly and they ran off, giggling with the high spirits of the young who had been waiting far too long for Christmas Day to arrive. She shook her head in exasperation but smiled and went inside.

'Effie, is that you?' Alice called from inside the pantry. 'Wrap the seaweeds in the damp dishcloth, will you?'

Effie did as she was asked, keeping some back for herself. Alice used it for her poultices and ointments. Effie liked to paint it.

'Why are you wearing Walter Danby's coat?' Alice asked, as she bustled into the kitchen. Her sharp eyes narrowed suspiciously as she looked at Effie. 'Your husband is away and I didn't think you the type to carry on with another man.'

'I'm not carrying on with Walter and you know it,' Effie said indignantly. 'I've been faithful to John for our whole marriage.'

John Cropton was ten years older than his wife and had been a bachelor longer than many thought he should, given his looks. He was shy and particular in his ways, and it had surprised everyone in the village when he asked Effie to marry him. People were perhaps less surprised at why when Effie's belly began to swell after too few months of wedded bliss for the numbers to add up.

Whether Effie had trapped John or John had trapped Effie into marriage was the subject of some debate among those who enjoyed speculating. Perhaps neither of them had intended to trap or be trapped, but the end result was the same. The man whom the village had believed would end his days a bachelor found a wife, and Effie had fallen from the middle to the working class.

Despite the beginnings of their marriage, Effie and John were content with each other, especially when John departed on the *Serenity*. Effie liked her husband well enough and relished the nights in their bed, but she quickly discovered that his reputation for shyness was in part because he had few opinions to express and was dull-witted. She was careful to keep such thoughts to herself, knowing that bold opinions might be frowned upon in a young wife. The voyages brought Effie two months of welcome solitude where she was free to wander along the shore, gather shells and seaweeds to sketch and please herself with when and what she ate and had no puzzled expression to contend with when she devoured the periodicals and books Walter lent her. She always welcomed John back with a kiss and she was reasonably confident he never suspected she enjoyed his absence as much as his presence.

'I met Walter by accident on the cliff path, if you must know.'

Effie's cheeks coloured slightly. It had been an accident on her part, though she couldn't swear the same on Walter's behalf.

She went to greet her son. Jack was sleeping in the cradle before the fire. Effie had been rocked in this cradle as a babe, as had her father before her. Seeing her son in it gave Effie a warm rush of contentment, tinged with sadness that both her parents had been taken by influenza before they had met their first grandchild. John, too, had lost his father to the sea and his mother to the resulting grief before he had married Effie. She stroked Jack's head and decided to let him sleep a little longer so she could enjoy a chat in peace.

'Walter gave me his coat to keep me warm because I couldn't wear my shawl. Look.'

She unwound the shawl and revealed the baby. The girl was sleeping, her arms and legs tucked up and her head burrowed down against her chest, reminding Effie of a mouse huddled in its burrow. Effie stroked the girl's head as she had done with Jack and caught a distinct odour of the sea. The child shifted, close to waking up.

Alice's eyes narrowed. 'Make tea and tell me everything.'

Effie explained the events of the afternoon. All the while she spoke, Alice sat silently and listened, never taking her eyes from the soft brown head.

When Effie had finished her tale, Alice put down her teacup.

'Show me her properly,' Alice said.

Effie loosened the shawl and laid the child, still wrapped in her fur, down on the rug in front of the fire. Alice held her hand about an inch above the girl's body and passed it slowly from head to toe and back again. She sucked her teeth loudly.

'There are easier ways to be rid of a baby,' she muttered. 'And you saw no one in the water?'

'I couldn't see any trace of where she had come from,' Effie said. 'No boat of any kind.'

'I didn't mention boats.' Alice fixed her granddaughter with sharp black eyes. 'Mayhap she is from the sea itself.'

Effie laid down her cup. 'From the sea? Do you believe in mermaids casting their children out?' She shook her head and gave a soft laugh.

Alice didn't smile.

'You used to believe when you were younger,' she said, eyeing Effie seriously.

They both glanced at the shelf where Alice kept her only four books: A Bible, a well-thumbed copy of Mrs Beeton, Tennyson's *Idylls* and Macdonald's *Dealing with the Fairies*.

'I'm not a child any longer and this isn't a fairy story, Grandmother. We are but twenty years away from the twentieth century,' Effie said gently.

Alice said nothing, only looked back at the child who gazed up at them both with those unnerving, knowing eyes. Effie shuddered. Too long in her grandmother's company and she might start to believe there was some truth in such nonsense that the strange eyes were the sign of a changeling.

'She was put there deliberately,' Effie said. 'And whoever did it – by which I mean a person, not a nymph or sprite or mermaid – took the trouble to keep her warm and safe in the basket and fur.'

She stroked the child's hand and the girl gurgled. 'She was loved, at least to some degree.'

They were prevented from any further discussion because Jack woke and began to wail from his cradle in the urgent tone that Effie recognised as hunger. The cry was immediately taken up by the baby on the rug. Effie brought Jack back to the chair and began to nurse him, but the cries of the other child couldn't be ignored. She put the girl to her other breast and contrived by holding the babies awkwardly beneath her arms, to feed them both together. She looked at the two heads, the tawny brown of the baby beside Jack's lighter colour. The girl's pull was stronger but she kept feeding until Jack pulled away, sated, before she too loosened her mouth. It seemed to Effie that she had waited until the boy finished before deciding to stop. Did babies have an instinct for that sort of thing? It was most likely coincidental.

'I'll take her home with me tonight,' Effie told Alice. 'She'll need feeding again.'

Alice poured Effie another cup of tea. 'Aye, she will, and you've taken the burden on. I hope you don't find you've taken on more of a duty than you intend to.'

Effie shook her head at the ominous tone. No wonder the villagers thought what they did of Alice with her talk of portents and unearthly creatures.

'Walter Danby said he would try to find out where she might be from. And it won't be the sea itself.'

The storm that had been on the horizon when Effie had left the beach had found its way to shore and Effie narrowly escaped a drenching, but the light was already fading when she reached the neat cottage that stood apart from the village. She slammed the door shut and bolted it, lit the oil lamp, and threw a shovelful of coal into the iron range to wake the fire. John had lived all his life in the cottage and Effie loved it. It was all on one floor, with a large room that served as dining room, kitchen and sitting room in one. There was a small pantry and a separate bedroom to the back. Enough for the needs of a couple and a small child.

When the chill left the room, Effie put both babies side by side on the rug to kick their legs while she cut a slice of bread and a chunk of creamy cheese. She ate her supper beside the babies and watched with amusement as their kicking brought them into contact with each other and their eyes grew wondrous as they realised they were not alone. When they began to grow fractious and tired she put them to bed, top to tail, in Jack's cradle.

The fire had taken quickly and the room was snugly warm. Effie hung her dulse and toothed-wrack to dry out on lines above the stove. They waved in a draught, long strands trailing and leaving shadows like fingers across the walls and tables. Effie intended to sketch them before they dried, in preparation for adding colours when she had the chance, but as she sat with charcoal and paper, her mind kept returning to the basket and the fur. She laid down her stick and unfolded the sealskin, which was now completely dry.

It was so soft as she smoothed it out on the table that Effie had the urge to bury her face in it. She ran her hands over the full shape of it and lifted it to her nose. It had the same sea-salt tang as the baby's head. It was an odd choice of protection for the child to be wrapped in. Before she went to bed, she folded it neatly and placed it in the basket, which had all but disintegrated. She put them both in the cupboard in her bedroom on the high shelf next to the linens and forgot about them.

Chapter Two

W alter knocked on the door of Effie's cottage the next night, just as the bells at St Stephen and All Saints were ringing the start of Evensong.

'I'm sorry for disturbing you at such an hour, but I have some news.'

His face was grave. Effie shivered. Even if he had been smiling warmly, the fact that the devout young man was here and not attending the service would have indicated something was amiss.

'Please, come in. It's always good to see you, Walter. I'll make some tea. Or would you prefer coffee?'

'Nothing, thank you,' Walter said.

Then after a pause, 'Yes, perhaps a cup would be welcome. Will you take one yourself?'

'Of course. You know I never pass up the chance.'

Walter gave her something like a passing smile, but it was so unlike his usual warm one that Effie's stomach tightened with anxiety. She bustled around filling the iron kettle and putting it on the stove. Walter stood by the door. He was wearing his heavy winter coat and it reminded Effie that she still had his riding jacket. She told him to take a seat by the fire and went into her bedroom to take it from the chair where she had folded it neatly.

The two babies were sleeping peacefully, heads at either end of the cradle. Effie moved quietly so as not to disturb them and paused to look down as they slept.

Jack lay neatly swaddled, but the foundling girl had wriggled free of her covers and lay with her hands thrown up beside her head. She had taken a long time to settle to sleep and had been fitful all day. Effie pulled the blanket around her, hoping she would not wake. Whatever Walter had to say would be best said without a wailing infant.

Walter had not sat down but now was warming himself by the fireplace, watching the flames through the grate. He thanked Effie for the coat and folded it over one arm.

'Have you discovered something about the child?' Effie asked.

Walter's grey eyes grew serious. 'Can we wait until the tea is ready before speaking?' he asked.

Feeling more uneasy by the minute, Effie spooned leaves into the teapot and glared at the kettle. A watched pot never boiled, Alice was fond of saying, though Effie pointed out that it made little difference to the water if it was being observed or not. This pot did seem to be taking much longer than was necessary out of spite and as the flames licked the underside of the kettle, Effie's sense of foreboding grew greater and greater. She poured two cups and handed one to Walter. On her own she would have used one of her pottery mugs, but Walter merited use of her mother's china tea set.

'What have you discovered, Walter? I know there's something. I can tell.'

'I rode to Whitby this morning and asked about any news of a shipwreck.'

He took another sip of tea and placed the cup and saucer on the mantelpiece. Effie wanted to shake him and snap at him to hurry with what he wanted to say, rather than draw it out so tortuously. She reined herself in. Walter raised his eyes.

'You were right. There was a shipwreck. News arrived this morning that the *Serenity* has been lost with all hands. Effie, I'm so sorry.'

Effie sank onto the chair. Her legs felt as if they had not the strength to support her. Her hands began to shake. The china cup rattling on its saucer filled her ears, making far too loud and harsh a sound for such a small object. Tea splashed over the rim of her cup and landed on her skirt. She gave a loud cry of exasperation. Walter reached out and gently took the cup from her hand.

'No survivors?' She looked at him pleadingly. 'Are you certain? If it was only this morning...'

'None have been discovered,' Walter said gently. 'A smaller boat came across the wreckage drifting at first light.'

He stopped abruptly and finally sat down, taking the chair opposite Effie's – John's chair, which he would never sit in again. A sob welled up in her throat, bursting out loudly.

'I'm sorry. You don't need to know that,' Walter said. He thought it was the detail that pained her. How could she explain that it was the chair without looking foolish or making Walter feel guilty?

'Tell me everything. I want to know,' Effie insisted. 'Was it the storm?'

'I don't think it was.' Walter looked doubtful but continued his tale. 'There was said to be a great crack in the hull that split the wood. It must have grounded on something with prodigious force, but no one could say what it was. They weren't near the Brigg.'

The Brigg was treacherous, being mainly below the water, but the captain and crew knew the waters well, having sailed them since they put on long trousers. They knew where the currents pulled strongest and which routes must be avoided in bad conditions.

Effie put her face in her hands. John was gone. It was scarcely believable, though every woman whose man worked on the sea lived with the possibility that her husband would not come back, from the moment they parted until she saw him on dry land and safely back. A sailor's life was hard and hazardous and a sailor's wife waited for this news whenever her man set sail.

She felt she should cry. She wanted to, but no tears came. She reached for her tea and drank what remained. The stain had spread across her skirt, leaving a patch of deep brown. It scarcely mattered. She would be wearing black from now on.

'The crew who found the *Serenity* said it was almost as if something rose up from beneath and struck the ship,' Walter said.

He sounded intrigued. It was a mystery, but not one that Effie had any inclination to consider.

'Thank you for coming to tell me,' she said, pressing Walter's hand.

His cheeks flushed. 'I'm sorry I had to bear such evil news.'

'I'm glad it was a friend who told me,' Effie said. She rose and picked up Walter's teacup – a subtle hint that it was time for him to leave. Thankfully he took it and picked up his extra coat.

'If I can be of any help in the coming days, or weeks,' Walter said, 'please don't hesitate to call. I am at your service.'

'Thank you.' It was an acknowledgement rather than an acceptance and she hoped he took it as such.

'If you wish to come to church with me in the morning I will gladly pray at your side. I know you aren't accustomed to going, but...'

'Thank you, but no,' Effie said, a little more briskly. 'John is – was – the churchgoer, not I.'

She didn't know whether to be affronted or amused that Walter saw her loss as an opportunity to bring her into the fold he so greatly valued. She edged Walter to the door, not caring if it was rude. A newly widowed woman must be given some dispensation for her conduct.

At the door, Walter paused. 'As a result of the terrible news, I forgot to mention the baby to anyone,' he said apologetically.

Effie glanced back at the bedroom door. Whatever tragedy had befallen the *Serenity* must have caused the baby to be set adrift too. It was chilling to think that while Effie was wading into the sea to rescue the child, the same waters were claiming John and his crewmates. One life saved in place of all those lost seemed an inadequate exchange.

'That can wait,' she sighed. 'A day or two more won't make any difference.'

She watched Walter make his way carefully along the uneven path until it widened and he increased his pace, striding out purposefully; a tall figure, confident that he had done his painful duty in the best way possible and no longer needing to hunch his shoulders and demonstrate his empathy.

Effie closed the door and only then cried for her lost husband. She wept harder and longer than she would have expected. Their marriage had its faults and trials, as most did, but he had been a kind man, hard-working and even-tempered. She found it now easy to forget they had shared little in common and decided she could not have asked for a better husband.

Once she had done weeping, she dried her eyes and went into the bedroom. The two children were beginning to stir as their bellies told them to wake. Effie washed in what was left of the hot water from the kettle and pulled on her nightgown. She took both children into her bed and pulled the blanket and counterpane up around her legs. She put the babies to her breasts and closed her eyes as they suckled. Both drank until they were sated and their milk-slack lips dropped open.

Effie's eyes filled with tears as she gazed down at Jack. He would not remember his father. She looked from the blond head to the darker one. The girl would not remember either, and no one could say who should be mourned in any case. She stroked both children's heads, taking comfort from the downy softness.

The room was chilly. The fire had died down and Effie had forgotten to bank it up for the night. Her feet were warm in their woollen socks and she couldn't face crossing the room on the bare floorboards to put the children back in Jack's cradle. She laid the babies side by side on the bed, close together for warmth, and tugged their caps down snugly. She tucked the blankets around the children then lay on her side and brought her knees up, cocooning them with her body to stop them from slipping down between bed and wall.

Outside, the storm swelled again. The waves and wind combined to create a cry that sounded almost human in its keening grief. It echoed along the length of the coastline, but Effie and the children slept soundly without hearing.

There were no children gathered at Alice's gate when Effie visited on the first morning of her widowhood, but someone was leaving. The visitor was a woman not much older than Effie. There was something in the furtive way she backed out of the door and glanced around before scurrying off towards the harbour cottages with her head bowed and a paper-wrapped parcel clutched to her breast that told Effie this had not been a social call. Alice's expertise at mixing home remedies was almost wholly responsible for her reputation as a witch and even if Effie did not believe in the type of witchcraft practised by her grandmother, there were plenty who did. As well as tinctures and tonics for childhood ailments and other day-to-day complaints, Alice had no qualms about providing elixirs for the lovesick to give themselves hope, and other, darker, remedies for when the love potions resulted in unintended consequences.

She let herself into the cottage and called a greeting. Alice bustled out of the pantry carrying a block of black dye. She gave Effie a look of sympathy.

'I thought you might need this.'

Effie had held back her tears since the night before, but now she laid the babies on the rug and fell into her grandmother's waiting arms. The older woman said nothing while Effie sobbed. Alice had lost a husband to the sea, as well as burying Effie's father and three other sons along the way. She knew how Effie's heart would be cracking.

When Effie's tears were spent, Alice unwound her arms and wiped Effie's face on the hem of her apron as she had done throughout Effie's childhood.

'Tea's in the pot,' Alice said briskly. 'It'll be well stewed by now. I'll fetch the cake; you pour.'

Effie put down her baskets and sniffed the spout, never

sure whether the brew would be the usual sort of leaves or something concocted from herbs designed to ease a bilious stomach or a fever.

'That's not what I gave to Prudence Maynard, don't fret,' Alice called.

Reassured she would be drinking proper tea from China, Effie poured two cups. Alice bustled back out of the pantry, wiping her hands down the front of her red and green striped apron. She put a slab of heavy fruit cake on the table.

'Her monthly courses were blocked and she needed something to return the flow. An infusion of raspberry leaves and nutmeg should help.'

Effie busied herself arranging the mugs on the table, knowing full well what the probable cause of the blockage was. The Maynards already had four children aged under seven. No wonder poor Mrs Maynard had looked so shifty when she left. Ah well, better the business be dealt with quietly and before things went too far to be kept hidden.

'Sometimes I wonder how different my life would have been if I had asked you to help me,' Effie sighed.

Alice gave her a sharp look. 'Do you wish you had?'

Effie closed her eyes. 'I don't know. It would be wishing Jack out of existence, and I love him dearly.'

Alice wiped her hands briskly on her apron. 'Then you made the right decision. Many disagree with what I do, which is why it is important that only those who ask me and know their mind get it.'

Effie twisted her hair around her forefingers and thought back to that first sickening realisation that she was with child. However dull she had found John's company at times, he had not abandoned her when she had broken the news to him. In fact he seemed pleased to be a father. She was going to miss him.

'Poor Prudence,' she said. 'Whatever she does, someone will disapprove of her choices.'

'Only if they discover she had to make them,' Alice said.

Effie glanced at the baby girl who was lying awake but silent on the mat before the fire, watching the dust motes. Not every woman had ready access to someone with Alice's knowledge or skills who could aid her in the grisly but practical ways Effie preferred not to dwell on. Newspapers carried discreet advertisements for remedies to do the same job but that carried the risk of discovery.

Had casting the child out to sea been an attempt to be rid of an unwanted baby? Such things happened, no doubt, but there were workhouses where a child might be given a chance to live. And, in any case, why provide a raft if there had been such a grisly purpose? It didn't make sense, however much Effie thought of it.

When they'd finished the tea and cake, Alice accompanied Effie back to her own cottage. Together they dragged the copper bath before the hearth and put water on to boil so they could dye Effie's Sunday dress black for mourning. She couldn't afford the luxury of new crape and veils, but that didn't cause her any worry. Today she would not be the only widow in the village making the best of what she had.

On the rug, the baby girl played with her feet while Jack lay on his back and babbled.

'I expect Walter Danby didn't remember to ask about her,' Alice remarked when they had left the wool dress and linens soaking in the copper.

Effie shook her head. The girl stretched, regarding Effie solemnly as if she knew she was the subject of the conversation, and it was at that moment that Effie came to a decision. It was one she might have been building up to in any case, but with the scent of mourning dye in her nostrils and her eyes sore from weeping, the girl's steady gaze was soothing.

'I'm going to keep her,' she told Alice. 'Jack will have no father, but he can have a sister to keep him company.'

She expected Alice to offer reasons why it wasn't practical, but the old woman nodded slowly.

'Aye. That's the proper way of things. You found her; she's in your care.'

Alice knelt beside the babies on the rug and passed her hand over the girl's head as she had done the day before, hovering slightly above the body and moving slowly while mumbling beneath her breath. Effie tried to hide her exasperation. Alice's ways were odd but harmless.

'There will be a proper way to go about it,' Effie mused. 'I'll ask Walter to help.'

'He'll be more than willing, I expect,' Alice said.

Effie ignored the slight note of disapproval in her grandmother's voice. Even if their friendship ran deeper on Walter's side, he wouldn't expect any return of affection from a widow of one day.

'He's the best-placed person I know, unless you think I should ask Reverend Ogram for help,' she said, suspecting quite rightly that Alice wouldn't countenance a man of the church becoming involved, especially one whose daughter had so recently been visiting for dark purposes.

When Walter returned to visit, as he surely would, she would ask him how best to proceed with fostering the girl. Until the unlikely time that someone appeared to claim her, Effie would treat her as her own.

Chapter Three

On Christmas morning, Effie and Alice attended church. It was the only day in the year that they did. In a village as small as Allendale Head, *not* to be present in the pews would be unthinkable. Effie was aware that even after almost a decade living there she was still viewed as an outsider, though her father had been born in the village.

John usually sat beside Effie and held her hand throughout, overjoyed that for one day of the year at least, she conceded to partake in something he valued and believed in so deeply. The Book of Common Prayer was the only volume he ever picked up and even though he stumbled over the words, he could recite the middle verse of psalm 66 by heart.

A lump swelled in Effie's throat. No God had saved these sailors and her husband would have no grave in the churchyard. He would share a memorial stone at St Mary's in Whitby alongside the rest of the *Serenity*'s crew and countless others lost at sea. Morrow and Settle, the company who owned the ship, would see to that.

Neither Effie nor Alice believed in their hearts that what

Reverend Ogram preached with such sincerity had any real truth, but as she sat in the pews at the back with a child in each arm, the story of a baby seemed particularly relevant to Effie this year. The hymns and carols she had learned in childhood had the capability of moving her more deeply than the sermon and lessons. Listening to the village children singing of a child with no crib in which to lay his head, she looked around at the congregation through a film of tears.

There were three women of varying ages newly dressed in black, whose husbands had also been lost aboard the *Serenity*. After the service they gathered together in the vestry and spoke briefly to Reverend Ogram, his wife and daughters. Effie sidled closer, never feeling at ease in the church or the company of the village women who had known each other since birth, but now wanting to offer her condolences and share in their communal grief. While John had stood at her side she felt less of an outsider, but now she felt very alone as she waited to be noticed. Walter was standing with his parents, deep in conversation with the doctor and his family and she could not look to him for support. She was close to leaving the vestry when she spotted Mrs Maynard standing beside the pew looking pallid and distant. Effie watched her surreptitiously. Whatever treatment Alice had given her must be having the desired effect. Mrs Maynard noticed Effie watching and an expression of anxiety flitted over her face.

Effie moved around and whispered, 'The pain will pass quickly, so I'm told.'

'I don't know what you're talking 'bout.'

Mrs Maynard's eyes flickered and she walked away hastily.

Reverend Ogram finally bid farewell to his more devoted parishioners and turned his attention to Effie. He offered words of condolence and what he truly believed were comfort.

Blushing at being spoken to, Effie found her tongue and thanked him, and he turned his attention to the children. He raised his brows as he regarded the two babies. Effie explained where the child had come from.

'Young Mr Danby said he would help me arrange matters so I could foster her until someone claims her,' she explained.

Reverend Ogram pursed his lips.

'Perhaps for a short time, although the parish might want the child to be placed in a home with more means to tend to all her needs, practical *and* spiritual.'

Effie ground her teeth behind her smile. A home where the child would daily be taught the catechism and receive the good Christian upbringing that Effie was failing to give her own son.

'I'm sure Mr Danby will advise me on the best course of action,' she replied. 'Now my son is an orphan, it will be good for him to have some company besides myself.'

~

As it transpired, there was very little officialdom involved in Effie being given custody of the girl, as Walter explained when he visited her three days into the new year.

By then, Effie and the two children had developed a routine and she was already becoming adept at nursing them both at the same time. After the first exhausting days when the children nursed constantly, her milk had increased to compensate for the extra demand and now both drank their fill contentedly. The girl had fitted seamlessly into their lives.

'I think the Parish Overseers of the Poor are quite happy to be relieved of the burden of an extra mouth to feed,' Walter explained. 'They offered no argument against you continuing to care for her.'

Effie gave him a genuine smile, one of the few she had been able to muster since John's death.

'Reverend Ogram won't be happy,' she said. 'He is worried for the child's spiritual care.'

Walter's expression grew serious. 'As he is right to be. We don't even know if the child has been baptised.'

She opened her mouth to protest, but Walter continued, 'Effie, I know your feelings on religion, and though I hope one day your heart opens to the Lord, I shall put no pressure on you. However, if you would allow me to play what little part I can in her life, I would deem it an honour to be allowed to oversee that aspect of her upbringing.'

His offer was open and generous. 'Thank you, Walter,' Effie said slowly. 'When you visit us I shall have no objection to you reading her some suitable stories, but I will not take her to church, and it is not my place to have her baptised.'

'For once I agree. The child is not yours and you are right not to make that choice on behalf of her parents.'

Walter reached into his coat pocket. 'I have something to give you.'

He pressed a small box into her hand. It contained a plain mourning brooch made of Whitby jet. He began blushing furiously. 'I wasn't sure if you have the means…'

Effie cut him off. 'Thank you. It's a kind thought, but I can't accept this from you.'

'Please. Consider it a gift from a friend.'

Effie shook her head and handed it back to him. 'I can't accept a gift from an unmarried man when I am so newly widowed, especially not one so personal. It would cause comment in the village.'

Walter nodded and reluctantly put the brooch back into his pocket.

'If there is anything else I can do to help you? The parish will pay a remuneration for the child's care but it won't be much. It will barely cover linens and whatever other matters children need. My sister's child is older than your two; I will see if she can pass down what Millicent has outgrown. She is always looking for charitable causes to support.'

Effie blinked at being described in such a way. Walter grew red.

'Oh dear, I do have a way of saying the wrong thing. That wasn't what I meant to say.'

Effie patted his hand. He had been tactless rather than sneering and, besides, she was not in a position to object to the description when she was accepting charity.

'Thank you. You've done more than enough and I would be happy to accept anything Eliza can spare. As you say, I don't have the means and I'm not too proud.'

'What will you do for money?' Walter asked. 'Will Morrow and Settle pay out a sum for insurance?'

Effie's stomach churned with anxiety. She and John had lived comfortably on the wages from the company, but now she had no husband to bring in an income she would need to earn her own. Gathering seaweed provided some food, but her diet would be dull if she relied on that, and seaweed wouldn't buy clothes for two babies.

'They offered each of us a mangle in compensation. What are we all to do with them? One in the village would be useful but all four of us can scarcely make ends meet doing a quarter of the village laundry.'

She detested laundry and even the promise of a mangle to speed things up didn't mean the idea was less of a chore.

'You turned it down?' Walter asked.

'I did. It doesn't make any sense for them to give us all

mangles, and if that is how they suggest we earn our living we will just be competing with each other. If I had a mangle and Mrs Penney had a wash board and dolly, for example, it would have made more sense.'

She broke off, aware that she was ranting and looked guiltily at Water. Anyone else might have been disapproving at her clear lack of gratitude, but he was grinning.

'I'm sorry. I become heated when something irks me.'

'Don't apologise. I suppose you are right, it doesn't make sense. I have no connections with the company, but I could ask my father to mention it to Crispin Morrow. It won't help you, but if there is another tragedy it could benefit another widow.'

'Thank you, Walter. If they had asked me before, I would have told them,' Effie replied, 'but I doubt it would occur to them to consult a woman and now I look ungrateful.'

'Fortunately some of us recognise that your sex can talk sense and I am always happy to represent you.'

Effie smiled at him, though her jaw clenched. Yes, Walter was more progressive than most men, but his first thought was to speak for her, not encourage her to speak for herself.

'What will you do?' Walter asked.

'I'm not sure. I'll think of something. We'll manage.'

After Walter left, Effie sat, brow knotted, and gave full rein to the apprehension she felt. Walter's offer had been generous and no doubt he would continue to help her if he could, but she was determined not to take his charity. Although there had been no obvious strings attached to his offer or his gift, she knew his affection for her outweighed hers for him. It might lead him to hope she might repay his kindness with her time and company. Although many women married again after the first year of mourning was over, Effie's sorrow at John's death was sincere and deep. It was far too early in her widowhood to be contemplating a remarriage and the idea of another husband was too much to imagine. She put that thought away and turned her attention back to the children.

'You need a name for the official papers,' she said to the girl who was lying on the rug trying to bite her feet. The girl looked up and Effie peered into her green-brown eyes, but nothing sprang to mind.

$\sim$

Effie had become a widow at the age of twenty-four. With no family beyond Alice, the first year of her widowhood was as hard as she had expected it to be. She took in sewing rather than washing, though most women did their own and couldn't afford the expense. Some of the more well-to-do villagers did what they could to pass work her way. The doctor's wife sent hers, saying that her fingers were too arthritic to manage, and Walter's mother obliged occasionally. Effie was not insensible to their kindness. At first the distraction of the work gave her brief respite from her grief and cares, but the work was so monotonous, and Effie was such a neat seamstress that after the first hour or two of working on shirt hems her mind was free to wander.

When Effie was not tending to the children or sketching seaweeds and plants, Alice did her best to keep her occupied, asking for help making powders and medicines.

'My hands and eyes aren't what they were,' she muttered. 'You're doing me a favour and I like to see the babies when you bring them around. It makes me feel young again.'

Effie didn't believe her grandmother's words. Or perhaps she didn't want to believe them. She had been orphaned at an early age and now she was widowed. Alice was her only kin, besides Effie's mother's sister who lived on the borders of Scotland. This distant aunt had sent only the briefest of condolences when Effie's parents had been taken from the world, being more concerned with assuring Effie she would pray they were reprieved from the fires of Hell for their irreligious ways. Effie did not even bother to inform her aunt of her own recent loss. To lose Alice would set Effie adrift. She kept the fear to herself, but loneliness consumed her nights.

The babies were a joy, but they were only babies. They grew stronger and more able with each passing week, becoming interested in the world around them. Effie lived quite contentedly with her son and foster-daughter, but no name seemed to suit the girl, either fancy or plain.

Effie tried not to fret.

'A name will suggest itself eventually, chick,' she told the girl. The girl seemed agreeable enough to this as she shuffled after Jack on her bottom.

The months passed, and as the shock of her widowhood and the manner of John's passing subsided, Effie's grief settled. It was as if she had tightened her corset another inch and had to wait until her body became accustomed to the new restrictiveness before she was able to breathe again.

At Midsummer she travelled to Whitby and wept at the memorial stone set up to the lives lost on board the *Serenity*. She bought new mourning crape to dye her striped summer skirts black while the children rolled on the rag rug and giggled in their own private language. By now the weight of her loss was ever-present, though not particularly debilitating. It helped that John had been absent at sea for long periods. She could convince herself he was only gone temporarily and would be back before long.

When October came and the mists drew in, Effie had

earned enough from her mending to buy a bolt of black wool to make herself a dress for winter. She caught herself humming while she sewed by lamplight after the children were in bed.

Walter visited when he returned from Manchester in early December, bringing a fresh pile of clothes from his sister and gifts for the babies.

'Next year we'll have a tree and proper decorations,' she promised the children, though neither of them had any notion of what she meant. Jack flapped his hands and squealed in the odd way he sometimes did, but the girl looked at Effie with something like approval, or at least that was what the tired young mother decided the expression meant.

Walter stood before the range and ate a slice of pound cake while the children clambered over the gaily wrapped box he had brought them. He'd brought a drum for Jack (for which Effie thanked him through gritted teeth) and a soft-bodied doll for the girl.

'Mayhap you'll find it easier to name the doll,' he said with a grin at Effie.

Effie sighed. 'I know, but nothing feels right. She's not a Victoria. Not Dora nor Jane nor Sally. My full name is Euphemia but I couldn't curse her with something like that. I'll have to choose something soon though. I told Alice I would decide before the year is out.'

Walter scratched at the whiskers he'd grown since Effie had seen him last. He looked older and more serious, though his eyes still gleamed with boyish enthusiasm as he described the fascinating developments in the Manchester sewage system.

'Could she be an Alice?' he asked.

Effie shook her head. 'I've tried almost every name I can think of. Most of the time I call her chick, which she seems happy enough with. If she had been a boy I would have called her John and made the name stick.'

She bit her lip as a stab of unfamiliar misery took her by surprise. It was rare she spoke his name aloud. The first year of deep mourning was almost over. After Christmas she would be able to reduce the amount of crape she wore. She would be able to enter society – such as existed in the village – a little more. Not that she minded her seclusion. In the company of the prim wives of the church she felt as out of place as among the forthright, loudly spoken fishermen's wives.

Walter placed his plate on the table and gave Effie a penetrating look.

'Do you ever think about remarriage? Would you consider it?'

It was the most blatantly he had ever referred to marriage. Such boldness was new to him. She sometimes missed the company of another adult in the house, but more crucially she missed the presence of a man in her bed. When half the visitors to Alice's door came seeking relief from the pains of pregnancy or impending childbirth, she was glad she was spared that and the idea of remarrying lost its appeal a little. She stared back at Walter frankly.

'I don't have time to. The children keep me so busy. I'm content as I am. With the stipend from the parish and what I earn from sewing I have enough income to stop us ending up in the poorhouse.'

Effie took Walter's teacup and walked him to the door. After he left she stood staring at the sea until the wind started up and forced her to close the door.

If Walter hoped Effie would come around to his way of feeling, he never showed his disappointment that she continued to treat him kindly but with a formality that gave him no opportunity to mistake her actions or words. Oddly enough, that discretion made her feel more fondly towards him than if he had professed love. But while Effie had the occasional craving for a man, she had no similar hankering for a husband.

~

A year to the day since she had found the basket, a knock on the door disturbed Effie's evening. Walter had called that afternoon to bring cut greenery to decorate the mantelpiece and news that seals had been sighted off the Brigg. He had stayed until dusk, singing Christmas carols to the children while Effie baked mince pies for Christmas Eve. When the knock sounded, Effie assumed it was Walter again and was a little ashamed that her heart did not speed up at the thought that he might have returned.

She was fond of him so why couldn't that feeling tip over into love? He was kind and intelligent and had grand ambitions to improve the lives of the alum workers. If this led him to be a little too serious, that was only natural and couldn't be avoided. That afternoon she had seen that he had the ability to loosen his collar and enjoy himself. The cottage had been full of laughter and spicy, Christmassy scents. Effie had felt happier than she could remember and had even indulged in a brief daydream that it could last for longer. Walter would undoubtedly marry her if she gave him enough hope to pluck up the courage to ask. Maybe she had to take a leap of faith and her feelings would grow as the marriage progressed, much like they had for John Cropton when she had been given no choice. Next time Walter mentioned marriage she might not reply with such a forceful no. It would be the sensible thing to do and they would be content, especially if she could encourage the light-heartedness she had seen.

She had been preparing for bed when the knock came and her hair hung loose. She removed the linen cloth from around her shoulders that she used to protect her dress from the oils and dust that were removed from her locks with the vigorous brushing. She gathered her hair and twisted it into a knot, securing it with one comb at the nape of her neck. She opened the door a crack and peered through.

It wasn't Walter. The man who filled the doorframe couldn't have been less like Walter unless he had two heads. He was dressed in a heavy black wool coat with the collar turned up and a fisherman's cap shading his face. His appearance would have been unremarkable but for the fact that over the top of his coat he had wrapped a dark-brown fur.

'It's late,' Effie said cautiously. 'Do you need some help?'

He raised his head and stared at her with dark-brown eyes flecked with the glass-green hue of a winter sea. Effie's heart stopped beating then sped up to double time.

'I come to speak of a child.'

The stranger's accent bore a touch of Scottish with a hint of something from further away at the edge. His voice was low and slow and made Effie think of cowrie shells and surging tides. The tone sent ripples undulating up and down her spine and spreading out along her limbs, but his words made her belly clench.

'Are you from the Parish Overseers' Committee?' she asked, trying to keep her voice from shaking.

The man gave a swift bow and stared at Effie. 'I am not from any committee, Effie Cropton.'

'Then of which child would you be speaking?' Effie asked.

She wondered how he knew her name if he had not come in any official capacity.

'I speak of the child who possesses a sealskin.'

He gestured to the fur draped across his shoulder. His pupils grew darker and larger and when he spoke next it was with a commanding tone.

'That child is mine.'

Chapter Four

Effie's hands tightened on the frame. No one had come forward to claim the girl in a year and now someone appeared in such outlandish garb under cover of night. She wished she were not alone. She wished that Alice – or better still, Walter – was at her side.

'And who are you?' Effie asked.

'My name is Lachlan.'

He removed his hat and shook out thick, dark hair, the same colour as the fur, before bowing gracefully once again. If he thought such pretty manners would appease Effie, he was about to find otherwise.

'I'll need to see some papers,' Effie said. She folded her arms. 'Who sent you? How did you know she was here?'

'No one sent me. I came myself. You ask a lot of questions, Effie Cropton, so here is one for you. Where is my daughter?'

'How do I know she is yours?' Effie said. She locked her knees to prevent her legs from shaking and stood tall. 'And it's Mrs Cropton, if you please. I have no proof you have any claim over her. Come back tomorrow.'

She bit off her words, swallowing her breath and waiting for his response. The man held her gaze. A shiver ran down Effie's spine at the intensity of his expression. She had stood up to him and yet he didn't appear angry.

'Look at me, Mrs Cropton, and then look at my daughter and say we are not kin.'

She couldn't deny it. His features were the same shape as the girl's with narrow lips that were deeply clefted, a straight nose and the same intense expression in the dark eyes. He was perhaps thirty, or a little over, with small lines at the corners of his eyes and around his lips. His eyes suited his age more, looking less uncannily ancient than they did in a child's face, but they still made Effie shiver.

'You've waited a pretty amount of time to claim her, Mr Lachlan.' Effie folded her arms, blocking the doorway. Her heart thundered, though whether from fear or because of his captivating eyes, she could not tell.

'Just Lachlan will do, if you please,' he said.

He scowled. Even with his face crumpled in frustration he was exceedingly handsome. More so than John had been. More than any man Effie knew.

'I would have come sooner had it been in my power. I had no choice but to wait.'

Something in his tone caught Effie's heart. There was sorrow beneath the frustration. She felt herself growing sympathetic, which was dangerous.

'I must take her tonight. The Midwinter tide turns and I cannot stay longer.'

Effie looked him up and down. As well as the heavy coat, he wore trousers of black moleskin and boots like the ones worn by the fishermen in the village.

'Do you have a ship waiting?' Effie asked.

He laughed unexpectedly, but his eyes remained serious. 'Something like that. Please give me my child.'

The children had not woken at the sound of voices. The wind was bitter and as she opened the door a little more it stoked the coals in the grate, causing shadows to dance over the ceiling.

'Can't you come back in the morning? She'll be sleeping now.'

'She isn't.'

He spoke with absolute conviction that made Effie frown in annoyance. He had no idea how long the children had been asleep. Following the excitement of Walter's attention, the girl had taken a long time to settle, and Jack had woken as soon as she had dropped off. It had taken over an hour for them to finally submit to tiredness. It had been a difficult evening. She glanced over her shoulder and as she moved, Lachlan ducked and slipped past her to the right and into the house with a swiftness she did not expect.

Effie had seen mild-tempered bitches snap at a hand that threatened their litter and now she understood why. The protective urge rose inside her. She followed Lachlan with an exclamation of fury and strode up to him, brandishing her finger in his face. Her hand was shaking. Only extreme anger at his invasion gave her the courage to confront a man such as he.

'How dare you force your way in here! Get out of my house!'

'Not without my daughter.'

He folded his arms and placed his feet apart. His bearing and manner suggested he was used to giving orders rather than receiving them. She glared at him and mimicked his stance. Anger and fear made her shake and her heart thumped so loudly she thought the sound might deafen her. Her eyes darted round the room, looking for anything she could defend herself with if necessary. They fell on the vegetable knife draining beside the sink. Lachlan followed her gaze and frowned.

'I mean you no harm.'

He dropped his hands to his sides and held them palms up, stepping back. 'I shouldna' have done that. I'm no' so used to polite company as I should be. I just want to see her. I've travelled a long way.'

The Scottish lilt was more pronounced. How far had he come? Then again, how far would Effie go to find Jack if he were taken from her? She unfolded her arms.

'If you disturb her she won't sleep again tonight.'

'She's awake. Go and check if you don't believe me.'

His voice held a note of authority. Reluctantly, Effie opened the bedroom door. Light from the moon streamed in, illuminating the corner where the cot was. Jack lay sprawled on his back, arms stretched above his head but, sure enough, the girl was peering between the bars with sleep-bleary eyes.

She babbled something incomprehensible.

'Hello, chick,' Effie whispered. 'Everything is all right. Mama is here. We have a visitor.'

The girl nodded slowly whilst yawning. Effie cradled her close. Her eyes pricked at the idea she would have to say farewell to the girl she had grown to care for.

'Does it have to be now?' she whispered against the girl's head. She closed the door softly behind her so as not to disturb Jack.

Upon seeing the girl Lachlan's face lit with relief and joy. Some of the lines around his eyes and jaw smoothed out. He held his arms out and the girl leaned towards him, but as Effie took her closer, the child whimpered and burrowed down against Effie's breast.

'Hush, chick,' Effie soothed. 'This is your papa, come to see you.'

She looked at Lachlan over the top of the girl's head. He couldn't take his gaze from her. There was such adoration in his eyes that Effie was no longer in any doubt that this was his child. She needed no papers from the authorities or any other proof. A man who looked at the girl in that way couldn't be anyone other than her father. Their eyes were so similar and the expression uncannily alike. His were a much deeper brown, bordering on black, but their expression was so similar Effie could not deny they were father and daughter. She slipped closer and motioned for Lachlan to touch the girl. He reached out a hand hesitantly then withdrew it.

'Would you like to hold her?' Effie asked.

He looked uncertain. 'May I?'

Effie gave him a small smile. 'She's your daughter; of course you can.'

With gentle movements unexpected in a man of his size, he eased his arms around the child, brushing against Effie as he did, and lifted her free. The girl looked infinitely smaller in his broad hands. He held her awkwardly as if he had no idea what to do with her. It struck Effie that most likely he didn't. She felt a rush of sympathy that he had lost his child and been searching for so long.

'Put your hand here,' she instructed, motioning towards him. 'And the other there. That's right.'

Lachlan bent his head close to the child's and spoke in a low, deep whisper into her hair. Effie didn't understand the words. A Scottish dialect, she presumed, but it was a tone Effie had heard Walter use to calm his gelding when something spooked it. Perhaps he worked with animals. The girl's body relaxed and she leaned against him, but she didn't put her arms about his neck as she did with Effie or Alice.

He buried his head in her embrace then looked up sharply, a shocked expression on his face.

'You gave her milk. Your milk?'

Effie nodded. 'Of course. She was famished when I found her, poor mite.'

Lachlan ruffled his hand through his hair and gave Effie a rueful look.

'Do you realise the bond you created? No matter. There is nothing that can be done now to undo that.'

'And *I* could do nothing else when I found her,' Effie said, jutting her jaw out. 'Do you know how I found her? Wrapped in a sealskin and naked as the day she was born. She could have frozen to death.'

She held her hands out. 'Give her back to me, if you please.'

Lachlan surrendered the girl. Effie tried not to feel triumphant when she immediately slipped her arms about Effie's neck, holding on tightly as if she would never let go. Effie avoided Lachlan's eyes, not wanting to appear mocking.

'Mama?' the girl crooned.

The girl had only begun speaking in the past fortnight and every time she called Effie that, Effie's heart swelled with fierce love. Lachlan looked as if he had been struck across the face.

'She calls you Mother.'

His voice was a harsh whisper of betrayal. Effie floundered.

'I'm sorry. She's been mine for a year. I've raised her with my son.'

Lachlan's expression became warmer.

'You did everything for the best of reasons.'

He stepped close and put his hand on the child's cheek. She

stared at him with the same dark eyes. His mouth twisted downwards and he looked so careworn that Effie had to resist the urge to offer consolation.

'Put her back in her bed,' he murmured. 'I shallna' take her tonight.'

Effie slipped into the bedroom and laid the girl down. She straightened Jack's arms and tucked the blankets around them both. She watched for a few moments while the girl's eyes drooped and she fell asleep. Effie kissed her fingers and put them to each child's cheek in turn.

When she returned, Lachlan was standing in the centre of the room and looking about him with interest. Effie lifted her chin and stared at him. His clothes were good quality, for all that they were plain. Maybe he was used to grander surroundings than a two-room cottage. Effie's furniture might be old, the crockery mismatched and the rug shabby, but the house was clean and neat. He would find nothing to criticise.

'Do you live here alone?' he asked.

There was curiosity in his voice rather than judgement.

'With my son. And your daughter,' Effie added.

'Where is your son's father? Do you have a husband?'

Effie gestured to the black skirt she wore.

'My husband drowned in a shipwreck. Almost a year to the day.'

She blinked as grief welled up, fresh and raw.

Lachlan's eyes narrowed then filled with sympathy. 'In foreign parts? He travelled far?'

An odd question but Effie answered it anyway.

'No, barely out of harbour from Whitby.'

'Ah. My condolences. My wife also…'

Lachlan tailed off and his face creased with visible evidence of deep sorrow.

Effie recalled Walter's report of a crack in the hull of the *Serenity* caused by some large object. The vessel carrying the child and her mother must have been in the same vicinity for the basket to float towards Allendale Head. Perhaps both ships had fallen foul of whatever it had been.

'I'm sorry,' she murmured. 'I never understood how the babe came to be in the sea. Would you like some tea?'

Lachlan lifted his chin. 'Thank you, but no. I am already under enough obligation to you for what you have done for my child.'

'It's only tea. There is no obligation,' Effie said. 'You just looked cold.'

She glanced at the seal fur that was draped over one arm. It matched the one in which she had found the girl wrapped and wondered where they had got them. Perhaps he was a seal hunter.

'Your daughter had a fur like that,' she said.

'Had?' He leaned forward urgently. 'What happened to it?'

'Nothing. I kept it safe,' Effie answered, slightly taken aback at the alarm in his voice.

'Good.' He pulled a stool back and sat at the table, resting his hands together on the edge.

'Mrs Cropton, we have a predicament. You have nursed my child and looked after her. You took her in and gave her your milk. You have cared for her for a year and she calls you Mother.'

He rubbed his eyes with his fingers. They were long and slender and looked as if they had never seen hard labour. He gave Effie a wry smile.

'You have as much claim to her as I do.'

'I'm sorry,' Effie repeated. 'I did what I thought was best.'

'And you did it well. You love her, don't you?'

Effie nodded.

Lachlan exhaled loud and long.

'You had no understanding of the bonds you were weaving or the obligations you have created but I cannot take her from you. If I leave her, will you continue to care for her as you have done?'

Effie hid her elation. 'Of course I will.'

'What have you named her?'

'I…'

Effie felt a blush rising to her cheeks. She'd been defensive and accusatory, but now had to admit that a year had passed without her naming Lachlan's daughter.

'Nothing seemed to suit her,' she admitted.

Lachlan didn't seem angry at this but his shoulders tensed. 'Then you have not had her baptised, I assume?'

'No.' Effie met his eyes boldly, staring into the inscrutable depths. If he condemned her for this he would not be the first. 'I'm not a churchgoer myself and it didn't seem right without knowing who she belonged to.'

'That is well. My people are also not of that faith. I would not have another barricade set between us.' He gestured to the fur around his shoulders. 'Where is her skin? I would like to see it before I leave.'

It was an odd request. Effie narrowed her eyes suspiciously, wondering if he planned to make off with it. Sealskins were prized but this fur was so small it couldn't be particularly valuable. The basket was where she had left it a year ago on top of the wardrobe in the bedroom. It had continued to disintegrate and was now little more than a pile of loosely woven stalks and reeds. By the light from the open door she stood on tiptoe and pulled it down, trying to keep silent so as not to wake the children.

She placed the remains of the basket on the kitchen table and unfolded the fur. Dust filled the air. Lachlan ran his hand over the pelt and closed his eyes. Effie remembered the softness and how it had felt warm under her palm even when cold and damp. She stroked the edge with her fingertip. In the bedroom, the girl stirred and whimpered softly as if she were dreaming.

Lachlan looked round at the sound. He crept to the cot and held his hand out over the sleeping children then withdrew it slowly. He bowed his head. Effie left the room, not wanting to intrude.

When Lachlan emerged, he walked to Effie and tilted her chin back. His hands were so cold, the shock of it almost outweighed the surprise of being touched by a stranger. He regarded her seriously and she suddenly felt very young.

'Effie Cropton, will you keep my child safe?'

She nodded. 'I will.'

Lachlan took her right hand. He pressed something cool and hard into her palm and curled her fingers round it. Effie opened her hand to discover a large pearl. She blinked in surprise. It must be worth double the sum she received from the Poor Committee each quarter year.

'We have a compact, you and I,' he said. 'I will return at Midsummer's Night on the turn of the tide and I'll bring you another pearl in payment.'

Lachlan paused at the door and looked back at Effie, dark eyes flashing.

'Her name is Morna.'

Effie clutched the pearl and watched as he slipped away. He headed away from the village, along the beach towards the Brigg. The moonlight followed him, but when the shore curved away the shadows claimed him and he was lost from sight.

Chapter Five

Alice was grinding something in a pestle and mortar when Effie visited the next morning. The cottage was filled with a sweet, slightly cloying smell that Effie half recognised. Camphor was definitely involved somewhere. Her own house had contained the faint trace of the sea when she'd woken, and a deeper underlying scent that made her think of the seal furs. She'd half thought Lachlan's appearance and his strange manner had been a dream until she saw the dust balls on the rug from where she'd brought the fur down from the wardrobe.

'What are these for?' Effie asked, running her fingers through the dried blossoms and lifting a fingerful to her nose. They crumbled beneath her fingers. Alice snatched the bowl away with a chuckle.

'Something you would neither believe in, my girl, nor approve of,' she replied, arching her eyebrows.

Effie put the babies on the hearthrug and drew up a chair. 'Do you really believe in love potions?' she asked. 'Or do you just trick the girls into believing?'

Alice gave her an enigmatic smile. 'Are you so certain there is nothing to believe in? Maybe the power is in their head rather than in the bottle. Maybe it is a combination of the two. What if there is a world beyond ours that we can't understand, a world that leaches some of its power through.'

'Fairies and sprites?' Effie laughed. 'It seems unlikely. I'd rather trust leeches, unpleasant things as they are.'

Alice laughed at the pun and Effie tailed off as her mind melted into an image of a single white pearl lying in a nest of hairpins in the pot on her dressing table.

Alice gazed out of the window towards the sea. 'Perhaps they're unlikely, but when I was a girl younger than you, I used to dance along the shore and throw shells into the waves in the hope a merman would come and visit me. I left bread out for the boggles and sang to the fairies.'

She sighed and closed her eyes for a moment and the wrinkles on her face smoothed, giving Effie a glimpse of the young woman her grandmother had once been.

'You might catch another husband if you were to do the same,' Alice said, whipping her eyes open and staring at Effie sharply.

Effie blushed to hear such direct words. 'Who says I want one?'

'Every woman wants a man,' Alice replied.

'You don't have one,' Effie pointed out.

Alice's husband had died before Effie had been born and Alice had never remarried.

'I never needed one. You do though. I can tell your body longs for comfort and company.'

Effie began to blush more furiously. She was all set to deny it but a gentle quivering in her belly reminded her of the larger tremor that had passed through her limbs when Lachlan had taken her hand the night before. She had craved something which she had not thought of for a long time. She wasn't sure she had ever craved it with such raw urgency, even when she had allowed John's sweet words and twinkling eye to tempt her.

To cover her embarrassment, she left the table to check on the babies. Morna was sleeping. Jack gurgled and waved his arms as Effie picked him up, trying to bat at the curls beside her ears.

'Have you been speaking to Walter?' she asked.

'Walter Danby?' Alice asked. 'Should I have been speaking to him?'

'He thinks I should remarry too,' Effie admitted.

'Would he be wrong?' Alice took Jack from Effie and held the pestle out to him. He reached for it and began chewing on it. Alice saw Effie frown. She put him back in the pen. 'Don't worry, the paste won't do him any harm. If his gums are hurting it'll soothe the pain. Walter can't have more than a year left of his studies before he'll be returning to Allendale Head to take on his father's business. He's been a good friend to you.'

Effie nodded. 'A good *friend*,' she repeated with emphasis.

Effie was saved from having to continue the conversation further because Jack gave a loud wail. Morna had spied Jack's pestle and was determinedly trying to wrest it from him.

'Morna! Stop that at once!' Effie took the pestle from the girl and gave it back to Jack, who began chewing. She knelt and looked sternly at the girl who glared back, red-faced and furious at being thwarted. Perhaps her teeth were hurting too.

'Do you have a spoon?' she called to Alice.

Alice leaned over and gave a wooden spoon to the girl who immediately started gnawing on the bowl. Effie sighed. If they were both teething she would be in for a few broken nights.

Alice knelt at Effie's side and peered at the children.

'Morna, is it?' she asked. 'That's a pretty name. Unusual too. How did you decide upon it?'

Effie chewed her lip. The name had slipped out without thinking.

'It just came to me,' she said, aware how strange that sounded. 'Mary Ogram brought me an old copy of a periodical last week with a pretty baby's cap design. I might have read it there.'

Alice nodded. Effie wasn't sure she was convinced, but she held her grandmother's gaze, hoping she was exuding truthfulness.

'It's good she has a name finally,' she said. 'Do you realise she's been with me for a year.'

'She's growing up bonny. They both are,' Alice said. 'They'll be helping around the home before you know it.'

Effie looked at her children, both sitting contentedly side by side now that each had something to chew. A rush of love filled her. If she told Alice of Lachlan's visit her grandmother would probably advise informing the authorities. It was better to keep it to herself for the time being. If Lachlan returned in six months' time as he had promised – and Effie was not entirely certain she believed he would – then she might consider admitting it.

∼

On Christmas Eve Walter visited. He too received the news of Morna's newfound name with a raised eyebrow.

'I did not expect you would choose a good Biblical name, but I didn't expect you to think of something so whimsical. Did Alice suggest it from her book of folk tales?'

'I thought of it myself,' Effie said defensively. 'And it isn't whimsical. I think it's Scottish. It reminds me of the sea.'

As she spoke, a vision filled her mind of long moonlit sands and endless violet skies; of eyes as black as Morna's staring at her from beyond cresting waves. Lachlan's accent had put that in her head, of course, but there was no foundation in such imaginings. For all she knew he lived in the shipyards of Glasgow and worked on the docks.

Walter was watching her closely. She shook her head to rid herself of the thoughts. Perhaps she was being whimsical. Too many days in Alice's company listening to the stories she told Jack and Morna had turned her fancy.

'What would happen if Morna's mother or father came forward?' she asked.

'After this long I would be surprised if they were to do so,' Walter said. He shook his head sadly and sighed.

'But if they did?' Effie prompted. 'If they travelled and had only just returned to England they might seek her out.'

'Then by rights he or she should claim her.'

'What if he or she didn't want to? Or couldn't. If her father was a seafaring man he might not be able to care for her.'

Walter patted her hand. She was two years older than him but he had the manner of an elderly patriarch at times – no doubt the influence of his father.

'I expect you would be allowed to keep her if the parent agreed. The Poor Committee would expect them to pay for her upkeep, of course,' Walter continued. 'A child should not be a burden on the parish when those who are duty-bound to support her are able to do so.'

He lifted his chin and grew stern, reminding Effie of his father. Effie thought of the pearl again. By rights she should admit Lachlan's existence, sell the pearl, and use the money from that to clothe and feed Morna. It was such strange payment though, and the way he had pressed it into her hand and talked of a compact in such a serious manner made her pause. Whimsy again. How unlike herself she was being.

'I have something for you,' Walter said. He tilted his head to the side, showing the occasional bashfulness that Effie found endearing. He delved into his bag and produced a shallow rectangular parcel wrapped in plain brown paper and a red and green tartan bow. His eyes were apprehensive.

'I thought if I wrapped it prettily you might not refuse it. It's a gift, but nothing as personal as the brooch. I realise now that was too intimate.'

Effie took it hesitantly. She'd accepted clothes from Walter's sister, and his father had kindly sent down glasshouse strawberries in early summer and plums at harvest, which had no doubt been Walter's idea. But a personal gift was a signal that their friendship was moving to another level of intimacy.

'Tartan,' Walter pointed out, rubbing the end of the ribbon between finger and thumb. 'Scottish like Morna's name. You see, it's an omen. Don't wait until Christmas night; open it now. Please.'

Effie swallowed down her unease. Walter's gentle persistence was as difficult to resist as the waves biting away the cliff edge. She undid the ribbon and slid the paper off. The parcel contained four brushes of different thicknesses and a selection of inks.

'Walter, thank you,' she breathed. Her throat felt slightly choked. Her paints had gradually been running out, but replacing them was not something she could afford to make a priority.

'I had an idea,' Walter explained. 'I was talking with one of the fellows in Manchester, and in the faculty of Natural History there is a great craze for Botany. I thought perhaps you could send drawings of some of the plants found along the coast here. The payment wouldn't be great, I'm afraid, but I suspect you'll prefer this to a mangle.'

'They would pay me?'

In her excitement, Effie clutched his hand and squeezed tightly. To earn even the smallest income by painting was like a wonderful dream. Walter looked startled, his eyes widening and a hint of pink appearing beneath his whiskers. Now she was the one being too forward. She dropped his hand and picked up the brushes, running her fingers over the soft tips. Dear, considerate Walter, who understood her so well.

'Thank you. I couldn't have wished for a nicer gift and I would be honoured to paint for your friends. I'm afraid I have nothing for you in return.'

'I want nothing from you, Effie. Nothing that you could package in ribbons, at least.'

His meaning was clear. Effie stood and smoothed down her skirts. Still black. Still a widow's garb, though now she was permitted to leave off deep mourning. Lachlan's words came back to her. Obligations they had created on Midwinter's Night. She couldn't make a stepfather for Morna without the child's father knowing. He might react badly and decide to take Morna away and Effie did not want that.

'Walter, I know what you are asking and I'm sorry. I cannot give you what you want. I shouldn't accept your gift.'

'You should. It comes with a ribbon but no strings. I am not asking for your hand in marriage today, though you know I could wish for nothing better. I haven't the means at the moment to support a wife or children. I just want you to know how deep my regard for you is and how highly I value our friendship.'

He reached for her hand once more, holding it by the fingertips. He lifted it to his lips and swiftly kissed the back. Effie smiled but she couldn't help comparing it Lachlan's touch. Her skin did not flutter when Walter's lips touched her, and the only shiver was a result of his whiskers tickling somewhat disagreeably.

'To see you smiling and to know you are living adequately is gift enough for me,' he said.

'You really are a good friend to me, Walter. A true friend.'

Walter winced and Effie felt a twinge of guilt. 'Of all the compliments a woman could bestow on a man, that is the cruellest. I bid you and the children a happy Christmas.'

Effie walked him to the door and bade him goodbye. Outside, the night was still and quiet save for the waves sighing as they spilled back and forth over the beach. She stood until he disappeared back along the path, then watched the clouds tumbling over the moon. She sighed. Walter's gift had touched her deeply. If only she were able to feel the same degree of affection he did. She had no doubt he would make a kind husband. Perhaps by the time Walter was in a position to marry, her feelings might have grown deeper.

The year passed. Effie sent three small paintings of oarweed and carrageen to the Manchester address given by Walter. She received the sum of twenty shillings in return. Walter had been right about the amount being meagre, but it all helped feed and clothe the children.

On Midsummer's Day she waited, not quite sure whether Morna's father would return, but return he did.

Just as the bell in St Stephen and All Saints pealed out nine,

Lachlan came into view, a lone figure cast into silhouette by the setting sun as he walked along the beach.

'Is Morna well?' he asked, standing on the doorstep. He'd declined to come in and Effie was happy for him to stay there.

'Very. She's an easy baby.' She didn't think he would want to hear the trials of sore teeth and weaning. 'Would you like to see her?'

Lachlan's eyelids flickered, dark lashes momentarily obscuring black pupils. He looked wistful but shook his head. 'No. It's enough to know she is cared for.'

He drew out a pearl and held it between his thumb and forefinger. His hand was uncalloused and Effie revised her opinion that he might be a labourer. 'Do we still have our compact, Effie Cropton?'

Effie took the pearl. Small and smooth in her hand, it felt cold to the touch. 'Yes of course. When will you return?'

'Midwinter's Night, as before.'

The year moved on. Morna was first to walk unaided, pulling herself up at the gate to look at the beach and simply stepping away as if she could have done it any time she chose. Jack followed a month behind, determined to follow his foster-sister everywhere.

Effie looked forward to sharing this progress with Morna's father, even treating him to a demonstration of Morna's walking, but his visit at Midwinter's Night was brief and late. This time at least he crossed the threshold into the house with Effie's permission, his decision doubtless encouraged by the sleet that hammered down relentlessly. He stood at the cot's side and smiled over Morna as she slept, reaching out a slim finger to brush a lock of hair from her cheek as Effie described the child's favourite games, the words she knew and the way she clutched onto Effie's hand to walk along the beach.

Again, Lachlan gave Effie a pearl. Again, he asked the question of her. Again, he vanished into the night.

Again, there was that lingering sense of need in Effie that followed him out of the door, tugging her towards him.

The driving sleet swallowed him almost immediately, leaving no sign he had ever been there. Next time he wouldn't pass in and out of their lives like sea foam over the sand, Effie determined. She had looked after Lachlan's daughter for two years now. She was happy to do so, but it was time the girl met her father properly.

～

The spring winds were finally starting to ease and it was an unusually warm first week in June. The stretch of beach closest to the village was teeming with people. Children raced along the shore, hurling pebbles that sploshed into the waves while their parents sat on rugs and drank bottled ginger beer. Courting couples wandered side by side, discreetly whispering endearments and vows they no doubt intended to keep.

Effie and Alice sat beneath the cliff on their rug, enjoying the warmth of the sun on their faces. Even a widow was allowed some enjoyments. Jack lay on his back, staring at the gulls circling overhead and cooing with delight as he reached his hands out to them. Effie gazed at him fondly but couldn't rid herself of the hint of anxiety that bubbled in her breast whenever she considered him. The birds caught his attention more than anything else. It was rare he could be persuaded to show interest in any of the playmates to whom Effie tried to introduce him.

Morna began toddling determinedly towards the sea. Though slightly younger than Jack, she was more active than Jack who seemed content to stay where he was put, only trying to reach a toy if it was dandled before him. Effie scooped her up for the third time and put her back on the rug.

'I've told you to stay here, chick,' she admonished.

Morna gabbled a reply, regarding Effie with a solemn expression. Jack rolled onto his belly, reaching his hand out to grab his sister's foot.

'She loves the sea,' Effie told Alice with a sigh. 'Every time we come here I spend most of the day trying to stop her running into it.'

Alice said nothing, but she looked out to sea with a thoughtful expression. Her hands moved deftly in and out of the basket of white dead-nettles they had brought with them, twisting flowers off, parting leaves and laying stems in bundles.

'I wonder if she can remember the basket and floating along?' Effie said. 'Maybe that's why she's so determined to reach it.'

'She'd be more likely to be terrified if she did,' Alice retorted briskly.

Effie lay on her front and played pat-a-cake with Morna in an attempt to distract her. She got the sense her play was merely tolerated, because Morna's eyes constantly slipped beyond Effie to the source of her true goal.

'Do you think she'll ever grow into her eyes?' she asked Alice. They were still uncannily old-looking and seemed out of place on a child who was less than three years old. It struck Effie she should have asked Lachlan when Morna's birthday was and put it in mind to ask him when he returned. She felt the unsettling shiver in her belly, like a pot of water coming to the boil, that happened each time she thought of the strange, dark man.

'She will grow into her eyes when she's ready,' Alice said. 'She'll most likely look odd as a child then grow into a beauty. Here, you do the nettles; I want to shred them and dry the stalks and leaves tonight. Can you put some above your stove? They're for a respectable purpose. Nothing you'd disapprove of.'

Effie agreed. Although she refused to have anything to do with Alice's love potions – or the darker brews used to deal with the resulting troubles – she was happy to help with the preparation of eye lotions and teas to help monthly cramps. She became so absorbed in the task that it was only when Jack started to wail and she turned to soothe him that she realised Morna had gone. She sprang to her feet, scattering nettle blossoms everywhere and began looking around, panic rising in her throat.

'Morna! Chick? Where are you?' She turned to Alice. 'Watch Jack.'

Calling Morna's name, Effie ran to and fro along the beach, looking at all the groups before finally spotting the girl almost at the edge of the waves. She had given up her unstable waddle and was determinedly dragging herself across the shingle, back legs flopping and scrabbling as she edged closer to the water. Lifting her skirts, Effie raced down and seized the child barely moments before a particularly strong wave crested over where Morna would have been, leaving arcs of foam on the sand.

Effie clutched the girl tightly, trembling at how close the child had come to being washed away. Deprived of her victory, so close to finally achieving her goal, Morna threw her head back and screamed with anger.

'Sea! Morna go in sea!'

She twisted in Effie's arms, flailing her limbs wildly and arching her back. The sound was a shriek that drowned out the gulls overhead. People were starting to stare. A mother with four children sitting close by shook her head in disapproval.

'Give in to them now and they'll rule you for ever,' she told Effie. 'A firm hand is what's needed when they show disobedience.'

Effie nodded, too distracted to bother arguing that a child of that age could hardly be expected to understand right from wrong. She walked back to where Alice and Jack waited. Morna was now scarlet-faced. Her usual agreeable nature was nowhere in sight and the black eyes were burning with fury. Even when she was laid next to Jack she continued to scream with frustration and before long Jack joined in until Effie could do nothing but sit and watch helplessly. Tears brimmed in her eyes and she would have gladly wailed herself if she had been in private.

'Give them a nettle bud to suck,' Alice suggested.

Effie twisted a couple of engorged flowers from the nettle stem and squeezed so the nectar swelled to the base. She gave one each to the children and, finally, mollified by the sweetness on their lips, the cries died away. Effie looked to Alice gratefully.

'Perhaps there is some magic in the world after all.'

Alice snorted. 'Of course there is, girl. You've just got to know what form it takes.'

Chapter Six

For the rest of the day Effie's mind returned to the sea; pictures of Morna reaching towards the waves distracted her from everything else. Morna had not been scared, even if Effie's heart had almost stopped with fear.

At dusk, Effie left Jack with Alice and returned to the beach with Morna. Most of the day-trippers and villagers had left and it was almost deserted. The tide had come in and the lovers' names scraped into the sand along the shoreline would be gone before long. She dropped to her knees and put Morna on the sand that was still dry.

'Let's have a look at the waves seeing as you like them so much, chick.'

Morna's face set with determination and she began to toddle towards the water. When Morna was almost at the edge of the waves, Effie tucked her skirts up and kicked off her clogs. The sensation of her bare feet sinking into the cool, damp sand was delightful. She breathed deeply, filling her lungs. It was as if life itself was being drawn into her body because she felt vibrant, golden, alive. No wonder the child, new to the world and all the wonders it held, was fixated on the beach.

'Shall we get your feet wet?'

The girl gurgled in appreciation. 'Yes.'

'Look at the waves,' Effie cooed. She picked Morna up and held her close. The waves crested and Morna reached out to them, giggling. Effie held her out safely so that when the next gentle wave came in to shore it covered her feet.

The water was cold enough to make Effie dance back out of the way. Morna shrieked at the new sensation, but as a second wave caught her the squeals turned to delight and she laughed.

'Again!' she cried.

They spent a happy ten minutes splashing in the water, with Effie kneeling in the sand and jumping Morna over the foam of the waves so the water came up to the girl's knees. Effie's petticoats and skirt were soaked, reminding her of the day she had strode into the sea and pulled Morna out. When the sun dipped down behind the clifftop and the light grew dimmer, Effie picked her up and cradled her close. The tide was coming closer and rivulets of water were beginning to swell and course down the beach. Effie would be walking through streams if she didn't hurry.

'I'm sorry, chick, it's getting too cold now.'

Morna shook her head. 'Again, Mama.'

Effie kissed the child's soft head and wiggled her feet back into the clogs. 'We need to go home. Jack and Alice will be waiting.'

Morna pushed out her lower lip and screwed up her face, turning red. Effie had to walk up the beach with her ears ringing from Morna's increasingly frustrated wails. Her jaw tightened and she was about to speak sharply to the child but then she remembered the severe words of the mother of four and took a deep breath.

'We'll come again another day,' she soothed. 'We'll bring Jack too. Would you like that?'

Morna paused in her screaming long enough to nod. Then her mouth wobbled. She threw herself against Effie's bosom and began to sob in earnest. Effie ignored the soft gulps that continued to erupt from Morna as they made their way along the beach, but she felt like the cruellest mother in England. It had clearly been a mistake to bring Morna to the beach. How could a babe that young understand it was concern not cruelty which deprived her of what she wanted most?

By the time they reached the jetty, the sobs had become yawns and Morna sat placidly with her arms wrapped around Effie's neck; by the time they reached the cottage, Morna's tantrum had burned itself out. While Effie dressed her for bed, she giggled and repeated the words *'sea waves, sea waves,'* over and over until it became nonsense, much to Jack's delight. He sat beside her, doing his best to repeat the sounds himself which made Morna giggle even more.

Her head was drooping and her eyes would barely stay open long enough for Effie to spoon porridge into her mouth. She fell asleep almost the instant her head touched the pillow.

Effie changed into her nightgown and hung her wet skirt and petticoats on the clothes horse by the range. She dozed off in the chair with her feet tucked onto a warm brick and when she woke in darkness, her only memories were of a confusing dream of Lachlan and Morna swimming side by side as the waves sang to them.

Midsummer's Day was golden and glorious with the daylight never seemingly going to end. Lachlan had arrived after dark on his first visit. Would he wait again for night to fall? From mid-afternoon, Effie was restless and nervous. In the six months since she'd last seen Lachlan, she had managed to calm her heart down so it beat with a regular rhythm whenever she spoke or thought of him. She doubled her resolve not to let him leave so abruptly but to spend time with his daughter. How would she explain to Morna who he was? She'd have to trust that the girl would recognise her father by instinct as she had seemed to before.

When the knock finally came at the door a few minutes before six, her heart leaped into her throat, beating a double-time jig at the thought of coming face to face with him once again. She whisked the napkins from around Jack and Morna's necks and wiped the mess of jam from their cheeks. She smoothed her hair down, adjusted the ribbons on her apron, then removed it completely, stuffing it beneath the pile of mending. Cross with herself for being so foolish, she mussed her hair up slightly before crossing to the door and opening it.

Walter stood on the doorstep. His smile deepened as he met Effie's eyes.

'What are you doing here?' Effie exclaimed.

Walter's smile dropped.

'That's hardly a greeting for a friend.'

'I'm sorry,' Effie said. 'Of course it's nice to see you, I just didn't know you were home.'

'I arrived at noon. I was paying a call on Reverend Ogram and his family. The sea looked so beautiful from the churchyard I thought I would suggest we might go for a stroll along the clifftop and look at the birds. It's hours until the sun goes down.'

'That's very impulsive of you,' Effie said with a gentle laugh.

Walter looked pleased. 'I feel impulsive today. I've received my degree and am free to begin my life.'

He twisted the hat in his hands and gave her a warm smile. His blue eyes sparkled. Effie had forgotten how attractive he could be.

'Did you know it is Midsummer's Day? Tonight is the longest night of the year,' Walter said.

'I know.'

They both regarded the sky for a moment. It was truly splendid, a canvas of bronze and mauve in a cloudless sky that transformed the sea into a canvas of silver and violet. The sight made Effie want to rush for her paints and brushes. Any other day she would have loved to walk along the cliffs and feel the breeze on her face, but Walter's mention of the date reminded her that Lachlan would be here soon and her pulse raced again. If she had revealed his existence to Walter after the first visit matters would be different but now there were too many questions it would raise.

'I'm sorry, Walter, I can't come with you today.' Effie tried not to peer over his shoulder too obviously. Lachlan might arrive at any moment and she didn't want the two men coming face to face. 'Another day, I would love to join you. I need to put the children to bed. I have washing to fold, mending to do…'

'All that can wait, surely?' Walter said breezily. 'Lay the children down quickly. They will be safe in their beds while we take a brief walk. I have a lot of news to tell you.'

'I'm sorry, but no,' Effie repeated. Walter had no idea how

long it took to settle a child and she was starting to grow irritated at his refusal to take her rebuff seriously. She put her hand on her lower belly and looked pained.

'I'm feeling a little under the weather tonight. I might even have to resort to one of Alice's teas.'

Walter's eyes flickered downwards. Understanding crept across his face and he flushed a little. He was a sensitive young man and was no doubt embarrassed at the thought of any matters of the female body, however natural. It was a little unfair to resort to such a tactic, but if he had accepted Effie's refusal the first time it would not have been necessary.

It was another two weeks before her courses were due and a small flicker of need sputtered into life in Effie's belly. Not for Walter, but for the idea of someone holding her and making love to her. She wondered if he was still a virgin. Manchester must be full of opportunities for a young, well-looking man to meet women who would oblige. Then again, Walter's faith was sincere, and he might be one of those rare men who adhered closely to the scriptures and was waiting for the sacred chains of matrimony.

She had treated her friend a little meanly, so patted his arm.

'Come on Sunday after church. I can bring the children and we can make an afternoon of it. I really would like to hear your news at a better time.'

Walter looked a little pacified, though no doubt he had not intended to make it a family outing.

'You could always join me for the service,' he said hopefully. 'Your attendance would be welcomed.'

Effie grinned. 'I commend your opportunism, but no thank you. I think my permanent absence has been accepted, even if it causes disapproval in some quarters.'

She stood silently and kept smiling until Walter tipped his hat and finally left. Effie shut the door and sighed with relief. She put the kettle on the stove and returned to her pile of mending. She resumed darning the hole in Jack's Sunday smock while the children chased each other about the room. They would tire themselves out and speed the bedtime process.

Not more than a quarter hour passed before there was another knock at the door, a little softer this time. Effie opened it a measure and peered through the crack. Lachlan stood there, an enigmatic smile on his face.

'Good evening,' Effie said. She opened the door and stepped back to allow him to enter.

He paused. 'You don't have any visitors?'

His eyes flickered and Effie wondered if he knew the answer already. Had he been watching her conversation with Walter? How close had he been?

'A friend called a short while ago but he couldn't stay.'

Lachlan nodded. 'I saw. You were formidable in the face of his obstinacy.'

'Were you listening?' Effie folded her arms and gave him a sharp look.

Lachlan held his hands up as if to ward off an attack. It was a playful gesture, one that she was unaccustomed to.

'No. I wasn't that close. I thought it best if I waited until he had gone. But I could tell from the way you both stood that you had very different ideas about what should happen.' He grinned suddenly and his features became almost boyish. 'I'm glad you prevailed.'

He gestured to the door.

'Will you invite me inside?'

'Of course. Please come in.'

He entered the cottage. It felt like a ritual had been completed. Effie mused over his words as she closed the door and followed him. Had it been so obvious that Walter had an attachment to her? She was glad her own body did not suggest it was returned.

'Will you sit down?'

Lachlan hesitated, then sat at the table and folded his sealskin neatly on the floor beside his chair. He was wearing a thinner coat and beneath that a collarless shirt of faded blue with thin white stripes. To still be carrying the heavy skin seemed odd, given how hot the weather had been.

Morna and Jack had noticed the visitor and peered round the edge of the table leg. They stood hand in hand with Morna leading, as always. Lachlan broke into a smile and leaned towards them. Both children came closer, eyes wide with shyness.

'What should I do?' Lachlan asked, glancing at Effie.

'She's your daughter.' Effie hid a smile at his nervousness. How like a man not to know what to do with infants. Walter was much more at ease with them, but he had nieces and nephews to learn with.

'Talk to her. Show her you're happy to see her.'

'I came to observe her progress and welfare,' Lachlan said. 'I don't need to touch her to ascertain that.'

'She doesn't know that.' Effie gently pushed Morna towards Lachlan. 'You leave too quickly. She needs to know who you are. Hold her or play with her. Children like to be held.'

Lachlan shook his head.

'It's enough to know she is safe and happy,' he said. 'Who was the man who came calling?'

Lachlan's tone was suddenly demanding. His broad frame looked tense.

'Tea?' Effie asked, ignoring his question. Lachlan could wait for an answer if that was going to be how he started the conversation.

'No. But thank you. Who was your visitor?' he repeated. There was a hint of something in his voice Effie hadn't heard before.

He was inquisitive, which was fair enough considering his daughter lived in the cottage. Anyone who visited Effie would encounter Morna too and her father was right to be watchful that no harm would come to her. But there had been something else beneath it that she couldn't quite place and that gnawed at her mind.

'My friend's name is Walter Danby. His father part owns the alum works a mile inland.'

'He's a rich man, is he?' Lachlan raised a brow.

Effie considered the question. The works had expanded over the past year, so she assumed it was profitable. 'His father is. Not that that has any bearing on our friendship. Walter has been a good friend to me over the years.'

'How good a friend?' Lachlan asked.

His eyelashes flickered. It was then that Effie realised what the tone beneath his words had been. It was jealousy. A frisson of excitement raced over her skin at the thought he might be interested in whether another man liked her. She sat opposite him in her usual chair and sipped her tea before answering.

'Very good. When I lost John, Walter was the one who broke the news and comforted me. He helped me to keep Morna rather than take her to the poorhouse. His sister has given me clothes for both children when hers have outgrown them, and he has provided the means for me to support myself.'

'All to his credit,' Lachlan said. 'And to his benefit. You obviously care for him.'

Effie paused before answering. 'Yes, I do.'

'And you call him by his Christian name.'

'As I call you by yours,' Effie retorted.

'Mine isn't a Christian name,' Lachlan said. His forehead wrinkled, a slight line appearing between his brows and following the line of his nose.

'Your given name, then,' Effie answered. She picked up her cup and took it to the sink. Lachlan settled back, glowering slightly at Effie but saying nothing. Effie frowned back, thinking it was insufferable to have two men in one evening who were prepared to sulk at her.

'I'll leave you to look at your daughter. Observe how well she is growing. Count her teeth if you like.'

She went into the bedroom and began folding clothes, straightening the counterpane, and shaking blankets vigorously until she had shaken off her agitation too. She walked back into the kitchen.

'Walter came to ask if I wanted to go for a walk with him. I declined because I knew you were coming. If I had known you were in such a temper I would have left the door on the latch and accepted his offer!'

Lachlan pushed himself from the chair.

'Did you want to accept?'

'I don't see why that is any of your business,' Effie snapped.

Lachlan's eyes widened in surprise as they met Effie's. The heat in the look that passed between them could have boiled water. He dipped his head.

'You're right, it isn't. Please accept my apology.'

'I did like the idea of a walk,' she admitted. 'Not with Walter in particular, but it is such a fine evening.' She fanned herself with her free hand. It had felt thundery all week and now the pressure had lifted, replaced by heat.

'I've been busy for most of the day, which incidentally has been the first bright one in a week, though the air has been close. The children have been fractious and...'

Effie stopped talking and gave a great huff. Now she had started, all the irritations that had been weighing her down burst forth, overwhelming her. The weight of responsibility threatened to crush her. When had she last felt carefree?

'Shhh...'

Lachlan held out a hand to Effie. After a brief hesitation she took it. His skin was cool as it had been the first time they had touched. She wanted to keep holding his hand to see how long it would take to warm up. The same frisson of excitement caused the hairs on her arm to stir and wake.

'I'm sorry you've had a hard week, Effie. Would you like to come for a walk with me to see the sunset? There's still a little time before the light fades completely.'

Her heart was too eager for her to accept, leaping high in her chest and suffocating her attempts to decline.

'You don't need to leave? Usually you're so quick to go.'

Lachlan glanced towards the window, his sharp eyes studying the sky. 'I can wait a little longer.'

Effie felt her resistance crumbling. She tried one final excuse.

'Jack and Morna need to go to bed. They should be asleep by now.'

'It willna' take long to settle them.'

Lachlan smiled in the direction of the children who were

lying side by side on the rug. They did look sleepy. The chasing around the table and curiosity at the visitor had tired them out. Effie changed them into their nightshirts and laid them in their cot, then pulled the curtains tightly shut until only a sliver of light peeked round the edge.

She turned to find Lachlan had followed her into the room and was standing close behind her. She started in surprise. No man had ever accompanied her into her bedroom besides John. Perhaps in Scotland people behaved differently and Lachlan saw nothing unseemly in his behaviour, or maybe life at sea had made him unused to the company of women. She put her finger to her lips and glanced towards the children.

Lachlan nodded. He laid his hand on Morna's brow and began to sing:

Dèan an cadalan 's dùin do shùilean.
Mo ghaol, mo ghaol.

The words meant nothing to Effie, but the tune was slow and soothing and the melodic baritone wove a spell around her. She sat on the edge of the bed, eyes beginning to close as Lachlan sang the children to sleep and feeling the tightness leaving her neck and shoulders. When his voice became a whisper and the last note died into nothing, Effie sighed with regret. Both children were sleeping peacefully, breathing in long, even breaths. Lachlan put a hand on her shoulder and she looked up at him through dream-heavy eyes.

'They will be safe from any harm and we won't disturb them,' Lachlan said. He held out his hand and fixed Effie with an intense gaze. She swallowed nervously and tried to ignore the bed she could see from the corner of her eye. Her husband had been a creative and vigorous lover but the fire that leaped to life in her breast as Lachlan faced her had never once grown so fierce in John's presence.

'Will you walk with me now, Effie?' Lachlan asked.

A walk. Cool evening air. Far from the heat and the room's associations of loss and lovemaking.

'Yes,' she said. 'I will.'

Chapter Seven

While Lachlan took another look at the sleeping children, Effie left the bedroom quickly. She smoothed her hair, hoping she did not look as flustered as she felt. If Lachlan commented on it, she would have to blame it on the heat of the evening. She tucked her light woollen shawl around her shoulders. Lachlan draped his sealskin over his shoulder. Together they walked to the beach and onto the sand. The tide was still out and the way would be quicker on the damp sand but, conscious that they might be spotted, Effie led Lachlan to the back edge below the cliffs. Being seen with a strange man would lead to gossip that she could do without. Moreover, if it reached Walter's ears he would be hurt and she didn't want that. They picked their way over the rocks. Some of them contained fossils – small creatures that looked like insects from so far back in time Effie couldn't contemplate it.

'Have you found any?' Lachlan asked when she told him.

'No, but I've seen the ones other people have picked up. Maybe I don't pay enough attention.'

'I imagine you pay more attention to things than most do,'

Lachlan said, tipping his head to one side and giving Effie a thoughtful look.

The breeze was still warm from the heat of the day. Effie wrapped her shawl over her arm rather than wear it. Her neck felt sticky and she longed to feel the air on her skin. She undid the top button of her blouse and then the one below that and loosened her collar to let the breeze do its best to cool her. Lachlan had draped his fur over his arm. It looked heavy and hot, but he didn't seem to mind.

The beach curved away from the village towards the inlet called Boggle's Cove. Effie and Lachlan walked side by side until they reached the stream that trickled down to join the sea from the cove between the rocks. The bay was sheltered and out of sight of the village. They would only be visible from the sea itself. Any worries that they might be seen melted away.

Lachlan selected a large, smooth boulder. He spread his fur out and sat on it before gesturing to Effie.

'Will you join me?'

The boulder was not large and they would be sitting intimately close. Her heart gave another thud, quickly followed by a shiver that ran down through her stomach and settled low in her belly. He had no idea what effect he had on her but, given his brief show of jealousy over Walter, she wondered if she was having the same effect on him.

She spread her shawl out next to the skin but not touching, and sat on it. She twisted round to face him and where his collar fell open she noticed a blueish-green circle about the size of a thumbprint. At first she thought it was a bruise but it was too regular. It must be a tattoo of some sort. She wondered what the rest of it – the part concealed by the shirt – looked like.

'You seemed ill at ease with Morna,' she said.

'I'm not used to children. I don't know what to do with them.'

'You'll grow better. You did well tonight soothing them to sleep.' Effie patted his arm. 'The song you sang was beautiful.'

Lachlan ran his hands through his hair and over the back of his neck.

'Tell me about Morna.'

Effie thought before answering. How to conjure a child's life in a few words for a father who seemed reluctant to know her in person.

'She's wilful,' she said, smiling as she added, 'and I don't mean that in a bad way. She's strong and determined to get her own way as all children are. She likes strawberries but not in jam. She fights going to sleep. At least usually she does. If I could sing to her like you did I'd have an easier time.'

'I could teach you the tune, but the words are harder to learn. The language is ancient,' Lachlan said. 'Tell me more.'

Effie chatted easily now, listing the new words Morna had learned since his last visit, how well she could walk and how close she and Jack were. Lachlan nodded in encouragement, asking questions and before long Effie had almost forgotten her awkwardness.

'Children grow so quickly. If you came more often you would see the change yourself,' she said.

'I can't do that.'

A breeze blew the warm scent of saltwater across the beach. Effie inhaled with a satisfied sigh and was instantly consumed by the urge to wade into the depths. She looked towards the sea.

'If you want to go in then do it,' Lachlan murmured.

She turned to him in surprise.

'How did you know that is what I was thinking?'

'You have a very expressive face. Also, I was thinking the same thing.'

She kicked off her clogs then turned her back to Lachlan and discreetly peeled off her stockings. The sand was cool and she burrowed her toes in it with a sigh of pleasure. She picked her way over the shells and pebbles to the edge of the water and stood close enough for the gentle waves to lap at her toes as they washed in.

Lachlan was still sitting on his fur watching her with a look of longing on his face.

'Will you join me?' she called.

After a moment he pulled off his boots and came to stand beside her at the water's edge. He rolled up his trouser legs, revealing well-shaped, smooth calves that were lightly tanned. He took a couple of steps further out than Effie. This brought them to the same height so that when he turned back his eyes were level with Effie's. He smiled and the edges of his eyes crinkled.

The sea was chilly but not as cold as it would be by morning. It felt refreshing. Invigorating. Her skin came alive. Effie wished she could lift her skirts and wade in as deep up her legs as Lachlan. Wished she could spread her arms and fall backwards into the waves.

'Morna loves the sea,' she said, smiling at him. 'She makes it her purpose to reach it at every opportunity.'

Lachlan looked at her sharply.

'Has she managed it?'

Effie took a step back, surprised at his sudden ferocity. 'I take her to play in the waves. It doesn't do any harm. She was so determined, it seemed cruel to deny her. She wanted to do it so much, I was worried that forbidding it would lead to her trying all the more.'

'Did something happen to make you suspect that?' Lachlan asked. His voice was soft once more, inviting her to tell him.

Effie gazed out to sea as she told him of the terrible day when she had lost sight of Morna and how the child had almost gone headfirst into the foam. While she spoke, Lachlan stood rigidly, face carved from granite and eyes never leaving the sea.

'I'm so sorry,' Effie whispered. 'I should never have taken my eyes of her. If she had drowned…'

She swallowed the end of the thought, a painful knot tied in her throat. She stumbled back to the rock and sat on it, her head in her hands. Warm tears bubbled at her eyes. She felt Lachlan draw close and looked up.

'It wasn't your fault. It is in her nature. I had hoped…' He broke off and gazed out to sea. 'It matters not. The fault is mine.'

'How could it be yours?' Effie asked. 'You weren't even here. I was distracted, but it won't happen again. I've never let her out of my sight since. Tonight is the first time, in fact.'

She glanced in the direction of the cottage. She and Lachlan had spent longer than she had intended.

'Morna and your son are safe, but we should go back. This night is passing and I canna stay for much longer.' Lachlan picked up his fur and gazed at it for a moment, then slung it over his shoulder.

'I need to think.'

Lachlan said nothing as they walked. Effie purposefully dropped behind to give him the chance to think over whatever was troubling him. He was right to be furious that Effie had put his daughter in danger, but there seemed to be more on his mind and she burned to find out what it was.

When they reached the turn of the beach and the village

came into view, Effie stopped and looked in dismay. The tide had come in further than she had expected and the way was blocked with water that was already knee deep. They would get soaked. The sun had dropped now, replaced with a pale half-moon that cast the beach into a palette of greys and purples.

'We'll go over the rocks,' Lachlan said and walked towards the back of the beach. The rocks at the base of the cliff had fallen decades ago. They were larger and more jagged than the ones the sea was able to stroke smooth. Clambering over them would be difficult without tangling or tearing her skirts. Lachlan had already begun to climb. When he looked back to see Effie standing there, he looked at her questioningly. She gestured to her skirt in explanation. He strode back, sure-footed over the rocks, and held his arms out.

'Give me your hands.'

She did as he asked and found herself lifted off her feet and swung up. She scrabbled her feet against the uneven rocks and wobbled, lifting onto her tiptoes and throwing her arms wide. Before she could slip down again, Lachlan caught her around the waist and held her to him. Effie looked into his eyes and saw reassurance radiating from him. He shifted and lowered Effie to her feet, somehow finding a flat surface to rest her on amid the jagged folds of rock. She dropped from her tiptoes onto her flat feet, feeling more stable.

'I've got you. You won't fall,' Lachlan murmured.

Effie nodded. Lachlan moved the hand that had been on her waist a little higher so that it settled in between her shoulder blades. Slowly, Effie put her hand to his chest, her eyes never leaving his. His body was firm and warm. Beneath his shirt, Effie could feel the contours of well-formed muscles. It had been so long since she had touched anyone in such an intimate manner or been held close. She gave an involuntary shudder as her mind filled with the notion of running her hand over more of him and discovering what other intriguing marvels were hidden beneath his clothes.

Her ears began to buzz with the speed of the blood rushing through her veins. Lachlan had bent his head to speak to her. His lips were so close to hers now. She looked in fascination at the smooth, fine shape of his mouth and the deep cleft in his upper lip. For such thin lips they were extraordinarily sensual.

For the first time in longer than she could remember, Effie Cropton wanted to be kissed. She could lift her head and bring her lips to Lachlan's. Would he release her or kiss her back?

Lachlan answered the unspoken question for her. He dipped his head and his lips skimmed across hers with the lightest touch, so soft Effie was not entirely sure it wasn't her imagination supplying what she craved or if the kiss was really happening. Either way she was not going to pass up the opportunity.

Lachlan's tongue brushed against the inner of Effie's bottom lip. He tasted of salt and iced water.

A gentle greeting.

An invitation.

She put her arms around his neck and kissed him again, letting her tongue meet his; a spark igniting in her. She felt him go stiff in her arms and he pulled his lips away from hers. Had she been so clumsy that she had repelled him? It had been so long since she'd kissed anyone; she must have forgotten how. She cringed with embarrassment. She stole a glance at Lachlan, expecting to see him laughing or revolted but he was looking shamefaced.

'Forgive me. I shouldna' have done that. The moment and the moonlight.' He shook his head. 'I have no justification.'

'You don't need one,' Effie said. She let out a long breath. Her lips were still throbbing from his kiss and she found forming words strange, as if her lips demanded to return to their previous activity. 'As you say, a beautiful evening like this can make people behave oddly.'

Lachlan tilted his head a little to the right and held her gaze, unblinking. His dark eyes grew blacker as his pupils widened, almost obliterating the green surrounding them.

'Even so, it was wrong of me. I should have been stronger willed.'

He held himself responsible, not her.

She dropped her eyes, feeling as shy as she had on the night she had first met John. Her heart was thumping and her skin felt prickly, as though she had run through nettles.

'And I should have protested. But I didn't. It was only a kiss after all.'

He stared at her solemnly with the large, serene eyes that drew her in, pupils large and black, rimmed with irises as green as the rock pools beyond the Brigg. He reached out and ran his thumb over her cheek, brushing against the corner of her lips with the cool digit. Oh, to be touched again in that place his lips had so recently been! He was right to go now. If he stayed, Effie wasn't sure what might happen.

Or she knew only too well exactly what would occur.

Her cheeks grew hot with shame, but her blood raced at the idea of being touched even more intimately. She stepped back from Lachlan hastily and glanced up again to find him staring at her with an intensity that took her breath away. She wanted to kiss him again, more fully and for longer. She wanted to do so much more but sensed his resistance. At the moment they were friends; if she pushed him, that could change, but something in his face was warning her there was more to his reluctance than she understood.

'Why does it matter so much?' she asked. 'Why was it so wrong?'

He fixed his eyes resolutely on the sea.

'We should go back to the house,' Effie muttered. 'We've left the children for too long.'

She clambered down the other side of the rock unaided, cheeks flaming with shame and desire that welled up inside her from a seemingly unending pool of lava.

Lachlan stood staring at her for a minute before leaping gracefully down and landing beside Effie in a crouch. He stood and faced her. Effie felt a blush rise to her cheeks. He talked of strength, and she knew he had been referring to moral strength but she couldn't ignore the energy he exuded. She pulled her shawl tightly over her shoulders. It was black, like all her clothing – a widow's dress. Perhaps that was the cause of his reluctance. It wasn't immoral to have kissed Lachlan. John was gone and, while she mourned him, she knew deep inside her that the place he held in her heart was only a small part of a greater emptiness that cried out to be filled.

'I'll go now,' Lachlan said. 'Farewell, Effie Cropton.'

'You're leaving just like that?' Effie exclaimed. After the kiss she felt flustered and more than a little cheated that he was not going to repeat the experience. 'Without saying farewell to Morna?'

'Morna is sleeping. If I returned to your house it would not be for her benefit. Are you still happy to keep Morna in your care? Do we still have our compact, Effie Cropton?'

'Of course. I love her as if she were my own. I'll care for her as long as she – or you – need me to.'

He dipped his hand into his pocket and produced another

pearl. It seemed to glow from within in the fading sunlight as he held it between his shapely fingers.

'Where do you get these?' she asked.

Lachlan smiled and pressed the pearl into Effie's palm. 'I hunt for them.'

She rolled it round with her fingers. It was slightly larger than the one she already had nestled in her drawer. It felt like a drop of ice. Lachlan turned to face the sea once more. Silhouetted against the sunset, his profile was smooth and sharp, reminding Effie of a figurehead from an old ship. She could imagine him dressed in his fur, standing on the prow of a ship as it ploughed through the Baltic waters. Not a modern steamer but a low, open vessel powered by oars. A seal trapper and oyster fisher. It seemed romantically old fashioned.

He turned back to Effie.

'What passed between us tonight… I hope it won't cause a breach between us.'

The kiss may have meant nothing to him, or as much as it had to Effie, but something in his manner was building a wall between them and she couldn't let it rise any higher.

'You're full of secrets,' she said irritably. 'I don't want a breach between us either, but you are keeping things from me and I don't like it.'

His expression was solemn, sad even. 'Go and see to the children. We will meet again when half a year has passed.'

He shrugged the sealskin over his shoulders and walked away. Effie stared after him with a mixture of fury and confusion. He was heading towards the beach, not the town, retracing their steps. There was no other village for miles. Had he left a boat moored somewhere? They had walked quite a way and if he had a rowing boat in Boggle Cove she hadn't noticed it. He was full of mysteries and Effie wanted to unravel them more than she had wanted anything for a long time. Barely stopping to think, she ran after him, reaching out a hand to grasp the pelt that swung down his back in order to stop him leaving.

'Half a year is too long without answers!'

He stopped and spun around, his eyes dropping to the pelt in Effie's hand. She let go.

'I want to know everything,' she said. She held the pearl out. 'If you want me to keep your daughter, tell me the truth.'

'Are you sure you want it?' Lachlan asked.

'So there is something you aren't telling me,' Effie said.

'Aye. And if I tell you, things will change between us. Maybe between you and Morna. Are you sure you want that?'

She hesitated. Nothing Lachlan could say about Morna would change Effie's love. It was a mother's love; unwavering and endless.

'Yes.'

She closed her fist over the pearl. Lachlan's eyes followed.

'Tomorrow morning I'll come to you and you'll hear it. Farewell for tonight, Effie Cropton.'

He walked away, and this time Effie let him go, watching until he was out of sight.

Even with Lachlan's strange response and sudden departure, the kiss had done Effie's spirits good. When she returned to the cottage she found the children were awake but lying placidly.

'What do you think your dada will tell me?' she asked Morna, mischievously. 'Do you think he is a pirate? A smuggler? The lost heir to a foreign kingdom?'

Morna blew bubbles and considered the question gravely. 'Boggle.'

Jack repeated the word over and over in his sing-song voice and Effie laughed.

'Now that would be funny.'

She tried to remember the song Lachlan had sung to lull the children to sleep. She was fairly sure she had remembered the tune but perhaps half the magic was in Lachlan's voice because when she sang it the children smiled up at her but did not fall under the spell as quickly as they had earlier.

'When your dada comes back tomorrow, I'll have to get him to teach me the words,' she said as she tucked Morna under the patchwork quilt. It didn't matter how snugly she started the night, by morning she was atop all the layers with her feet up against the footboard.

'Da,' Morna said, sleepily.

Effie smiled. Neither child spoke much, although they communicated to each other in their own way.

'Ga,' Jack echoed. Effie's smile faded. She pressed her lips together feeling a wash of melancholy. Jack had no father coming back to him.

'Good night, my treasures,' she whispered, closing the door and leaving them to sleep. She gathered her workbasket and the ever-increasing pile of mending and altering and sat outside the cottage on the front step.

The air was fresh and salty and the night was warm. Midsummer's Day had passed and slowly the heat and light from the sun would begin to diminish, but for now she could believe it would be summer forever. Gulls circled effortlessly on the horizon over the placid sea. She wondered whether Lachlan could see them from wherever he was now. The idea of him made her frown even as it caused her lips to throb in memory. Tomorrow he would no doubt spin her some tale of why he shouldn't have kissed her. Was it due to the curious tattoo on his chest perhaps? Tattoos were commonplace among seafaring folk, but these were the oddest she had seen. Her mind went to Charles Dickens' *Great Expectations* and the convict in the marshes who had left his daughter with another woman. Did Lachlan's skin bear brands of punishment of some sort? Had he been a criminal?

Whatever the answer was, there would be a rational explanation, but waiting to discover it was almost unendurable. The pile of mending went untouched as Effie's mind filled with doubts.

Chapter Eight

The next morning promised another fine day ahead. After breakfast, Effie dressed the children in clean smocks and straw hats and put them in the garden to play. Movement caught her eye. Lachlan was making his way back across the sand, his timing perfect. Effie left the door open and poured herself another cup of tea from the pot and sat at the table. She placed a second cup beside the pot, leaving it up to Lachlan to decide whether he was going to continue his strange habit of refusing anything she offered.

Presently, Lachlan tapped on the door and waited until Effie bade him enter. He took the chair opposite hers, steepled his fingers beneath his chin and regarded her with a solemn expression.

'What do you want to tell me?' she prompted.

He remained silent as the minutes passed and Effie had to force herself not to ask again but eventually heaved a sigh.

'You've asked me and you have the right to know. There is something I need to tell you about Morna's birth. About her mother and about myself. Something I should have told you long before.'

Effie thought of Prudence Maynard. Of the brews Alice made which worked or not depending on luck and timing as much as on the effectiveness of the contents. Of the children born to mothers who had no choice but to carry them. Was Morna the result of such an association? Did Lachlan have a string of lovers with unfortunate scraps fostered out up and down the coast? Jealousy stung like a wasp.

'Tell me,' she said.

'Have you noticed anything unusual about Morna? Odd habits, strange urges?'

Effie wrinkled her brow. It was Jack who concerned her. He didn't speak as well and rarely seemed to respond when people spoke to him, preferring to spend his time repeatedly drawing spirals or looking at the birds. The only thing that marked Morna out as unusual were the dark, old eyes that she had still not grown into, but she could hardly say that to Lachlan when their twins gazed at her so intently now.

'She's perfectly happy and normal. The only urge she persists in is trying to get into the sea at every opportunity.'

Lachlan made a noise in the back of his throat and jerked his hands together. Effie took a sip of tea and tried to remain calm in the face of his strange behaviour.

'Lachlan, what are you trying to say? Why was it so wrong to kiss me? Why should Morna seem odd? If there is an illness you share that I should know about, tell me.'

'No illness,' he said. 'Effie, I havena' been honest with you. I should have been but I was scared you'd reject her. For that I apologise, but you'll see why when I tell you what I have to.'

Lachlan walked to the window and looked out at the children. They were running in circles, heads back and mouths open, squawking like gulls. They were having great fun. Effie had done the same as a child. She glanced at Lachlan, who had the purest look of sadness on his face.

'What are you hiding?' she whispered.

He reached out, fingers touching the pane of glass.

'You have seen how Morna craves the sea? I had hoped she would not. Or would not so soon.'

He looked at Effie and his face was bleak. A chill ran through her.

'We are of the sea, she and I. It calls to her as it calls to me.'

Effie bit her lip. Sailors often talked of the sea calling them but Effie suspected the urge was in themselves, not in the water itself. Lachlan obviously expected a reaction to his words but she wasn't sure what to supply.

'What are you trying to tell me?'

'We are not the same as you or your son, Effie. There is not a person here in this village who is the same as Morna or me.'

Lachlan carried the teapot and cups – his untouched – to the sink. He took off his sealskin and spread it over the now-empty table. It looked much larger spread out. He ran a hand over it, fingers burrowing into the brown depths.

'This skin is mine, Effie. It is part of me. When I don it, I become the seal. When I remove it, I become the man you see before you. Morna is the same. The name for our kind is Selkie.'

Effie felt for the dining chair, pulled it out and sat, digesting his words.

'You become a seal when you wear your fur? Morna could become a seal?'

'Aye.'

Such fanciful stupidity. Lachlan must think her feebleminded to tell her such a thing.

'You expect me to believe such a foolish story as this?' she said coldly.

Lachlan blinked. 'It isna' a story. It's the truth.'

Effie gave a scornful laugh. 'Of course it is. You transform into a seal. So will Morna.'

'Aye.'

Effie's stomach clenched with anger. She leaned across the table and looked into his eyes, mustering all the contempt she could.

'Lachlan, I'm a grown woman. I don't believe in fairy-tales. You're insulting me now, for whatever reason of your own. If you regret kissing me, please be man enough to say that.'

'You think I'm telling you this because I regret our kiss?'

'Yes!' Effie felt tears pricking at the corners of her eyes. 'Tell me you've got another woman, or that I'm too old for your taste. Or that I was clumsy and you felt nothing. But such a fanciful lie demeans us both.'

'None of those things are true!' Lachlan exclaimed. His mouth jerked into a rueful smile, his lip curling slightly. 'You are a fascinating woman, Effie Cropton, and I feel your pull as strongly as a spring tide. That's why last night was a mistake. For my kind to become involved with yours is doomed to end in tragedy.'

He dropped his head, steepled his long fingers and gazed intently at them before lifting his gaze once more and meeting Effie's eye. 'You don't believe me. That's to be expected. You are, as you say, a grown woman and fanciful things are beneath you. What would it take, Effie Cropton, to make you believe in something?'

His eyes flashed, pupils large and black, irises green as moss on wet rocks. With his high cheekbones and straight nose, the smooth brow and black hair gave him a sleek profile.

Effie shivered, though the morning was hot. A bead of perspiration slowly made its way between her shoulder blades. If it weren't such nonsense, she could almost believe he belonged in one of Alice's tales along with boggarts and pixies.

'You still have Morna's skin kept safe?' Lachlan asked.

'I do.'

'Please bring it to me,' he commanded in a low voice.

Effie went into the bedroom and pulled the basket and fur down from the top of the wardrobe. Dust flew everywhere, making her cough and blink it away; a couple of spiders would be homeless, judging by the cobwebs that stuck to her fingers. She was slovenly when it came to cleaning things that were out of sight.

The basket disintegrated in her hands, rushes and reeds crumbling and drifting to the floor. She took the remnants and the fur to Lachlan. He held the fur tenderly and brought it to his face as Effie had longed to do herself when she first discovered Morna.

'If I were lying, you'd expect to see what you saw before, you agree? A fur only big enough to wrap a newborn babe?'

Effie nodded. Her stomach fluttered and she pressed her hand to it firmly as the first inkling of doubt awoke. Surely Lachlan couldn't continue his pretence any further? He moved his own pelt out of the way and spread Morna's in its place.

'Look and tell me if I speak the truth,' he said, stepping back to the wall so there was space at the table.

Effie did as he bid her.

The colour had deepened, but, more disconcertingly, the pelt had undoubtedly grown. Whereas before it had been just the size to cover a newborn baby snugly, now it was double that. Big enough to comfortably wrap a child of three or four. Effie bit her bottom lip and lifted the fur with fingers that shook. The pelt was as soft and warm as she remembered. She held it to her cheek. From the garden outside she heard Morna giggle.

A coincidence, surely?

Effie spread it out on the table again and frowned at Lachlan. He could not be speaking the truth. He couldn't. Her mind refused to comprehend it. She ran her palm over it and Morna giggled again, louder, as she did when Effie tickled her.

'This can't be the same fur. You've swapped them somehow.'

Lachlan laughed softly. 'How would I have done that?'

He walked over to her, reached out and brushed a grey smattering of cobwebby dust from Effie's hair where it had landed. He held his fingers up to show her the spun silk that glinted in a beam of light.

A chill crept over Effie. The fur had lain undisturbed for the last two years where she had left it in the remains of the basket on the shelf. Untouched since Lachlan had requested to see it on the night he first appeared. The dust bore witness to the passing of time. It was unquestionably the same fur, yet it had grown. That could be proof he was speaking the truth, but her mind rebelled.

Lachlan ran his hand over the small skin with the reverence of a priest touching a relic. When he spoke, his voice was brimming with love. 'This is Morna's skin. It will grow with her as she grows. The other is mine.'

Effie had asked for proof, and like Thomas doubting Christ she had been given it. She laid her fingers on the fur again. Faced with evidence of the impossible, her mind threw a hundred different thoughts at her. Fear pinned her to the spot. Lachlan was standing close, staring at her with a watchful expression, his frame tensed.

To flee or attack her?

A seal.

An animal.

Not human.

He held out his hand to touch her. 'Effie?'

His voice was even and low, as if he were speaking to a jittery animal. And just like a frightened lamb, she jumped back out of his reach. He stepped forward. Spurred on by terror she lunged forward and shoved him hard.

'Monster!'

He didn't fall, or even seem to be affected, but his face twisted in distress. He picked up Morna's fur and held it to him, lovingly. Seeing her chance, Effie bolted past him and into the bedroom. She slammed the door and pressed her back to it, panting. Her breath wouldn't come and she was growing faint. A soft knocking on the door made her jump.

'Talk to me.' Lachlan spoke soothingly, his voice still low and quiet. Effie used the same tone when trying to soothe the children.

Her heart seized.

Jack was alone in the garden with Morna. Effie had left her child at the mercy of these creatures. Her legs began to shake. Only the thought that Jack was outside gave her the energy to stand upright. She counted to three, took a deep breath and opened the door. Lachlan was standing directly on the other side with his hands spread wide on the frame. He toppled forward, taken unawares. Effie ducked beneath his arms and ran to the front door.

'Effie, wait, please. Listen to me. You have nothing to fear from me.'

He caught hold of the back of her skirt as Effie threw the door open. She cried out in fear and anger. Jack and Morna stopped their game and looked up in alarm. Effie spun to face Lachlan with her fists raised and he dropped her skirt. His pelt was lying over the table where he had spread it. Effie clutched at it, raising it before her like a shield to ward him off. Her fingers curled into the rich-brown warmth and the nails dug deep. Lachlan's face twisted. Effie dug her fingers tighter until the nails bit deeper. Lachlan stumbled. He clutched his side, closing his eyes with a grunt of discomfort.

'Don't…'

Until that point, even though her mind told her Lachlan must be telling the truth, Effie had not truly believed in her heart. His reaction was the proof she needed. She loosened her grip and looked at the fur in horror. She'd caused him pain. Tears blurred her vision. She had grasped the nearest fur but she might equally have used Morna's and caused her daughter to scream in pain. Her stomach heaved. Whatever Morna was, Effie could never intentionally hurt her.

She laid the fur back over the chair and stood trembling before Lachlan, arms around her as a shield.

'What are you?' Her voice was a whisper, strangled by tears.

'I told you. But we are nothing to fear.' He held both hands out, palms upwards in a gesture of surrender and stepped closer. 'Last night you greeted me warmly. You walked on the beach at my side.'

She remembered the night before and what else they had done on the beach. What else she had wanted to do.

'You kissed me,' she whispered. 'I kissed *you*, and you let me do it, knowing what you are!'

The memory of the kiss came back to her, but this time it was sullied. She groaned in disgust and wiped her hand viciously across her lips as if that could rid them of the trace of him. Lachlan looked pained.

He looked human.

He had felt human, and the kiss had not felt like anything other than a normal kiss, and a very good one at that. Effie lowered her hand and bunched it in her skirt.

Lachlan looked at her gravely. 'Every time we have met I came close to telling you, but I lacked the courage. When you and I kissed last night I knew I could no longer deny you the truth.'

He reached a hand up, then withdrew it hastily and clenched his fist to his side. The kiss *had* meant something to him, Effie understood, but he had stopped. She had wanted to continue, but he had been stronger. She couldn't hate him for that.

'The kiss should never have happened but the memory wouldna' fade. You wouldn't fade, Effie Cropton.'

Lachlan stepped towards her and took her gently by the shoulders. She stiffened as he touched her, but didn't protest. When she looked into his eyes she saw no threat, only the same warmth she had always seen when he looked at her. The same brown eyes with the sea-green flecks.

'I knew I could not keep the truth from you any longer. I resolved yesterday to tell you, whatever the cost.'

'What are you?' she asked, her voice shaking.

'We're called Selkies.'

He'd said it before. The word meant nothing to her but hearing there was a name for what Lachlan claimed he was made her shiver. He guided her to the table, a hand firm but gentle on the small of her back. She let him. Her legs didn't feel like hers. She felt like she was wading through the sea, slightly buoyant and dragging against resistance. When she was seated, Lachlan poured out a cup of tea and placed it before her. She sipped it slowly. The tea had gone cold in the pot, but the earthy sweetness was comfortingly normal. A lighthouse, guiding her through treacherous waters. Lachlan sat silently opposite her, watchful.

'You feel better?'

She smiled faintly. 'I've often joked with Alice that there was magic in the leaves. Now I wonder if there truly is.'

Why not, she mused, when a creature from a folk tale was sitting opposite her. The corner of his mouth twitched upwards. It occurred to her that he was as apprehensive as she was. She put the cup on the table and faced him.

'How many are there like you?' she asked.

'Two hundred or thereabouts that I know. My clan are scattered between islands in the north of Scotland. Mine is named Skailwick.'

He waited for her to comprehend his words. Almost the same number as lived in Allendale Head. She struggled to imagine her village filled with men and women who could change their shape at will.

'There are others across the sea in Ireland and Iceland,' Lachlan continued. 'Maybe five hundred in all that I know of. In other parts of the world, who can say. I'm trusting you with a lot by even telling you this, Effie.'

'Trusting *me*?' she exclaimed. 'You tricked me, not the other way around. Why have you waited so long to tell me?'

'I didna' want to tell you the first time we met.'

'You wanted to take Morna then,' Effie said. The anger was rising again. She fought it down. 'If you had told me this at the start I would never have stopped you. Why didn't you tell me then?'

'You're right. If I had taken Morna away as I had planned I

wouldn't have had to tell you anything and you would have been none the wiser, but she'd drunk your milk. You had a claim on her.' Lachlan looked regretful. 'I should have told you but when I saw how you had already grown to love her, I knew this was the right place for her and I feared you'd refuse. Whatever or whoever she is, she loves you and you love her.'

Effie glared at him. 'So you concealed the truth.'

'Yes. If there had been another way, I would have taken it.' Lachlan sighed deeply. 'Once I saw the bond that had developed, I knew she belonged to you as much as to me. More, even, because I cannot provide a mother's love that you can, or the care a woman can give a child.'

'You should still have told me the truth when you first came,' Effie said. She folded her arms and looked sternly at him. Hearing him speak of mothers and love tore her heart. She did love Morna, whatever she was.

'If I had told you, would you have rejected her?'

Effie hung her head, the truth in her heart a shameful thing. 'Probably, yes. Or I wouldn't have believed you. I'm still not sure I believe you now.'

Her eyes fell on the pelt she had inadvertently used to injure him. And Morna's.

There was no doubting Lachlan's words.

'Right now I've half a mind to send her with you,' she said. 'I don't know what I've brought into my home. What if she harms Jack?'

'She won't.'

Lachlan walked over to the window and his face softened into a smile. He beckoned Effie to join him.

'Come. Look at the children.'

Reluctantly she joined him and stood at his side. His eyes flickered over her and his brow furrowed. He wasn't human.

He might look like a man – and there was nothing about him to hint at anything otherwise – but she didn't quite trust him not to transform into something other. He moved aside from the window and Effie took his place. Jack and Morna were giggling together and looked as perfectly content as ever. Morna stopped occasionally to turn and stare at a particularly large wave that crashed on the shore. She seemed uncannily able to spot them before they broke.

'The sea calls to her,' Lachlan said softly. 'It is in her nature to try and answer.'

He sounded forlorn.

'When she crawled to the sea, what would have happened if she had reached the waves and I hadn't been there?' Effie asked. The memory of the terrible minutes spent searching hit her like a punch to the belly. The responsibility was so enormous. 'Would she have drowned or swum?'

Lachlan took his time before answering.

'I don't know. In her seal form, swimming would come as naturally as breathing. Even in human form we have an amazing ability to hold our breath and swim. But if she hasn't been taught…'

He shuddered.

'Thank you for keeping her safe once again.'

He glanced at the sky.

'We both have lots to consider. I think I will take Morna for a walk by the shore. The tide won't turn for a while yet and we can go past the rocks.'

Without waiting for Effie's answer, he gathered the two pelts from the table.

He left the cottage. Effie didn't stop him.

He paused to speak to Jack and patted the boy on the head. Jack wriggled his shoulders and returned to his game. Lachlan spoke to Morna. She stared at him with her solemn eyes then put her hand in his. Effie watched as they walked around the bend in the path. Her heart gave a lurch, the invisible rope tugging her after them. What if Lachlan had decided to leave and she never saw Morna again? What if she never saw either of them again?

She went into the garden. Lachlan and Morna had already disappeared from view by the time she reached the gate. Would they use the pelts to transform into seals?

The idea intrigued rather than repulsed her. She tried to picture how the transformation took place. Clearly just being in the presence of the skin wasn't enough or Morna would have appeared as a seal, not a human child, in the basket. There were so many questions she wanted to ask. Were there magic words? Did they have to be naked?

She blinked and coughed, wondering where that last thought had come from but found she couldn't rid herself of the image of Lachlan removing all his clothes until he stood naked. Was he a man in every sense?

Her face and neck grew warm. She turned her eyes to the sky, hoping for a cloud to appear in the endless blue to hide the sun and cool her. To bring her to her senses, for she had doubtless lost her wits for desiring him.

She sat on the step and picked Jack up, holding him close. He allowed her embrace for a brief moment before giving a wordless babble and leaning away. She put him down reluctantly. He seemed content in his private world and any attempt to show him affection was merely tolerated. It felt traitorous to admit it but, whatever she might be, Morna was more affectionate than Effie's own flesh and blood.

Chapter Nine

There was nothing to be accomplished sitting and waiting for Lachlan to return. Effie could pace and wait, but it was a fine drying day and there was washing to be done. Something normal would help ease her mind.

Lachlan and Morna still hadn't returned by the time she had washed and wrung the linens. As she hung them on the line that stretched from the privy to the cottage where they wafted gently in the breeze, she glanced down the beach. The only people there were a handful of older children leaping over the surf and the two middle-aged spinsters from the house at the top of the hill, who walked arm in arm as always.

'Jack, shall we bake apple pies?' she asked. He blew a bubble of appreciation. Mentions of food always caught his attention. Effie made pastry while Jack stood on a chair and watched. She was helping him press out the circles for the bases, holding his small hand over the cutter to help him press hard enough, when the gate creaked. Lachlan and Morna came through the front door, hand in hand.

'Baking. Morna will bake!'

Morna squealed in excitement and let go of Lachlan's hand. She ran to Effie, who opened her arms to help her onto a chair. She knew, as the warm bundle squirmed against her, that she would never deny the girl a home or love. Morna and Jack began a tug of war over the pastry cutter while Effie tried to roll up Morna's sleeves, put an apron on her and stop both children from tumbling to the floor.

Lachlan stood watching in the doorway, his face solemn as he watched the mess unfolding before his eyes. In his arms he held both furs, and now that Effie saw them side by side, she could see that the smaller one was slightly lighter. She caught his eye and he smiled uncertainly but didn't move closer.

'I wasn't sure if you were coming back,' she said.

'Why not?' He sounded genuinely surprised.

'You took your... the furs.'

'When I leave I will always say goodbye,' Lachlan said. 'That isn't why I took them.'

'Did you swim?' She couldn't bring herself to say 'transform'.

'No. We played in the sand and splashed in the waves, but, for now, Morna doesn't need to know what she is.'

He looked likely to remain standing in the doorway for ever, half in and half out. The irony was not lost on her.

'Come in properly and shut the door behind you.'

He raised an eyebrow but did as he was told. Morna triumphed in the tug of war and seized the metal disc from Jack who began to wail. Lachlan flinched, perhaps fearing Effie would take this as proof that his daughter was a danger to her son.

'No! You must share,' she told them sternly, removing the cutter from Morna and pocketing it.

'Children quarrel over the slightest thing,' she reassured Lachlan.

'Aye, that's the same whether human or not.'

Morna and Jack both began pulling on Effie's apron, trying to reclaim the treasured cutter. She'd wanted to ask Lachlan all the questions she had spinning in her mind, but she could see that wasn't going to happen now.

'Will you help us?' she asked. 'They can both cut but I can't help them both at the same time.'

Lachlan glanced at the table strewn with flour and pastry shapes, looking slightly taken aback.

'You're under no obligation to eat the pies,' she added.

The corner of his mouth twitched upwards. He crossed the room and laid the furs over the back of the chair by the hearth, rolled his sleeves up and took Morna from Effie's arms.

'What should I do?'

Effie had intended a stern cross-examination of Lachlan. Instead she found herself filling pastry cases with fruit while the man who claimed to also be a seal supervised the children, in a scene of domestic harmony that would not have looked out of place in an illustrated story. And she was having a nicer time than she could remember for years.

When the pies were in the oven and the children had been sent out into the garden, Effie turned to Lachlan. The afternoon of fun had only been delaying the inevitable.

'We need to talk,' she said.

'Yes, we do.' His solemn manner was spoiled slightly by the dab of flour on his right cheek. Effie's fingers twitched to wipe it off. Lachlan motioned to the chairs by the stove, but Effie pulled out the one she was standing by and pointed to the one at the other side of the table. He sat obediently and laced his hands together on top of the table.

'If I asked for proof I couldn't deny, would you give it to me? Change before my eyes, for example?'

Lachlan's brows shot up. Effie's cheeks burned. She was reasonably sure she had just done the equivalent of asking him to strip naked.

'I won't ask that,' she said hastily. She tried to summon the anger she had first felt. 'I'm still furious that you didn't tell me before now.'

'And you are right to be,' Lachlan admitted. 'I did you a grave disservice in not telling you when we first met.'

'Yes, you did.' She stared over her shoulder at the furs. 'Though I wouldn't have believed you, I imagine.'

She looked into his eyes. The brown was dark and the green highlights sparkled. The pupils were perhaps slightly larger than normal, but he stared back at her evenly and there was no trace of anything untoward that she could see. Nothing animal. Effie pressed her fingertips to her eyelids. There really was no other explanation for the change in Morna's fur, but to allow the acceptance of that into her life opened up doors to all sorts of things she had never believed in.

Effie walked to the window. Jack was piling pebbles one on top of the other while Morna stood by the gate. Her face was pressed to the slats as she stood staring at the sea, one arm reaching through. Effie sensed Lachlan come to her side. 'Do you want to break up their happiness by parting them?' Lachlan asked.

Effie shook her head. Jack responded to Morna in a way he didn't to anyone else, even his mother. The knot of worry in her breast loosened slightly.

'Morna will never harm Jack, will she?' Effie said quietly. It wasn't really a question.

'No,' Lachlan said. 'Nor will she harm you. And neither

will I. You and Jack will be perfectly safe. The danger is to Morna and me. I was not exaggerating when I said I am trusting you with our lives. There are countless tales among my people of our kind being tricked by yours. If I told them all to you it would take days. It is enough to say that throughout history we've been met by hatred or resentment, used and enslaved. We have more to fear from you than you do from us.'

Effie looked at him. Lachlan was strong and well-built and she couldn't imagine him being harmed. Morna was different though; a child without any means to defend herself. The recollection of Lachlan wincing when she dug her nails into the skin made Effie's skin crawl. She could have hurt Morna herself if she had seized the wrong pelt.

'I won't tell anyone what you are. Please believe me,' she said.

'I believe you.'

He took hold of her hand. Her initial instinct to recoil vanished almost immediately beneath a frisson of yearning at being touched.

'How does it work? How can you exist?'

Lachlan smiled at her, a gentle upturn of his lips that made the hairs on the back of Effie's head prickle.

'How do any of us exist? How does a bird fly or a caterpillar become a butterfly? We have always existed for as long as I know. There are legends that stretch back to the time of knights and castles of encounters between my kind and yours.'

The watercolour sketch she had done of Lachlan sprang to Effie's mind, not sailing the familiar Yorkshire waters, but navigating far-off tides dressed in his fur, under a sky of iron clouds and black waters. She hadn't suspected anything out of the ordinary when she had painted it, but something had whispered in her mind and she had captured it without realising.

'I've never heard any stories like that,' Effie replied. Alice's book sprang to her mind. There were no seal people in any story as far as she remembered, but it had been a long time since she had read more than a page or two.

'Perhaps another time I shall tell you one,' Lachlan said.

Another time.

'I have to go,' Lachlan said. 'My journey is a long one and I am already a day behind.'

'Behind what?' Effie asked.

'Behind my clan. We travel to the islands off the Netherlands at the summer and winter solstices.'

Effie stared out of the window at the sea which stretched to where the horizon blurred and tried to picture a colony of seals gliding through the water before shedding their skins. It made her shiver with longing to see such a thing.

'Are you happy to keep Morna for me?' Lachlan asked.

Effie gave him an uncertain smile, wrinkling her brow. There was the problem: she did care for Morna deeply. But knowing what the child was threw up problems she could not put into words. He hadn't told the child what she was. Effie couldn't either, but sooner or later the girl would become aware of her differences. Raising her as a human didn't seem fair. Lachlan must have sensed her reluctance.

'Keep Morna for another six months. I won't ask more than that. At Midwinter I'll return. If you still have doubts, I will take her and we'll leave.'

'That's fair,' Effie agreed.

'Then I'll be going. Will you walk to the rocks with me?'

Effie gathered the children and together they made their way along the beach, Morna on Lachlan's shoulders and Jack holding Effie's hand and jumping over clumps of seaweed. At the long line of rocks, Lachlan took Morna down from his shoulders and stroked her cheek. When he stood, his eyes were sad. This parting must be even harder for him, knowing that Effie knew his secret and her doubts.

'I'll care for her well. She won't come to any harm,' Effie promised. 'Six months will pass quickly.'

His lip twitched into a small smile at the corner of his mouth. 'Does our compact still stand, Effie Cropton?' he asked.

She'd just agreed it did and the formality struck her as odd, but she guessed this was part of whatever arrangement she had made.

'We still have a compact, Lachlan,' she replied.

He reached into his pocket and drew out another pearl.

'You gave me my payment last night,' she said.

Lachlan closed her hand over the pearl and held tight to her hands. 'That was payment, this is a gift. To say thank you. No conditions are attached to it.'

His fingers were cool. Desire surged in her belly, catching her unawares. Her mind might comprehend he wasn't human, but her body made no such distinction. Their eyes met and Effie blushed.

'Thank you,' she murmured.

He released her hands and clambered up onto the lowest rocks. He looked back once before pulling his skin higher over his shoulders. Effie walked back to the village with the children running ahead of her. She watched them carefully. Six months must be long enough to decide what to do about Morna and see whether the child's nature would begin to show itself. Six months must be long enough to think of all the questions she hadn't asked of Lachlan and which would need answering to give her peace of mind and satisfy her curiosity.

Walter visited Effie after the Sunday morning service as planned. He was wearing his best coat and hat and looked every bit the country gentleman he would one day become.

'Walter! I'm so sorry. I've been busy and it clean went out of my mind that you were coming today,' Effie exclaimed when he opened the door.

His face sank, causing Effie no small amount of contrition. She could hardly explain that the news that her daughter was part seal had consumed her mind. She gestured to the kitchen.

'There are apple pies and I'll put the kettle on to boil.'

Tea was the answer to everything.

Walter was dressed too formally to walk along the beach so they sat on chairs outside Effie's cottage while Jack and Morna threw pebbles into a chalk circle on the floor. Walter detailed the sermon Reverend Ogram had given and though Effie was not overly interested, the conversation was reassuringly mundane. After the extraordinary revelations that had accompanied Lachlan's visit, she was grateful for Walter's conversation. A normal man with nothing to trouble her.

He drank a cup of tea then laid his cup and saucer on the step.

'I wanted to speak to you the other night because I have something important to tell you.'

Effie's scalp prickled. After Lachlan's astounding revelation, Effie half expected Walter to announce he was a unicorn or transformed into an owl at full moon. She suppressed a giggle, though there was nothing to laugh at. She wasn't entirely sure she hadn't lost her mind and imagined the whole incident.

Walter looked at her oddly.

'I'm sorry. I was thinking of an unrelated thing. Please, continue.'

'It will go around the village like wildfire soon enough and I wanted you to hear it from my lips.'

Walter broke off and poured a second cup of tea, stirring the spoon round in the cup twice before taking a sip.

Effie sat forward, affecting patience while she burned to hear what he had to say. How like Walter to break off at such a moment and leave her to imagine what he meant. Marriage to an unsuitable woman? The family was bankrupt and would have to sell the alum business? He was seriously ill?

'For goodness' sake, Walter, you can't leave me hanging on your words while you pour tea! I'm imagining horrors and scandals. Have you got someone with child or fought in a duel?'

His eyes creased with amusement. 'Nothing so dramatic, thankfully. My father intends to send me on a grand tour of Europe. I won't return until next spring at the earliest.'

'How exciting for you,' Effie breathed. 'Where will you go? When do you leave?'

'You shan't miss me?' Walter asked. His smile became a touch less wide. He put his tea down and linked his fingers together across his chest.

She squeezed his hands. 'Of course I will miss you. You are my dear friend, but I've grown used to you being away at university so it won't be a change for me. I'm only thinking of your good fortune. The chance to travel will be an opportunity you can't miss and I won't be happy unless you write to me at least once a month to tell me what you see and do. Now, tell me everything you have planned.'

Walter looked a little mollified.

'I will be travelling with a group of friends from university.

We leave on July the fifth and our first port of call will be Dieppe. From there we'll visit Paris. We'll be taking in all the cultural sites: the opera, the galleries, the ballet...'

'The opera singers and the *corps de ballet*,' Effie interrupted, laughing.

Walter looked scandalised. 'Goodness me, no! At least I won't be. I can't speak for my companions, but I hope I have judged them well enough not to have fallen in with a couple of rakes.'

'Well I do hope you have a wonderful time,' Effie said. 'It might do you good to have a little excitement and kiss a few opera girls.'

'I don't want opera girls, Effie. I want you. I'm not asking you to enter into an engagement now. I could not dream of holding you to a promise for so long in my absence. Nor could I ask you to leave Jack and Morna to travel with me as my wife, though I would dearly love to share Europe with you. All I ask is for the hope that you will be thinking of me fondly while I am gone, and that when I return you might entertain the thought of becoming my wife. A hint would be enough to sustain me.'

He stopped and drew a deep breath. He sounded so eager that Effie didn't know what to do. She worked her hands free, privately thinking that Walter should rely less on hints. She laughed gaily.

'Walter, you're being foolish. You don't know who you might meet. I would not want to hold *you* to a promise that you would wish to break.'

'Who would I meet that I like better than you?'

'A hundred women,' Effie said. She waved her hands around as if trying to conjure them on the path. 'Women more respectable than an opera girl, and better suited to being the wife of a gentleman than a poor sailor's widow with two children.'

Walter grimaced.

'As if I cared for that. A man or woman's worth does not come from their station in life but from what they do and what they give. If that is all the impediment, I will say now that I would marry you whether you were desolate and in the poorhouse or the daughter of a duke.'

'That's very nice of you to say, but...'

Before she could continue, Walter swept the hat from his head and pulled Effie from her chair and into his arms. It was the second time in a week she had been kissed without warning and again she reacted instinctively, pressing her lips to Walter's. He drew back and his face was suffused with such joy and triumph that Effie's heart raced.

'Does this mean you will wait for me?' he asked.

'Goodness me! Walter,' Effie breathed. 'You kissed me, and it was very nice, but a kiss is not a promise of marriage.'

His face fell.

'I should go; that was improper. I let my feelings get away from me.'

Effie picked up his hat and placed it gently on his head, tipping the brim forward. 'Go, but not with a sense of shame. Travel and discover the world, and when you return I will be pleased to see my dear friend.'

Walter straightened the brim, pushing the hat back so that a lock of hair fell free.

'When we meet again, perhaps you will be as pleased to see me as I shall be to see you.'

'Perhaps I will,' Effie said.

She had made her answer as clear as she could and, thankfully, Walter took this hint and left.

Effie gathered up the children and went to visit Alice.

Her grandmother looked her up and down on the doorstep and her eyes gleamed sharply. 'Well now, I can see something has happened. The kettle has just boiled. Put the tea on to stew and tell me all about it.'

'Why do you think there is anything to tell?' Effie asked with a shake of her head.

'I'm not going to give away my tricks,' Alice cackled. 'Kettle, girl.'

Effie did as instructed, wondering at Alice's intuition. No wonder her reputation as a witch lingered even in these days of science and learning. While she made tea, Alice settled Morna with a knitted fisherman's sweater to unravel and wind the wool to be used again. She gave Jack a teasel and told him to brush her cloak, starting at one edge and working along. Methodical, repetitive tasks suited him well and he hummed as he worked.

'Tell me,' she instructed Effie, sitting back in her chair.

There was no point pretending there was nothing to tell. She couldn't tell *all*, so she selected the events that wouldn't see her confined to a madhouse.

'Walter is leaving for Europe soon. He asked me to wait for him until he comes back and not to marry anyone else. Then he kissed me.'

'How did you feel about his kiss?'

Effie thought about it as she poured the tea. It had been a bolder kiss than the one Lachlan had initiated, and yet not as accomplished.

Pleasant was the word she would use to describe it.

Nice.

It left a tingle of excitement on Effie's lips, but the sensation did not come close to replicating the wave of excitement that had overcome her the previous night. It was not Walter's fault; he was young and, apparently, completely inexperienced, whereas Lachlan had been a husband and had more understanding of pleasing a woman. How good would the kiss have been if he hadn't been worried about Effie's reaction and the reticence caused by what he knew. How good would he be at lovemaking?

'It was good enough if your expression is anything to go by,' Alice chuckled.

Effie pressed her lips together. She'd stopped thinking about Walter as soon as Lachlan had come to mind, but had no intention of telling Alice anything about him. Where would she even begin?

'Do you think you should – or could – wait for him to return?' Alice asked.

Effie sighed. Had Walter's kiss been stirring enough to keep as a beacon until he returned? Honestly, probably not.

'I don't know. My head says it would be a sensible thing to do. I like Walter well enough and he clearly likes me. We have a lot to talk about always so I have no doubt that we'd be as happy as John and I were. Besides, I don't exactly have a wide choice of other men offering me marriage, do I?'

Alice narrowed her eyes and scrutinised Effie. 'I can see that, unfortunately. What else is bothering you?'

Effie poured the tea. She hadn't even told Alice of Lachlan's existence, and after that kiss she did not want to complicate things even further.

'I don't know,' she sighed. 'I'm thinking of travel. Of men going to explore the world while I wait here. Could you imagine if a woman decided to sail off to the frozen north or get up and visit every country in Europe? It would cause a scandal.'

'Not if she was wealthy enough to thumb her nose at society. Walter will go into his father's business and he'll prosper. If you marry him he'll keep you well. You could travel together,' Alice pointed out.

Effie wrinkled her nose. That was another point in Walter's favour, though it felt mercenary. Thumbing her nose at the world was appealing, even without money, but Walter definitely wouldn't approve. It felt like she had been infected with a fever that made her blood run hot.

'That isn't what I mean. I need something to do. I think while I was grieving for John my mind was full, and now it isn't.'

She broke off, realising she had just admitted that her grief had almost ended. She took a sip of tea, bending over her cup to hide her face. 'That sounded terrible, didn't it?'

Alice patted her hand. 'No, it sounds natural. You've grieved in your way and your time, and now your life needs to go on. Did you know that in Egypt they say that the pharaoh's wives were buried along with the pharaoh when he died? Fortunately we don't have that custom. You should live while you are alive.'

The next day, Effie set up her easel and painted for the whole afternoon, filling sheet after sheet until some of the passion within her ebbed. Not careful copies of flowers or seaweeds to send to Manchester, but scenes that filled her mind with frozen cliffs and Italian lakes, great pyramids, and rock-strewn seas. She added figures and it was only when she examined her creations later as she laid them on the table to dry that she realised she had painted men who looked very like Lachlan and Walter.

She pulled a chair close and examined the paintings as if

she had not been responsible, eyeing the figures with as dispassionate an eye as she could.

The two men were both different. Who could say whether Walter's kiss would have moved her more if she hadn't been kissed so recently before? It could have been the novelty of Lachlan's lips that had made his kiss stick in her mind the longest.

When the pictures were dry, she stowed them away and did her best to forget about the men they represented. Walter would have her but he was to be gone for almost a year. Lachlan... well, she sensed he wanted her – the attraction had been obvious – but he was gone for six months and he had his reasons for keeping away that were perfectly understandable. She didn't want to examine the part of her that wanted him back despite knowing what she did about him. Not that it mattered. Neither man was here, and neither man would provide the companionship she craved.

She had not been buried with John and was damned (she slid her eyes away from the direction of the church as she thought that blasphemy) if she was going to bury herself waiting for something that might never happen.

Chapter Ten

That summer, leading into autumn, the mood of the village changed. Mr Danby was expanding his alum quarry, drawing more custom from further afield. Railway lines were being laid to reach the site and brought trouble with them.

'There was fighting again outside the Queen's Arms last night,' Mrs Ogram told Alice as the women gathered outside the butcher's shop door. 'They come to spend their wage packets on strong drink and provoke our men into brawling.'

There was no need to ask who 'they' were. The rail workers were strangers to the area, moving along as they changed the landscape.

'Surely Reverend Ogram wasn't provoked?' Effie asked. Although he delivered some hellfire in his Sunday sermons, the vicar was a mild, kind father and husband and Effie couldn't imagine him throwing a punch.

Mrs Ogram threw Effie a rancid look. 'Are you suggesting my husband would frequent a public house?'

'Of course not. You misunderstand me,' Effie assured her. A

voice inside her screamed in mortification that she had spoken so forwardly. Where had such impertinence sprung from?

'I meant, was he provoked to write a sermon denouncing such behaviour? Perhaps the word I should have chosen was *inspired*.'

She heard Alice give a gentle snort that she turned into a cough. Effie determinedly didn't meet her grandmother's eye for fear she would begin to giggle.

Mrs Ogram threw her a dirty look again.

'You would know the answer to that if you ever stepped foot inside the church. Your presence would be welcomed with open arms. You should give serious consideration to the children attending at least some of Reverend Ogram's services. It is never too young to learn how to live a good Christian life. A tarnished soul can always be washed clean.'

'The only thing dirty about my children is their faces,' Effie retorted indignantly, gesturing to the children who were each licking a sugar mouse enthusiastically. 'And that can be washed off easily with soap and water in my own house.'

Mrs Ogram drew herself up to her full height and nodded at Effie. She leaned into Alice and spoke in a mutter. 'I'll see you in the morning, Mrs Millbourne, when I call to get my package. Good day to you both.'

'A good Christian woman who isn't above purchasing mixtures to help with her change in life from a reputed witch,' Effie muttered as they watched Mrs Ogram walk up the hill.

'I thought you didn't believe in witchcraft,' Alice said.

'I don't, and I'm not sure you do either,' Effie retorted. She bit her lip. A month had passed since Lachlan's revelation and not a day went by that Effie didn't watch Morna carefully for signs of something out of the ordinary. Who was Effie to say that witches weren't real too?

'I've said before,' Alice reminded her, 'sometimes the magic is in the believer. But in any case, my remedies should ease her troubles, and perhaps improve her mood.'

Effie laughed and they walked down Harbour Hill together in good spirits. When they came to part, Alice gave Effie a measured look.

'I'm surprised at you, my girl. You delighted in antagonising Mrs Ogram back there. You never would have spoken to her in such a manner a year ago. I sometimes wonder if you care anything for your standing in the village.'

Effie shifted her basket. Facing Mrs Ogram didn't seem so terrifying any more, not to a woman who had confronted a Selkie and demanded answers from him. She had stood up for her children today and the world hadn't ended.

'She won't give up trying to bring me into her fold. When Walter asks me to go to church with him, or when John did, I don't mind so much. She grates on my nerves with her condemnation and talk of tarnished souls. I don't believe in what she does and I'd be a hypocrite if I sat there and prayed and sang along.'

Alice shook her head. 'Do you think everyone who goes believes as fervently as the Ograms? The church is more than that for many. It's where they go to meet friends. You could do with a few of those. You've not had any visitors since Walter left over a month ago and you need company.'

'I have company. I see you all the time,' Effie protested.

'Company of your own age. Other girls to chat to or women to help with the children. You've always been a loner but you've never been this alone.'

Effie bit her thumbnail, with Alice's words bubbling in her head. She had never minded solitude but now she was lonely and hadn't done much to make friends in the village. It was months until Lachlan was due to return, and goodness knows when Walter would be back. She did enjoy the occasional gossip with Mary Ogram and her younger sister, and the children needed companions of their own age too.

'I won't go to the services,' she said eventually. 'But perhaps I'll consider joining one of Mrs Ogram's societies. That should be bearable and I'll be doing some good.'

'I'll do what I can to help you,' Alice said, patting Effie's hand. 'But you'll have to do the hard work yourself.'

Effie smiled. Hard work had never been a problem for her.

Alice proved as good as her word. The following Wednesday afternoon, she asked Effie to take her place at an afternoon tea with Mrs and Mary Ogram, and a handful of the other women from the village. The intention was to conclude to which of sundry suggested charitable works the women would contribute. It sounded dull but worthwhile so Effie agreed to attend, leaving the children in Alice's care.

Her appearance in the sitting room at the vicarage was greeted with raised eyebrows by the eight occupants and she almost backed out. She'd always been aware that the village had been divided between the families who fished and the families employed at the alum works. At a higher social stratum were those for whom the villagers laboured or who held professions not related to the sea or mines. This room contained only the latter matrons. Effie recognised the doctor's wife and daughter. Sitting beside them were a deceased colonel's middle-aged daughter and her companion, who lived together in the grand house at the top of the hill. Even Mrs Forshawe, the wife of the minister at the Wesleyan Chapel, was present. Effie shyly took a seat between Mary and the postmaster's wife.

'I'm sorry for being late. We've been swimming and Morna took exception to having the salt combed out of her hair. I had to battle with her. Children of that age are so strong willed, aren't they!'

She looked at the other women, hoping for some sign of motherly solidarity but was met only with indifference.

'Why on earth are you so determined to get those children in the water?' Mrs Forshawe asked in a puzzled tone.

Because my daughter is half seal.

'To stop them drowning,' Effie replied. She gave Mrs Forshawe a wide smile. The minister's wife was at least a decade younger than Mrs Ogram, sensible and personable. If Effie ever did have the urge to attend a service, she felt Mr Forshawe's style of ministry would suit her temperament better.

'And because they enjoy it. We all do.'

Since the scare when Morna had found her way to the waves, Effie had been determined that no danger could befall the children in the water. Lachlan hadn't known whether she would drown or swim and that scared Effie. Both children seemed able to follow instructions so Effie had chanced letting them into the sea and had fashioned outfits that allowed the children to kick their legs and splash about. Effie herself stood up to her waist in loose bloomers and a skirt and held their hands as they splashed.

'The water is wonderfully bracing and I'm sure it is good for the constitution,' she explained to the doubtful faces. 'I can quite see the attraction of sea bathing as a pastime. Perhaps one day the beach at Allendale Head will be as fashionable as Brighton or Lyme Regis. If the new railway lines bring people to the area, we could become quite the bathing attraction. I could become famous for starting the trend and we could have rows of bathing machines on the shoreline.'

There was a murmur of enthusiasm from the doctor's daughter and the companion. Mrs Ogram rattled her teacup in the saucer and the room fell silent once more.

'Infamy for such unladylike behaviour, more likely. You might treat your reputation in a cavalier fashion, but you will never see me or my daughters in bathing costumes. We have more productive things to do with our time than splash about in cold water.'

She coughed delicately and looked around the room at the other women. 'Besides, so far all the railway lines have brought is uncouth working men. Which brings me to our business. These men are living in encampments without ready access to a place of worship. I propose…'

Effie let her mind drift as she half listened. Mary Ogram caught her eye and gave her a discreet smile. Mary had been the one to lend Effie the periodicals and ladies' papers containing designs for bathing costumes. Effie suspected she was not as averse as her mother was to the idea of a fashionable resort and lace-trimmed bathing caps. She noticed a couple of the other women had not agreed so readily with Mrs Ogram either, though now they were all nodding along with the suggestion of luring men into church with the promise of hot meals.

Her mind was still elsewhere when Mary nudged her arm and she recollected herself. Mrs Forshawe repeated her request for Effie to contribute weekly biscuits to the cause. She could ill afford to spare butter and flour in order to tempt men into the church or chapel (Effie would like to be a fly on the wall when Mrs Ogram and Mrs Forshawe came to the matter of where the intended worship would take place) that she had no intention of attending herself. She frowned, not sure what to say. Mrs Forshawe's usually cheerful face fell at her obvious reservation.

'If you feel such work is beneath you, Mrs Cropton...'

'Not at all. I simply don't flatter myself that my baking will convert many heathens,' Effie said, with a laugh to cover the awkwardness that had arisen. 'I simply wonder if there is a way more of the men might be tempted to take a more active part in village life. A swimming contest or football game, perhaps?'

Mrs Ogram leaned forwards and looked down her nose at Effie. 'I am telling you this in a spirit of friendship, Mrs Cropton. You have a reputation for giving yourself airs and this attitude does nothing to help you.'

'Airs?' Effie felt anger rising through the astonishment. It was the prerogative of the vicar's wife, a woman senior to Effie by many years, to speak freely about her character, but it rankled to be so publicly chastised.

'Hoity-toity. You turned down the offer of a mangle when you could have supported yourself through your widowed state taking in washing,' added the doctor's wife.

Effie sat up. 'I don't need a mangle. I support myself with what I earn from my paintings for Mr Danby's friends.'

'Well that's another matter,' Mrs Forshawe said primly.

'What do you mean?' Effie asked, wrinkling her brow.

'Everyone says you have a mind to get Mr Danby to marry you,' Mary said quietly.

'Well I don't,' Effie retorted. 'I paint because Mr Danby asks me to, not in an attempt to entrap him into marriage, I might add, and I spend half my days helping Alice with her work.'

Mrs Forshawe pursed her lips. 'Then there's your strange

foster child, and your own boy has an odd manner. He is a simpleton. Your determination to teach them both to read and write is causing gossip, never mind your eccentric insistence on the swimming.'

'My children are fine.' Effie's stomach twisted. This was the first time anyone had voiced what she had worried over privately. Jack was behind where he should be. Morna's past was enough to cause comment, but she also had a wildness to her that Effie was finding hard to tame. If anyone discovered the truth...

The afternoon had taken a nasty turn and she felt as if she were in the dock awaiting sentencing. It was becoming hard to hold back the tears. *Wait until Alice hears this*, she told herself. Venting and gossiping over a pot of strong tea would be a sure cure for the anger and confusion she felt. She bestowed a particularly steely smile on Mrs Ogram.

'Excuse me, but I really must be going. I promised the children I would take them to Boggle Cove to say goodnight to the boggles and we don't want to keep them waiting.'

Mrs Ogram drew herself up high. Effie reflected on how professing a belief in boggles would meet with disapproval yet turning up to the church on Sunday would result in the opposite. She picked up her bag and left without waiting for the maid to be summoned to collect her cloak and hat. She was halfway down the steep, winding road through the town before tears welled up and blurred her vision. It had been a disaster from start to finish.

She didn't want to appear at Alice's door crying, so she sat on the steps of the quayside and watched the fishwives hauling boxes and slitting fish open to clean the guts out. They were joking with each other in loud, cheerful voices and looked much more appealing company than Mrs Ogram's circle, but they would have seen Effie as above them, given John's position on the *Serenity*.

Caught between mug and teacup, as Alice had once told her.

The injustice of Mrs Ogram's words stung her afresh. She was raising two children alone without calling on the parish for aid beyond the small stipend they paid her to look after Morna. So what if her work didn't involve visible effort? She thought of the pearls Lachlan paid her with, lying undisturbed in her drawer. She had no idea how much they would be worth, but if she somehow converted them into money she would have to work even less.

Lachlan.

It was so easy for him to walk away along the shore and leave Effie behind with the responsibilities he evaded. A pearl and a kiss were not enough remuneration for that.

'Mrs Cropton?'

Effie looked up at the sound of her name spoken hesitantly. Mary Ogram stood behind her, holding Effie's bonnet and cape.

'I'm so sorry about Mother; she can be unbelievably rude. Sometimes I wonder what has come over her. She never used to be so outspoken before her change in life started.'

Effie scowled, but Mary's expression was sincere. She took the clothes and moved up to make space on the step for Mary to sit down.

'Maybe your mother is right. I don't fit in with the respectable women. I like living on my own and doing the things I do. Walter is almost the only one who will tolerate my oddness.'

Mary twisted the end of her ringlet. 'I think you're so brave to turn your nose up at the world. I wish I could live my life as freely as you do.'

Effie looked at the vicar's daughter with fresh interest.

'Do you find your life difficult?'

Mary sighed. 'Mother is desperate for me to make a good marriage. I don't think she will be happy unless I wed the Archbishop of York himself.'

'Is there someone you'd prefer to marry?' Effie asked.

'I may not wish to marry anyone,' Mary said quickly, before clamping her mouth shut. Effie noticed the way her lips tightened. If there was a man Mary had her eye on, she wasn't about to share the name.

Effie patted Mary's hand. 'Will you come with me to Alice's house? I have to relieve her of my children.'

They walked to Alice's cottage where they were greeted by Jack and Morna, hurling themselves at Effie's legs.

'You have beautiful children,' Mary said, bending to greet them.

'I can only take credit for one of them,' Effie reminded her. 'I don't know what Morna's mother must have looked like, but I imagine she was very beautiful to produce such a child.'

They both regarded Morna with interest. She was losing some of her childish roundness and her hair was now to her shoulders, and sleek chestnut-brown in colour. She must have had her mother's colouring because Lachlan was darker. The shape of her eyes and the intelligence that made them glint like black opals were all his, however.

Mary sighed. 'Poor child to be orphaned so young. How fortunate that she found you.'

Effie smiled, though a flicker of worry stirred inside her. Morna was not completely an orphan. One day Lachlan might decide she was old enough to go with him to his home in the north. For all her irritation at Lachlan leaving without a care, when that day came Effie was not sure she would be able to bear the loss.

The two women parted on the steps, Mary to go back to the vicarage and Effie to take the children to Boggle Cove as promised.

'Do you really believe in boggles?' Mary asked.

It was such an unexpected question that Effie laughed.

'Of course not. I don't believe in Alice's magic either. Or fairies. Or anything of that nature,' she said, possibly far too forcefully because Mary blinked in surprise. She laughed. 'I might be wrong of course, but I'd have to meet a boggle face to face to satisfy myself.'

'Do you believe in anything?' Mary asked. Her face grew serious and her hand went to the small cross she wore at her neck. Effie thought carefully before answering. She suspected talking so flippantly about the supernatural to the daughter of a vicar was bordering dangerously close to criticism of the divine. Then again, what would Mary say if Effie presented her with proof that there was more in the world than she could possibly suspect?

'I think I believe that giving people something to hold onto is where the magic lies. It makes the children happy to leave bread for the boggles, even if the gulls really eat it, and that's what counts.'

Mary smiled, dimples appearing in her cheeks.

'I think you're very wise. I know Mother disapproves of you, Mrs Cropton, but I like you. I would be honoured if you would allow me to call myself your friend.'

Effie filled with delight. 'I would be honoured too, and please, if we are to be friends, you must call me Effie.'

Mary's resulting smile was so warm that Effie's entire mood brightened. Alice, standing in her doorway, winked at

Effie and she wondered how much her grandmother had intended this very outcome. The afternoon had not gone to plan, but she had somehow ended up with a friend after all.

Mary and Effie grew closer over the months that followed and by late autumn Effie considered her a firm friend. The vicar's daughter had a lively mind and was amusing company. Despite her mother's disapproval, she often spent afternoons with Effie and Alice. She delighted in playing with Jack and Morna and teaching them to recognise their letters and singing them songs, which Jack hummed back to her almost instantly. Effie privately thought it was a shame she did not have children of her own, but who in the village was there for her to marry?

When Mary discovered Effie's talent at painting, she was entranced.

'Will you paint me?' she begged. 'I would love a portrait. I could give it to my parents for Christmas.'

'I'm not very good at faces,' Effie said apologetically. 'I'm better at plants. That's why Walter bought me the paints after all.'

Mary continued to wheedle, so Effie rummaged through her portfolio and found a quick watercolour sketch she had done of Walter. He was standing before the entrance to the Jardin de Luxembourg, wearing a summer suit and sweeping his hand out towards the path. She held it out to Mary.

'See, I was painting Walter from memory but it barely resembles him, whereas the trees are much better even though they are only from his description in a letter.'

'It may not look exactly like him but it captures his

manner,' Mary said. She took the painting and examined it carefully. 'He's very keen and earnest. Any second now I can imagine him opening his mouth to tell you the history of France in immense detail.'

Effie grinned affectionately. 'That's true. "Earnest" is a very apt description of Walter, but at least he has ideas and thinks women are worthy of hearing them.'

Effie took the picture back, feeling a brief pang of pining as she regarded Walter's image. She had painted this portrait from his description and her imagination and had been pleased with how she had captured French morning sunlight playing over Walter's hair and face. She wondered where Walter was now. He had written twice, once from Paris and again from Lyon, mentioning the Paris opera and promising he had not been swept away by the *corps de ballet*.

'Now this one is very interesting,' Mary murmured, drawing another sheet from the case. 'It looks like something from a fairy-tale, but all blues and greys.'

Effie glanced over to see which one she was talking about and her heart skipped a beat. It was a painting of Lachlan standing in the prow of an old-fashioned fishing boat with towering cliffs of ice in the background. He was wrapped in furs and his face was turned towards the observer with a look of challenge. She had done it before she had realised the significance of the sealskin, of course. Watercolours were a poor medium for the setting. Mary would not see it, but Effie had captured his resemblance much better than she had with Walter's portrait.

'This isn't Walter. Who is it?'

'Just a face I must've seen,' Effie said. She wanted to take the painting back, but Mary walked over to the window where the light was better. She raised the paper and examined it closely.

'He looks a little like Morna.'

Effie's jaw tightened. She forced an indifferent tone to her voice. 'He does, I suppose. Maybe that's where I found his face.' Her fingers twitched possessively. She held her hand out to take it, but Mary was still gazing at Lachlan. She sighed dreamily.

'I wish a man like this would come to life. Can you imagine what he would say?'

'I can't.' Effie took the picture from Mary and put it back in the portfolio, feeling thoughtful. So Mary liked the look of Lachlan, did she? Effie wasn't sure she was happy about that. She felt slightly possessive, which wasn't at all fair on Mary who had only shown curiosity at a strange painting. She would think again if she knew what he was.

'I can try and paint you if you like,' she offered. 'Maybe with a hat, standing on the quayside or outside St Stephen's and All Saints so your parents will know it is you.'

She wondered if Lachlan would like to see his picture, but the thought of admitting she had remembered his features and bearing so accurately would be excruciating. It would be Christmas in just over a month. Already the nights were smelling colder and the air was damp. Perhaps she should do Lachlan a sketch of Morna to take with him as a gift. She wanted to give him something.

As Christmas drew nearer, Effie's skill at drawing people did not increase, but she discovered that she could do a passable attempt if she did not exactly try to capture them. When the subject was surrounded by nature, it was easier. On rare bright days when the children were playing, she spent her time painting. Morna showed no interest in drawing, but Jack was fascinated more than he was with any other thing Effie attempted to show him.

Jack worried her, especially after Mrs Ogram's harsh comments regarding his development. He still spoke very rarely and became distressed when Effie commanded him to look her in the eye to follow her mouth movements. He sat sprawled at her feet, drawing with charcoal and stubs of pencil, colouring birds and fish that were alive with feathers and scales that seemed beyond the ability of his age. Was he more slow-witted than his father had been, or just taking his time to grow? Alice simply told her he would find his own path and Mary doted on him, irrespective of how he behaved.

She was satisfied in the end with three paintings: one of Morna by the waves, surrounded by the shells and seaweed she loved to gather, a second of both children running beneath the cliff (a gift for Alice) and, lastly, Mary standing before the church gate surrounded by roses.

'I can't believe there is only one week until Christmas,' Mary said as she breezed into Effie's cottage bearing a basket of paper chains. Will you come to church on Christmas morning? I'd like to see you and tell you if mother and father loved my picture. I am sure they will.'

'You know I will,' Effie assured her. 'It's the one day of the year I'm happy to be there.'

It didn't matter that she didn't have faith in God any more than she didn't believe in boggles or fairies or Christmas ghosts. Somehow the stories and songs, the lights, and the company, combined to create a sense of wonder.

She took the basket from Mary and together they hung the chains around the chimney.

'I love Christmas,' Mary sighed. 'You must love it too now the children are becoming old enough to enjoy it.'

They both regarded the children, who were rolling chestnuts across the floor and trying to get them into the coal scuttle and giggling madly each time they succeeded. They were brimming with excitement at the thought of the roast rabbit and plum suet pudding that would make Christmas Day a treat. Effie offered Mary a pastel-coloured sugared almond. They had arrived in a painted wooden box from Walter, along with other confections so pretty Effie could hardly bear to ruin them by eating.

'He is spending Christmas in the Italian Lakes. I've been very tempted to hide these from the children and keep them all to myself,' she told Mary.

'I would too,' Mary answered. She gave Effie a long stare from underneath her pale eyelashes. 'Do you miss him? Did he say when he will be returning?'

Effie closed the lid of the box. 'No, he didn't.'

Yes, she did miss Walter and was looking forward to his eventual return. It would have been the thing she was most looking forward to, but for the small quivers of anticipation at the thought of Midwinter's Night and Lachlan's return. That set her stomach rolling until she was unable to eat.

She had questions to ask, but, more than that, she wanted to see the man himself.

Chapter Eleven

When Midwinter arrived, Effie's emotions were at their highest. The children must have picked up on her mood because they were both agitated, running to the window and door frequently.

'Dada is coming tonight, Morna. Are you looking forward to seeing him?' she asked as they scrubbed the hearth. Morna nodded eagerly and pointed at the knitted stockings which Effie had already hung by the window ready for Christmas morning.

Effie opened her mouth to explain but closed it again. How could a child distinguish between the fantasy figure who brought presents once a year and the strange dark-eyed man who visited every six months? Morna must have only the barest memories of him. Nothing like the memories Effie had of conversations and the brief kiss which brought him alive in her mind with far too much vividness.

To the child's mind, with a short memory and such a little life behind her, Lachlan, with his strange songs and softly spoken ways, must be just as fantastical as Father Christmas.

Midwinter's Day brought a storm with it. Clouds gathered, black on grey, throughout the morning and almost on the chime of the midday church bells, the sky cracked and torrents of rain lashed the village. The turn of the beach towards Boggle Cove was barely visible. From half past three when the faint sun vanished, Effie found herself watching the door. Four o'clock came and she fed the children toast and sardine paste for tea, trying to hold in her anticipation. Five o'clock passed, six o'clock too.

She told herself that, of course, Lachlan would not arrive so early. He never came before nightfall. When eight o'clock came she was growing fearful and her hands slipped as she bathed the children, getting soap in Jack's eyes which caused him to wail. She put the children to bed and sat by the fire, taking up some darning, and tried to silence her voice of foreboding.

The darning remained untouched. He wasn't coming. He had decided this year not to. He had decided his revelation had been unwise and was leaving Morna for ever.

No, Effie told herself firmly. He had promised to return and would not abandon Morna, so something must have delayed him. That thought was worse because the unknown obstacle could mean danger. She felt as agitated as the children waiting for Father Christmas, except the pit of her stomach was filled with anxiety rather than excitement. The sea was so rough and rain lashed the cliffs. Her mind returned to the shipwreck that had claimed John and a bitter taste filled her throat. She took the oil lamp and placed it in the window; a beacon to help Lachlan find his way. It was a pointless gesture; if he was close enough to see the dim flickering, he was not in danger, but it made her feel better to know it was there.

It was somewhere close to ten when there came a faint tap at the door. Effie threw down her darning and rushed to open it, ready to greet Lachlan with demands of why he was so late and expressions of relief, but her words died on her lips when she saw the man standing before her. Lachlan was hunched over, with his right arm against the door frame and the left hanging at his side. His head was bent and as he raised it to look at Effie his eyes were blank with exhaustion. As always, his seal fur was draped over his neck but tonight it was sodden and looked ragged, hanging loosely about his shoulders. The journey had clearly been an ordeal and Effie felt guilty for even feeling irritated at his lateness.

'You look exhausted! Come in out of the rain before you catch your death!' she exclaimed.

Lachlan limped as he passed the threshold, holding himself awkwardly with his left arm now crooked up and pressing against his right shoulder, deep beneath his fur. His usually healthy complexion was sallow and he was breathing heavily.

'You're injured!'

She reached a hand towards Lachlan. He flinched, as might a wounded animal. She took him by the shoulders and drew the fur aside. Her fingers met bare skin on his neck. So cold. He tensed and she felt the muscle contract powerfully.

'What happened?'

Lachlan shook his head. His brow creased in pain and he jerked the breath into his lungs sharply. He took a couple more steps into the room, slowly fumbling his way. Effie rushed to close the front door, which was whipping back and forth in the wind. When she turned, Lachlan was still standing where she had left him. His pelt trailed on the floor and the fingers of his right hand were pale with the effort of gripping it. Thank goodness he had not arrived while the children were awake. They would have been terrified at the sight of him.

'What happened to you?' Effie asked again.

Lachlan's only answer was to clench his teeth. He swayed, and without hesitation Effie ran to catch him in case he fainted. His eyes met hers, pupils huge and black, causing her to blink as a crack of desire as dangerous as any bolt of lightning speared her.

'Were you attacked?'

Visions of Lachlan being set upon and beaten flooded Effie's mind. He seemed strong, but against a gang of three or four he would stand no chance.

The light was not bright, but it was good enough for Effie to see what she had not noticed on the doorstep. It was not just rain that caused Lachlan's shirt to cling to him. His fingers were bloodstained and he was holding his hand against his shoulder to stem the flow. He was still clutching his fur with his other hand. Effie picked up the trailing end to take it from him and Lachlan's eyes flew open. He stared determinedly at her and tightened his grip. Effie saw for the first time that blood crusted the side of the soft brown fur, surrounding a long gash that had ripped down one side of it.

'It's badly torn,' she said in dismay. She ran the fingers of her free hand gently over the ragged edge, wondering if she could repair it. Lachlan sighed and his hand went slack as he relinquished it.

'It'll heal,' he said gruffly.

Effie set the fur to one side, feeling sick at the sight of the rough gash. The fur was part of Lachlan. If he had been wearing it when he was injured the wound must be equally severe on his body. Not a beating. Knives or some other weapon had been used here.

'Who attacked you? Mr Danby will hear of this as soon as I'm able to speak to him.' Walter's father had been furious to learn of the previous trouble, threatening to have any culprits dismissed from the alum works and replaced by men who had taken the vow of temperance. He should know the kind of men he was employing.

'No attack. An accident.' Lachlan spoke for the first time. He spoke in clipped sentences, his accent thick and heavy.

'How?'

Lachlan looked at her and his eyes were bleak.

'Nets. Hooks.'

Effie guided him to the fire and settled him in what she still thought of as John's chair.

'Can you explain?' she asked gently.

He leaned back and closed his eyes, his expression a mixture of exhaustion and agony. Effie caught sight of a long scrape running from beneath his ear to underneath his collar. His hair was slicked back, plastered to his head by the rain, giving him a sleek profile.

'Hard journey today. Rough seas and rain. Lost direction and concentration.'

'Were you...' She hesitated before finishing the sentence. 'Were you in your seal form when you were injured?'

He nodded. 'Nets had been abandoned under the water. Hooks and ropes were drifting and I wasn't expecting them to be there.'

It sounded like he was describing fishing trawls, sunk to the sea bed. He would have swum into them, become caught and been dragged down. Effie gave an exclamation of anger. 'Sometimes the alum workers come down to try to fish but they don't know how and they abandon their equipment.'

Her throat constricted, imagining Lachlan fighting to free himself, being dragged down to drown beneath the waves. Seals could not hold their breath underwater indefinitely. He could have died. The thought upset her far more than she imagined.

'Let me see,' Effie said. She knelt beside him and slipped her hand to his collar to see how low the wound went. Gently but insistently she prised his hand away from the shoulder that he was trying to cover.

'Take your shirt off,' she instructed him. 'I want to see how severe your injury is.'

He sat forward and began to unbutton the shirt with one hand. He winced as he twisted his arms and Effie had to help him slip it off, kneeling up at his side and easing it over his shoulders and arms. The last time she had touched him was when they had kissed, and the surge of emotions now rolled over her with an unsettling mix of desire and concern.

Lachlan was naked beneath his shirt, wearing no vest or undershirt, but Effie had no time to be coy. She'd seen the extent of the damage to the fur so knew what to expect, but even so the sight of the wound made her gasp. A deep gash stretched in a diagonal line from Lachlan's right shoulder across his chest, skimming beneath his left nipple and ending just below his left rib. It continued over his back and down to his shoulder blade.

She sat back, hand over her mouth.

'Bad?' Lachlan asked.

He must feel the pain. The confirmation was for her benefit. Oddly enough, now she had seen the severity of the wound, Effie became calm. Jack had once fallen and landed face first on the path from the jetty, leaving him with a lump the size of a pigeon's egg and a huge graze across his nose and chin. Effie had screamed at first, but then an inner person had taken over, ensuring she picked him up calmly, not showing him her distress as she bathed the wound and picked grit out of his forehead. The same voice spoke to Effie now.

'You need a doctor. We have a new man since Doctor Ackroyd gave up his practice. Let me go and fetch him,' she said.

'I want no doctor.' Lachlan gripped her wrist, his voice as firm as his expression.

'You need someone. The wound is so big I can't do more than bathe it.'

Lachlan's grip tightened on her arm. He couldn't realise it was hurting her, and compared to the suffering he was enduring, it was insignificant.

'I just need to rest.'

'You can afford it. You bring me pearls, for goodness sake!' she exclaimed. She would pay herself if necessary. Lachlan shook his head.

'Not that cost. I want no men of science to examine me.'

Would a doctor be able to tell Lachlan wasn't human? Effie doubted it, but it was not her decision to make.

'Something needs to be done. The loss of blood could kill you.'

The sound of voices came from the bedroom, followed by a thump. Morna had recently learned how to climb over the side of the cot. Lachlan jerked his head to the door.

'She canna' see me like this, it would frighten her.'

They were in agreement about that. Effie hurried to the bedroom and scooped Morna up just before the girl reached the door.

'Dada?'

'Dada is very tired. Don't disturb him now.'

Effie tucked Morna back into bed and gave her a quick kiss

on the forehead. 'Be an obedient girl now and you shall have an extra plum twist tomorrow.'

Morna nodded, her large eyes growing wide with longing. She'd spent all afternoon hanging on Effie's skirts as she and Alice had baked treats for Christmas.

The solution came to Effie in a flash, so simple she didn't know why she hadn't thought of it immediately. Alice would be able to help Lachlan. She must have poultices or something that could ease his pain at the very least. She closed the bedroom door.

'I'm going to get my grandmother. She helps people but she isn't a doctor.'

'She'll ask questions,' Lachlan murmured. His speech was slower and the bloodstain on his shirt had spread. Effie rolled up a tea towel and pushed it against his side, pressing on it with his hand, then picked up the lamp she had put in the window.

'Don't worry, I won't tell her what you are.'

When John died, Effie had kept his oilskin coat. It was too big for her, but ideal for just this weather. She pulled it on, closing her ears to any of Lachlan's anticipated protests but he was silent. She opened the door and looked out. The rain was still pelting down but the temperature had dropped dramatically and it was turning to sleet. Effie shivered. She would be as drenched as Lachlan by the time she reached Alice's house.

'I'll be back as soon as I can.'

She ran as quickly as she dared to Alice's house, blinded by the rain and with her feet sliding on the cobbles. Alice's front door was unlocked as always. Alice was sitting by the fire, her crochet on her lap. She started as Effie burst in, soaking wet and breathless.

'You have to come with me!'

Alice dropped her work into the basket at her side and stood up in alarm.

'Are the children hurt?'

It struck Effie now that there was more to explain than she had planned. Lachlan had been right.

'Morna's father is in my cottage and he's been hurt. He refuses to see a doctor, but he's bleeding and I don't know what to do.'

She gestured to her torso, fingers describing the path of the wound. She could hear the edge of panic in her voice.

If the news of Lachlan's existence surprised Alice, she kept it well hidden. She smoothed down her cap and stood.

'I'll find my bag of things and come right away. Go back and get the kettle boiling.'

Effie returned home to find Lachlan where she had left him, but the two children were no longer in their cot. They had climbed out and were standing in the doorway to the bedroom hand in hand, staring solemnly at the visitor in the chair. Lachlan had a little more colour now but was lacking the vigour she associated with him. He was bare-chested but had dragged the fur across his uninjured side and sat, legs sprawled out on the hearth; a long, lean figure who looked out of place in such an ordinary setting as a cottage kitchen. Effie dropped her heavy coat onto a chair and put a shovel of coal into the range to heat the hotplate for the kettle.

'Shall I get you something to drink?' she offered. 'Tea? A glass of brandy? There's a little left over from making the pudding.'

'Nothing, thank you,' Lachlan said. He moistened his lips with his tongue.

'Some bread and cheese? Some water?'

'Not even water,' he replied.

She felt a hand on her arm. Alice had arrived and crept behind Effie unnoticed. She had no idea how long Alice had been standing there. She had a habit of entering rooms quietly and waiting to be noticed.

'Alice, this is Lachlan, Morna's father. Lachlan, this is my grandmother.'

She watched as the two sized each other up. Lachlan straightened in his chair but didn't stand.

'Good evening, Mrs— Not Cropton, I think?'

'Call me Alice. Lachlan, you say? From up north?'

'That's right.'

Alice moved closer. Effie stepped aside to allow her access to her patient. She seemed shocked, unusually quiet rather than bustling around and taking charge as she habitually did when there was someone to treat.

'Morna's father?'

'Aye.'

Alice looked over her shoulder at the children, then back to Lachlan. She gave him a measured look up and down, her arms folded and a look of extreme interest on her face. Lachlan watched her back, his face unreadable. She gestured to the seal fur that lay loosely across him.

'Yours?' she asked in a voice that was barely more than a whisper.

Lachlan nodded slowly. 'Aye.'

Alice pursed her lips. Her cheeks grew red. She glanced at Effie then back at Lachlan and her brows came together. He stared back. They were having a whole conversation without speaking and Effie had no idea what it entailed.

'Effie, take the children into the bedroom,' Alice said without turning her head away. She gestured to the fur again.

'May I?'

Again Lachlan nodded, but now Effie noticed the smallest hint of a smile curling about his lips. Alice picked the fur up carefully and held it out at arm's length, letting it unfurl like a banner.

The tear in the thick, lustrous fur was visible. Wanting to do anything to help, Effie crossed back to Alice's side.

'I'm good with a needle. I can try to mend it.'

'No,' Lachlan said tersely. 'No needles or thread.'

'Can I do anything to help?' Effie asked, feeling useless.

Alice took her by the arms and steered her to the bedroom again. 'You brought me and that's the best help you could give him. Take the children and comfort them. I'll call you when I need you. Some of these herbs sting when they're applied and I don't want the sound of him groaning to upset them. I'll work here alone.'

'I willna' make a sound,' Lachlan said indignantly, rousing himself slightly.

Alice glanced over her shoulder. 'Would you like her to stay while I work? While we talk?'

Lachlan looked away.

'What do you know of this man whom you have invited into your home and to whom you offer food and drink?' Alice was wearing the familiar expression that meant she had thoughts she was not prepared to share. Well, there was plenty Effie couldn't share either.

'Not very much,' Effie said cautiously. 'I look after Morna and he comes to check on her every six months.'

She was beginning to feel foolish.

'I'm sure he isn't a threat to us,' she insisted.

'We'll discuss it later. Leave us be now.'

Effie knew there was no point arguing, though she disliked

being banished from her own kitchen. The main thing was that Lachlan's wounds were dressed before he grew ill from the injury and that Alice left, so she ushered the children inside. She closed the door to the bedroom but not before she heard Alice say to Lachlan, 'Now, my young fellow, let's be having a look at you and we'll have a little chat, shall we?'

She sat on her bed and sang Christmas carols to Jack and Morna in a hushed voice, but her mind was not on the songs. Alice had seen something in Lachlan's face or words that had made her cautious of him. Effie just had to hope as best she could it was not the truth.

Chapter Twelve

It felt like hours before Alice's voice came softly from the other side of the door telling Effie to come out. She put the children in bed, still wide awake, and snuffed out the candle. The kitchen was filled with a sickly, rich aroma that made Effie's eyes water. She was able to pick out one or two of the herbs but not all.

Lachlan was now wearing his shirt again although the buttons were undone and it hung open. Over his wound was a large bandage, presumably to hold in place the strong-smelling poultice or paste that Alice had applied.

He smiled on seeing Effie and his face was less pale than when he had arrived. A small bowl on the table indicated he'd been given one of Alice's pain-relieving draughts, no doubt with something to help him sleep added.

Until that point Effie hadn't given much thought to the greater implications of Lachlan's injuries and the impact on his routine. He came and left. That was how it was.

'You want him to stay here?'

'Well he can't go anywhere else,' Alice pointed out. 'I've

done what I can but the best healing comes with rest and sleep.'

'I'll go,' Lachlan said. He struggled to his feet and his face drained of colour. He swayed slightly and Effie suppressed the instinct to rush forward and catch him before he fell. Too much time in the company of unsteady children, she reasoned. He sank back into the chair and ground his teeth, obviously frustrated by his weakness. Beads of perspiration covered his chest which, she noticed now the urgency was over, was smooth and free of hair. The muscles of his abdomen and pectorals were well-formed and toned, with a deep tan as if he spent most of his time shirtless outdoors. She longed to trace her fingers over them. He was slighter than the workers who toiled to build the railway lines or hauled alum around and his body reminded her of one of the marble sculptures in Walter's books. Lithe, was the word that sprang to her mind. Where the wound in his side had been dressed, the shadows and curves of his muscles tapered to his hips, disappearing below the waist of his trousers and drawing Effie's eyes downwards. She blinked, conscious that she was staring right at his most intimate parts and lifted her head. Lachlan's eyes flickered up and met hers. He'd been watching her looking at him. If he had any sense of what she had been thinking, he gave no sign of it.

'How long will it take for the wound to heal?' she asked. Let him think she had been examining him with the eyes of a nurse rather than imagining what the rest of him looked like.

'A day or two,' Alice answered.

It must be nigh on midnight. He couldn't reasonably go away. He'd have to stay here. Close by. The first man who had slept under her roof since John died.

'You can stay,' Effie decided. 'You can take my bed.'

'Where will you sleep?' Lachlan asked.

Was he suggesting she might sleep beside him? A shiver raced down Effie's spine, her skin quivering. To lie at his side. To rest her head on that smooth chest. To fall asleep with the gentle breathing of another in her ears. Longing tore at her whole being.

'I'll take the chair by the fire.'

Lachlan shook his head. 'No, I'll take the chair. The children will be used to your presence in the room and mine will disturb them.'

He sat back and folded his arms, stretching his legs out towards the hearth. Clearly he didn't intend to discuss it further and Effie was more than happy with that.

Alice smiled with satisfaction. 'You'll be right in Effie's care.'

Lachlan bowed his head as if Alice were a queen. 'I'm sure I will. I am indebted to you, Alice.'

'Yes. You are,' Alice said, 'and as such I'm sure you won't object to taking a glass of wine with me, will you? I will consider it your debt cancelled.'

Lachlan stared at her, then shrugged. 'Very well. It's an odd payment but I accept.'

Alice reached into her basket and produced a small bottle with a wax cork. Effie recognised it as her homemade nettle wine.

'Three glasses, Effie, if you please. Lachlan, I'm sure you have no objection to sharing my hospitality in Effie's house?'

'Not at all,' Lachlan said, grinning slightly.

Alice smiled triumphantly, as if she had won something. She poured three glasses of the butter-yellow liquid and handed them round. She held hers up to Lachlan.

'To your good health and healing.'

'To your health,' he replied.

'And to Effie's contentment and fortune,' Alice said.

Lachlan raised his glass in her direction and smiled. 'To Effie's contentment and fortune.'

It was an odd toast to be subject to, but by now Effie had so many thoughts whirling round her head, she didn't care. She drank, looking into Lachlan's dark eyes over the rim of the glass. He did the same, holding her gaze steadily, radiating trustworthiness. He was very good at communicating without speaking, Effie decided.

Some things needed to be said aloud, however.

'Where is Morna?' he asked. His voice was starting to slur. Alice's medicine was already starting to have an effect and before long he would fall asleep. 'I want to see her.'

'She's in the bedroom. Do you think it's wise?' Effie asked.

'I won't frighten her now the blood is gone.'

Effie brought Morna. 'Be mindful of your dada,' Effie cautioned. 'He has a poorly side.'

She showed no fear but clambered onto her father's lap and snuggled down, legs and arms going everywhere, and put her arms around Lachlan's neck.

'Poor Dada. Morna kiss you better.'

Effie smiled to hear the child suggest the remedy she most frequently offered the children. Over the top of Morna's head she met Lachlan's eyes. They smiled at each other. Morna burrowed closer to him and a look of adoration crossed his face. Effie had only planned to let the child stay for a minute, but they looked so contented she changed her mind. Lachlan needed a blanket, so while they sat together Effie brought him one and added another shovel of coal to the fire to keep him warmer for longer.

Alice was gathering her jars and bundles from the dining table. Effie scooped up the wads of bloodstained linen and put them in the soaking bucket. Alice raised her eyebrows and cocked her head towards the door. Her meaning was clear and Effie supposed she was owed an explanation.

Alice pushed a pot into Effie's hand. 'There is enough paste to redress the wound in the morning and again tomorrow evening. Put it on the front step to keep it cool overnight. Lachlan will sleep soon.'

'Will you come and do it?'

Alice shook her head. 'That's a job you can do. You can manage, can't you?'

Effie pursed her lips and Alice gave her a stern look.

'I don't believe you're a coward, Effie Cropton. I'm sure you can bring yourself to care for him.'

'I'm not a coward,' Effie protested indignantly.

It wasn't that she feared what he might do but to apply the poultice meant to touch Lachlan with his shirt off. It was an intimacy that had held the essence of attraction until she had known what he was. Alice knew full well what nursing him involved.

'I'll do it.' Effie hugged her grandmother. 'Thank you. I didn't know what else to do. He was so insistent we should not get a doctor.'

'Yes he was, wasn't he.' Alice gave her an odd look. 'I wonder why that may be? Do you have any thoughts?'

'The expense I suppose, or perhaps that he didn't want anyone to know he was here?' Effie suggested, keeping her voice light.

Alice sucked her teeth, leaving Effie with the impression she had given the wrong answer or somehow failed a test.

'He'll be asleep soon. Let him speak with his daughter. In the morning you'll come to mine and we'll have a chat, just the two of us.'

Effie watched Alice walk along the path in the rain until she was out of sight then returned to check on Lachlan. Morna was lying on top of Lachlan. Man and girl were fast asleep, brown heads touching. If Effie tried to move Morna back to her bed she would risk waking them. Effie put another shovel of coal on the fire.

Lachlan's fur lay spread on the table. Effie ran her fingers lightly over the tear in the side. Lachlan shifted in his sleep and opened his eyes. Effie took her hand away, remembering how Morna had once done the same. The connection between the person and the skin was something she still didn't understand.

'I'll take her to bed,' she whispered.

Effie leaned in and gently untangled Morna from his arms. Her face was buried in the seal fur and her arms and legs were limp in Lachlan's good arm.

'I miss the scent of peat. Coal doesna' smell as sweet,' he said, slurring his words.

'Is that what you use?' Effie asked.

His eyelids were growing heavy again thanks to Alice's brew, and the look he gave her was drowsily sensuous. Effie felt a little shiver run down her back. Even drugged he was extraordinarily attractive.

'When you're stronger you can tell me about your home,' Effie said.

'Aye. One day, perhaps...' he yawned.

She carried the sleeping child into her room and went to sleep wearing her clothes in case Lachlan needed something in the night. If she was going to be spending the night with a half-naked man a dozen steps away, she was not going to be in any state of undress.

~

It was not even light when Effie woke, but she was immediately alert, sitting up and staring at the door almost before her eyes opened. The door was closed, as she had left it. The night's events tumbled round her head; events as muddled as if they were a dream. She knew they weren't. Lachlan was asleep in her kitchen.

She swallowed, her mouth feeling uncomfortably dry. The last thing she'd drunk had been Alice's nettle wine at the toast that Alice had insisted on. In a night full of strange events that had seemed one of the strangest. Alice's insistence they all partake and the formal words she had used had sounded almost ritualistic. Effie could imagine an archbishop speaking with such heavy solemnity in church.

The children were still fast asleep in their beds and looked set to stay that way for the time being. They'd never had such a late bedtime before, but then again it had been an unusual night for everyone. Effie slipped through the door into the kitchen.

Lachlan was asleep in what Effie still thought of as John's chair. His head was slumped onto his chest. He'd wake with a crick in his neck, though that would be the least of his worries. In the night he had slipped his shirt back on and covered himself with his fur. Effie regarded him for a moment. Until he had arrived she had been unsure how to greet him or whether she even wanted him in the house. The moment she realised he was injured, all reservations had vanished.

She was longing for a cup of tea and slice of bread. Usually the job of emptying the ashes from the stove was Morna and Jack's, but Effie did it herself this morning. She moved around stealthily, trying not to wake the sleeping man, taking the pan outside and tipping the ash into the bucket that stood inside the privy door. She made use of the privy while she was there and rinsed her hands and face in the stream that ran behind her house down the hill into the village. It was bitterly cold outside and the air smelled like oncoming snow.

Lachlan had woken while Effie had been outside. He was sitting upright and greeted her with a smile. Effie smiled back cautiously. At least now he was awake there was no need to be stealthy so she shovelled charcoal into the hob grate until the embers were glowing and put the kettle on the ring.

'I'm making tea. Would you like a cup?'

'Nothing, thank you.'

Effie recalled his refusal to eat or drink anything the previous night. She faced him, arms folded.

'So you'll drink Alice's wine but you won't accept tea from me?'

Lachlan furrowed his brow. 'Your grandmother healed me. I was under obligation to her.'

There it was again, the peculiar old-fashioned language.

'As you please. I expect you won't want any breakfast either.' She turned her back on him and began mixing the ingredients for griddlecakes in a bowl.

'Does Alice know what you are?' she asked.

'Your grandmother is a rare woman,' Lachlan answered. 'She has insight. Do you have any Scottish blood in you?'

Effie turned back to him, surprised at the question. 'Yes, a little. My grandmother's mother was born in Killin but she married my great-grandfather and they moved to Middlesbrough.'

'So you have a touch of Scottish yourself, even if only a trace.'

'I suppose so.' Effie shrugged and carried on whisking the batter. She'd never thought much about the line that stretched from her father to Alice Millbourne, through Eliza Jefferies to the great-great-grandmother whose name she had forgotten. She rested the whisk in the bowl and came to sit in the chair opposite Lachlan.

'You both behaved so strangely; I was very confused. I think she can't be sure whether or not I know what you are.'

Lachlan scratched his chin contemplatively. It was remarkably smooth, considering how dark he was. By morning, John, even as blonde as he had been, had to shave away the growing whiskers. A man as dark haired as Lachlan would surely be stubbled and unshaven by morning, but maybe he had no need of hair when he had fur.

'As I said, your grandmother is a rare woman. More perceptive than most. Of all the people you could have brought last night she was the best. She knows how to keep secrets and she knows enough old remedies that many don't.'

That reminded Effie of something.

'Alice said to apply the ointment again this morning,' she told him. 'I should fetch it now while the children are still asleep and won't get underfoot.'

She fetched the jar and was about to hold it out to him when she hesitated, remembering Alice's hint that she was a coward. He would be able to apply ointment to his chest and the wound beneath his arm but would not be able to reach his own back. Effie would have to apply it for him there, and if she could touch him there it would be churlish to refuse to apply the rest of it.

'If you remove your shirt I'll do it now. Come over to the table where the light is better.'

Lachlan stood at the dining table and slipped his shirt off. Alice had covered the wounds with long strips of linen which were now bloodstained. As he unravelled them Effie tensed, uncertain how terrible the sight would be, but already the bleeding had stopped and the edges of the wound were looking less angry.

Years before, Effie had spotted the tattoo at the base of his throat. Now she realised nearly his entire chest was tattooed. An assortment of very pale blue and green inked circles of different sizes began in a cluster over his heart. The largest was the size of his thumb, the smallest a mere pinprick. They ran down the centre of his abdomen, in and out of spirals, and vanished beneath his waistband. She'd seen sailors who had been covered from neck to waist in designs, but these were unusual.

'What are these?' she asked.

He glanced down at his chest. 'Clan markings. We are given them on reaching manhood and at other significant times. Each of us bears some that are the same and some which are unique only to us.'

Effie stared at them, thinking she could see a pattern but then losing it, and wondering which were Lachlan's exclusively.

'Did it hurt?'

He chuckled. 'Aye. But that's part of the tradition. At least I didna' ruin them last night. A lot of work went into them and the Record Keeper would be annoyed with me. She's got a sharp tongue on her.'

'She? A woman did this?'

Lachlan grinned. 'Aye. You of all people aren't surprised at a woman artist, are ye?'

'A little surprised at one who uses men as a canvas,' Effie admitted. She dipped her two fingers into the pot. She bit her lip. The moment she would touch Lachlan had taken on an unbearable significance.

You're nursing him, she told herself, *nothing more. Get your mind in order, girl.*

She tried to channel Alice's voice. 'This won't be as painful as tattooing, but it might sting,' she said.

His eyes crinkled. 'I'm ready.'

'Lean forward. I'll do your back first,' Effie said.

Lachlan obeyed, resting his hands on the table, bowing his head, and curving his spine outwards. Effie unscrewed the lid of the jar and dipped her fingers into the thick mixture. She held them above his wound, smelling the pungent herbs and trying to identify them. A seaweed of some sort, from the saltiness. Goldenrod, from the hint of aniseed. Others she didn't recognise. She stood behind him and gingerly smeared the paste over the wound. As her fingers touched Lachlan he tensed and drew a short breath between his teeth.

'Does it sting?' Effie asked, pulling her fingers away.

'Aye. But carry on. It needs to be done. Tell me what you'd paint on me,' Lachlan asked.

'I'm not sure,' Effie answered. She ran her fingers over the length of the wound on his shoulder blade. His back was lean and as he inhaled she felt the tautness of his muscles. It was the first time Effie had touched any man so intimately besides John. Her husband had been broader, his body toned from hauling ropes and suchlike. Lachlan was different, with a sleekness that suggested a different form of exercise had given his body its strength.

'Now let me do the front.'

Lachlan turned to face her. He drew his shoulder blades together, arching his spine to stretch. His movements were sinuous, elegant almost. She smoothed the ointment over Lachlan's side and chest; down one side of the rip and up again.

His chest was smooth and hairless in contrast to John's thick, dark thatch and again she couldn't help but notice the firmness of his muscles beneath her fingers. But why would a seal man have hair, she reasoned, when his skin was lying beside him.

'I'm done,' she said, taking her hands away. Alice had left fresh linen and Lachlan obediently turned this way and that as Effie wound it around him as best she could.

'Thank you, Effie,' Lachlan said in a low voice. 'Can you help me to stand?'

He held his hands out and Effie pulled him to his feet. He swayed slightly and she tightened her grip, moving closer. The fragrance of Alice's poultice was sweet and mingled with Lachlan's own warm scent. The last time they had stood this close Lachlan had kissed her. She had kissed him. She wanted to again. Knowing his nature couldn't compete with the longing for him that proved she was just as much an animal as he was.

Lachlan cocked his head to the bedroom door and gave her a smile in which she read regret. 'The children are awake.'

Effie had heard nothing, but to prove Lachlan's point the children began calling for their mama. His hearing must be much better than hers. She wasn't sure whether to be relieved or disappointed at the reprieve. She slid her hand from his and stepped back. She stooped to pick up the used bandages, giving her an excuse not to meet Lachlan's eyes.

'I'll take Morna for a walk along the shore while you visit Alice,' he said. 'She'll be waiting.'

'Are you in pain? Are you well enough to walk?'

Was he well enough to leave?

'I'm well enough. I'll return soon,' Lachlan said. He buttoned his shirt – Effie turning away to stop herself staring at the distinctive marks on his belly – then wrapped his fur around himself. He waited while Effie wrapped Morna warmly in her coat then man and child walked out of the door. It was starting to snow. Gentle flakes of grey dotted the sky. They seemed mild enough now but could grow heavier as the morning went on. Effie shook her head in exasperation. If he chose to catch a cold to add to his misery, that was up to him.

She let the snow settle on her hair. The path was covered with Jack's charcoal scrawls, not yet washed away by the torrents of rain. Shells and seaweed. And what might be an unskilled attempt to draw seals. Despite his protests, Effie pulled Jack into her arms.

'Come on, my pet. Let's go and see my grandmother. There are a few things we have to discuss.'

Chapter Thirteen

Alice took one look at Effie's face and crossed her arms, her chin rising. She was bubbling with barely concealed annoyance.

'You knew what he was before yesterday, I gather, if you're here sporting that guilty expression. Why didn't you give me a hint of what to expect?'

Effie hung her head, feeling like a child being scolded. 'What would I have said? Come and treat my visitor; he changes into a seal at will.'

Alice sighed. 'I'll set the kettle to boil.'

Effie followed Alice into the kitchen and deposited Jack on the floor by the hearth. She'd been holding back tears and now a violent sob burst free. Jack began whooping in his high-pitched voice and clapping his hands together as he sometimes did when sounds startled him. Effie held his hands together and breathed softly on his face until he stopped making noises. It always seemed to work and had the double advantage of calming her down so the urge to cry subsided. She needed to be rational when she spoke to Alice.

Alice had taken a seat in the wooden rocking chair and was knitting. When Effie turned away from Jack, she laid her needles down and crossed her hands in her lap.

'You didn't know when you first found Morna, I trust?'

'Do you think I'd have let a creature like that into my house if I'd known from the start?' Effie exclaimed.

Alice's eyebrows shot upwards. Effie pressed her lips tightly together, slightly shocked herself at the ferocity of her protestations.

'I didn't know,' she said in a softer voice. 'I didn't even suspect any such thing could be possible.'

'When did you find out?'

Effie sank onto the soft chair and recounted the events of the morning back in summer where Lachlan had shared his secret, leaving nothing out. As she described the way she had squeezed the skin and Lachlan had winced, she began to feel ashamed to admit how she had reacted.

'Even now it seems so outlandish I can hardly believe it,' she said, sagging back against the cushion. 'I keep telling myself Lachlan is playing some sort of trick on me.'

'Why would he? What purpose would it serve to make you less likely to keep his daughter? It sounds like he risked a lot by telling you and he didn't have to yet.'

It had been the kiss that had prompted his admission, but that was a fact Effie had not shared with Alice.

'I don't know,' she said, throwing her hands out wide in exasperation. 'Seals don't become people and people don't become seals.'

'Explain the change in Morna's pelt. Explain the wound in the pelt that matches the one on Lachlan's body.'

'I can't.' Effie rubbed her eyes. A problem shared is a

problem halved, they said, but she found that now she was discussing it openly with Alice, it seemed less real.

'Why did you believe him, Alice? You guessed before he said anything, didn't you?'

'The fact he refused a doctor and refused any hospitality from you with such insistence. The fact the pelt was torn in the same places as his injury and yet his shirt was untouched.' Alice clicked her tongue. She placed her knitting down and folded her hands over her stomach, giving Effie a self-assured look.

'Sometimes I wonder if you see what is before you.'

'It was all a rush. I didn't look too closely at the pelt,' Effie admitted.

Alice pursed her lips. 'The pelt was the proof, but something in his eyes gave him away. Have you ever looked closely into his eyes, my girl?'

Effie chewed her fingernail and didn't answer. Lachlan's eyes had burned in her mind for more nights than she cared to admit. Alice took her hand and squeezed it.

'Tea, I think.' She filled the teacups and looked at Effie over the top of the sugar bowl as she dropped lumps into her own cup.

'What contract have you entered into with this man?'

'I will raise Morna for him. He will visit when he is able. He's come twice a year so far, on Midsummer's and Midwinter's Night.'

'Powerful times,' Alice said, sucking her teeth. 'And what form does his payment take?'

'He gives me a pearl each time.'

Alice nodded in satisfaction.

'Those types place significance on that sort of thing. Still, that's safer than some would give you. What have you done with the pearls?'

Effie sipped her tea. Alice was speaking as if treaties with creatures from a child's story were commonplace.

'I haven't done anything with them. I can manage to feed and clothe Morna well enough without having to use them. I don't really know where to exchange them without having to explain how I came by them.'

Alice nodded again. 'Pearls can be returned. If he'd given you wishes or kisses that would be harder to repay.'

'I would never kiss him!' Effie exclaimed.

Her neck grew hot and prickled at the lie. The collar of her blouse felt uncomfortably tight but she resisted the urge to pull at it to loosen the bow. Alice was already watching her far too keenly. She tried to dismiss the thoughts she had been harbouring since Lachlan had last visited, but the memory of his arms around her and his lips on hers would not be banished.

'You've thought about it though.' Alice chuckled.

The blush was spreading further, rising up above Effie's collar and spreading to her cheeks. She couldn't hide it, and putting her hands to her cheeks would only draw attention to it. At least Alice suspected it was shame at the thought, not remembrance of the deed. She swallowed a mouthful of tea and banged the cup down in the saucer. Alice gave the sort of cackle that would have seen her burned at the stake two hundred years previously. Right now, Effie would have cheerfully held the first brand to the kindling!

'Well I wouldn't blame you for that. They're said to be powerfully beguiling and Lachlan is a handsome one. I only regret that I never met him when I was young and beautiful enough to weave a spell of my own, but I was married for too many years.'

'Alice, stop it! That's disgraceful, and you're talking as if this is commonplace, as if the world is filled with fairies and changelings.'

'When I was sixteen I met a man on the shore at Alnmouth one night who claimed to live between worlds. I don't know if he told the truth but I always wondered. His eyes were like polished jet in the moonlight and his kiss tasted of the ocean.'

Effie raised her head in surprise and saw a wistfulness on Alice's face she had never seen before. It was impossible to imagine Alice as the young and carefree girl her grandmother was clearly remembering. She'd always been old to Effie, but wasn't that true of everyone? Sometimes Effie felt ten years old and sometimes like she was fifteen and blossoming for the first time. When she was seventy, perhaps she would dream of her stolen kisses on the beach with Lachlan.

She pushed back her chair and went to Alice's shelf. She picked up the book of fairy-tales, turning the pages rapidly.

'How many other things in this book are real?'

'Who's to say,' Alice said with a shrug. She picked up her knitting and began again, needles clicking rapidly. Looking at Effie over the top, she spoke. 'The more important question now, my girl, is what do you intend to do next?'

'I don't know. When Lachlan left, I told him I would decide by this visit. I must think of Jack. What if Morna hurts him?'

Jack had been lying on his side looking at the flames in the grate. He raised his head at the sound of his name then lost interest and lay on his back, singing wordlessly to himself.

'Would taking away his sister hurt even more?' Alice asked.

'She isn't his sister.'

'Not by blood, but by every deed you've done, every kiss

you've given her and every word of love you've spoken to her. Where are Lachlan and Morna now?'

'Gone to the beach. They took the skins. *Their* skins.' Effie laughed slightly wildly and ran her fingers through her hair, twisting the curls which had come loose from the knot. 'I can't believe I'm saying that aloud.'

Effie walked to the window and leaned against the frame, peering out. Beyond the harbour walls the sea was grey as iron, streaked with white where the currents surged and pushed the waves aloft. The idea that there were creatures out there who could slip unnoticed between land and sea was astonishing. Were the man and child out there, moving through the water as seals, fur sleek and brown? A hand clutched at her heart. Lachlan had been hurt. What if it happened again and he was too far away for her to help? What if something happened to Morna?

That was the answer when it came down to it.

'I love Morna, whatever she is. It would break my heart to lose her. Jack's too. But Lachlan… I don't know. He lied to me for months. A child won't do us any harm, but he's a grown man. I let him stay last night because I didn't have any other choice. Am I doing the right thing by letting him stay in my house?'

'You're doing the kind thing.'

'Will he be well enough to go soon?'

Alice held a finger up while she counted the rows then smiled at Effie. 'The ointment works quickly. He's had two applications now so he'll be well enough to leave by the end of today if you apply a final layer around dusk. If you can bear for him to stay until tomorrow morning that will be better. Unless you don't want him to, for some reason.'

Effie bit her lip.

'I lied before. I did kiss Lachlan the last time he was here and I've thought of nothing else since.' She raised her eyes hopefully. 'Do you think he's put an enchantment on me? Is that why I can't get the kiss out of my mind?'

Alice chuckled. 'You could ask him, but I don't know of any enchantments that would do that. The magic, if any, is in the fact that he is a powerfully attractive man and you've been a widow for three years.'

Her lined face grew serious. 'I'm not saying you should, but I'm not saying you shouldn't. Few in our world mix with theirs and it doesn't always end happily. Then again, I know of enough marriages between men and women that end with tears too. He seemed a man of honour to me and there are precious few of those about, whatever shape they take.'

'It was only a kiss,' Effie said.

'In that case there's no harm done. Now, girl, go back to your house and decide what you're going to do. Lachlan is under no obligation to you and nor are you under any to him. Make sure you get all the answers you want. He's a guest in your house and he'll answer straight if you bid him to. When you've discovered what you need to know, you know where I'll be if you want to talk again.'

Alice took her by the hand and held it tight. The hand on hers was frail, but it was the same hand that held Effie as she sobbed when her parents died. They were the hands that helped without asking anything in return. Effie would trust she was right.

'Remember, bid him to give you plain answers.'

'I will,' Effie said.

Effie left feeling slightly happier than when she had arrived. No questions had been answered – in fact she had left with more – but Alice's blend of matter-of-fact briskness, coupled with her acceptance of the impossible, left Effie determined not to be cowed.

Lachlan and Morna were back at the cottage and there was a smell of frying fish when Effie returned. Her mouth watered. She decided not to ask how Lachlan had caught it. She stood on the threshold inhaling the scents that mingled together. Familiar coal and wood smoke, soap and bread were edged with Alice's poultice and an unfamiliar salty, fresh note that she associated with Lachlan. The commonplace and the unlikely under her roof. She walked inside and forced a smile.

'You'll not eat with me but you'll use my kitchen.'

'I can eat what I cook because then the obligation is not on myself.'

'But what obligation is on me?' Effie asked. She smiled to show she was joking, but there was a worry underlying it. Obligations clearly mattered. Alice knew that too.

'Any obligation I could place on you with a bite of fish would be light in the balance compared to what I already owe you,' Lachlan said. 'But if you like, I will swear now I share it with you freely.'

Lachlan rolled his shoulders back and raised his arms, testing the movement. He winced and looked apologetically at Effie.

'Alice said you would need to stay another night. Is that correct?'

His jaw tightened. 'I can endure the soreness, but I couldn't swim far or row yet.'

'You can stay tonight. I don't want you to risk further injury or falling ill.'

'That's kind of you,' Lachlan said.

Effie shook her head. 'It's the right thing to do. Besides,

how would I explain to Morna that her father died because I wouldn't have him in my house?'

At Christmas of all times, she thought to herself, where even one who is not a Christian should practise kindness to strangers.

Effie nodded and hung her cloak on the peg. 'In that case I'll lay the table.'

The fish was hot and the freshest Effie had tasted in a long time. She watched the children licking the peppery, buttery flecks from their fingers and was sorely tempted to do the same.

Something that had been tugging at Effie's attention finally succeeded in capturing it. Since their last meeting when she had discovered his true nature, she had wanted to ask so many things that would be intrusive. Or perhaps the answers would scare her, she wasn't quite sure.

'If you accept food or drink it places you under an obligation, but what about Morna? I've fed her for years now.'

'You placed my daughter under an obligation the moment you put her to your breast,' Lachlan said quietly.

'I didn't realise. I'm sorry.' Now she understood the shock in his voice when he first visited. 'If I had known...'

'Then she would have gone hungry,' Lachlan finished her sentence. 'No matter. You did what needed to be done. But be aware that she belongs to you until you decide otherwise. That's why I could not have taken her even if I had wanted to.'

'Do you want to take Morna away?' she asked once they had finished the meal.

He shook his head. 'No. Are you happy to keep her? I'll admit, the way I arrived yesterday willna' have done my cause much favour.'

'I am happy to carry on, truly. But I don't understand why

you want her here. At Midsummer you said you were both more in danger than I was. Those tales of your people being enslaved and suchlike... if we are a danger to you, why do you want Morna to live among us? She's not a nursing babe any longer. Surely a woman in your clan could foster her?'

Lachlan drummed his fingers on the table. 'It's possible I could find a woman to do that. As you say, there are those in my clan who would welcome my daughter, or her mother's daughter into their homes.'

They'd probably welcome Lachlan too, Effie thought. A widower who was as handsome and charming as Lachlan must be a catch for a woman, assuming his kind thought him handsome. She had no idea what the others looked like, but couldn't imagine him ever being called plain.

'Here Morna has an opportunity that is rarely granted to my kind,' Lachlan continued. 'She can learn to live in your world as an equal. The world is growing smaller year by year and I fear for our eventual discovery. When we live among you – and it has happened before – it is always as an outsider, or with our true nature known. Here she could be one of you.'

Effie digested his words. There was sense in them. To have two worlds at her fingertips would be better than only one.

'Will you tell her what she is?'

Lachlan steepled his fingertips and gazed thoughtfully at Morna. 'When I visit next she might be old enough, but children that age find it hard to keep secrets. For now it's best not to tell her.'

His words made sense, even though Effie doubted anyone in Allendale Head would think it any more than a fanciful child's story.

By early evening Lachlan's presence had become almost normal. He sat in the chair by the fire while Effie and the children ate barley broth flavoured with ham bones. Again he declined to eat and Effie did not press him. Sharing the fish had been a step forward, and perhaps he was simply not hungry. Jack and Morna ran around the house in excitement at their new companion and by their bedtime Effie was run ragged.

'Are they usually like wild things?' Lachlan asked from his position by the fire.

Effie counted to ten before answering. She might be hearing criticism where there was none intended.

'They're so excited because it's almost Christmas, and with you being here and everything else that has happened over the past two days, well...'

She waved her hands about to encompass everything that had happened. The clock read seven. It was hard to believe the day had gone on so long.

'Would you sing them to sleep like you did before?' she asked.

'I can sing them a song or I can tell them a story if you like,' he replied.

'Story!' Morna said. She ran up to Effie. 'Story, please!'

'Very well, a story it is,' Lachlan said. 'Jack, come here if you would like a story too.'

Jack turned at the sound of his name. He was doing that more and more which always cheered Effie. 'Story, Jack?' she asked.

He giggled in his high-pitched voice and walked over, wiggling his fingers in excitement. Effie settled back in the comfy chair opposite Lachlan and both children climbed onto her lap. Lachlan met her eyes. She held them for a moment, looking keenly for any trace that he was not all human, but however hard she searched, all she could see was a man. She'd wager he would give Alice's moonlight stranger at Alnmouth a run for his money when it came to sparkle.

Lachlan cleared his throat and began to speak. Both children were rapt with attention. Effie settled back to listen as Lachlan's deep, rich voice filled the room.

Chapter Fourteen

There was once a seal maiden who lived in the foam where the sky was widest and the waves tumbled and danced around the rocks. The sailors of these parts were tough and hardy with calloused hands and weathered faces and held no attraction for the maiden. But one day a stranger came to the village nearby, a bard from Edinburgh who came to capture the rocks and the waves and the seals. To walk on the cliffs that rose in the moonlight high above the sand and sit on the rocks that sank deep into the waters while he pinned down the world with his words. The seal maiden saw the bard and because she was young and because he was handsome, she fell in love with him. She knew that no good could come of giving him her heart, but one night she swam to where the bard was sitting and staring up at the waxing moon. She took off her skin and walked along the beach to meet him, and because the bard was young and because the seal maiden was beautiful, he fell in love with her.

'I will be your wife if you want me,' she told him, holding out the skin so he could see what she was.

'I do want you,' replied the bard, accepting the fur from her arms.

So on the beach in the moonlight they kissed and did more besides until she was a maiden no longer. And so they became man and wife.

Lachlan paused and his eyes flickered to Effie. She felt a blush creeping round her neck as she smiled back. The children were settling, growing heavy in her arms and an atmosphere of peace filled the cottage. The wind screamed over the chimneys and the window catch banged, but she felt snug and safe in the cottage lit only by the oil lamp hanging above the table and the gentle glow of coals through the grating in the range.

Lachlan resumed his tale.

For seven long and happy years the seal woman and the bard lived as man and wife in the village by the shore. The bard kept his wife's skin in the wedding chest at the end of the bed. While other men might have hidden it so she was bound to his side, he told her where it was because he trusted her to stay through love. The village women liked the seal maiden, and, if they knew what she was, they said nothing against her. They liked the bard too, but the fishermen observed his smooth skin and uncalloused fingers and turned their noses up in scorn.

'Come and fish with us,' they told him as they sat in the inn late at night. 'Do a man's job for a day then go back to your songs and pipes.'

The bard always declined, but after the seventh year ended the men wore him down and he agreed to set sail on a boat heading out for a month to catch cod in the cold Icelandic waters. The seal woman begged her husband to stay on land, but he kissed her and patted her cheek as he laughed and told her not to be silly.

'I'll be back in a month,' he said. 'Keep my bed warm, my darling.'

Effie's throat tensed. She had a sense of foreboding at how the story was going to turn out. Story or not, whenever men went to sea they faced danger. She didn't think she had made a noise but Lachlan paused once again and looked at her questioningly. She couldn't recall if she had told him of John's fate, but didn't want to interrupt. She shifted Jack a little in her arm as an excuse to explain why she had moved and settled down again.

Lachlan raised an eyebrow. Effie nodded in answer and he began again.

That night the storms came, fierce and full of hatred. The boat the seal woman's husband was on was tossed to and fro until the inevitable tragedy struck and it was dashed to pieces on the rocks, leaving no survivors. When the seal woman heard of his death she wailed and wept until she could weep no more. Then she unlocked the chest at the foot of her marriage bed, took her fur and walked out of the cottage, leaving the door wide open, for she had no more cares of what would become of it.

She walked down to the beach and put her skin on. With one last look at the village she had come to think of as home she dived into the sea and returned to her people.

Lachlan sat back and folded his arms across his belly.

'Is that the end?' Effie asked.

'What more should there be?' Lachlan looked surprised.

'I don't know. A happy ending? Fairy-tales should have happy endings.'

'It isna' a fairy-tale; it's a folk tale. There is no requirement for a happily ever after. Besides, at least she didn't become foam like Andersen's mermaid. She lived her life to the natural end.'

Effie swallowed down a lump that had formed in her throat. Drowning sailors and grief-stricken widows were too close to her own life for comfort.

'Maybe there was a happier ending when she returned

home,' Lachlan said gently. 'Perhaps she found love again with a man of her own kind, or she might have made peace with her widowhood. But that's the end of the story as I know it. Look, the children are asleep.'

Effie craned her head down and saw he was right. Morna and Jack's heads were touching, their bodies limp and faces slack and reddened with sleep.

'I had better get them to bed,' she whispered. She carried the children into the bedroom, balancing them precariously on her hips. They were almost too big to carry at the same time. She laid them in their cot and kissed them. Before she left, she glanced at the box on top of the wardrobe where Morna's fur lay wrapped in newspaper. Morna would need to learn of its existence one day.

When she returned to the kitchen, Lachlan had spread his own pelt out over his knees. Effie drew close, then hesitated and stepped back. The moment seemed very personal. Lachlan folded over the skin and found the spot where the deep slash was. He ran his fingers along the edges, then put the same fingers to his shoulders. He raised his head and gave Effie a satisfied smile.

'Already it begins to heal as I do.'

Effie stared down at the skin. It didn't look much different to her, with the long tear running through it. If she peered closely she might imagine that it had healed on its own. The tear was still long and deep, but the edges were smoother than she remembered them being. The fur, like Morna's, had changed since Effie last looked properly at it. The knowledge thudded in her brain that this was a living thing, a part of the man before her as surely as his foot or eyes were.

'Is the part of the story true about the fur holding the woman captive? That she couldn't leave without it?' she asked.

'It's a child's story. How much do you think is true?'

'I've been asking myself that since Midsummer,' Effie said frankly.

Lachlan's eyes grew solemn. 'That part is true enough. I keep mine with me always. Do you remember I told you our kind is at risk from yours? If you were to take my fur and hide it away I would have no choice but to stay in this form and at your side.'

'But you could go and live anywhere, couldn't you?' A traitorous little voice whispered in the back of Effie's mind that it would not necessarily be a bad thing to keep Lachlan close to her.

He shook his head. 'Not without a great deal of discomfort. The further we are from our skin, the greater our anxiety. Where the fur goes, we go. If it is taken from us, we belong to that person until they choose to return it, or until we win it back through cunning. We are easily enslaved.'

'Is that true or just a legend, though? I'm not sure I believe in magic,' Effie said.

'Even when it is presented to you in broad daylight?' Lachlan asked. He leaned against the table and folded his arms. 'But before you would have sworn you definitely didna', so that's a change. I wouldn't say what we are is magic, however. We just are.'

'Is that why you wouldn't take tea or eat anything I offered?' Effie asked. She remembered tales from Alice's book where humans were ensnared using such means by fairies and goblins. Of Proserpine in the Underworld for six months of the year. It had never occurred to her that the charm could be used both ways. Were those stories true too?

Lachlan smiled. 'Yes, there are certain obligations that a person can be put under. I don't think you would deliberately try to charm me, but once I accept hospitality from you I am under obligation to you.'

Effie raised an eyebrow. 'You're under considerably more obligation by giving me your daughter to raise than if you drank my tea!'

'That's true.' Lachlan gave her a warm smile that made the hairs on the back of her neck stand up. 'And, in that case, I wonder if I might be so bold as to beg a drop of something to drink now. I've got a powerful thirst.'

Effie looked at him. This was a test of some sort, but she wasn't exactly sure who was being tested. She was about to put the kettle on the stove but changed her mind and fetched a bottle that was half-filled with sloe gin and put it on the table along with a couple of glasses.

'You can pour. We don't stand on ceremony here. I don't know if that will lessen the obligation.'

He grinned, revealing even white teeth. The canines were slightly more pointed than Effie's or anyone she knew. He had a nice smile now he was showing good humour. He handed her a glass of gin.

'Thank you.' She nodded toward his cup. 'I place you under no obligation by drinking it.'

He lifted his cup to his lips and looked at her over the rim.

'Do you give this freely without the prospect of favour?'

It was an odd phrase, but clearly the form of the words was important to Lachlan. It was no less odd than the repeated phrases in the catechism, Effie supposed.

'I give it freely without the prospect of favour,' she said.

She lifted her own cup and drank, wondering what the scene would look like to an observer. It felt like an old ritual was being enacted. Lachlan's smile deepened and the fine lines at the sides of his eyes crinkled. His forehead and nose made a straight profile and the deep-brown eyes were hypnotic, but there was nothing she could see that would mark him out as anything other than a handsome human man.

'Thank you. There's no more obligation than I choose to place myself under by accepting it.'

He drank, keeping his eyes on Effie as he did so. It was disconcertingly sensual to watch his lips enclose the rim of the glass and she found herself imagining what it would be like to kiss him, now she knew what he was. Would she be able to forget, and would it matter anyway if she did not?

Lachlan sighed in satisfaction and placed the glass back on the table.

'Yours or Alice's?'

'Both. We picked the sloes together. The children pricked them with darning needles before bottling. Talking of needles, should I stitch the tear in your pelt? I have a neat hand and you'd barely see the mend.'

'I'd feel it,' Lachlan said. 'Every prick of your needle.'

Effie ran her fingertips along the ragged edge. Lachlan shivered and blinked.

'Did you feel that?' she asked, taking her hand away hastily.

'I did.'

'Did it hurt?'

'Not in the slightest.' He gave her a small smile, a quirk of the corner of his mouth that contained something he didn't need to say aloud. The rolling surge awakened within Effie again. The need that called for his touch. She lacked the courage to ask what sensation her touch had evoked, though from the look that had passed between them she had an inkling.

Effie looked him up and down out of the corner of her eye

174

for evidence of strangeness. He should have webbed fingers or pulled-back ears or something to make him less attractive. It would help her considerably if he did.

'I need more of Alice's ointment applying, but if you'd rather I tried to do it myself I will.'

'I don't mind doing it,' she replied. 'I'll fetch it from outside.'

She opened the door and stood on the step, gulping a couple of lungfuls of cold air. By the time she had returned Lachlan had removed his shirt and had started unwinding the wrappings. Taking another breath to steady herself, Effie crossed to him and began to apply the ointment, smoothing it over the wound as she had done previously. Again, her eyes were transfixed by the markings on his chest. She wanted to fit her fingertips into the circles and work her way downwards. She thought of Morna's mother, the woman who had lain with Lachlan to create the child, and jealousy crept into her heart.

She concentrated on his injury, keeping her eyes down, but was aware of his gaze on her as she let her fingers explore the shape of his form. She concentrated on the task, talking as she moved her hands over Lachlan and describing the condition of the wounds. If she did that, she would not be able to think about what else her hands could be doing.

'The bleeding has stopped. I think tonight it would be best to leave the bandages off and let the air get to the wounds,' she said.

'Aye, that's a good idea. I'll be warm enough like this,' Lachlan agreed. He reached for Effie's hand. 'Thank you, Effie.'

Her fingers were still oily from the ointment. Lachlan rubbed his thumb across a stray smear on the cleft between her first and second fingers. Such a light touch but it sent her head spinning. She had to keep reminding herself he was not a man, because the desire was as strong as ever. She lifted her eyes to meet his and found desire shining back. Effie was aware she was breathing hard, her heart beginning to race as his fingers laced through hers.

'Effie, I think it's only right to tell you that I'm wanting to kiss you,' Lachlan murmured.

'I know,' she replied. 'I want to kiss you too.'

'Even though I'm a monster?'

Shame burned, the heat almost eclipsing the desire.

'You aren't a monster. I'm sorry I ever called you that. When I think back I'm ashamed of myself.'

'You have nothing to be ashamed of,' Lachlan said. 'It was a natural response to what you'd just learned.'

He glanced towards the bedroom.

Silence.

Now there would be no interruptions from the children waking. They smiled at each other. Lachlan put his hands to Effie's cheeks. Hesitantly, he leaned towards her and kissed her very softly on the mouth. The room spun around her as the gentle pressure of Lachlan's lips sent waves of excitement pulsating through her veins. She buried her fingers in his hair, curling them into the waves. It was as soft, thick, and fine as his pelt.

Lachlan increased the pressure slightly, his tongue skimming the inside of Effie's lower lip. She opened her mouth wider and let hers meet it, increasing her grip in his hair to hold him closer. His hands slid downwards, fingertips brushing over her neck and further down to encircle her waist. Their lips moved in harmony, and if Effie had planned to watch out for indications of his true nature, she soon forgot that idea as she lost herself in bliss. All too soon for Effie's liking, Lachlan drew away. His eyes were heavy-lidded and brimming with desire.

'I'm greedy,' he said, shaking his head. 'I always have been, but I'll never take what I'm not offered.'

Effie's stomach tightened at his words. He had judged correctly that she was coming close to offering him whatever he wanted, but if she did there would be no going back from that moment. The story of the seal maiden and the bard flitted through her head.

They kissed and did more besides.

'Thank you,' she whispered, finding her voice again. 'I'll see you in the morning. Sleep well, Lachlan.'

It was too early to go to bed but if she didn't go now and go alone, she would most likely end up inviting Lachlan with her so Effie lay in the bed she had shared with her husband and tried not to think of the dark-eyed man on the other side of the door.

Lachlan left on Christmas Eve at six when the bells of the church were pealing to herald the start of the service. The village came alive as the congregation headed excitedly up the steep hill towards St Stephen and All Saints. Alice joined Effie and the children, and the party of five walked along the back of the beach on the shingle where the tide hadn't reached. When they reached the first rocky outcrop that forbade any further passage, they stopped.

Lachlan took Alice by the hand. 'I owe you my life, Mrs Millbourne. That is a debt I can never repay.'

'In time you might,' Alice replied briskly. 'Pay me back by doing what is right.'

He nodded. 'I strive to do that anyway.'

He picked up Morna, slightly awkwardly in his weak arm, and held her close. He whispered something to her in the language Effie did not understand. Morna put her thumb in her mouth and stared at him with the green-brown orbs that were so like his. He put her back down on the sand and faced Effie. Neither of them had made any mention of the kiss. It had seemingly satisfied them both and drawn a line beneath what had been a very odd couple of days.

'Midsummer's Day, Mrs Cropton?'

'Midsummer's Day.'

He shrugged his pelt around his shoulders and walked away.

It was only when the children were opening their presents on Christmas morning that Effie realised she had not given Lachlan the portrait of Morna she had done for him.

Chapter Fifteen

'Effie, I have a proposal for you.'

Mary laid down her pencil on top of her sketchpad, holding it firmly to stop the winds blowing both away. Her eyes were brimming with excitement.

'I intend to start a school for the girls of this village and the nearby ones. Now that education is compulsory, we need a school here. Whitby is too far for many of them to walk. I would like you to be my assistant in that task.'

Effie laid down her pencil and looked at Mary with interest. The women were sketching each other in the garden of the vicarage. 'Don't you already run the Sunday school with your mother?'

'Yes, I do, but this would be more than that. A proper school that teaches the children to read and count, and the fundamentals of History and Geography and the great empire we have created. I have been reading—'

She broke off and bit her bottom lip, a look of guilt flashing over her face. 'Well, it doesn't matter what I have been reading, but I have concluded that I am not as educated as I would like to be. My school was excellent at teaching me to sing and embroider. Less successful at teaching me art, I'll admit,' she added with a laugh as she looked at the slightly top-heavy sketch of Effie on her lap. 'But knowing nothing of the world around me, I would like to know more. And I believe the children of this village – the girls included – would also like that. You could bring Jack and Morna. They could even begin their lessons and be our first pupils.'

Effie looked at the two children. They were walking backwards and forwards across the churchyard (Morna in the lead as always) gathering snowdrops which had started to peek through the ground. It was the third of February and the first day which had not been too bitterly windy or rainy to endure staying outside.

'I don't know,' Effie said uncertainly. Her eyes followed Morna. Effie spent a good part of every day studying Morna to look for any indication of her true nature starting to develop. She had found none, but Morna had few companions besides Jack, Alice, and Mary. Any difference might become more apparent when in the company of other children. Then again, even Alice had admitted nothing in Morna's behaviour or look had led her to guess before she knew of Lachlan's existence.

'What does your mother say?' she asked.

A mischievous glint appeared in Mary's eyes. 'I haven't told her, but I have discussed it with Papa. He agrees that if I am determined not to marry at present – which I am assuredly not – I should have something to keep me busy. If you agree to help, he will suggest it to Mother as his own idea. He knows men on the Education Board at Whitby and will speak with them to find out what I must do.'

She reached out and took Effie's hands. 'Please say you will. There's no one I would rather have with me than you.'

Effie could feel herself weakening to the flattery. There was no reason why she should not. Time seemed to be moving more slowly than it had done and she was conscious that she was falling into the trap of counting down the days until the return of Lachlan and Walter in the same manner she had when John had gone to sea.

'Tell me everything you have planned and I'll think about it.'

～

Of course she agreed.

Reverend Ogram persuaded his wife that it would be an excellent venture for Mary and even allowed the use of a room in the vicarage that was no longer used as his study. Mary and Effie excitedly set about planning a syllabus for the children. A lengthy discussion at one of Mrs Ogram's ladies' groups concluded that whereas many of the older ones could either not be spared from working with their families or could manage the walk to Whitby, the youngest children could be given basic tuition in numbers and the alphabet. Their absence from the family home would allow mothers to work or clean without them underfoot.

In the first week of March, Effie received a letter from Walter. He had now made his way to Switzerland and would be spending a month in Lausanne on the shores of Lake Geneva. She wrote back to the hotel address he had supplied, telling him about the scheme. She was glad that for once she had more to report than the children's health and an account of the paintings she had done. Walter's reply came almost by return, full of praise for their socially minded enterprise and promising to write the same day, entreating his father to supply any materials the women needed.

He was true to his word and a week after receiving Walter's letter, a large box was delivered to Effie, compliments of Mr and Mrs Danby. It contained a dozen slates and slate pencils and five primers of instructional and moral stories for young children.

Walter's letter also contained passages of a much more personal nature: a page and a half praising Effie's nature and character and reminding her of Walter's own philanthropic inclinations. He strongly hinted that together their combined zeal for public good could be more than the sum of its parts. He hoped to be back in England by the end of July and looked forward to hearing everything from Effie's own lips.

So, he still had not found anyone to fall in love with, she mused. She folded the letter and put it in the drawer where she kept the pearls Lachlan had given her. They were wrapped in the folds of one of John's handkerchiefs. Effie picked them up and laid them on her bed one by one. She looked around her bedroom. The children were almost too big for their cot where they still slept top to tail. Often, Effie woke in the night to hear them complaining at each other when their feet collided.

She wasn't sure how much an individual pearl might be worth but if she sold one pearl it might be enough to buy another bed, as well as some new linens for all three of them. She still wore her mourning clothes for John, though that was as much because the skirts and dress were still serviceable. But the thought of a new dress for summer that was perhaps a dark blue or grey rather than black appealed. With the other pearls she could afford to equip the school room with as many books and slates as they could possibly need. She held the pearls in her hand, remembering Lachlan's touch as he had given them to her. Alice had said that the pearls could be returned if she decided to end their agreement, but these had already been earned. Besides, the nature of their relationship had changed. He had accepted her hospitality and was a stranger no longer.

She laid them out in a row again from smallest to largest. They were all similar in size and colour. She picked out the one in the centre and put the others back.

When Reverend Ogram next went to Whitby, Effie went along with him and paid a visit to the pawnbrokers. She entered the shop nervously, pausing to let a woman clutching a package wrapped in brown paper pass by her and exit. It was Saturday and most likely the woman was redeeming the Sunday best clothes for the following day. The shop was neatly ordered, with lamps and ornaments on shelves along one side, clothing hanging displayed on the other and a cabinet with watches, jewellery, and other more valuable pledges towards the back. There was a bottle-green skirt that looked to be her size labelled as four shillings and fourpence. It was fuller than was currently fashionable, but that wasn't a great concern and she wasn't too proud to wear second-hand. If she were offered enough for the pearl, she'd buy it.

In the stories Effie had read, pawnbrokers were always greasy-haired or crooked-backed and inclined to cheat unwary customers, but the proprietor, Mr Harrelsen, was a homely-looking man with curly grey hair, smartly dressed in a brocade waistcoat and grey suit. He sat at the counter towards the rear of the shop with a newspaper spread out over the top and a mug of cocoa. He kept his attention on the paper, occasionally underlining passages with a pencil until Effie approached him.

'My mother had a pair of pearl earrings. She sold one but left me the other…'

Effie began her tale but Mr Harrelsen cut her off. Clearly he wasn't interested in where his customers obtained the goods they were pawning, presumably to aid deniability should the police show interest in any of the objects in his shop. He took the pearl and examined it under an eyeglass, then fixed his eye on Effie.

'The quality is exceptional but it has no setting. No marks at all in fact to show how it was set into an earring. This isn't from any jewellery I can imagine. Where did it really come from?'

Effie smiled sweetly. 'It was given to me by a seal man who travelled from the islands of northern Scotland.'

Mr Harrelsen narrowed his eyes.

'The music hall is two streets up if you want to play the comic. I'll give you nine shillings and eleven.'

Effie gritted her teeth. The pearl must be worth far more than that but that wasn't the reason for the offer. Anything below ten shillings could be sold if she didn't reclaim it. Anything above would have to be auctioned with all the inconvenience involved.

'If I see this in the window it will be for four times that, even without the setting,' she argued. 'Two guineas ten at least.'

Mr Harrelsen grinned good-naturedly. 'This is my business, madam, and I have my children to feed. I like you though. You have gumption. I can go to two pounds exactly.'

That was a week's wages for a clerk or secretary in Mr Danby's office. It was better than nothing, though Effie wondered if Lachlan realised how little his half-year's payment was considered to be worth.

'Done, if you'll excuse the penny to purchase the ticket and throw in the green skirt for four shillings exactly.'

She stuck out her hand. Mr Harrelsen grinned widely and shook it. As he wrote out the ticket he remarked, 'Somehow I don't think you'll be back to reclaim this, will you?'

'Probably not,' Effie agreed as she placed the ticket and money into her purse. She considered the transaction could have gone worse. She completed her other purchases and re-joined Reverend Ogram, bearing bundles and packages. It was just as well, because she would have a lot of sewing to do.

'It's only a week until Midsummer's Day. I think we should have a party to celebrate,' Mary announced. 'We can gather in the churchyard and crown a Summer Queen. Perhaps even have a bonfire in the evening.'

The two women were walking arm in arm along the clifftop path, enjoying the warm sunshine. Jack and Morna walked ahead in the company of five other small children. Their task was to gather five unique objects each and keep them safe in their smock pockets.

Only a week! With all her time spent organising the school, Effie hadn't been keeping track of the days. The year had gone so quickly and for the first time she was not spending her days anticipating Lachlan's return. She had even slipped a letter from Walter into her apron pocket and forgotten about it for two days. It was exactly as it should be, but it did mean she hadn't spoken much to Morna about her father's arrival. At bedtime she would have to make sure to remind the child. Six months was much longer for her than for an adult.

A bonfire sounded fun but not on that day when Effie and Morna had other arrangements.

'Isn't that rather pagan?' she asked uncertainly. She had no objection in that regard herself but Mary was a vicar's daughter after all.

Sure enough, Mary looked anxious. 'I don't know. Perhaps I should ask my father for advice.'

Effie took her hand. 'Why not suggest the children gather flowers in the afternoon and leave it at that? We could have a picnic and play games in the churchyard. If they enjoy it we can do more the year after.'

'That's a good idea. So much better than mine. I'm so pleased you're helping me with everything,' Mary said, hugging Effie. Effie hugged her back. It was good to have a friend, and even better to have one who listened to her ideas without asking too many questions.

Midsummer's Day started dull and drizzly, but by lunchtime it had brightened enough for the children to enjoy their picnic. Effie wore her green skirt and matched it with a spray of flowers in her straw hat. No one had criticised her starting to leave off mourning wear and she had resolved to buy another skirt when the weather became colder again. The games were a success and the weather held off long enough for the children to gather blossoms. At six, the clouds began to gather again and Effie left the children with Mary and the other mothers as she raced home to collect her bed sheets in from the washing line.

It was just as well, because as she came to a halt at the gate, she saw Lachlan was waiting on the doorstep. His pelt was slung over one shoulder and in his hands he held something grey and shiny. He smiled at Effie as she approached.

'You're early. It's not dark yet,' Effie said in surprise.

'Should I go?' He looked uncertain. Effie caught him by the arm. She'd been uncharacteristically rude.

'No! I'm sorry, I just wasn't expecting you so early. You normally wait until later. 'It's good to see you again. How is your injury?'

Lachlan flexed his arms and rolled his shoulders back. 'Completely healed. There's a scar, but nothing that causes me discomfort.'

Effie glanced back to the beach where there were still people walking along the shore. He could have been seen coming to the cottage and a stranger wearing a seal fur and carrying fish in his bare hands – for Effie realised that was what he was holding – would attract attention. She pointed at the fish and raised her brows.

'I thought we might eat together.'

It was a thoughtful gift, meaning they could share a meal without any of Lachlan's worries about obligations. Lachlan held out the glistening body and Effie held her hands up.

'Thank you, but I'd rather not touch it. I need to get the washing in. The door isn't locked. Please, go in while I gather the sheets before it rains,' she told him. When she came in with her arms full, Lachlan had found Effie's oval serving plate and laid the fish on the table.

'I'll do the filleting so you don't have to touch it,' he said with a grin.

He was forgetting she lived in a fishing village and had long since lost all squeamishness about touching raw fish, but if it made him happy she wouldn't object.

'Where is Morna?' he asked.

'The children are up in the graveyard gathering elderflower blossom with Mary and some of the other children. I'm going to teach them how to make it into syrup. They'll be back soon.'

'Which children are they with? Who is Mary?' Lachlan asked.

As he gutted and cleaned the fish with remarkable skill, Effie told him about Mary and the progress the two women were making with the school. Lachlan listened with what appeared to be genuine interest despite not knowing any of the people she mentioned, interjecting with questions at some points.

'It's an admirable endeavour. Learning is important,' he said when she finally came to an end. 'Perhaps I should invite your Mary to visit Scotland with me and establish a school there.'

Effie suppressed a twinge of jealousy that he spoke of taking Mary and not her. 'Don't you have schools? Can you – Selkies, I mean – can you read and write?'

'We have no school, but many of us are literate,' he answered. 'Those of us who deal with the humans who live nearby tend to be more so. Others prefer to remember things by word alone and keep to themselves. We're all different but all of us value learning in whatever form it takes.'

Like the families in the village, with different degrees of literacy and interest in the world outside Allendale Head, Effie considered. Her thoughts were interrupted by the arrival of the children, who ran into the house bearing baskets brimming with tiny white flowers. The cottage was suddenly filled with the scent of tart sweetness and loud voices. Effie relieved the children of their baskets and sent them outside to wash their hands.

'They've grown tall. Both of them,' Lachlan remarked.

'And louder,' Effie added.

When they returned, Effie guided Morna towards Lachlan. 'Look who's here. Dada has come to visit.'

Morna slipped behind Effie and buried her face in Effie's skirt. 'Now, don't be shy,' Effie instructed.

Lachlan squatted on his haunches and held his hands out.

'Hello, Morna, do you remember me?'

Morna shook her head. 'No! Go away.'

'Morna!' Effie exclaimed. The girl had never shown such obstinacy before. She drew the girl out from behind her and lifted her onto Lachlan's knee. Morna reached back to Effie and gave a plaintive wail as she stretched her arms out.

'Mama.'

'Greet your dada,' Effie said gently. She gave Morna a gentle push in the small of her back, but Morna shook her head and craned her entire body away from him.

'Morna wants Mama.'

Effie winced: Morna could speak perfectly well and usually only referred to herself by name when she was distressed or tired. Lachlan looked desolate at her words. He held the squirming girl out at arm's length.

'Take her. Please. She doesn't want me.'

Effie took hold of the child and put her on the rug. Lachlan slumped into the chair and dropped his head, looking defeated.

'She fears me. What have I done wrong?'

'Nothing that I can explain,' Effie said.

Lachlan pushed himself upright.

'I should go. This is a mistake.'

Effie took his arm. 'No, stay and eat. If you go now, whatever the problem is won't get solved and next time you come she'll be even more reluctant. Bring the fish over to the stove. I'll heat some butter to fry it.'

He did as she asked but with a reluctant expression on his face. Morna sat on the floor by the bedroom door, knees drawn up and watching his movements with a suspicious look on her face. Once she ventured as far as the chair by the fire and stared intently at Lachlan's fur but retreated as soon as Effie gave her a smile.

Chapter Sixteen

I t was not the relaxed meal Effie and Lachlan had been anticipating. Morna sulked and still refused to meet Lachlan's eye.

'I don't like fish,' she muttered angrily when the fried fillet was put in front of her.

'Yes you do. She does,' Effie hastened to assure Lachlan. 'She's just being contrary.'

Jack, on the other hand, behaved perfectly; using his fork to shovel food into his mouth instead of his fingers and grinning around the table.

'He's a good-looking boy, Effie,' Lachlan said. 'Is he much like his father?'

Effie gazed at her son, the unaccustomed glow of praise warming her. 'In looks, yes. In manner, no. Jack is…'

She hesitated, unsure how to describe him. 'He doesn't speak much, but I think he listens and understands more than he shows. Don't you, Jack, my pet? He isn't as quick at his letters as Morna, but he holds chalk and draws well.'

'Morna, do you know your letters?' Lachlan asked, pride

creeping into his voice. She buried her face in her hands and, despite Effie's cajoling, refused to look up or eat any more of her meal. Effie could feel the urge to banish her daughter to bed rising steadily.

'I'm sorry. I don't know why she's being like this.'

She lifted Morna from her chair and led her into the bedroom, shutting the door behind them.

'What are you thinking of, being so rude to your dada?' she demanded. 'He's come a long way to see you.'

'Is he my dada?' Morna asked. Her bottom lip stuck out and she screwed her eyes tight. 'I have no dada. Jack has no papa.'

Her voice was no longer sulky but plaintive. Effie sat back on the bed and closed her eyes. Of course it was hard for the child to understand. Lachlan had only visited a handful of times and Morna would barely remember most of them. The last time he had come in pain; there had been shouting and blood. Now her mother was forcing her to greet him and getting irritable. Of course Morna was wary. Effie had blundered by trying to force the issue.

'He is your dada,' Effie reassured Morna, drawing the child onto her lap and rebraiding one of the plaits that had come loose. 'He's a good man. You need to get to know him a little.'

Morna looked stubborn again. 'He smells of the sea. He doesn't smell like me.'

Effie's hand froze, mid twist of a braid. She'd been aware of Lachlan's scent when they had kissed but this was the first time Morna had mentioned anything. Was the girl's sense of smell more acute? Animals knew each other, didn't they, and a mother sheep would reject a lamb that had been handled by a person. What if that was happening now? She hugged Morna tightly, sadness welling up at the thought.

'He smells like himself and like he always has,' she reassured Morna. 'Will you try to be kind to him? To please me?'

Morna nodded reluctantly. Holding hands tightly, Effie took Morna back to the kitchen. She gathered Morna into her arms and sat opposite Lachlan, leaning forward so the child was close but still held by the mother she trusted. Morna picked up her fork and toyed with the fish, lifting a piece to her mouth with her eyes firmly on Lachlan.

'She is nervous of you because she doesn't see you often enough,' Effie explained in a low voice. 'Children go through those phases. Jack had two weeks when he wouldn't let me leave him with my friend Mary, even though he knows her well. I suppose when you visited at Christmas she might have got scared and only thought about it afterwards. Let's take a walk to the beach. It's still hot and light but most people will have returned home.'

'What about the children?' Lachlan asked.

Effie eyed him sternly. If he thought there was going to be a repeat of the kiss they had shared, he was mistaken. Wasn't he?

'I meant with the children.'

He acknowledged her tone with a gentle laugh and dip of his head. Effie brightened. The evening could be saved still.

The beach was almost empty, but they walked along until it curved away in case anyone spotted them. The clouds still hung low in the sky; oppressive and stifling, but there was a slight breeze. In an hour's time the temperature would drop and it would be cool and more tolerable. Jack and Morna kicked off their clogs and ran into the waves, jumping over the white crests and squealing with laughter. The air was a little fresher down by the shore, carrying the scent of salt and seaweed. Effie took a deep breath, drawing the aromas into her lungs, and inspiration struck her. If Morna thought Lachlan smelled of sea, then she should smell the same.

'Morna, shall we show Dada how well you swim? I bet you swim better than he does.'

Morna loved swimming more than anything else in the world. She beamed at the adults and splashed further into the waves, fully dressed. Once she was waist-high she kicked her legs out behind her and began to paddle, arms and legs moving rhythmically. It was not an elegant style, but she was quick.

'Remember, only along the shore, not out further,' Effie cautioned. She took off her own shoes and walked barefoot into the sea. She lifted her skirt and petticoat to keep them out of the water as much as possible, glad that she was not one of the fashionable ladies in Mary's magazine with an elaborate bustle or train. Lachlan would be able to see her calves if he bothered to look, but his eyes were on Morna.

'It's lovely and cool. Come and join us,' she called.

He shook his head, but Effie stared at him until he sighed reluctantly and grinned. He kicked off his shoes, rolled his trouser legs up and waded in up to his knees, holding his hands out to Morna. Morna dived under the water and swam to him, throwing herself against her father's leg. Lachlan scooped her up gingerly and walked back to the shore. He sat her beside him on the sand and draped his fur over his shoulders. Morna reached a hand out and touched the edge with a fingertip, closed her eyes and smiled. At that moment Jack strode out of the water and Effie hastily held him back before he could interrupt. Lachlan looked up and caught Effie's eye and gave her an almost imperceptible nod. She smiled back, feeling a knot in her throat.

Lachlan began humming softly and when Morna shyly peeked out from beneath her fringe he changed the tune for a lively melody. He lifted her onto his knee and bounced her up and down as if she were riding a horse. Soon Morna was giggling and doing her best to clap along. Jack stood at Effie's side with tears springing to his eyes, bereft at losing his playmate. Effie scooped her son up and hugged him tightly. She seldom thought of John with any sense of grief these days, but seeing her boy with no father to sing to him twisted her heart. Jack should have a papa to jog him up and down and sing shanties. She hummed a nursery rhyme but Jack carried on sobbing. Effie bit her lip, overwhelmed with sadness.

Lachlan looked at her over the top of Morna's head and his eyes filled with understanding.

'Would you like a song too, laddie?' Lachlan asked, gesturing to his other knee. Jack nodded slowly, putting his first and middle fingers into his mouth. Gratefully, Effie passed him down to Lachlan.

Lachlan began a new tune; livelier and merry. He jiggled the children up and down until they were both squealing with excitement.

'I'll go back to the cottage and wash the dishes,' Effie said to Lachlan. 'Bring them back when you've tired them out. Or they've tired you out.'

She glanced over her shoulder once or twice as she picked her way across the shingle. Lachlan was now bucking his legs up and down alternately, sending each child high, but his dark eyes were watching Effie. She waved and left them to play.

She was in the process of drying the final dishes and heating milk when they arrived home, Lachlan in the middle with a child holding each hand. All three of them were laughing. The children were soaked to the skin. Effie brought them towels and started getting the children out of their clothes and into nightgowns.

Lachlan was not as wet, but she brought him one too. His hair had already started to dry into slight curls and the occasional water beads made their way down his forehead and cheek. His shirt clung damply to his body in what Effie considered quite an indecent manner, emphasising the sculpted muscles of his chest and arms.

He gathered the children's damp clothes and spread them over the drying rail that hung on ropes above the stove, while Effie poured warm milk into their cups and sat them at the table. She held her breath in case Morna decided to be obstinate again, but she drank enthusiastically. Effie cleared away the mugs and as she stored them in the cupboard a pencil on the side reminded her of something. She fetched her art case and found the portrait of Morna. She held it out to Lachlan.

'There was something I meant to give you at Christmas, but with everything else that happened I forgot.'

His eyes widened. 'You did this? The likeness is remarkable. You have real skill.'

Effie blushed with pleasure. 'She's changed already.' They both looked at Morna who was sitting by the window playing with a pair of peg dolls, making them dance up and down. It was true; her face had lost the baby chubbiness and her hair had grown longer since Effie had painted her.

'I did it for you as a gift, but now I'm thinking if I did one of you for Morna it would help her to remember you.'

'That's a good idea. Could I suggest you do one of both of

us? Morna and me, I mean. That way she will see the likeness between us.'

'Of course. Shall we do it now before she goes to sleep?' While Effie collected her brushes and paints, Lachlan began looking through Effie's portfolio. He picked up a portrait she had done from memory of Walter and studied it closely.

'This is your friend who visited last year, isn't it? The one who annoyed you by suggesting a walk.'

'I did it from memory. He's been travelling in Europe for almost a year now.'

Lachlan's mouth twitched. 'You must have an excellent memory to capture his likeness in so much detail. He must feature clearly in your mind.'

There was an edge of something to his voice. Effie resisted the urge to rip the paper from his fingers.

'I've known Walter for many years so I can remember him well. As to how good the likeness is, I couldn't say. My memory might be completely false.'

Lachlan handed it to her. 'Possibly, though probably not.'

He sat by the window and placed Morna onto his lap. As Effie sketched, he asked about the other paintings and she explained how she had begun and the work she did for Walter's friends in Manchester.

'One day you should travel to Scotland and paint some of our plants. We have flowers quite unlike anything else.'

'Maybe one day I will. I could bring Morna and Jack to visit you. She should see where she was born.'

'Possibly,' Lachlan said, though he sounded as if he had reservations. His brother might tolerate Morna living with humans, but he would not tolerate humans entering the clan. Morna's head had begun to droop as Effie sketched and the light was fading. She put her pencil down.

'I'll stop for now. I have enough of both your likenesses that I can complete this another time.'

'Of course. I'll look forward to seeing it when you've finished.'

'Children, it's time for bed now. Bid your father goodnight, Morna.'

Morna stood beside Effie and waved. 'Sleep tight, Dada. See you tomorrow.'

Lachlan's face darkened. 'Not tomorrow, lassie, I'm afraid. I'll be back at Midwinter.'

Morna turned to Effie. 'Sleep tight, Mama. Will you be here?'

'Of course I will,' Effie said. She bent and kissed Morna's cheek, did the same with Jack and led them into the bedroom.

When she returned after settling Morna, Lachlan was staring out of the window once again. He looked deep in thought.

'I should go. Thank you for persuading me to stay.'

'I'm glad you did, and I'm pleased tonight turned out well.'

His mouth jerked downwards and he tensed.

'Am I doing the right thing by visiting her? Would it be kinder to let her forget me?'

'No. Morna got to know you better, but she needs you in her life more. Even the fishermen who go off to sea and leave their families for weeks or months at a time spend more than one night at home before they leave again.'

'What are you saying?' Lachlan asked.

'I'm saying you need to stay longer or visit more often if you want Morna to know you. Children need to know their parents. If you could come more frequently she would recognise you better and become more pleased to see you.'

Lachlan shook his head. 'I canna do that.'

A future stretched ahead of Effie where Lachlan came into their lives only for a brief period every six months. She could start a hundred schools but she knew without question that whatever else she did to fill her days, the intervening months would be spent waiting for him to arrive. Morna would wait for a father she barely knew and Effie would wait for... what, exactly? The chance to spend an hour or two in the company of a man who made her heart leap, in the hope that their brief kisses could be repeated.

Was that the way it had to be?

'Why not? I know you can stay for more than one day because you did it twice in succession. Last summer and again at Christmas when you were injured. Couldn't you stay tonight? Longer, even?'

Lachlan raised an eyebrow. 'How long? And where would I stay?'

'I'm not saying stay in the house with us – I know that wouldn't be proper – but last summer you stayed somewhere.'

'Could you imagine me living here?' Lachlan asked.

'I only meant a night or two, but if it comes to that, why not?' Effie replied. 'There are more strangers in the village than there used to be now it is expanding. You probably wouldn't pass for an alum worker; your complexion is more that of someone who works outside, but you could easily pass for a fisherman if anyone questioned you.'

Lachlan walked to the window. His pelt hung loose about his shoulders. He gestured to it.

'This place is not for me. I don't belong in this world.'

'But you're expecting your daughter to fit in,' Effie said sharply. 'If it's good enough for her, why isn't it good enough for you? The woman in your story lived with her husband for seven years.'

'That was a fairy story!'

'A folk tale. One you said was based on reality.'

He regarded her for a moment with a speculative look in his eyes.

'You've changed since I first met you, Effie Cropton. I remember when I first walked through that door to claim Morna. You faced me but I could tell you were terrified. Now we are all under your command.'

'Do you prefer me the old way?' Effie asked. She walked around the table and leaned against it, closer to him.

'No. I've always liked women who know their own mind, however much that causes difficulties for me.'

'If I can change, why can't you?' Effie said. She bit her lip and looked him in the eye. 'I think you *have* changed, but Morna will need you to change more.'

He looked obstinate. Effie folded her arms.

'If we matter – if Morna matters – enough to you, you'll do it.'

'I have… responsibilities.'

'You have responsibilities here too,' Effie pointed out. She walked to the window and stood beside him. 'I don't see you as the sort of person who shirks his obligations. What is really the problem?'

She held his eye until Lachlan dropped his head.

'I'm not sure I should get too fond of her,' he said quietly.

'Why ever not? She's your daughter. She's young now but don't you intend to take her eventually?' The thought made her stomach clench.

'I don't think that would be wise,' Lachlan said. 'Where would I take her?'

Effie frowned. 'Back to your people and home.'

Lachlan gazed out to sea, his profile stern. His eyes took on a faraway look.

'You may be right. What if it would be best for Morna to stay here and try to live a life with you and Jack?'

Effie wrinkled her brow. 'You said the sea calls to her.'

'But she doesn't have to answer. Not yet. Maybe not ever. With you she has a chance to live as a human. My world is shrinking while yours grows larger. What parent would not want the chance to see their child have a better life?'

He reached into his pocket and produced a pearl as usual. When he held it out to Effie, she shook her head firmly.

'I don't want it this time. I want a different sort of payment.'

He cocked his head to one side, eyes narrowing suspiciously.

'Oh? And what would that be, Effie Cropton?'

'Answers. To questions. I know almost nothing about you,' Effie said. 'Do you have a family? More children? How do you fill your days?'

He blinked. 'Those are your questions? You'd forego a pearl to find the answer?'

'I would.'

He rolled the pearl between his fingers, his eyes thoughtful. Finally he slipped it into his pocket and beckoned Effie to his side. He leaned against the windowsill and folded his arms across his chest.

'I have no children besides Morna, nor anyone to have them with.' His eyes crinkled and heat prickled the back of Effie's neck. 'As to how I fill my days: I carve wooden figures for the prows of rowing boats, I mend what needs to be mended. And I'm a storyteller in the clan when we gather together.'

He said the last part with a touch of pride and Effie was swept back to the winter's evening by the fire listening to his tale of the Selkie wife. If he was as skilled in his other roles as that one, his work must be a sight to see.

'That's a lot of jobs,' Effie remarked.

'You raise two children, teach others and help Alice,' he answered. 'My elder sister Firtha is the chief of our clan. My younger brother Seathan and I act as her advisors when she's in the mood to listen to advice.'

'Your sister!' Effie remarked, his words sparking interest in her. 'A woman leads your clan?'

'Yes, she is the elder of the three of us,' Lachlan said.

'And the rest of you don't mind being ruled by a woman?'

'Not at all, and, even if we did, she's the eldest child so that is how it is.'

'I think we have a lot to learn from you,' Effie said. She gave him a wide smile. 'This is so refreshing! If I said these things to any of the men and most of the women here they would tut and raise their eyebrows at my forwardness. Even Walter would seem anxious at the thought of such radical ideas.'

They met each other's eyes.

'Aye, well we are different in a lot of ways but my people see the value of a strong leader, whatever their sex.'

Something in his voice changed, became darker. Effie was an only child but sibling fighting wasn't rare. 'Does your sister know about Morna?'

'She does, and about Morna's mother's death. In fact, Seathan was with me when—'

He broke off and gazed out towards the sea. 'But never mind. I've told them about you.'

His lip curled into a wry smile. 'Seathan was not pleased I

had left Morna with a human at first. Now he sees that it is working, he is happier with the situation.'

'Is it working?' Effie asked.

Lachlan took her hands, sending ripples over her arms that lifted the hairs and caused the skin to become sensitive.

'We are making it work, you and I. Every obstacle in our way we have overcome together.'

He was right. There were things they still needed to negotiate, but it was working in its odd way.

'Ye-es, but for how much longer? Morna will want answers too before long. If you try to deny her them, it will only end badly. Sooner or later you'll have to tell her the truth about what she is before she discovers it herself.'

His mouth twitched. He raked his fingers through his hair and looked out towards the sea.

'I'll think on your words. And now I shall leave.'

He leaned forward and left a light kiss on Effie's cheek.

'Farewell, Effie Cropton. Keep safe and happy until I see you again.'

He strode out before she could reply.

Chapter Seventeen

Morna did not seem affected by her encounter with Lachlan and did not seem curious where he had gone. Effie's mind eased, though it caused her a little sadness to think that Lachlan went out of Morna's life without any lasting effect.

Alice, on the other hand, was becoming a worry for Effie. She had started walking with a pronounced limp and increasingly talked about her own demise.

'I don't need a new cloak,' she grumbled on an unusually damp and chilly August evening, when Effie suggested her current one was becoming threadbare. 'This one will see me out.'

'For pity's sake, Alice, please stop saying that,' Effie exclaimed. It was at least the third time she had heard that gloomy prediction. 'You talk as if you'll be in your grave by the end of the week.'

Alice gave her a solemn look. 'None of us can say that we won't be. And with that in mind there are things I need to teach you. When I'm gone someone will have to know how to fix things for people. You're going to have to do it.'

'Me? Doctor Douglas, who has taken over, seems perfectly good and doesn't charge more than he needs to.'

Alice waved a hand. 'Oh, I dare say he is but there are some people who won't go to a doctor on any occasion and some things that a woman won't discuss with a man. No, my girl, I'm going to teach you at least some of the things I know.'

'But there are advertisements in papers for… for *that* sort of thing,' Effie said.

Alice's expression grew blacker than Effie had seen for a long time.

'And nothing that I would pay good money for or that won't do more damage than good. Chalk and aloe at best, arsenic at worst! What I make works and has done since time began. Besides, not everybody trusts these new ways. What if your Lachlan turns up again with another injury or illness?'

Effie laughed, though her skin tightened at the memory of the blood seeping through Lachlan's shirt and his insistence that she did not call a doctor. 'He's not going to need the sort of thing you make. And he's not *my* Lachlan.'

'Isn't he?'

Alice gave Effie one of those inscrutable looks that in no small way contributed to her reputation as a wise woman.

Effie set her jaw. 'No, he's not. He belongs to himself.'

It wasn't just rhetoric. Until or unless Lachlan gave his skin to another, he was entirely his own person. It had crossed Effie's mind what she would do if he did propose such a thing. Just like when Walter had asked her to marry him, she had no idea how she would respond.

'Very well,' she said. 'Show me some of what you do and

I'll try to learn. Some of the ones to treat children might be best. Mary and I will always find a use for those in the school.'

~

'Someone has taken the old fisherman's cottage at Boggle Cove.'

Mary announced her news over an afternoon cup of tea at Mrs Ogram's Women's and Young Mothers' Society. So far, the members consisted of Mrs Ogram, Mary, Effie, Mrs Forshaw and Mrs Newbury, whose husband ran the grocer's shop.

'I'd hardly glorify it with the description of *cottage*,' Mrs Ogram said, placing her cup on the saucer and picking up her knitting with a steely glance towards the other women's abandoned work. 'If it doesn't leak in half a dozen places I'll be very surprised. Are you sure it is properly let and not a vagrant who's taken it upon himself to occupy it? There are more and more unsavoury types since the whaling industry began to ebb and there is less work for the lower classes. Really, we need a constable to patrol the shores and streets to keep us safe in our houses.

'Quite sure,' Mary said, smoothly interrupting her mother's flow. She picked up her knitting needles. Despite not being a mother, as the patron of the society, she had taken it upon herself to dictate the first activity, which was to supply the children of impoverished families with knitted stockings. 'I heard it when I took your medicine bottle back to Alice, and Mr Peters pointed the man out himself. He was just leaving Mr Peters' house.'

Mary turned to Effie, who was sitting on the sofa beside her and her eyes grew wide.

'It's the strangest thing, Effie. Do you remember the

painting you once showed me of a seal hunter on the ice floes? The man looks almost exactly like that!'

'A whale hunter,' Effie corrected. 'But what a strange coincidence.'

She couldn't ignore the frisson that shimmied across her body at Mary's words. A coincidence was all it was. It was only August, and Lachlan wasn't due to return for another four months. All the same, she found it hard to focus for the rest of the afternoon and the meeting could not end soon enough for her. She agreed readily to every proposal put forward involving stocking distribution and other matters that suddenly felt very unimportant to her wandering mind.

Morna and Jack had been playing with Mrs Newbury's twin boys in the garden. Or at least, Morna had been playing while Jack sat and pored over a book of pictures of birds.

'Mama, I want to go and see the boggles tonight,' Morna said as soon as Effie called her in.

'Goodness me, what an imagination the child has,' Mrs Newbury said, looking along her nose at Morna. 'Don't you know there are no such things as boggles, child?'

Morna pouted rather rudely. Effie mildly admonished her. Whether boggles were real or not, there was no need for Mrs Newbury to be quite so patronising. She wondered what the sensible storekeeper would think if she knew that the child she was correcting was not even human.

'There may or may not be. We never see them, do we, Morna? Why do you want to go there tonight, chick?'

'I want to go and see the house,' Morna said.

Effie tried to hide her surprise. What did Morna know? The window was open so she must have heard what the women were talking about.

Although Effie would never have revealed it to the

children, she was keen to visit Boggle Cove and see whether the mysterious tenant really was Lachlan or not; as such, she allowed herself to be cajoled quite easily by Morna.

Jack threw his weight behind the argument by tugging meaningfully on Effie's skirts. He still barely spoke, preferring to communicate with actions not words and had started occasionally to add growls and chuckles to his repertoire. It was something Effie tried not to dwell on, but as the children grew it became more and more apparent he was lacking something that Morna and most of the other village children had. Despite that, he seemed to show just as much pleasure in life as his foster-sister, as the two children raced ahead over the beach after they had eaten their supper.

'Careful! The tide will be going out soon and I don't want you to get swept away,' she called as Morna ran full speed towards the waves.

'The tide won't take me, Mama,' Morna shrieked. 'He wouldn't dare to try.'

She danced closer to the waves and Effie tried to bury her fears. The girl was a strong swimmer, and even though she had never taken seal form she slid through the water as if born to it.

Effie picked a path where the larger pebbles met the sharper shingle but which was easier on her feet. As they neared Boggle Cove, the scent of fire mixed with the seaweed and salty air. A plume of dark smoke was rising from around the curve into the inlet. The fire had been lit inside a circle of small rocks.

A man was sitting cross-legged on the shingle beside it with his hands busy working at something. He had his back to Effie and the children, but as they approached he lifted his head and grew still then turned round.

Effie's heart began fluttering as if it had grown wings and was about to rise skywards.

It was indeed Lachlan.

Chapter Eighteen

Lachlan had been sitting on an upturned wooden crate in front of his hut, weaving a fishing net when Effie arrived with the children in tow. He smiled widely as Effie and the children drew close. Jack ran to his side and picked up the net. He began looping it around his hands like a game of cat's cradle.

'I'll teach you properly, laddie, but don't tangle it now.'

Lachlan took the net from him and put it beside the fire before stepping towards Effie.

'Effie! What a surprise and pleasure to see you so soon. Did Alice tell you I was here?'

'You've seen Alice?' Effie asked in surprise. 'No one tells me anything.'

A small flame of betrayal flickered in the pit of her belly, scorching the wings from her heart until it became a lump again. Lachlan had gone to see her grandmother first, and not Effie and the children.

'Actually, that isn't quite fair. Mary Ogram mentioned a tenant but nobody told me it was you.'

'I saw Alice when I went to arrange the lease on the hut. Not intentionally, but she was passing as I left. I didn't intend to tell anyone I was here because I wanted to make the hut fit for visitors before you saw it. As it is, that might take longer than I first expected.'

Effie looked at the building that was set back against the cliff at the point a stream came down the narrow, forested gorge. She had walked past it a hundred times or more and never taken notice. The abandoned hut was just part of the scenery.

Mrs Ogram had been right in her assessment that a shack would be a better description than a cottage. It was a small dwelling that had, at some point in the past, been occupied by a fisherman. There was only one room by the look of it, and it was in a poor state of repair. The roof was covered partly over with oiled sackcloth to block holes where the slates had fallen in. The window had pieces of driftwood nailed across the frame.

'Is it true you are staying here?'

Lachlan nodded. 'I don't know for how long but you were right when you told me I needed to play a greater part in Morna's life.'

Morna came over at the sound of her name and stood beside Effie, pulling Effie's skirts around her to hide in. Effie gently but firmly untangled her and drew her round to stand in front of her. 'Do you remember your dada?'

Morna gazed at Lachlan solemnly. Jack had John's eye colour and shape rather than Effie's, whereas Morna's eyes were entirely Lachlan's in every respect. What must it be like for him to see his own eyes reflected in another's face?

Lachlan knelt down so he was level with Morna. 'Hello

again, Morna. I would like to get to know you better than I have. Would you like that too?'

Morna shook her head. 'No,' she said seriously.

'She doesn't have to talk to me yet,' Lachlan said. 'There's going to be plenty of time.'

Even so, his face had fallen and Effie felt sorry for him.

'How long?' she asked.

'I don't know. I've taken the lease until the end of the year but I don't know if I'll need it. It all depends how things work out.'

Jack had been piling pebbles into a heap and finally realised Morna had gone. He took up his position on the other side of Effie.

'Will you look at this fine laddie!' Lachlan said, smiling down at the boy. 'He's grown so tall since last I saw him.'

Jack gazed up at Lachlan solemnly. Effie put her arm around Jack's shoulder. He already reached past her waist. 'He takes after his father. He was tall too.' A little of the worry she had been feeling regarding her son ebbed away under Lachlan's praise.

Jack pointed to a pan Lachlan had put on a fire, containing a large, glossy mackerel. He spoke in a rumbling voice.

'Fish.'

'Aye, laddie. My supper. Perhaps you'd like some?' Lachlan held out a hand to Jack and to Effie's amazement Jack went willingly. Lachlan led him to the fire and held a frying pan over the heat.

'Fish,' he repeated in his rumbling voice.

Effie blinked, feeling her eyes start to well up. She wiped her sleeve across them and Lachlan looked concerned.

'He doesn't talk much,' she explained to Lachlan.

'He talks to me,' Morna pointed out indignantly. 'We just don't always use words.'

'You don't always have to,' Lachlan said. 'There are plenty of other ways of showing what you want to say. Now, Jack, will you hold the pan steady so the fish doesna' burn?'

He helped Jack hold the long handle, keeping the boy's hands clear of the flame. Morna left Effie's side, clearly unable to bear being left out and went to stand close to Jack. Lachlan acknowledged her with a nod of his head, but didn't remark on her being there. A cautious approach worked and before long she was kneeling beside Lachlan at the fire. Effie settled onto a rock nearby and watched the man and children as they cooked. It was a mild evening and pleasant to feel the breeze and listen to Morna chatting. Lachlan was barefoot, dressed in plain trousers and a fisherman's sweater. He would fit in easily in the pub in the village or among the labourers on the railway.

The door to the hut stood open. In the darkness Effie could make out the shape of a bed frame. A large leather bag stood by it with something folded on top.

'Do you have everything you need?' she asked.

'I'm afraid the house isn't fit for visitors,' Lachlan said. 'My needs are few and while the weather is good I'll cook and eat outside. The roof won't leak and the bed is comfortable. That's all I ask.'

Effie met his eyes and saw something in them that she'd seen before, when they had shared intimate moments. Just like when she had applied the ointment to him, and when he had held her tight as she tried to flee him, the memory of his body against hers rose inside her, igniting a flame. It was very true; there were ways of speaking that required no one to open their mouth. Beds weren't just for sleeping and Lachlan's eyes betrayed him. She hoped hers were less easy to read because she knew how tempting it would be to share it with him. She drew her shawl around her shoulders.

'If you discover you are lacking anything, please ask me. For the house, I mean.'

All the while they had been talking, and she had been considering the matter of Lachlan's sleeping arrangements, Lachlan had been pulling the cooked fish from the bone onto a large tin plate. He held the plate out to her.

'Try some mackerel. I caught it myself.'

'With a net,' Effie asked, 'or in another way?' She put her hands to her mouth, aware of how intrusive the question was, but Lachlan only gave a deep-throated good-humoured chuckle.

'My usual way. Here, it's very good.' He broke off a piece and held it out to Effie between his fingers. The flesh was smooth and smelled delicious but Effie hesitated, remembering how Lachlan had first refused her offer of a drink.

'If I accept this, what obligation does it place on me?' she asked.

'No obligation. Eat freely as my guest.'

She leaned forward and Lachlan placed the fish between her lips. It was oily and smoky and every bit as delicious as she had anticipated.

'Even if I were to try to place an obligation on you, I am so indebted to you for caring for Morna and looking after me when I was ill that the balance would take more tipping than a single roast fish could accomplish.'

'It's very good fish. Who knows what it could accomplish,' Effie said with a grin. She licked her lips and helped herself to another piece before Jack and Morna devoured the whole plateful.

Once the fish had been eaten, Lachlan sent the two children

to wash and scrub the frying pan in the sea with handfuls of sand to remove the grease. He vanished inside the hut and reappeared with his skin and a blanket made of tightly woven wool in purple and moss-green checks.

Effie finally realised what was different about Lachlan. For the first time he hadn't had his fur with him all the time. She had never seen him without it. It was as odd as seeing a woman attending church with no hat or gloves and she understood how truly it was a part of him.

Perhaps now that he was settling in the hut and no one else was around, he had felt safe enough to leave it there.

He slung it over his shoulders and held the blanket out towards Effie.

'It's not cold yet, but the sun is going in and it will be chill soon. There's nothing as warm as wool from highland sheep.'

'Thank you.'

She held her hand out for it but, instead, Lachlan swept it around her shoulders for her, before sitting down beside her and stretching his legs out. He wriggled his toes into the coarse sand.

'If you're to eat with me every night I'll have to catch more fish,' he grumbled. He was smiling though, and his eyes crinkled warmly.

'I'll bring you teacakes in return,' Effie said with a grin. They watched the children, who were now arguing over who had the privilege of carrying the pan back up the beach. As always, Morna gave way the moment Jack started to become distressed.

'What changed your mind about coming?' Effie asked quietly.

Lachlan altered his position, shifting so his knees were drawn up and his elbows rested on them.

'You did.' He cocked his head towards Effie. 'You made me feel ashamed.'

'I didn't mean to,' Effie protested.

'Aye, you did,' Lachlan said, holding his hand up. 'But it is not the worse because of that. It's been easier to let Morna live here, and easier still for me to stay away knowing she is so well cared for. I've not had to think about the future.'

He inclined his head as he spoke. Effie acknowledged his words with a dip of her head that brought their faces close. Their eyes met and the world flooded away, the space filled by the need to be kissed by him. Lachlan drew away, as if realising what she was thinking.

'You are a remarkable woman, Effie.'

'How do you mean?' she asked.

'Accepting me and Morna for what we are.'

A little worm of guilt wriggled inside Effie. 'I didn't accept you straight away though. When you told me what you are, I tried to run. Then I tried to hurt you.'

'Aye, but you did neither.'

Lachlan stretched out his legs and rested back on his elbows.

'When I see you like this it's impossible to believe what you said is true,' she replied. 'I'm not sure I ever will until I see you in your other form.'

'Perhaps one day you will.'

Effie's hair had slipped loose at the side. She reached back behind her ear and pinned it into the bun which had started to come undone. Lachlan reached out and caught another strand.

'Your hair is like sunlight.'

Effie's face grew hot. Hair had no feeling, but the sensation building inside her seemed to be directly connected to

Lachlan's fingers. Perhaps this was what it felt like when she brushed her fingers over his sealskin.

'It's just a dull blonde.' She tucked the lock back into the bun, not wanting him to see the effect the compliment had on her.

'To you maybe,' he murmured. 'To me it is the sun on the water at dawn or the moon kissing it goodnight at dusk. Where I come from everyone is darker. And when I swim in the depths where no sun reaches, I remember the sight of it.'

The pulse at her throat beat violently. 'Do you think of me sometimes?'

'Aye, I do.'

'I think of you too,' she said. She dropped her hands into her lap, thinking of the painting in her portfolio of Lachlan on the prow of a ship.

'Tell me what it is like. I've never been that far north. Do you live on the beach like this?'

'Our homes are in better states than this hut,' he laughed. 'Some of us live in houses in the village, and some closer to the sea. Some of us live most of our lives on the land and less in the sea. Some almost never step foot on land, living in seal form for most of the day. The villages we live in are small and the humans either know and accept us, or don't believe we are what we are.'

'You live among humans?' That came as a surprise. Effie tried to imagine Allendale Head half-populated by Lachlan's folk.

'We've learned over the years that the best thing to do is not keep ourselves completely to ourselves because that provokes suspicion. Where suspicion starts, distrust quickly follows. Then comes persecution.'

'It shouldn't,' Effie said.

'No, but that's the way it is. And that's why I say you are remarkable for accepting me. It is one of the reasons Firtha agreed to me coming here.'

'You had to ask her permission?'

'Of course. I couldna' just up and go without her leave. I knew it would have caused her distress. She granted permission. Seathan was harder to convince.'

'But you've done it anyway.' Effie frowned. 'Lachlan, will there be trouble for you?'

'No. Don't fear that. I've told Seathan that it is to the clan's advantage to understand what life is like outside our islands. It took many long nights of discussion, but I think he finally believed me. At least, he was willing for me to come. If no harm befalls me, it might persuade him that our peoples can live together. He blessed my boat himself before I left.'

'You have a boat?' Effie asked in surprise.

'Yes, of course.'

'I imagined you in one once, but an old-fashioned one, like the Vikings had,' Effie admitted.

He laughed, but kindly. 'You are odd. Yes, I have a boat.' He gestured to the rocks at the far side of the cove where a small dinghy with a mast and furled sail was beached. 'How do you think I came this far?'

Effie wrinkled her brow. 'I thought you swam. Didn't you?'

'Not all the way. Sometimes I changed into my seal form and swam about the boat. How else would I carry my clothes and belongings?'

Effie looked at him. 'I don't know. I thought perhaps the clothes changed on you.'

Lachlan grinned. 'It would be useful if they did, but unfortunately not. When I change, I am exactly as I was made.'

His grin deepened. 'But no society would accept me walking around like that.'

Effie laughed, but her cheeks grew warm at the idea of Lachlan naked. She had never been able to put the sight of his smooth chest and curious tattoos from her mind.

'All the same, I'm glad your brother agreed to you coming without too much difficulty.'

'Aye, me too. He's a bit blockheaded at times, but he listens to sense when it is talked.'

Lachlan clambered to his feet and stood facing out to sea.

'The world is growing smaller, Effie, and bigger at the same time. It's changing. I fear for the day when we don't have the choice to live apart from the world.'

Effie sighed. 'I think my world is as small as ever it was. Since I came to live here aged fourteen, I have barely left the village beyond going to Whitby a few times when I had to buy what I couldn't get in Allendale Head.'

Lachlan turned back to her. 'You sound wistful. Do you wish to see more of the world?'

'Of course,' Effie said. 'I remember what Durham was like when I lived with my mother and father, but not very well. When you tell me what your home is like, or when Walter writes to tell me about where he is travelling, my heart feels like it might explode with envy.'

Speaking Walter's name filled her stomach with a pang of yearning. She hadn't heard from him recently.

'Sometimes I almost wish I had gone with him when he left for Europe. He said he would be back this summer, but he keeps extending his trip and I don't blame him for it.'

'I shall look forward to meeting him when he eventually returns.'

Effie sat forward. 'You intend to meet Walter? What for?'

Lachlan gave her a smile. 'I'm going to be living here. I am sure our paths will cross. With your permission I would like to know some of the other people in Morna's life.'

Effie chewed her thumbnail. Lachlan wouldn't be skulking on the beach like a hermit, but the thought of him meeting her friends and neighbours was odd. Alice had accepted his presence, but would the rest of the village? It would take some careful consideration.

'I'll introduce you to anyone you wish,' she said.

'Would you go travelling with your Walter if he asked again?' Lachlan said, giving her a narrow-eyed look.

'I don't know. I don't think so. Besides, I think he intends to join his father in business. He talked of plans he wanted to share with me soon.'

The sun had long since begun to set and the shadow cast by the cliffs was chilly. A dampness was setting into the evenings that insinuated autumn was imminent.

'I'd better take the children to bed,' Effie said. 'Thank you for sharing your fish with us.'

Lachlan pulled Effie to her feet. He didn't drop her hands immediately she was standing, but held them at shoulder height. He could slip his arms quite easily around her neck and draw her into a kiss if he wanted to. His eyes met hers.

'Would you come travelling with me if I asked?'

Effie's heart began to race. 'What would your brother say if I did that?'

Lachlan let go of her hands and scratched his chin. 'It's hard to say, but as Morna's foster mother your tie to the clan is almost as strong as blood. No one would refuse you hospitality and many would welcome you with open arms.'

Which left the unspoken implication that some would not. Seathan, perhaps?

As she walked back along the beach, she glanced back. Lachlan was standing at the turn of the beach, watching. It felt odd to be the ones leaving him behind for a change. She waved and encouraged the children to do the same. Lachlan raised a hand in return.

'That was fun, wasn't it?' Effie said to the children. 'We'll see your dada again soon, Morna.'

'More fish?' Jack asked.

Effie beamed at him. He had been listening to the conversation and had said something relevant. 'That's right, Jack. More fish.'

She took the children by the hand and together they ran home.

Once they were in bed, Effie sat on the doorstep and stared up at the sky. Lachlan was easy company and the evening had been a pleasure from beginning to end.

She had chosen not to go travelling with Walter, but if Lachlan asked, would she venture to the north with him and see where Morna had been born?

It was a tempting prospect.

Chapter Nineteen

Effie's plan was to introduce Lachlan into village life by stealth and, accordingly, she invited Mary to afternoon tea, along with Alice for security. Mary was the person least likely to ask awkward questions and would give Effie and Lachlan the chance to discover if their tale was believable.

Lachlan was already sitting at the table when Mary knocked on the door. He and Effie had already gone through the ritual assurances that the sultana buns and pot of tea would place him under no obligation. Both had agreed there should be no hint that Lachlan was anything other than a simple fisherman from the north of Scotland. He had arrived wearing his fur draped across his shoulder but had folded it and given it to Effie on arrival.

'Will you keep this in your bedroom while I visit, please?' he asked.

Effie took it from him with all the reverence of a simple village pastor receiving relics from the Archbishop of Canterbury himself. It was not anywhere near as significant an offering, but to her the skin signified a change in their relationship, however temporary or small. From the look in Alice's eye, and the way she said nothing when Effie returned from the bedroom, she had her own opinions which she was keeping to herself.

And so it was that when Mary arrived the three of them were already seated at Effie's table in readiness for the introduction.

'Mary, there is someone I would like you to meet,' Effie said as she took her friend's hand and led her inside to the table.

Mary's eyes grew wide.

'You're the man—' she began.

Effie had a horrible feeling Mary might admit to having seen the painting of him. 'This is Lachlan,' she interrupted. 'He is Morna's father.'

Mary stared at Lachlan for longer than was polite before giving him a sweet smile.

'Of course. Now I see you here beside Morna, you could not be anyone else. You look so much like your daughter. This is wonderful news.'

Between them, Effie and Lachlan told the tale they had agreed on of a boating accident and Lachlan's long search for his daughter. They skimmed over how Lachlan had actually come to discover Morna's whereabouts, and fortunately Mary's sweet and trusting nature did not compel her to ask. The only thing Mary remarked on privately as she said goodbye to Effie was how much Lachlan resembled the painting.

Effie smiled and gave a light laugh. 'I know. Isn't it strange? I must have imagined him somehow from looking at Morna. It's uncanny, really.'

Mary's cheeks dimpled. 'You're so self-possessed. He's very good-looking, in a slightly wild way. I'm sure if he had appeared at my door I'd have screamed and swooned clean away.'

Altogether, Lachlan, Alice and Effie agreed the first meeting was a success.

~

Lachlan visited Effie's cottage daily or Effie sent the children down to him on the beach, relishing the opportunity for an hour or two to herself. Before too long, word of his residence in the hut spread, and other small children gathered to see the mysterious man. By the end of his first week in the village, Lachlan had grown weary of inquisitive faces peering from behind rocks so began to sit leaning against the harbour wall where he could exchange words with the handful of older men who spent their days there. Effie sometimes found Alice sitting with him, resting on a rug with her eyes closed as they talked. Before another week passed he was on first-name terms with half of the fishing families.

Effie found herself jealous of how easily he had been accepted into the village. She had lived in Allendale Head for over ten years and was still viewed as an outsider, though she had to grudgingly admit she was not as personable as Lachlan.

Lachlan made good his promise to teach Jack how to make nets and the boy's small fingers were ideally suited to the task. Jack seemed to enjoy the repetitive nature of the task and, more often than not, Effie found him with lengths of hemp in his hand rather than chalks or charcoal.

To this skill, Lachlan added whittling. One unseasonably wet evening, sitting in Effie's cottage, he showed Jack and Morna how to take a piece of driftwood, shape it with a knife and tease out a form that was so lifelike, it was hard to believe the wood could have been anything else.

'It's as if each figure was waiting to be released,' Effie remarked, as she tried to shape her own piece.

'In a way that's true. The form of the wood suggests to me which animal it should be. This one for example…' He held out a short stubby piece of wood for Effie's scrutiny. 'This could be a cat or a dormouse but never an eagle or dolphin.'

Effie looked down at the mass of splinters and curls in her lap. She held up a piece of wood that she had managed to turn from a rough piece of driftwood into a slightly less rough but still irregularly shaped piece of driftwood. 'I don't think this is my talent,' she said ruefully.

Lachlan chuckled. 'Aye, maybe not. I'll see what it can become.'

A day later, when Effie opened her cupboard to fetch down the plates, she found a chubby seal staring out at her and knew before she touched it that this was her abandoned piece of wood. Unexpectedly, her eyes swam with tears. She waited until she and Lachlan were alone that evening, after the children were in bed, and sat beside him at the table.

'Lachlan, I think it's time to tell Morna the truth.'

'Why do you say that?' Lachlan looked up from his book, raising his brows.

Effie took the seal out of her apron pocket, cradling it in her hand.

'Because you said that everything can only be one creature but you are two, and so is Morna. She is happy with you now and trusts you. You've been here for two weeks. I can't think of a better time to tell her.'

Lachlan closed his book, marking his place with a gull's feather. He had discovered a love of reading and borrowed anything Mary would let him have. Currently he was devouring *Persuasion* by Jane Austen and Effie, delighted at once more having someone to discuss books with, was having to resist checking how close he was to the denouement.

He scowled, then pushed his hand back through his hair. 'The problem with you, Effie Cropton, is you're always right and I waste hours of my time trying to disagree when I should just submit to your better judgement. I've been putting it off, but I can't any longer. I'll tell her tomorrow.'

'We,' Effie replied. She bit her lip. 'We'll tell her. I should be there.'

Lachlan raised his brow. 'You would want to be?'

'Of course.' She couldn't believe he would think otherwise. 'Morna might be angry or scared. Or…'

She stopped and clamped her lips shut. She might take her skin and swim away, leaving Effie behind without a second thought. She couldn't say that aloud. She bunched her fist, trapping the wooden seal inside it.

Lachlan reached for her hand, closing his around it. He rubbed his thumb over her knuckles, his touch comforting her.

'I know what you're thinking, but Morna loves you and she'll never leave you.'

'She will one day,' Effie mumbled. 'All children leave their parents.'

'Aye, but not till they're grown and the time is right,' Lachlan said. 'Yet again you prove me an inconsiderate glaikit. You should be there when I tell her. It was thoughtless of me not to consider it. I wasna' sure you would want to be. Thank you.'

He stood and pushed his chair under the table. 'I'll go now. I have a lot to think about. How to explain. What to say.'

He put *Persuasion* on Effie's window ledge. He never took

the books back to his hut, saying there was no light to read by. Before he left he put his hands on Effie's shoulders and brought his head close to hers.

'Thank you for wanting to come tomorrow. I am very glad you will be there with me.'

He turned his head and left the lightest brush of his lips on Effie's cheek, then left. She did not find it easy to sleep that night. Her heart surged with each small contact with Lachlan.

The following morning, Effie left Jack with Alice and made her way to Boggle Cove with Morna. Effie carried Morna's skin in a basket covered over with a tea towel. She didn't want Morna to see it before Lachlan had a chance to speak. She wasn't sure how Lachlan planned to deliver the news but was prepared to let him take the lead.

Morna skipped ahead, stopping occasionally to gather particular shells or pebbles that caught her eye. Lachlan was waiting in front of his hut. His feet were bare. He wore his skin over one arm and across his back, the effect reminding Effie of statues of Romans she had seen when she was a child, and she told him so.

He smiled, but still looked nervous. His gaze flickered to the basket. Effie nodded. There was no need for words.

He bent down and squatted on his haunches in front of Morna. Effie stood close by, unsure of what part she would play.

'Morna, you know I'm your dada, don't you?' Lachlan began.

Morna nodded. 'I brought you a shell,' she said, offering one to him. He took it and examined it with keen interest.

'Thank you, Morna. Do you ever wonder why I don't live with you all the time?'

Morna shook her head. 'Betsey Barker's daddy goes on boats and comes back. So does Albert and Nellie's. I found a other shell even better than what I gived you.'

'Gave,' Effie corrected automatically.

Lachlan grinned up at her. 'You're very clever, Morna. You're right. Lots of fathers go to sea. But the people you and I come from live far away in the north.'

He took the fur from his shoulders and held it out. 'Do you ever wonder why I wear this?'

Morna poked a finger into it. 'It's soft.'

Lachlan's eyelids flickered.

Lachlan looked at Effie and gestured to the basket. She carried it to his side and took out the fur. Lachlan took it from her hands and held it out in front of him.

'Morna, do you know what this is?'

Effie held her breath. Morna's complexion paled. She reached out and hesitantly touched the fur with the tip of one finger. She withdrew it quickly and stepped back, looking alarmed.

'You can touch it and hold it, if you wish,' Lachlan said softly.

Again Morna reached out, this time stroking the fur with an open palm. She bit her lip and looked at Lachlan with an expression of fear and wonder on her face.

'This is me,' she said in the quietest voice Effie had ever heard her use.

'Aye, it is. It is a part of you that your mama has kept safe until you were old enough to understand. If you come with me, I will show you what we can do with them. Would you like that?'

He picked up his skin and gestured to Morna. Morna glanced at Effie, seeking permission. Effie's heart lightened, then plunged. Morna looked to her for guidance, but would she still do that once she learned what she was capable of?

'Go with your dada,' Effie urged. Morna picked up her skin and followed Lachlan down the beach away from Effie. Her eyes prickled. She would not cry. This was how things should be. But she couldn't bear to wait here.

'Lachlan!'

He turned as Effie called him and raised an eyebrow.

'I'll go home. Will you bring Morna back there when you're done?' she asked.

He strode back up the beach to Effie. He put his hands on her shoulders, squeezing reassuringly, and looked into her eyes. 'We will come back, don't fear,' he said. He leaned down and kissed her cheek.

'Go and visit Alice. Don't sit and fret at home. I know that's what you'll do.'

Effie pressed her lips tightly together, not wanting to shed tears in front of Lachlan. This was a joyful occasion for him and she did not want to spoil it. She wanted to caution him to keep Morna safe but she knew it was unnecessary. She purposefully walked away, resisting the urge to look back along the beach, leaving her heart behind with the departing father and child.

Chapter Twenty

A lice was dozing in her armchair when Effie arrived. Her mouth was half open and she was snoring softly. Jack was engrossed in weaving a net, humming tunelessly to himself. He acknowledged Effie's kiss on his forehead then went back to his task. A pan of crab apple jelly was on the stove, bubbling down. Effie gave it a stir, frowning as she spotted it had started to stick at the bottom. She heaved the pan off the stove and covered it with a lid before she shook Alice awake. It was not like Alice to leave a task halfway through, and that added to Effie's worries.

'Thank you, my dear,' Alice said when Effie told her what she'd done. 'I only intended to close my eyes for a moment. You saved me having to throw the batch away. I'll make sure to save you a jar when it's done. Can you pop the mint leaves in to infuse before I strain it?'

Effie did as instructed, then sat opposite Alice, perching on the edge of her chair.

'Lachlan has taken Morna and her skin.'

Alice's eyes filled with sympathy. 'And you're worried they will not come back?'

Effie bit her lip. 'Not exactly. Lachlan has told me they will, and he's a man of his word. I just worry that Morna won't want to come back. Lachlan once told me she's mine until I choose to release her, but if she asked to go then of course I would let her.'

'And that would be the right thing,' Alice said.

'I know that!'

Alice's brows shot up at Effie's sharp tone. Effie sat back and stared at the ceiling. 'It would break my heart to lose her but I'd let her go, if she wanted to go with him.'

Alice leaned forward and patted Effie's hand. 'Lachlan came to call on me this morning at first light. He told me you'd most likely be coming to see me today, but he didn't say why. He's a good man, Effie, and he cares about your needs. He won't do the wrong thing by you.'

'Yes, he's a good friend,' Effie agreed, feeling a little better. Her cheek pulsed as if Lachlan's lips were still pressed to it. She didn't think friendship had been on his mind when he had kissed her.

'A good friend indeed,' Alice mused. 'Men of his character are rare. I don't think he'll be ready to go back to Scotland as long as there are things to hold him here.'

Alice's eyes were clear and penetrating. There was something in her words that made Effie's stomach flutter. She hoped Alice was right, for, as much as she dreaded Morna leaving, she didn't want Lachlan to go either.

She spent the morning with Alice, helping to bottle the jelly and dusting cobwebs from the high corners Alice couldn't reach. Lachlan had been right to suggest she went there because it meant she didn't dwell on what Lachlan and Morna were doing. All the same, she was eager to return to her cottage by mid-afternoon and wait for their return.

She heard them before she saw them. Morna was singing a song Effie hadn't heard before. Lachlan had taught her other things besides how to swim, from the sound of it.

Morna burst into the house, slamming the door back on the hinges. She skipped up to Effie and threw her arms around Effie's waist. The fears Effie had been nursing that Morna would abandon her melted away. She hugged the child tightly, burying her face in Morna's tangled hair. She smelt of the sea. Of freshness.

She looked over Morna's head to where Lachlan stood. He smiled knowingly.

'Mama, I swimmed,' Morna whispered. She looked from side to side then put her fingers on her lips. 'But it's a secret and Dada says only you can know. I promised.'

She sounded so excitedly serious that Effie didn't have the heart to correct her grammar. 'I know, my chick. Look at your hair! It's come out of your plait. We'll have to comb the tangles out together.'

Morna pulled a face. She turned to Lachlan. 'Where is me?'

He held Morna's skin out and the child took it, burrowing her face in it. Effie longed to do the same. Morna held it out to Effie. 'Dada says you keep me safe.'

'I will,' Effie said. She took the skin from Morna's hands and stroked it. Morna yawned.

'I'm sleepy now. I swimmed a long way. Next time will you come, Mama?'

'I'd like to watch you,' Effie said. 'I can't swim as far as you and Dada though.'

Morna frowned. 'Where is your skin?'

Effie shook her head. 'I don't have one.'

'Why not?'

Effie held her hands out. 'Only you and Dada have them.'

Morna's mouth twisted into a pout. 'But I want you to have one.'

She ran to Lachlan and began scrabbling up his body to reach for his skin which was lying across his shoulder in his habitual fashion.

'Give Mama a skin,' she cried. 'Mama needs a skin.'

Lachlan's pupils grew large and black. 'I cannot give Mama a skin like ours. She doesna' have one.'

Morna began to wail. She didn't often have tantrums but when she did, she practically caused the windows to rattle in their frames. Lachlan had never experienced one and his expression of incredulity was terrible to witness.

'Morna, stop all this silliness and noise!' he snapped.

Effie shook her head. 'Don't be angry at her. She doesn't understand.'

His expression changed from anger to distress. Effie crossed to where he stood and knelt to put her arms around Morna.

'I'm not the same as you but I don't need a skin to be your mama.'

Morna buried her face in Effie's skirts, sobbing fiercely. Effie felt Lachlan's hand on her shoulder. She raised her head and met his eyes. He looked helpless. Effie felt the same. They stood silently until Morna's sobs subsided into irregular sniffles. Effie picked Morna up into her arms and stood awkwardly. She was growing so big and it was hard imagining her as the small armful Effie had first plucked from the sea.

Lachlan stroked Morna's cheek, rubbing his thumb across a smattering of dried salt. 'Morna, you're very young and this is confusing, but one day it will make sense. I promise you.'

Effie hoped Lachlan's words were true, but only time

would tell. She cocked her head towards Morna's skin which she had put on the table. Lachlan fetched it and held it out. Morna clutched it tightly in one hand. He put his arms around Effie and Morna together, encasing them both. His presence was comforting; solid enough to ward off the ills of the world. Effie could have stayed in his embrace for eternity. Morna must have felt it too because her sobs finally ceased. She buried her head against Effie's breast and reached one hand out to touch Lachlan's fur.

'I want Mama to have a skin, though,' she said plaintively.

In that moment Effie wished she could cast off her flesh and become what they were. 'I do too,' she said, hearing tears on the edge of her voice.

Lachlan smiled at her, but it was tinged with sadness.

'Morna, why don't you go and play with Jack in the garden. He has missed you while we've been swimming.'

Morna skipped off, calling Jack's name. Effie and Lachlan exchanged a glance that was part relief, part exhaustion. It seemed impossible that this was the same child who had been crying inconsolably only moments before.

Lachlan's lips switched into a smile. 'Without obligation, might I beg a drink of something? I'm feeling greatly in the need.'

'I think I'll join you in that,' Effie said. It was barely four o'clock but Effie fetched a bottle of blackberry gin and poured two good-sized measures. She handed one to Lachlan.

'No obligation upon you.'

They clinked glasses and drank. Effie flung herself down into her armchair and Lachlan did likewise in his.

'Do you think Morna understands what happened today?' Effie asked.

Lachlan took his time before answering. 'Partly. She

understands now what she can do, though demanding that you have a skin tells me she doesn't quite comprehend it.' He reached for the gin bottle and refilled his glass then held it out to Effie. She shook her head. 'I wouldn't expect Morna to understand everything so quickly. To us who are born with the knowledge and grow up with it, we see nothing strange, but to Morna her whole world has been tipped off balance.'

He toyed with his glass, holding it by the base and twisting it back and forth in his hand. 'I think to truly understand she'll have to see where she's from and meet others like her.'

'You want to take her there,' Effie whispered. Alice had been wrong. He was going to take Morna.

'I'm thinking of it,' Lachlan said quietly. 'But only for a visit, and not yet. When the lease of my cottage is up might be a good time.'

Effie nodded; her throat too tight to speak. She sipped the gin, letting the sharp fruitiness slip over her tongue and down her throat. 'I think that's a good idea.' She looked at him plaintively. 'You will come back, won't you?'

'Of course.' There was a slight edge to his voice. Effie wasn't even sure if he was aware of it, or whether he intended it, but there was doubt in his mind. 'Effie, thank you for today. Thank you for the years. You've done a grand job with Morna. I canna think of anyone I'd rather have trusted her with. You've done so much for her, and for me.'

'Don't,' she said.

'Don't what?'

She looked into his eyes and saw confusion. She looked away, dropping her head as sorrow welled up.

'You sound like you're making a farewell speech. I can't bear it.'

Lachlan was at her side the instant the words left her

mouth, kneeling beside her chair. He reached for her hand, holding it tightly, and lifted her chin so she was looking at him once again.

'I'm not saying farewell, Effie. I promise you. I just want you to know how much I value you.'

'We're friends, aren't we,' Effie said, recalling the conversation with Alice.

'Aye, we are.' Lachlan nodded slowly, but when he looked at Effie his eyes expressed so much more than friendship. 'Effie, I think the weather is going to be hot for the next few days. I wondered… will you come sailing with me tomorrow evening?'

'With the children?' she asked.

He held her gaze. 'No. Just you and me.'

The desire that always simmered just beneath the surface of Effie's consciousness when she was close to him bubbled to the surface. He felt it too, she saw. It had been so long since he had first kissed her, when they had walked on the beach together, but the memory was still there, unspoken. If she agreed to go sailing with him, she had no doubt he would kiss her again.

'Yes,' she answered, with barely a hesitation. 'I will.'

The following day dragged. It was washing day, so at least Effie had something to keep her busy, scrubbing and boiling and wringing out clothes and sheets. She didn't see Lachlan all day and Morna seemed happy, asking questions that Effie could not answer.

The day was hot and airless. No wind blew and Effie counted down the hours until she would be on the sea with

Lachlan. Out there, there would be a breeze even if there was none on the land.

Alice had readily agreed to sit in Effie's cottage and mind the children while she went with Lachlan. She had given Effie a knowing look that had been infuriating and had caused her stomach to twist with embarrassment. She wished she had asked Mary instead, as she had considered, but Mary would find it odd that Effie would spend an evening alone with a man she hardly knew. At least Alice's reference to courting was based on the knowledge that Lachlan and Effie had been friends for years.

In the days since his arrival, Lachlan had worked hard to improve the condition of his living arrangements. The windows to the hut now had bright-red striped curtains – provided by Alice – and the oilskin covering holes in the roof had been replaced and neatly nailed down. The fire was larger, built up with rocks to create a pit and support a three-legged iron trivet upon which stood a kettle.

Lachlan was sitting by his fire and the scent of roasting fish reached Effie before she saw it.

'I thought we might eat before we go sailing,' Lachlan said, standing to greet her. 'It won't get dark for an hour or two.'

He had spread out a blanket on the shingle. Effie sat and watched as Lachlan prepared the fish.

'Are you warm enough?' Lachlan asked, as he brought two plates and sat beside Effie.

'Perfectly.' Effie loosened her shawl. There was a breeze now that the sun had started to set, but the air would stay warm for an hour or two longer until it finally sank beneath the horizon.

'Do you feel the cold?' she asked, remembering how chilly

his hand had been the first time she had shaken hands with him on that winter's night.

'In this form I do,' Lachlan replied. 'In my other form, not so much.'

He glanced back at his skin which was lying folded on the rock beside them. Effie imagined how warm the rich-brown thickness must be and wished she could bury her fingers and face deep in it as Morna had.

Her curiosity brimmed over with questions. 'How does it work? When you change?' She waved her hands, miming removing a coat. 'Does it hurt?'

Lachlan laughed, but kindly. He looked upwards as if thinking how to answer. He put his hands to his chest between his heart and the hollow of his throat. The skin was smooth, and where the neck of his shirt lay open to reveal the top of his chest, she caught a tantalising glimpse of his tattoos. His fingers spread wide. Effie noticed how long and slender they were.

'I simply will it and take my skin off. It's hard to explain. It doesn't hurt, but it takes more effort than removing my shirt. The moment of transformation feels almost like a sneeze or a climax.'

Effie blushed at his words. Such matters weren't to be discussed or even alluded to outside the marriage bed. John had called it his 'joyful release' and it had been so long since Effie had experienced that release for herself, she was not entirely sure how accurate her memory of the sensation was.

'Which form do you prefer?'

Again, he took his time before answering.

'Each has its advantages and disadvantages.' His smile deepened as he licked a stray fleck of fish from the corner of his mouth. 'Right now I'm happy in this form.'

'Could you stay a human?' Effie asked.

Lachlan's eyes became serious. 'I'm not a human, Effie. I don't want you to forget that. Whatever form I take, I'm neither a true human nor a true seal. I'm a Selkie. Yes, I could choose to live as one or the other but neither is permanent as long as I have my skin.'

Effie dropped her head as confusion thickened her mind. To hear him speak in such a matter-of-fact way made it harder, not easier. She had to remind herself constantly that he wasn't the same as her, but it was so hard.

'Can I see it?' she asked.

'See what?'

'See you change?'

Lachlan raised his eyebrows in surprise.

'No one has ever asked me that,' he said. 'It's a very private moment. Would you be happy for me to watch you undressing or dressing?'

'Of course not!'

Effie's cheeks flamed hotter. Her throat grew tight. Such a thing was unthinkable, but at the same time, the thought of Lachlan watching her doing something so intimate excited her in ways she couldn't deny. She put her hands to her face, feeling her cheeks heat and wondering if her embarrassment was as visible to him as it felt to her.

They ate in relative silence after that. The fish was as good as ever; with crisp skin and tasting of the smoke from the fire. At least Effie could compliment him on that without raising awkward topics. When both their plates were empty save the bones, Lachlan took them to the sea and rinsed them clean. He put them neatly by the fire then collected his skin and held out a hand.

'Let's go sailing.'

Chapter Twenty-One

Willingly, Effie took Lachlan's outstretched hand and he pulled her to her feet. As always, his hand was cooler than hers, though now the blood that rushed through Effie's body felt like boiling water. Hand in hand, they walked along the beach past Lachlan's hut to where his small fishing boat was pulled up above the waterline.

'I'll get her into the water. Take off your shoes and stockings or they'll get wet,' he instructed.

While Effie kicked off her clogs (keeping to herself the fact that she had no stockings on in the first place) Lachlan dragged the boat down to the sea and turned it to the shore. He waded deeper until the rolled-up cuffs of his trousers were damp.

'Can you swim in this form?' Effie asked.

He laughed. 'Of course, though not as well. When I'm in this form I am everything that a human is. Ungainly. I feel the cold. I can be hurt. Everything is just the same.'

The swell of waves washed around him as he steadied the small boat. His loose shirt billowed in the breeze and the wind caught his hair, lifting it and leaving locks trailing across his face. He stood sure-footed with the light fading around him, making him seem more solid than the gauzy sky and sea. He looked wild, and finally Effie could believe he wasn't fully human. Ungainly wasn't the word she would use to describe him.

'Come on. It isna' too cold,' he said with a grin. Effie picked her way through the shallows and climbed into the boat. Inside were two wooden benches. She sat on one while Lachlan took the other and picked up the oars.

They set out with Lachlan rowing. He had a powerful and rhythmic stroke and the beach soon became distant. Effie reclined and trailed her fingers in the water, imagining she was on a gondola in the streets of Venice that Walter had described to her. She wrinkled her nose, feeling that to think of Walter was an intrusion.

'Where are we going?'

Lachlan indicated with his head further along the coast away from Allendale Head. 'I know a cove you can't reach by land. The only way there is to row or to swim. It's very peaceful.'

'Do you swim there?' Effie asked.

'Quite often,' Lachlan replied. 'When I want to think about things or when your world gets too much for me.'

'Does the world get too much for you?' Effie asked. He might decide Allendale Head was too much for him and leave. Her belly twisted at the thought.

He shrugged, but his eyes were sharp. 'Doesn't it get too much for you at times?'

'Yes. Seeing you accepted by the villagers so easily when I have struggled has been hard for me.'

'I think it is important to be welcomed in the community,' Lachlan replied.

Effie pursed her lips. 'Meaning I don't think it's important.'

'I'm not criticising you,' Lachlan assured her. 'It's important for my kind not to be ostracised. It leads to suspicion, which leads to danger. Men are more accepting in general and the fishing families are more like my own folk than the fine ladies up the hill. I imagine their judgement is fierce.'

'It is,' Effie agreed. 'Sometimes I still don't know if I want to be accepted or not.'

Lachlan sat back, rocking the boat gently and fixed his eyes on Effie. 'Is there any reason you have to decide yet? Just like Morna, you're in between something but there isna' a rush to settle.'

He laid down the oars and gave a great sigh of contentment. 'I have a sudden urge to be in the water. The sea is warm enough to cool you without giving you a chill but the weather is going to change soon and there can't be many fine days left.'

He looked at Effie side on. 'Will you come in with me?'

'I haven't brought my bathing costume,' Effie said regretfully. 'Have you got yours?'

She glanced at the skin that Lachlan had stowed beneath the seat. 'And I don't mean that.'

Lachlan laughed. 'If you mean that curious garment you wear when you're playing with the children, I am glad you haven't brought it. I canna imagine how such a weight doesn't drag you straight to the ocean floor. No, I don't have anything like that. When I swim, usually I wear nothing.'

The back of Effie's neck began to burn. She had spent hours idly imagining what Lachlan would look like naked. Again he laughed and she realised he had been teasing her.

'In this instance I can wear my shirt and drawers. I'm sure you must have a thin enough layer under all that.' He gestured to Effie's dress and she followed his gaze. Fashion was currently dictating that skirts should be narrow, but, like most women in her financial situation, Effie didn't have the money to comply and her skirts and petticoats were full and unfashionable.

'I could take off a layer or two,' she said thoughtfully. 'If you turn away while I do it.'

'I'll do better than that,' Lachlan said. 'I'll get in the water first. Close your eyes if you are feeling modest.'

Effie screwed her eyes closed and added a hand across her face for good measure. The boat rocked as Lachlan was obviously undressing. Effie peeped through her fingers and watched as he unbuttoned his shirt and slipped it off, leaving him wearing only a vest. When his hands went to the waistband of his trousers she closed her eyes tightly, her imagination supplying every detail of what she would see if she'd kept them open. The boat rocked more violently and then she heard a splash.

'You can open your eyes now.'

His voice came from somewhere behind Effie. She turned round to see his head bobbing above the surface at the stern of the boat, his hair wet and sticking to his forehead and cheeks.

'Is it cold?' she asked.

'Only at first.' He dived under and appeared at the other side of the boat. Effie couldn't help but think he moved through the water exactly how a seal or fish might, seemingly making no movements but cutting through the waves all the same.

'Join me. I'll swim around while you undress. Call my name when you're ready.'

He dived under again and within a couple of heartbeats, his head appeared in the distance. He moved so quickly, Effie would never be able to keep up with him. She quickly stripped off to her drawers and camisole. She hesitated at this point. Beneath her camisole she had a corset, and beneath that a chemise and drawers, but she could hardly swim with a corset on. Then again, could she really join Lachlan with only one layer of thin cotton covering her naked body? In the end she removed the corset but kept the camisole on.

'I'm ready,' she called.

There was no answer. She knelt up, and the boat wobbled a little.

'Lachlan, where are you?' She couldn't see him anywhere until his head appeared beside her, causing her to jump.

'You startled me!'

'I was giving up hope of you joining me. Are you ready?'

Effie leaned over and dipped her fingers in the water. They had rowed beyond the waves that crashed ferociously onto the shore and made the coast such a dangerous place. The surface of the water was more even, but hidden currents still caused the boat to occasionally pitch gently from side to side. The sea was steel grey and the bottom was out of sight.

'It's chilly!'

'Only at first. The quickest thing to do is to stand and leap in.'

'I'm not sure I'm brave enough. I'm not a strong swimmer.'

Lachlan held his arms out. 'I'll catch you. Trust me, I won't let you come to harm.'

He fixed her with an even gaze and she implicitly trusted him. She clambered to her feet, throwing her arms out as the small craft wobbled precariously. Lachlan kicked his legs and moved further away from the boat.

'Jump. I'll catch you.' He raised his hands out of the water, seeming to rise up with nothing pushing him. Effie took a deep breath and counted to three. She leaped up and out over the water towards him.

The coldness of the water hit her like a punch to her ribs. She plunged down and further down; feet together and hands trailing above her. Panic stilled her heart. She wasn't going to rise. She'd sink to the bottom and even Lachlan wouldn't be able to find her.

She wanted to scream, but a sensible part of her brain forced her to keep her mouth tightly shut. She had no idea how long her breath would last before she had no choice. At last she slowed and, to her relief, began rising again. She opened her eyes. The salt water stung and she closed them again rapidly, but the glimpse of light was enough to tell her she was almost at the surface. She kicked her feet and broke through the water, opening her mouth wide to drag air into her screaming lungs, and found herself gripped in Lachlan's arms.

His legs became tangled between hers as he held her close and she felt for his feet, resting hers on his as if they were solid ground. She opened her eyes to see him grinning.

'Goodness me, Effie. I didna' expect you to jump in with such enthusiasm!'

'I didn't think I'd go so deep!' She shivered and looked at him accusingly. 'It's cold here. You said it would be warm.'

'You'll grow warmer when you move,' Lachlan said.

He unwound his arms from Effie. She bobbed rather than sank and made a few experimental moves with her arms and legs. In her shift and drawers she felt practically naked, but so wonderfully free. Why on earth did she bind herself into her corset? Surely her spine would have enough support without the stiff whalebone?

Lachlan dived under the water and surfaced in front of her. 'Come to me,' he said, beckoning with both hands. She swam towards him, but when she neared him he kicked and moved away through the water, laughing. She gave chase again and again, but every time he remained elusively out of reach.

'That's not fair,' she said with a laugh. 'You're used to the water, I'm not.'

Lachlan's face fell a little. 'I'm sorry. It's a game my kind play. I forgot for a moment you aren't like me, Effie.'

She'd been growing warmer as Lachlan had promised, but now she grew cold inside. She was at such ease in his company.

'I had forgotten too,' she said quietly.

They had gone further out than Effie could ever have swum from shore. She glanced nervously towards the boat which bobbed in one place. Lachlan put one arm round her waist, drawing her close to his side. His body was warm and as she instinctively cleaved to him a bud of desire awakened.

'Take my hand. We'll swim together.'

She linked her fingers between his, noticing briefly the slightly larger flaps of skin between each finger that she had never noticed before. Had they appeared once he was in the sea? He squeezed her hand.

'Are you ready?'

Effie nodded. Lachlan began to swim and she was carried along in his wake, barely needing to move. They swam for what seemed like miles until the boat was a distant speck and she could see the village in the distance around the curve of the headland. The water didn't seem as cold now, though by rights Effie's legs should be stiff. Lachlan stopped and took hold of her other hand. They bobbed up and down, facing each other. He grinned and his eyes glinted.

'Are you feeling brave?'

Effie nodded and pushed a strand of wet hair back from her

face. At some point that she hadn't realised it had come loose from the bun and now trailed freely down her back. 'With you here I am.'

Lachlan released her hands then dived behind her and surfaced with barely a ripple. He wrapped his arms around her from behind.

'Take a deep breath.'

She did as he instructed and he dived down, bearing her with him. After her initial surprise there was no fear. His body was pressed to hers, his arms holding her close and she knew he would never let her go. He bucked and they dived further down. When Effie felt her breath was about to give out, she tapped Lachlan's arm urgently and felt him change direction. They broke the surface into the air again.

'Did you like that?' he asked keenly.

'I think so. It was strange.'

'Would you do it again?'

She answered without hesitation.

'Yes.'

This time he treated her to what felt like a display that tumblers in a circus tent might perform, rolling over, twisting around, diving deeper and coming up for breath every so often. He never let go of her and she felt completely safe; with her eyes closed, she experienced the world through darkness and movement. When they surfaced for the fifth time, the sun had dropped to the horizon, painting the water bronze, and the air was noticeably colder.

Effie put her arms around Lachlan's neck.

'Thank you. I think that's the most wonderful thing I've ever done. Is that what it is always like for you in the water?'

'Yes, though it's always better to share it with a friend.'

'With a friend,' Effie agreed. Something inside her

shrivelled a little. Part of her had hoped that Lachlan felt a little more towards her than friendship.

'It's even better with someone you are fond of,' he said in a quiet voice.

Effie raised her eyes to find him staring down at her with a look of intense longing. She smiled and he kissed her.

She put her arms around his neck and he wrapped his around her waist, holding her to him. They sank beneath the waves, legs intertwining. To Effie it felt like they were suspended in the water.

Suspended in a moment out of time.

They rose to the surface again. Effie opened her eyes to see Lachlan smiling at her.

'I thought you'd need air. I think it's time to get back in the boat, don't you?'

They swam side by side at a leisurely pace. When they reached the boat, Lachlan pushed himself up and in, the water seemingly aiding him. He knelt inside and lifted Effie in to join him. She landed on the bottom of the boat and sat up. Her clothes were clinging to her, displaying every inch of her form. She might as well have been naked for all the modesty her drawers and camisole gave her.

She shivered and hugged herself.

'Wrap yourself in this to keep warm,' Lachlan said. He pulled his skin from beneath the bench and passed it around Effie's shoulders. She nestled down, luxuriating in the warmth and softness of the thick fur.

It smelled of Lachlan. It *was* Lachlan, as much as the arms that had held her and the lips that had kissed her. Her stomach fluttered, sending a throb down between her legs.

Lachlan turned his back and took his undershirt off, then reached for his dry shirt. His back was slender and muscled.

Effie knelt, reached out a hand and touched his shoulder. He turned round and gave her a long, speculative look. She drew her hand away, observing how it quivered, but held his gaze.

The fire inside her was growing stronger, needing to be stoked. The angle Lachlan was at twisted his body, creating interesting curves from his neck and angular jaw, over his shoulder blades and down to the firm muscles of his belly. She could see a thin, pale scar that was the legacy of his injury. Once again, Effie reached her hand out, this time tracing the length of the scar with a fingertip before placing it over his heart. She knew full well that by touching him she was inviting him to touch her in return. His eyes never left hers.

'Effie, what are you doing?' There was a note of warning in his voice but he came closer so that her arm didn't need to be stretched fully out.

'I'm not sure,' she said.

'Aren't you?' He raised an eyebrow.

She bit her lip. Now was the time to stop. To put on her discarded clothes and return to the beach. Common sense told her to do it, but her heart was still racing from the swim and the kiss. It felt as if the entire evening – their entire acquaintance with every touch, look and contact – had been driving them to this moment. She spread her fingers wider and ran her tongue over her lips before answering.

'I know what I want and I think you want it too.'

Lachlan was kneeling at her feet now but seemed hesitant to touch her. She wondered if she had misjudged him. Maybe he didn't want to do what she wanted to do. Maybe he didn't want her.

'Am I wrong? We can go back to the beach…' she began.

Lachlan reached out a hand and caressed her cheek.

'Effie, you're not wrong. You have no idea how much I

want you. How much I've wanted you for longer than I can remember. I don't want to go back to the beach, but if we do this we won't be able to go back from it. It'll change us.'

'I don't care.' She frowned as a thought occurred to her. 'Is it even possible between your kind and mine?'

'It is. I'm a man in every respect, if that's your worry.'

She reached her arms out to him. The skin – Lachlan's skin – *himself* – fell back from her upper body. Lachlan moved closer, still kneeling but now moving astride Effie until he was positioned above her thighs. He leaned forward and put a hand on each shoulder, running his fingers down her arms, until he took her hands.

They laced their fingers together and she rose to meet him in a kiss. He manoeuvred his way around the small boat so that he was lying alongside her and began exploring her shape, caressing her, and feeling his way around her body. He slipped his hand beneath the collar of her chemise, edging the wet, clinging fabric away from her shoulder and breast. Effie's senses exploded into life. The recollection of how to relax enough to be touched, and how to touch a man, flooded back. It brought with it a sense of anxiety. She had been in this situation once before with John, and that had led to the conception of Jack and the hasty marriage that followed.

She wasn't aware of a change in her manner, but Lachlan paused his explorations and looked at her.

'What's wrong? Am I doing something you don't like?'

'No.' Effie leaned up on her elbow and faced him. Lachlan didn't know why she was not completely accepted by the respectable village matrons. He was the most tolerant person she knew and wanted no secrets between them, but if he condemned her conduct, the cut would wound her deeply.

'I made love to John before we were married and I got

pregnant with Jack. That was why we had to marry. My reputation was in tatters.'

'If you're having second thoughts about your reputation we can stop right now.'

'I don't want to stop,' Effie replied. 'I don't care about my reputation, you know that. I don't want another baby and I don't want to place you under an obligation if I had one.'

'I've never heard tell of a story of any offspring of my kind and yours. I don't think it is possible.' Lachlan stroked her cheek, leaving a trail of heat in the wake of his fingers. 'There's nothing I'm not doing willingly here. Tonight is tonight, and there will be no obligations resulting from it. If that's what you want.'

No obligations. No repercussions. Just a night of perfect pleasure at the hands of this man who had teased her senses for so long. Effie bit her lip and nodded.

'I do.'

Lachlan moved a little closer to her, wriggling his feet alongside hers. He leaned his head in, pressing his forehead against hers.

'What would you like me to do?' he whispered, his voice thick with desire and promise. 'Guide me.'

Effie took hold of his hand and pressed it to her breast. With his other hand she began to stroke down the curve from her waist to her hipbone until she felt him take over the motion himself, slowly and thoroughly, leaving no part of her unexplored.

She put her arms around his back and pulled him close, brushing her lips against his earlobe and biting gently as parts of her body that had been dormant for years began to awaken. His response was to increase the pressure of his hands and wrap his legs around Effie's. With efficient movements they peeled off their wet clothes until they were both naked.

Effie shivered as the breeze caressed her bare flesh. Lachlan reached out and drew his skin over them, enveloping Effie in his presence absolutely. The softness of the fur contrasted with, and complemented, the hardness of his lean, muscular frame.

Another part of his anatomy was swelling and hardening too, causing Effie to shiver with desire.

'I'm so hungry for you,' she whispered against his neck, driving her pelvis against him.

He turned his head and she wondered how she could be so bold as to say such a thing. Then his lips found hers, their bodies fused together, and Effie became incapable of wondering anything at all for some while to come.

Chapter Twenty-Two

Effie returned home at daybreak. The harbour was busy but Effie avoided the street and climbed up the cliff steps to return home. She hadn't intended to stay the night, but when Lachlan had lifted her over the edge of the boat at the beach they'd discovered neither could bear for him to relinquish his embrace.

Alice was kneading bread and didn't turn round when Effie slipped furtively into the cottage. The children were nowhere to be seen.

'I'm sorry. I went swimming and got wet and by the time my clothes were dry it was too late to walk home in the dark.'

She omitted to mention her clothes had dried in front of Lachlan's fire while their owner had lain naked in Lachlan's bed, warming herself in another way.

Alice looked back over her shoulder. 'I didn't ask.'

Effie tried to hide her smile but she felt like a flower blooming in sunshine after a hard winter. She should feel shame, but the emotion had no chance against the memory of the hours spent in Lachlan's bed.

Alice sighed and rolled her eyes. 'It's as well you asked me to mind the children, not Mary,' she remarked, giving the dough a vigorous, two-handed knead. 'She wouldn't have been able to stay the whole night without her mother fretting where she was. She'd have fretted where *you* were, for that matter.'

Effie gave her grandmother a hug. 'Thank you. I didn't intend for anything to happen but I got caught up in the moment.'

Alice turned to face Effie and looked her up and down. 'Caught up is one thing, caught out is another.'

'Lachlan says that can't happen,' Effie said.

'Do you believe him?' Alice folded her arms, leaving a trail of flour over her sleeves.

'Yes. He's never lied to me. He doesn't want complications any more than I do.'

'Well, the two of you have been making eyes at each other for as long as I can remember,' Alice said. 'I've been waiting for something like this. Is that the end of it?'

'I don't know. We didn't talk about it. I'll have to see what happens. He'll be gone before too long.' Effie slumped into her comfy chair by the fire. Her limbs ached from swimming and contorting into positions she hadn't realised they could make, and she hadn't had as much sleep as she needed. She gave Alice a wistful look. 'I'm a fool, I know.'

'You're a happier fool today than I've seen you look for a long time. For that I'm under more obligation to him than he knows,' Alice said. She transferred the dough to the bowl for proving. 'I'll be going home to bed. I never sleep well in a chair.'

'I'm sorry,' Effie said. Alice chucked her under the chin.

'The children are almost old enough to leave in their beds, I think. If you should want to go out at night again.'

She left, whistling under her breath.

The morning was cold. The storm didn't come but still hung in the air, making it dense and chilly. Effie began the daily chores, listening to the sound of gulls and remembering the touch of Lachlan's lips on hers, the pressure of his arms around her waist and his hand spreading on her lower back. Her legs ached from throwing them into positions she had not lain in for years, and some she had never before tried.

If Lachlan intended to visit today, he would have to fit in around her life. She eyed the washing copper. Filling it was an arduous job and one that left her arms and neck aching. Washday was two days away but she wondered if asking Lachlan to carry the water to fill it would be too much of a liberty. He had lifted her from the water into the boat (and later from the beach straight into his arms) with no trouble. The job would not tax him. She stood, lost again in the memory, until Jack pulled at her skirts and brought her back to reality.

She fed the children and put them in the yard to play. As she was checking the gate was secure she saw Lachlan appear at the turn of the beach. He raised a hand to her and cautiously she waved back. She looked in the other direction. Allendale Head harbour was alive with the usual activity of the morning: men hauling small fishing boats up the slipway, their wives waiting to sort the catch, children and dogs tussling over rope ends. Hopefully Lachlan would think to avoid the main street and come up the side steps instead to avoid notice. She waited until Lachlan arrived, then led him inside the cottage.

Lachlan had his sealskin draped over one arm and Effie eyed it with interest. He had been in the habit of leaving it in his hut when he visited and she wondered if there was any significance to its presence. Her heart gave a gentle throb. Was he intending to offer it to Effie to keep for him, as in the stories he had told? Did he see their actions the night before as something significant and binding? She wasn't sure whether the thought scared or excited her.

He had warned her that things would change between them and she had anticipated awkwardness. He stood opposite her. 'Hello, Effie.'

'Hello, Lachlan.'

They met each other's eyes and both broke into smiles. He put his hands to her cheeks and kissed her. Her legs turned to water, threatening to give way beneath her as their tongues met in the sweetest greeting she had ever experienced. She slipped her arms around his neck and pulled him closer.

'I wasn't sure…' she began.

'Sure of what? That I'd still want you once we'd satisfied our curiosity for each other?' His eyes crinkled then grew serious. 'Effie, we could spend years discovering each other and I wouldna' be bored. Last night we barely began to learn. If you want me, I'd very much like to continue.'

He took hold of her hands and her pulse fluttered like tiny moths were landing on her bare arms. Her skin felt doubly sensitive to touch and the simultaneous throbbing of her breasts and at the cleft at the top of her legs nearly caused her to swoon. She could no more turn down the prospect of undiscovered pleasures at Lachlan's hands than she could stop the tide from swelling over the Brigg.

'Yes,' she murmured, lacing her fingers through his so their palms were touching. 'I would.'

But when he left he still took his skin.

~

The first of October arrived with a vengeance, bringing storms and hail. Effie didn't care. Lachlan came for Morna each day, and when he brought her back he often stayed the night in Effie's bed. Together they strung up a cord in Effie's bedroom and hung a blanket to create a division between her bed and the children to give them some privacy.

Life was good. They made love together while the sea raged and the wind screamed through the eaves, blocking the weather out with murmured endearments and stifled gasps of pleasure. As Effie drifted into sleep with the weight of Lachlan's arm across her back, she couldn't imagine what might happen to change that.

She was to discover it sooner than she expected.

Despite her initial reservations, Effie had found that helping Alice was fulfilling work. She had always helped gather the plants but now she was learning how to combine them into tinctures and ointments to alleviate myriad aches and illnesses.

'You'd make a fine healer,' Lachlan told her as he stripped liquorice roots for Effie to pound into a remedy for indigestion while Alice dozed in her chair. 'Mairead, our clan's healer, would love to compare her remedies with Alice's.'

Effie looked at Alice and smiled to herself, imagining her grandmother and a seal woman deep in conversation as they sorted through piles of seaweed. Even though Alice seemed to physically tire more easily, she had lost none of her keen intelligence or enthusiasm.

She was returning from delivering a bottle of cough syrup to a patient who lived at the top of the village when a male voice called her name.

She turned back to see a man in a well-cut grey sack-coat and a bowler hat waving from the door of the bakery.

'Walter?'

He tucked a paper bag under his arm and strolled over to her, tipping the brim of his hat as he arrived at her side.

'How lovely to see you!' Effie seized his hands joyfully and squeezed them tight. He blinked, looking taken aback at her enthusiasm, then his face crinkled into an appealing smile.

'Effie, my dear friend! Goodness, I wasn't expecting such a warm welcome, though of course I'm overjoyed to receive it.'

He disentangled his hands, took one of hers and lifted it to his lips, bowing low over it, letting his lips settle on the back. Despite the dampness in the October air, Effie wasn't wearing gloves and his breath was warm against her skin. For the first time in ages she became conscious that her hands were rough, with short, practical fingernails. Not a lady's hands at all, not the sort Walter would be used to kissing.

He stood upright and gave her a beaming smile.

'See, I am quite European now in my manner. I could greet you in four languages and possibly converse about the weather in three of them.'

'Which one can't you?' Effie asked.

Walter's eyes sparkled. 'Italian,' he said decisively. 'It is the language of love, not meteorology.'

Effie giggled, feeling like a child again. She hadn't realised how much she had missed Walter until he was standing before her. He smiled widely, his blue eyes dancing. He'd thickened out. His blond hair was swept back at his brow and he had grown whiskers and a moustache. The last vestiges of puppyness that had followed him into his third decade had vanished and he was most decidedly a man now.

For a moment they said nothing, only looked at each other

with a slight awkwardness brought on by being apart for too long. Had there been a slight emphasis on the word *love* when Walter had spoken?

The street was filling up and Walter's arrival had been noticed by others. Old acquaintances smiled at him, some interrupting to wish him well, others merely tipping their hats or curtsying. He was a popular young man. The families employed in the alum works naturally looked on him favourably, but even the fishing families whose lives and livelihoods were not tied up with his father's business seemed pleased to see him.

Effie shifted her basket from one arm to the other.

'Oh, let me carry that for you. I'm so thoughtless sometimes,' Walter said.

He had always been self-deprecating, but now there was a veneer of charm over the top that practically forced one to contradict him. Effie hastened to assure him he was nothing of the sort as she passed her basket over.

'I have a meeting with Reverend Ogram in…' Walter pulled out a pocket watch, checked it and replaced it. 'In twenty-three minutes. If you are finished with your shopping might I accompany you as far as your cottage? I have an urge to see our shore again.'

'I was going to call on Alice but that can wait. She has started to teach me some of her remedies.'

Walter raised an eyebrow. 'I must say I'm surprised. You always seemed sceptical of her methods.'

'No I didn't,' Effie said a little too quickly. 'Many of them have worked for years and there is no reason to change them now.'

Walter's expression grew dubious.

'Let's walk down to the harbour,' she said. 'We'll be able to see the cliffs from there. The tide will be in at the moment so we couldn't walk far on the beach in any case.'

Walter offered his arm. Effie slipped hers through it and together they made their way down the hill. Walter had to stop so many times, put the basket down and raise his hat in greeting that their progress was slow. After a couple of turns down the hill, Effie removed her arm from his and took possession of her basket again to free him for the task. Walking arm in arm with Walter had already resulted in one or two raised eyebrows and knowing looks from the women they passed. In contrast, the gentlemen had included Effie in their greetings, presumably having no particular objection to their friendship. She was respectable by association.

As they rounded the final corner, Walter tugged gently on Effie's sleeve. She stopped and he waved his hand towards the beach.

'Look. As beautiful as the lagoon of Venice and the shores of the French Riviera are, I found nothing could compare to what I knew was waiting for me here.'

'It is beautiful,' Effie agreed.

'I was not only thinking of the sea.' He gave her a lingering look that set her cheeks growing warm. They had been friends for too long for her to protest modesty, so she grinned.

'You've learned to charm, I see.'

'You are no longer wearing mourning,' Walter said quietly.

Effie glanced down.

Since she had bought the green dress from Whitby, she had gradually eased out of mourning wear. Her current dress was an old one that had lain in Alice's drawer for at least a decade. The cloth was a light wool of narrow indigo blue and pale-grey stripes. She had agonised over wearing a pattern, but the weight was more suited to autumn chill than the green skirt which had seen her through summer. She had altered it to take account of the changing fashions and there had been so much cloth in the skirt that Effie had been able to fashion a shawl and a pinafore for Morna from the offcuts.

'It isn't disrespectful,' Effie had said. 'I know it is another three months before I can truly leave off mourning but I couldn't afford to buy more black cloth and I needed to replace my old dress.'

'I didn't mean to criticise. I'm sure you would never do anything intentionally inappropriate,' Walter said hastily. 'Blue suits you. Many widows choose lavender or plain grey, but you need a stronger colour to bring out the tone of your hair.'

Effie smiled and swallowed her concerns. So far, Walter had succeeded in criticising her choice of clothing and her work with Alice. He hadn't meant to, but all the same, Effie walked home with a slightly heavier step than she had left with that morning.

Walter's unintentional blundering continued the following morning when he came across them down at the beach. Even though Morna swam regularly with Lachlan in her seal form, she still enjoyed playing in the water with Jack. The sea was almost too cold to bear for Effie, but she could not bear to deny Morna – or herself – the pleasure of playing together.

Effie was standing up to her thighs in the water with the overskirt of her bathing costume ballooning around her. Jack and Morna were having a swimming race, following the line of the shore as they paddled beyond the waves breaking on the shore.

'What on earth are you doing?' Walter asked.

Effie cocked her head to one side. 'I'm teaching Morna to swim. She needs to learn.'

He frowned. 'Why?'

Effie waded back to the shore, noticing the way Walter's eyes fell to her lower half. Even with the voluminous skirt and petticoat, the way the wet layers clung to her legs meant her shape was more apparent. She chewed the inside of her mouth while she thought. The true answer wouldn't do.

'She might grow up to be a fisherman's wife and need to go out in a boat.'

'Jack won't. Why does he need to be in the water?' Walter asked. He gave the boy a pitying look. 'Jack won't be able to do any job that requires skills. He will most likely always be dependent on you or the parish for support.'

'He could do anything,' Effie retorted. 'He's only young. And if he is dependent on me, I don't mind. He likes to swim alongside Morna so I'm not going to deny him that.'

Walter reached for her hand but Effie moved it out of the way and crossed her arms.

'I meant no offence. Your care for your son is admirable, Effie, my dear, but it is a lot for you to bear alone.'

'I don't mind bearing it. Looking after Jack doesn't feel like a trial.'

It was a bit of a lie; often his stubbornness or the way he shrieked if he was prevented from doing something he wanted was hard. While he was a child it was not too hard but when he got to be ten, or fifteen, or twenty-five…

Walter was right: there would come a time when she couldn't cope with Jack alone and Walter's well-intended concern added fuel to the anxiety she tried to ignore.

'I'll think of something,' she said, lifting her chin.

'I'm sure you will. I have every confidence in you. I must go now. I have plans to discuss with my father.' Walter's eyes gleamed with excitement. 'I hope I'll be able to share them with you before too long.'

He bid Effie good day and strolled off along the beach, swinging his cane as if he imagined himself still on the French Riviera without a care in the world. Effie watched him enviously. It was lovely to have him back, even if he did leave her feeling slightly chastened after every conversation, as if he were channelling the spirit of Mrs Ogram. Effie turned her attention back to the children, who were still having a fine time in the water. A solution would present itself, she was sure.

Chapter Twenty-Three

Walter had returned from Europe with a zeal for improvements and reforms. His mind was consumed with them. One in particular was Mary's school, which he visited with Effie.

Mary was in a high temper when they arrived.

'It's Mrs Peel,' she fumed. 'The woman appeared on my doorstep on a Sunday morning to demand why her children were not more advanced by now.'

She tossed her head back and put her hands on her hips. Effie and Walter exchanged a surreptitious glance of amusement. They had never seen the usually placid Mary in such a temper before.

'I ask you! A Sunday morning! Knocking at the door of the vicarage immediately after the service ended! And the reason for the lack of progress? Well, I could give her a list as long as her sharp nose.' She snapped her jaw shut.

'I'll speak to her if you wish,' Effie said. 'I'll explain to her that if she wishes to complain to anyone on the Lord's Day she should come to me, heathen that I am.'

Mary grinned. 'Thank you, my dear.'

Walter, however, looked unsettled. 'I do not understand what is going on with you young women. You used to be so mild-tempered, and perhaps a little more decorous.'

Effie burst out laughing. 'Walter, we're nearly the same age yet you talk as if you are fifty.'

'Perhaps we are just tired of foolishness and less inclined to meekly accept it,' Mary said, arching her brows.

Walter looked flustered. Clearly being set on by women was a new experience for him.

'Do you think we should be otherwise?' Effie asked.

'No! I would never wish you other than you are! That is, I don't know. That is, I'm pleased to see you have solid convictions but I worry that you might both become the subject of censure or scandal.'

'I imagine I would survive the ordeal,' Effie said, giving him a grin. He looked worried.

'We are very alike, you and I, Effie. Both of us see nonsense and question it.'

'The difference is, you are not condemned for doing so, whereas I am,' Effie retorted.

Walter lowered his voice. 'It's the manner in which you do it. As if your opinions are on a par with Reverend Ogram's or the charity board's.'

Effie scowled. 'Do you think they aren't?'

Walter held his hands palms up before him.

'No, no. I don't mean that at all. You know how highly I value your opinions, only sometimes you speak them so directly that men who are less liberal than I am are taken aback at the sound of a woman expressing herself in such a way. They are wrong, of course.'

He straightened his collar. 'Regarding Mrs Peel, her

husband is one of the foremen in my father's quarry. I will speak to him on your behalf and suggest that he guide his wife towards a proper time to communicate that does not break the day of rest.'

Effie and Mary exchanged a glance.

Effie took his hand. 'Walter, that's very sweet of you but you don't need to appoint yourself our knight errant.'

'We shall deal with the matter as tactfully as our sex are able to do,' Mary assured him. Her face was straight, but Effie had to stifle a giggle.

Walter opened his mouth, no doubt to protest, so Effie cut in quickly, not wishing his feelings to be bruised.

'But there is a way your masculine experience would benefit us. We want to be able to provide a fire for the classroom in the middle of winter. Would you speak with your father about the possibility of us taking the children to gather fallen branches on his estate?'

'Of course,' Walter said. 'Anything I can do, my dear ladies, you know that.'

Effie put a hand on his arm. 'Of course we do. And you are a solid and generous friend to us.'

'I try to be.'

'Let us show you what the girls are learning,' Mary said.

Walter walked around the schoolroom where six girls aged between four and nine were painstakingly copying out the alphabet on slates. The visit was occasionally punctuated by the screech of chalk on board.

'This is an admirable undertaking, ladies.'

'Thank you, Mr Danby. I would like to extend my premises to allow for more girls,' Mary told him. She seemed mollified by the praise and her passing annoyance at Mrs Peel had ebbed away.

'The railway workers often bring their wives and families when they come to work in the area, but their temporary camps have no facilities,' Effie explained.

Walter frowned. 'If they did, perhaps there would be fewer disturbances between the village men and the newcomers. You're correct, the situation is far from ideal. I wonder...'

He stared off into the distance and Effie never discovered what he wondered because the door to the schoolroom opened and Lachlan entered, bearing a loaf of freshly baked bread in one hand and a basket in the other.

'Good morning! I hope you don't mind my intrusion but thought the children might like something to play with.' He placed both armfuls on the table at the front of the room.

'Good morning, Lachlan. It's nice to see you,' Effie said.

Walter had drawn close to her side.

'Effie, who is this?'

Effie hadn't intended to introduce the men in this way, but now they had accidentally come into each other's presence there was no better time.

'This is Lachlan, Morna's father,' she said.

'That is unexpected,' Walter said.

Lachlan held a hand out. 'You must be Mr Danby. Effie has talked of you often. I'm pleased to finally meet you.'

Walter inclined his head. 'I am pleased to make your acquaintance. I am overjoyed you have located Morna. Now you have come to claim her, the burden placed upon this excellent woman can be lifted and the parish need no longer support her.'

Effie suppressed a gasp of surprise. Walter did not seem interested in the hows or whys of Lachlan's sudden appearance at all, only the financial implications. It was rather disheartening in Effie's opinion, but perhaps men were more practical in their concerns.

'I don't know if Lachlan is here to take Morna,' Effie said uncertainly.

'Oh but he must!' Walter fixed his eyes on Effie. 'Your charity has been wonderful to behold, Effie, but you have other concerns now. After all, you only intended to keep the child until she was claimed and then you intended to relinquish her.'

He turned to Lachlan. 'Sir, you agree with me, I'm sure. A man with any sense of pride would not countenance his daughter being raised on the charity of others.'

'Aye, but there is no charity involved,' Lachlan replied, lifting his chin proudly. 'As to whether I take Morna, that is Effie's decision as much as mine. She has cared for Morna so has a stake in the matter.'

Walter blinked, either at Lachlan's words or tone. 'I'm sure *Mrs Cropton's* maternal feelings will be taken into consideration, whatever her "stake" might be.'

He placed a particular emphasis on the formality of his address. Effie realised he assumed Lachlan's recent arrival had been his first appearance in Allendale Head. He had no idea of the length or nature of their acquaintance and therefore was bristling on Effie's behalf at what he assumed was a stranger being overfamiliar in address.

'Mrs Cropton's opinion will always be taken into account,' Lachlan agreed pleasantly. He slid Effie a sideways glance. 'She has excellent opinions.'

Effie cleared her throat uncomfortably. Walter shifted his hands on the top of his walking cane. He wore yellow gloves that matched his scarf, and a dress coat in closely woven grey and black wool. Lachlan was dressed in a knitted fisherman's sweater and moleskin trousers. The two men could not have looked more different. There was a sense of animosity between them. They reminded Effie of a pair of dogs circling around and sizing each up before deciding whether to attack.

'The decision does not need to be made now,' Effie said firmly. 'Lachlan has a lease on the hut until the new year so we have plenty of time to reach an arrangement.'

She walked to the table to see what Lachlan had brought. The basket contained pairs of carved wooden animals: rabbits, horses, cats, dogs and seals.

'Did you make these?' Mary asked.

'Aye. It's something I like to do.' Lachlan looked pleased with her praise.

Walter walked over and pulled one of the seals out of basket to inspect it.

'These are beautifully carved. You work with great skill.' His praise was genuine and Lachlan accepted the compliment.

'Driftwood carving is traditional where I come from. The nights are longer and darker that far north and it is something to do when the sun goes down.'

'One day you must teach me the skill,' Walter said.

'I'm sure a gentleman such as yourself would have no need for these,' Lachlan said.

'I'm not yet fortunate enough to have my own child,' Walter replied. 'Though of course I hope one day that will be the case.'

He looked at Effie and Lachlan's eyes tightened.

'May I?' He held his hand out for the carving. Walter returned it and Lachlan took the basket to the children, who fell on it excitedly.

'Thank you, Lachlan. The children will love them. We might try sketching and painting them,' Effie said.

'I will order sets of watercolour paints to be sent to you,' Walter said. 'I would not see you using your own resources.'

Effie suppressed a sigh. Whatever animosity there was between the villagers and labourers was nothing compared to what she detected between the two men standing before her.

Lachlan cleared his throat. 'The waves look good for fishing. I'll be leaving. Will you bring Morna to see me this afternoon?'

'Of course. Good luck fishing. Try and catch me a mackerel.' She gave him a mischievous smile meant only for him, knowing no one else would suspect how he intended to catch his supper.

Lachlan bowed to Mary and Walter then left.

Walter covered her hand with his. 'I too must be going. Effie, will you walk with me to the gate? I would like a word in private.'

Effie rested her hand on his arm and walked with him, carefully ignoring the expression of excitement on Mary's face.

'What do you wish to speak to me about?' she asked when they were alone.

Walter cleared his throat. His expression flickered, growing anxious.

'Effie, it is not yet my place to say what you can and cannot do. I should, however, caution you that your association with Alice is drawing comment.'

'Comment from whom? What association? What do you mean, "not your place yet"?'

The questions tumbled out of Effie in no particular order.

'Alice is my grandmother. Of course I will *associate* with her, as you put it.'

Walter reached for her hand but she drew it back.

'I've heard Mrs Ogram and Mrs Forshawe saying that you

270

are aiding Alice in creating her… remedies. Do you know what the rumours are? I only tell you this for your own good. While I don't believe there is any harm in the occasional poultice, some of what she does flies in the face of all that is good and right.'

'Mrs Ogram is a hypocrite,' Effie said sharply. 'Why, she uses some of my grandmother's mixtures herself. How dare she criticise what Alice does! And as for you being in any position to prohibit what I do!'

She gave a loud sigh of annoyance and stepped away. Walter followed, much to her irritation.

'Effie, my dearest, I would never seek to control you. Or stem your vitality.'

She rounded on him. 'I'm very glad to hear it, because you are in no position to do so.'

'I know.'

He put his hands on her shoulders. She brought her head up sharply, meaning to rebuke him but he looked deep into her eyes with such an expression of remorse that she stayed her words.

'I know, and I wish constantly it were otherwise, as well you know. If I am overbearing at times, please know it comes from a place of deep affection. Effie, we are friends, are we not? This silly little dispute will not alter years of affection between us?'

He sounded so despondent and looked at her with the expression of a dog trying to please its master, so that she couldn't help but nod.

'Yes, we are friends, Walter.'

His relief was visible. His affection might be stifling, but knowing he cared warmed her heart.

'I will not trespass on your time or good nature any longer

but I wonder if you might agree to walk with me tomorrow. I have something I would like to show you. If you are unclaimed by anyone else, that is.'

'I'm unclaimed,' she said with a smile.

'Wonderful. You shall be the first to see it,' Walter said.

Effie smiled again. 'How intriguing. Tomorrow it is.'

She returned inside and leaned against the desk.

'Goodness me, Walter can be hard work at times. I thought he was very unwelcoming to Lachlan, don't you agree? I was quite surprised.'

'Perhaps he has heard the rumours in the village.'

Effie tensed. Lachlan no longer carried his skin everywhere. He looked human and behaved human so there should not be any gossip.

'What sort of rumours?'

Mary twisted the end of her hair ribbon, looking uneasy.

'Mary, what rumours?' Effie repeated.

Mary bent her head. 'Of him and you. They say he's been seen leaving your cottage very late at night or very early. That sort of rumour. They say you are lovers.'

'Oh!' Effie gave a careless shrug, though her stomach was clenching. 'Lachlan is Morna's father. He comes into my cottage, but that doesn't mean he's in and out of my bed.'

It wasn't exactly a lie. That Lachlan was Morna's father had no bearing on the fact that he and Effie made love together. It was a warning that they would have to be more discreet than they had been.

'Who are *they* anyway?' Effie asked tartly. 'The old gossips who sit in the front pews at church and act pious on a Sunday? I've weathered worse scandal so why should I care about them?'

'Walter will never ask you to marry him if he hears the rumours,' Mary said looking worried.

'Perhaps I don't want him to.'

Mary looked astonished. 'Why wouldn't you?'

Effie twisted the wooden cat in her hand. The thoughts and feelings she had towards Walter were nothing compared to the way her whole being glowed when she was with Lachlan. After Mary's revelation, she would walk barefoot over razor clam shells rather than admit it though.

'I'm not sure I could live up to the expectations of being the wife of such a respectable man. Dear Walter, describing himself so proudly as a modern-thinking man while simultaneously offering to speak for us. Sometimes he seems too like his father.'

'We should give him credit for trying to be and you will tease him into being less like Mr Danby,' Mary assured her.

Effie nodded. Walter was only just beginning that journey. Sometimes she wondered if she should marry him simply to try to nudge him all the way down the path towards becoming a champion of female equality. He might not have a passionate nature when it came to the fair sex, but he did for causes.

'Do you think we are becoming unfeminine?' Mary asked.

'Of course not,' Effie replied firmly. She grinned. 'Well, perhaps I am, but you are as lovely as you always were.'

Mary's face grew wistful. 'Sometimes I hate this village. I wish I could leave and find somewhere bigger to live where there are more like-minded women and no one gossips.'

Effie looked at her friend in a new light. This was the first time Mary had shown any indication she was dissatisfied with village life.

'Don't you have an aunt in Harrogate? You could pay her a visit for a week or two.'

'That's right. Aunt Cynthia is Papa's cousin rather than an aunt, but I'm sure she would be pleased to have me. Though Mama might not be so pleased to let me go. Aunt Cynthia believes in female emancipation and education. She never married because she vowed to remain a spinster until women had equal legal rights in marriage. She shares her home with a friend called Georgiana whom she has known since school, and breeds spaniels.'

Effie embraced her friend. 'I absolutely think you should go and stay with her. She sounds an ideal companion for you, in my opinion.'

'I shall write to her tomorrow,' Mary said decisively. 'I wish you could find some happiness too, my dear.'

'I am happy.' Effie bit her lip. Was she? She adored her nights with Lachlan but he had not given her any indication that he saw their association as more than a love affair. Sooner or later he would return to Skailwick and then what would she do? Wait for him to return infrequently like she had with John, counting the months until he came back to her bed? It was a life she had been forced into by her pregnancy but not one she would have chosen. She didn't want to be alone and perhaps marriage to Walter would be better than that.

Then again, as Mary said, Walter had not actually asked her.

Walter called for Effie the following morning at half past ten precisely. He was dressed in tweed with an overcoat and carried a stout stick instead of his walking cane.

'I hope you don't mind a lengthy walk,' he said.

Effie peered through the window at the sky. The clouds were grey and covered any trace of sun that might still be valiantly trying to break through, but they did not look like rain clouds.

'Of course. I'll wrap the children up warmly. They'll enjoy running around.'

'By all means bring them with you. They can run ahead while we talk.'

He offered Effie an arm as they walked up Harbour Hill and through the village. Walter gazed around, listing things which were different since before his departure for Europe. The newly painted sign on the Ship and Anchor Inn was now blue not green. The death of the elder Mr Marsh meant the baker's shop was now *Marsh* not *Marsh and Son*. Small changes, but clearly significant to Walter.

They reached the top of the hill and Walter turned to the clifftop path that led through the fields towards Whitby. He adjusted his hat and gave a shake of the head.

'I feel I have been away too long. I have obviously missed some important events. The arrival of Morna's father, for example. How do you know he is who he claims to be?'

'You only need look at them side by side to know they are father and daughter,' Effie said.

'And what of the mother? Where is she?'

'She is dead.'

'Is that what her father says? Do you know the circumstances?'

Effie shook her head. Lachlan had never told her and she had never inquired. Maybe she had been remiss.

'Perhaps you should ask him, unless you would like me to make enquiries on your behalf,' Walter said.

'No thank you. Any enquiries I choose to make, I can do myself.'

'I have noticed, since my return, a change in your temperament that I am not sure is for the better.'

Surely he was not intending to bring up her *unwomanly conduct* again? Effie narrowed her eyes and folded her arms. 'Would you care to explain what you mean?'

'You are more forthright than you used to be. Do you remember how I intervened with the Poor Commission when Morna first appeared? Why, now I believe you would march down to their offices and speak to them in person.'

'Perhaps I would,' Effie agreed. 'Would the world be worse if I did?'

'I fear I will outgrow my usefulness to you,' Walter said. He walked on ahead, stopped and lifted his eyes to the sky, looking troubled. When Effie caught up with him he gave her a wistful smile.

'Perhaps the fault is mine and I am behind the times, but I dislike change. I wish the world would stay as it always was when we were young.'

'The world is changing and only a fool would hope to turn it back,' Effie retorted. She heard the harshness in her voice and softened it. 'I don't think you're a fool, Walter.'

'I'm very glad to hear it.'

She folded her arms. 'Walter, did you only ask me to accompany you so you could caution me about Lachlan or was there another purpose?'

'Another purpose,' Walter said.

He pointed his walking cane towards a row of rusty iron railings set into a stone wall. It marked the grounds of an old manor house that sat, unloved, on the hill. A painted sign on the gate was barely legible thanks to the battering of the elements but Effie could make out the name.

Beacon House.

Walter raised his brows and gave her an excited grin, once more his old enthusiastic self.

'Here we are at my purpose. The side gate is unlocked. Shall we go in?'

Chapter Twenty-Four

B eacon House stood in grounds directly on the edge of the cliff. The iron railings that had once separated the lawns from the thin strip of scrubland on the other side had become overgrown and there was no difference now between the tangled grass on either side. Effie instinctively clutched Morna's hand tighter. Even though she no longer fought to be in the water, thanks to Lachlan's excursions slaking some of her thirst, the child's obsession with the sea could quite easily see her running to greet the waves and hurtling head over heels down the steep drop.

Walter bent down and lifted Jack, swinging him up and onto his shoulders. Effie shot him a grateful look.

'Let's look closer at the house,' Walter suggested.

A brickwork path was still partly visible. They followed it up to what would once have been a knot garden in front of grand double doors that opened onto a raised patio. They could not reach it, however, because the rose bushes had grown rampant, claiming the borders and mingling with brambles. Alice would be there with a basket to gather the fruit and leaves the moment she saw them.

'It's a castle,' Morna murmured.

Effie looked at her in surprise. 'What, chick?'

Morna gestured at the tangle of thorns. 'You know, Mama. Like the prince had to cut through in the story in your book.'

'You're right,' Walter said. He bent to put Jack down beside Effie and knelt, looking into Morna's eyes. 'Perhaps there is a princess waiting inside to be woken? Shall we go and see?'

Morna twisted her pinafore around in her hands.

'You aren't a prince and you haven't got a sword,' she said with a pout.

Walter's forehead creased, one thick line appearing between his brows. A look of irritation flashed across his face.

'Morna! Mind how you speak,' Effie chided. 'You are forgetting yourself.'

Walter blinked and the expression was gone, replaced with his customary good-natured smile.

'You are right, Morna, I don't have a sword. But I have something much more useful.' He dipped his hand into the pocket of his coat and produced a ring with half a dozen keys attached. 'I have the key to the front door. Would you like to be the one to open it?'

'Yes please!' Morna reached out her hands.

'Take the ring and see if you can find one to fit the door,' Walter instructed. 'Take Jack to help you.'

The children ran off hand in hand. 'That will keep them occupied for a few minutes while we take a turn about the garden,' Walter said with a grin. He offered an arm to Effie and together they walked down to the end of the path where a stone fountain stood. The cherub in the middle was covered in moss and seagull droppings. Walter shook his head sadly.

'In times gone by this was the site of a beacon to send messages along the coast. When the Spanish tried to invade in the reign of Good Queen Bess it was lit to warn of their coming. Of course, now we have much more effective methods of communication. My great-grandfather built this house for my great-grandmother, but she preferred to live in York.'

'It's very remote,' Effie commented.

'That was why my great-grandmother disliked it. But I have plans to change that. It would not take much effort to lay roads to the surrounding fields and build more houses. The land here is too wild to plant and too near the cliff for grazing. The railway line runs close enough to be walkable.'

He put his hand on Effie's shoulder and turned her to face away from the sea, looking past Beacon House and over the undulating bracken- and gorse-carpeted surroundings.

'Imagine a village here, as big and thriving as Allendale Head. With new, modern cottages for workers and their families. A school such as the one Mary wishes to establish but for all children. A church and shops. A park, even.'

His enthusiasm made his eyes light up endearingly.

'It sounds wonderful,' Effie agreed, giving Walter a warm smile.

'I have ambitions to do good in my lifetime. I've seen poverty and wealth on my travels. The slums of Manchester that put our great nation to shame. Deprivation and crime. Even the fishermen's dwellings in our beloved village are far from adequate. I know any part I might play will be small, but I want to do it.'

His zeal was infectious. He seemed to grow taller in stature before Effie's eyes.

'I'm sure you could accomplish anything you've set your mind to,' she told him.

'Almost anything. Some ambitions still seem beyond my capabilities.' Walter cocked his head and gave her an odd smile. 'Shall we go and see if the children have found the right key?'

The children were still trying keys in the lock. Walter took the ring, selected one and opened the door onto a shadowy hallway with rooms leading off to left and right and a staircase in the centre. Jack slipped his hand into Effie's. Morna ran to the stairs and stopped.

'There isn't a princess,' she said, her smile drooping.

'Perhaps the house is waiting for one to arrive,' Walter said. 'A queen too.'

He met Effie's gaze and his eyes filled with a suggestive light that made her blush. Subtlety was not his strongest attribute.

'It's dusty enough to have a princess sleeping in the attic,' she said, scuffing her foot in a circle and leaving a trail of grey on the stone floor.

'I know. My grandparents found tenants but the house has been unoccupied for almost twenty years. It will be in terrible need of modernisation. I doubt it has a single water closet and certainly no gas lamps. It would take a courageous and determined woman to become its mistress. Someone who wasn't afraid of hard work and didn't run screaming at the lack of a whitewashed scullery.'

Again, Walter caught Effie's eye.

'If that woman were to become Mrs Walter Danby I would see this wreck become the finest residence possible in the shortest time. Effie, dear, do you think you might be able to put aside the reservations you must have and consent to marry me?'

It was the first time he had directly asked the question. Effie looked about her, imagining herself mistress of an establishment of such size and grandeur. Her entire cottage could fit into the hallway and one of the rooms. She became aware that Morna was tugging at her skirt to attract her attention.

'I don't want to live in a dark house, Mama.'

'It's only dark because the curtains are half pulled and the windows are dirty,' Effie said. She glanced at Walter, who was frowning. 'Perhaps this is a conversation for another time, when we're alone.'

'That's not a refusal,' Walter said hopefully.

'It's not an acceptance either,' Effie cautioned.

They walked back to Allendale Head together. At the top of the hill, Walter bid them farewell with a tip of the hat and a request to Effie not to leave him waiting for too long. He carried on home while Effie and the children went down the hill.

The proposal had been odd, seemingly based as much on Walter's need for an assistant in his philanthropic endeavours as his feelings towards Effie. He believed she was capable of helping him fulfil his ambitions and that was flattering in itself. Wife of a man who regarded her highly might be a more sensible choice than lover of a half-man who might up and leave without notice.

Effie had intended to keep Walter's conversation and proposal to herself; she had not counted on the innocent, loose tongues of children. A dry morning two days later gave her the opportunity to take the children to the beach and let them run around. She was joined by Lachlan and Mary, and the adults sat on a rug, taking turns to read from Scott's *Ivanhoe*.

'Mr Danby asked Mama to live in a big house with him,' Morna said. She pouted. 'He said it was a castle with a princess but there wasn't a princess there. It was dark inside. I liked the view of the sea though.'

She went back to playing with her dolls, clearly unaware of the wasps' nest she had just poked. Effie looked up from the book to find both Mary and Lachlan looking at her keenly.

'He asked you to marry him,' Mary exclaimed.

Effie nodded. Her tongue felt curiously thick and heavy in her mouth and she didn't want to say the words aloud.

'Did you accept?' Lachlan asked. Effie searched his face for some hint of his opinion, but it was as neutral as his tone had been. She shook her head.

'Whyever not?' Mary exclaimed again. 'Just think of the life you could lead. Mrs Walter Danby. It sounds so respectable.'

'I know,' Effie said, finding her voice at last. 'I'm not sure it's the life I'm ready to lead just yet, even if I could do with the respectability.'

She put her paintbrush down with a sigh. 'Walter wants me to do good with him. He has a notion to build a new village for the workers in his father's quarry and the farm labourers. It's very admirable. He talked of what we could accomplish together. He has such grand vision.'

'Why on earth did you decline?' Mary asked, lifting her brows expressively. 'Are you not tempted?'

'By the man or the vision?' Effie asked with a slight laugh. She could feel herself growing hot.

Lachlan pushed himself to his feet. 'The children are getting too excited. I'll take them along the beach to run off their heads.'

Effie and Mary watched him go, the children at his heels like faithful dogs.

'What do you mean, Walter offered you respectability?' Mary asked curiously.

'Because of Jack,' Effie said. A faint prickle of annoyance caused the back of her neck to grow damp. 'Because he was conceived before John and I were married. I imagine your mother kept the gossip from reaching you at the age you were. Didn't you ever wonder why I was such a pariah in the village? No one could prove Jack was conceived out of wedlock, but many suspected it.'

Mary took her hand. 'You face the world so bravely. I know I couldn't.' She began to rummage in her bag and produced a letter. 'I wrote to my aunt. She says she would be delighted for me to spend a month with her and Georgiana. She has invited me to begin my journey on Monday.'

Effie forced a smile. 'I'm delighted for you, but that's so soon! I shall miss you.'

Mary threw her arms round Effie. 'And I shall miss you too, but I shall give you her address so we can write to each other, and I shall not be gone for more than a month.'

Effie hugged her friend back. Once Mary discovered the delights of a spa town she would be reluctant to return to the remote village. She would be in the company of young and interesting people. There was no doubt in Effie's mind that before the year was out, Mary would have fallen in love and would find reasons to stay.

Mary's news put Effie in a melancholy mood for the rest of the day. Alice and Lachlan spent the evening in the cottage with her and the children ran around excitedly, getting underfoot. To Effie's relief, Lachlan offered to walk Alice home.

She had seemed uncertain on her feet as Effie had accompanied her there. Effie intended to get the children washed and into bed by the time Lachlan returned, but they proved too lively and seemed intent on prolonging the evening.

Lachlan returned in time to hear Effie threatening no jam for a week if they did not obey her. He winked at her, scooped both children up under an arm each and sat them on his lap in his chair by the fire.

'If you promise to go to bed straight away afterwards, I'll tell you a story.'

The enticement worked and both children sat still. Effie brought her basket of darning and sat in her chair to listen as she worked.

There was once a seal maiden with hair as black as the ocean depths who was too adventurous, so her family said. One autumn morning she became trapped in a net belonging to a fisherman from the western isles. He freed her and recognised what she was.

'Can I see you in your womanly form?' he asked, and because he had freed her and had asked politely, she obliged and shrugged off her skin.

Quick as a salmon leaping upstream, the fisherman seized her skin and bundled it into his sack and tied the drawstring tight.

'Now you can be my wife and keep my home,' he told her. 'I'm so lonely living all alone.'

Although she begged and pleaded for her release, the seal maiden had no choice but to obey him because he had her skin, and so she clambered into his boat and wept salt tears as he rowed them both to land.

The marriage was not unhappy because the fisherman was gentle and had indeed acted through loneliness not malice, but the seal woman – now a maiden no longer – missed her own folk. Whenever

the moon was full she asked her husband to let her take her seal form
for a day and swim out to meet them.

'No,' he answered, 'because if I did you would not return to me
and I should be lonely again.'

The seal maiden wept because she was a creature of her word and
would have returned to her husband. After twelve months of asking
and refusal she changed her plea to an hour each month but the
answer was always no. When the fisherman left her alone in the
house she searched for her skin but could never find it. Every year for
five years she bore her husband a son.

'I thought you said that wasn't possible,' Effie interrupted,
sitting forward.

Lachlan shrugged. 'This is a story and things are different
in stories. I've never heard tell of it in real life.'

Effie's hand slipped to her belly. She'd had her monthly
bleeds since she had started sharing her bed with Lachlan, and
so far he had been proven right.

'What happened next? Dada, finish the story,' Morna said.

Lachlan took a sip of water and put the cup down.

One night, while the fisherman was out in his boat, there was a
terrible storm and lightning struck the lingonberry tree he had
planted on their wedding day. The tree fell and the roots twisted
upwards. The seal woman's oldest child, a boy of almost six, ran to
the roots and shouted, 'Mother, there is a box beneath the roots.'

The seal woman opened the box and there was her skin, lying safe
and snug. The seal woman wrapped her skin around her shoulders.
Then she picked up her youngest child and balanced him on her hip.
She took the next youngest child by the hand and each child in turn
took hold of his brother's.

Hand in hand, following their mother, they walked to the shore
and into the sea.

'I don't like that story,' Morna said. Her mouth began to tremble and she pouted.

'It's only make-believe,' Effie said, leaning forward and giving her a hug. 'Isn't it, Lachlan?'

He scratched his chin. 'Aye. It's only a story. They all are.'

Morna looked unconvinced. 'Stories should have happy endings.'

'It was happy for the seal woman. She was free again and the fisherman didn't deserve to be happy,' Lachlan pointed out.

Morna still did not look convinced, but she allowed Effie to put her to bed.

Late that night, once the children were safely asleep, Effie lay in her bed and listened to the rain hammering on the roof. Autumn was starting to become colder, but, despite their nakedness, she was warmed by Lachlan's body lying pressed behind hers.

Perhaps it was the story of the seal woman taking her children to sea, or perhaps the conversation with Walter that prompted her to roll over and face him.

'Tell me about Morna's mother.'

Lachlan raised an eyebrow. 'Now?'

'Why not? I see a lot of you in Morna but there are things in her that I don't see in you.'

Lachlan lay back and tucked his hands behind his head. Effie rested her cheek against the hollow of his neck and shoulder and put her arm around him. It was her favourite position to lie in, where she could stretch her body against the length of Lachlan's and feel his warmth. His lips moved, though he did not speak at first. Effie waited patiently for him to gather his thoughts. When he finally spoke, his voice was slow and dreamlike.

'I loved Lileas from the first moment I saw her tumbling through the water off the shore of Skailwick. She bewitched me. I could have been one of the foolish sailors in my stories. Our union was inevitable the instant I donned my skin and swam to meet her.'

Jealousy prickled Effie's flesh at the thought of Lachlan besotted by the fascinating creature.

'She was a wild thing. I see Morna's stubbornness as hers. Do you remember I told you some of us live more in this form and others live more in our seal form? Lileas would have spent all her time in her skin if possible.'

'But you don't. Did that cause problems?'

Lachlan nodded and swallowed.

'She lived briefly with me during our courtship, but the closer she came to the end of her pregnancy, the more time she spent in her skin. I wondered at first whether she felt I did not care enough for her. I had never tried to keep her with me. I never wanted her to feel she could not leave.'

Effie closed her eyes, listening to his story. Lachlan's words offered some explanation of why he had never given Effie his skin. He did not want to feel imprisoned by her.

'When Morna was born, I had hoped we might come to an agreement, but it only made things worse. Lileas wanted to raise Morna entirely in her skin. We quarrelled daily. I would have been happy to have Morna for even half of the time but Lileas wanted more.'

His heartbeat was increasing. Effie could feel it thumping in his neck where she rested her cheek against him. She stayed silent but slipped her hand into Lachlan's.

'We fought badly on the last day I saw her. I had to travel to a nearby village. That was another cause of conflict; she did not believe we should ever mix with our human neighbours. When

I returned home, I discovered she had gone. She had taken everything from our cottage and she had taken Morna.'

A sob broke from his throat. 'Can you imagine the desperation of not knowing where your child had gone?'

Effie squeezed his hand tightly but he moved it abruptly and wiped it across his face. Effie didn't dare raise her head to see if he was weeping. The sight of his tears would undo her even more than hearing the pain that cracked his voice.

'It took me a day to discover where she had gone, then Seathan and I, along with Lileas' four brothers, went after her in pursuit.'

Effie held her breath in anticipation, dreading what she would hear next. She already knew the outcome: a dead woman and a child abandoned to her fate in the sea. What part had Lachlan played in that? She could not imagine him as one of the brutish men who murdered his woman in a fit of rage, but the bitter truth was that many did not appear such until they struck the blow or wielded the knife.

'You don't have to go on,' she said.

Lachlan lay silently for a couple of minutes. Then he gave a long, drawn-out sigh and began to speak again.

'She had been spotted by a ship. The bastards on board decided to use her for sport, or perhaps to claim her skin. She was speared through the belly but somehow managed to break free and escape. We found her but it was too late. She was floating in her human form, almost insensible from loss of blood and the pain.'

He put his hand to his shoulder. Effie recalled the terrible injury he had suffered at Christmas that had still left its trace on his flesh and the gash in his skin that had healed.

'Could she have changed form? Would that have saved her?' she asked.

Lachlan gave her a sideways look.

'No. Her injury was too severe.'

'She told me she had saved Morna but could not tell me where the baby was. She died cursing the sailors. I swore to avenge her death, but she cursed me too, for driving her to leave Skailwick.'

His voice was harsh and full of barely suppressed anger that Effie had never heard before. She wanted to weep at the sound.

'But we avenged her nonetheless,' Lachlan said.

'What did you do?' Effie asked, her blood chilling at the darkness in his voice.

'We took revenge on the ship,' Lachlan said. 'We swam around it, making ourselves known and suspecting that if the crew had tried to get themselves one pelt, the prospect of six would be hard to resist. We were right. The ship changed course and followed us and when we were close to the Brigg, we scuttled it.'

Effie felt bitterness rising to her throat at the thought of Lachlan doing something so brutal. It was followed by a wave of nausea as she began to suspect whose ship it had been.

'And this was a fair judgement on them?' She sat up and pulled her knees up to her chest, hugging them tightly.

'Was it fair that they murdered Lileas?' Lachlan asked. 'Was it fair that they left her to die while her babe drifted out to sea, to die a cold and lonely death?'

He put his hands to his temples and pressed firmly, as if he were trying to banish the memories from his brain. 'I'm not saying it was balanced or rational, but those men murdered Morna's mother.'

The feeling of nausea in Effie's belly intensified. She had to force her next words out through a throat full of bile. 'I think one of those men was my husband.'

Lachlan grew very still.

'John's ship was found wrecked with all hands lost on the day I found Morna. No one could explain the circumstances. Until now.' She pointed an accusing finger at Lachlan. It trembled and she lowered it, bunching a fist. 'You murdered them.'

'They murdered Lileas,' Lachlan said. He pushed himself to a sitting position facing Effie.

'They didn't know she was your wife,' Effie snarled. 'At best they thought they were killing a seal. It was a fishing vessel. They thought she was just an animal.'

Lachlan turned his head sharply. 'Aye, just an animal. I suppose that is what I am.'

'That's not what I meant. They didn't realise they were killing a woman.' Effie bit back a sob, tasting bitterness. The man in whose arms she had lain could be so brutal. The feeling of betrayal was unendurable.

Lachlan grimaced, baring his teeth. Now she could imagine him beating at the underside of John's boat, feeling no remorse as the water filled the breached hull. Watching the men gasp their final breaths. Effie's head spun. Her heart would not pump. Her lungs would not inflate. She was drowning on land.

'Did you know who you had killed? Did you suspect that the husband I had lost was on board that ship? Did it mean anything to you when you took his place in my bed?'

'No! I mean, no, I didn't realise it was John's ship. It means everything to me to share your bed. Effie, I wouldna' hurt you for the world.'

He held a hand out, his expression bleak, but Effie shook

her head. She had opened her heart to Lachlan. Built a friendship and more that she now discovered was on no firmer foundation than the water itself.

'You told me that we were a danger to you, not the other way round. You lied, just as you lied to me about what Morna was. It doesn't make you an animal to want revenge, but to feel no remorse makes you a monster.'

She realised as the words left her lips that they were a mistake but it was too late to unsay them. She'd called him a monster once in fear, but this was in rage and disgust.

Lachlan's eyes locked onto hers, black and angry. Without another word, he clambered from the bed. Ignoring his discarded clothes, he threw his skin over himself and walked out of the room.

'Mama?' Jack had awakened and was pulling himself from his bed. Morna too was stirring. By the time Effie had settled them and had followed Lachlan, there was no sign of him on the beach, only a dark shape heading out to sea.

Chapter Twenty-Five

Lachlan did not call for Morna the following morning. Effie did her best to drag her attention to the household chores but could not find the vitality she needed. She sat on the rug and read to the children, bundling them onto her lap so they would not see her mouth wobble as she read the stories of duplicitous wolves dressing in human clothing. Her emotions lurched from horror at what the crew of the *Serenity* had done, to disgust at Lachlan's brutality. When Morna snuggled against Effie's bosom and held her breath at the scary part, Effie could not feel anything other than rage at the men who had orphaned the child.

Mary visited mid-way through the afternoon and noticed immediately that her friend was out of sorts.

'Has something happened with Walter? Effie, I don't like to see you sad, especially when I am leaving you alone.'

'It isn't Walter. Lachlan and I had a quarrel. We spoke harshly to each other, and he left.'

Mary wrinkled her brow. 'Was he upset over Walter's proposal?'

'Should he be?'

'I would consider it peculiar if he was not.' Mary adjusted her gloves briskly and gave Effie a coy look. 'Anyone can tell from the way Lachlan looks at you that he is love-struck. The idea that you might marry Walter must be unbearable for him.'

Effie turned away. Her heart had thudded when Mary called Lachlan love-struck. He had never expressed any emotions as strong as love. Even if he did, she could not imagine they were durable enough to withstand the words she had spat at him or the knowledge of what he had done. Nor could she explain to Mary what had occurred without omitting so many details that would reveal their secrets.

'It wasn't over Walter. We talked of Morna's mother, and of John.'

'I am sure you will mend your quarrel soon,' Mary reassured her. 'I doubt the fault is on your side alone.'

Effie bit her lip doubtfully. She regretted her words, but not the judgement she had passed on him. What Lachlan and his companions had done was abominable. He was changed in her eyes.

'I do not know if we can be friends again, nor if I even want to be.'

At that, the tears spilled over. She pulled out a chair and sat at the table, weeping into her hands. Mary knelt and threw her arms tightly around Effie and kissed her cheek.

'I wish I was not going to Harrogate. You need me by your side. You should come with me. I'm sure Cousin Cynthia will welcome you.'

'Thank you.' Effie sniffed. She wiped her eyes and swallowed. 'I could not trespass on your cousin's hospitality, but, even if I could, I would not expect her to play hostess to two children. Besides, Morna needs to live here by the sea and be where Lachlan is.'

She sat back and gazed around with a sigh. 'The cottage is full of memories of Lachlan and John that blur into one.'

The chair Lachlan now claimed in the evenings had belonged to her husband. The bed they made love in had been her marriage bed. She could not see anything without thinking of both men and how their actions had unknowingly shaped each other's fate. The association was distressing.

Mary rested her head on Effie's shoulder. 'If you will not accept my proposal, perhaps you should accept Walter's. Nothing would give me greater happiness than knowing you are happy too.'

Effie promised to consider it. Happiness seemed too great an ambition but the safe, comforting companionship Walter offered might be exactly what she needed to mend her crushed heart.

Lachlan came the following morning. Effie made no attempt to invite him in and he did not ask. His face was expressionless and his manner as wary as on the first night he had appeared at her door.

Effie folded her arms. 'Morna missed you yesterday. I was not sure what to say to her. She has become used to you being here. Should I be preparing her for that to change?'

'I don't know. For now I'll come for her daily as always.'

Effie sent Morna out. She ran to Lachlan, clutching her skin in one hand, and threw her arms around him.

'Dada, I missed you.'

Effie watched man and girl depart with a sour taste in her mouth. It was her fault that Lachlan had not come.

No, she told herself firmly, not entirely hers. Lachlan was equally culpable. It twisted her guts to realise how quickly they had become like strangers. She could run after him and apologise and things might return to normal, but now she could not see him or look upon the skin without associating it with what he had done to John's boat. She would need to find it in her to forgive before she could ask forgiveness.

Morna thankfully did not appear to notice the frostiness between Effie and Lachlan. For the next week she was as happy as ever to go with him and return to Effie.

'We swam almost to the Brigg today,' she told Effie proudly on Saturday evening. 'Dada says next time we'll go even further.'

Effie looked at Lachlan, who was standing at the gate. 'You took her that far?'

'Aye. She is stronger now. She can go further still.'

Effie's throat tightened. 'Are you planning to take her further still?'

His lips tightened. 'Perhaps.'

'To Skailwick?'

He looked away.

'You won't take her without telling me, will you?' Effie asked fearfully.

His expression softened for the first time since he had stormed out of her bedroom.

'I'll tell you.'

He blew a kiss to Morna, then left. Effie put her arm around Morna, forcing herself not to hold the child too tightly. She was Lachlan's daughter and he had the right to take her but Effie was not prepared for that day to come so soon.

~

Before that possibility, there was the certainty of another departure. On Monday morning Mary left for Harrogate. Effie climbed despondently up Harbour Hill to bid her goodbye. Morna skipped ahead, excited to give Mary the posy of dried flowers and seaweed she had made. Jack walked holding Effie's hand and murmuring to her. Effie couldn't tell how much he understood or cared about Mary leaving, but he responded to Effie's sadness. A pony and trap was waiting outside the vicarage to take Mary and her father to the railway station in Goathland. Reverend Ogram was accompanying his daughter as far as York. Jack and Morna petted the pony while Mary and Effie hugged tightly and wept on each other's shoulders. After her estrangement from Lachlan and Mary's departure, her friendship circle was rapidly diminishing.

Walter had come down the hill to bid her farewell and stood beside Effie to wave Mary off.

'I shall miss her,' Effie said.

'You will have me for company whenever you desire it,' Walter assured her. He slipped his arm through hers and they began to walk along the street with the children ambling behind. 'My mother would very much enjoy having you to afternoon tea one day. You shan't be lonely.'

'Thank you, Walter dear,' Effie said affectionately. He patted her hand and opened his mouth, but, before he could speak, they were accosted by a red-faced man wearing a heavy woollen jumper and a fisherman's cap. He took the cap from his head and twisted it in his hands, bobbing a bow.

'It's Mrs Millbourne. Mrs Cropton, you must come quickly; she's had a fall.'

'Where?' Effie let go of Walter's arm.

'She was on the rocks beyond the harbour. We think she must have slipped. My brother took her back to her cottage. My wife went with him.'

'Walter, I must go,' Effie said. 'Will you watch the children for a few moments?'

She picked up her skirts and began to run.

'Effie, walk. Take care you don't injure yourself,' Walter called after her.

He was right and she slowed her pace. Harbour Hill was steep and winding at the best of times, but the rain turned the cobbles to glass, making it doubly treacherous. She would be no good to Alice if she twisted her ankle.

Alice's front door was open. A woman Effie recognised from the harbour was standing in the doorway, twisting her hands in a fish-stained apron. Her anxious expression turned to relief when she saw Effie. Effie wished she knew the woman's name. Lachlan would have.

'She's been asking for you, Mrs Cropton.' She put a hand on Effie's arm and shook her head solemnly. 'She's in a bad way. I'm glad you're here now.'

Effie's stomach tightened. How bad?

Alice was lying on top of her bed. Another woman Effie didn't recognise was with her. She sat on a stool and was pressing a tea towel to Alice's temple. Alice turned her face to the door and moaned faintly when Effie entered the room.

'What happened?' Effie asked. 'I hear you've been giving these good folk a scare.'

She kept her voice light so as not to alarm Alice, but inside she was gasping in horror. Alice was so pale. Her nose was swollen and her eyes were surrounded by bruises.

'What did you fall on?'

The woman beside the bed answered for her. 'She went

over on some rocks. She didn't trip, if that's what you mean. She was walking along, then she stopped and sort of wobbled and put her hand on her heart. Then she dropped to the ground face first.'

Effie knelt beside the bed and took hold of Alice's hand. The skin over her wrist was translucent and papery thin, and the pulse in the blue vein that showed through was faint and rapid. Alice's eyes flickered open. She moistened her lips.

'Effie, it's my time.'

Her voice was little more than a breath.

'No it isn't,' Effie said. 'You just need to rest for a day or two.'

Alice shook her head faintly. 'I am ready to rest,' she whispered.

A male voice came from the outer room. Walter had arrived.

'I sent a message to Dr Douglas. He should be here within the quarter hour. My mother is minding Jack and Morna.'

'I want no doctor,' Alice mumbled. 'Save your money, Effie, my girl.'

Walter cleared his throat. 'If it's the expense you're worried about, I will bear it.'

'I can afford it,' Effie said. The precious pearls would pay for any treatment. She'd sell them all if it would help Alice live.

'No doctor at this time. Nothing to do with the cost,' Alice said, her voice gaining strength with the insistence.

Walter reached for Effie's free hand. She took it, glad for the comfort.

There was another voice from outside. Effie recognised it and her skin prickled. Lachlan was here. He walked into Alice's bedroom, but stopped short when he saw Effie and Walter, his eyes briefly settling on their joined hands. Effie dropped Walter's hand. Lachlan walked to the bed and knelt at Alice's side, taking her hand.

'Can I do anything for you? Fetch a draught to help your pain?'

Alice shook her head. 'No draught can help me now. I've expected this day for a long time now.'

Walter moved to the end of the bed. 'You don't know that, Mrs Millbourne. Would you like me to pray with you?'

Alice opened her eyes. For a moment they filled with indignation, and Effie had the vain hope that she was rallying.

'No prayers. No doctors. A song perhaps, laddie, if you will.'

Walter looked startled at the request, but by the term she had used, Effie knew she meant Lachlan.

'Please, Lachlan, will you?' Effie asked quietly. It was the first time she had used his name since their quarrel.

Lachlan cleared his throat and began to sing. The tune was similar to the lullaby he had sung to Morna and Jack, but it was faster and with a pulse that made Effie want to dance despite her burgeoning grief. Effie's mind filled with a vision of painted men walking side by side, shields and spears in their hands. Tears flowed freely down her cheeks. She let them fall.

Alice licked her lips to moisten them. 'If I was half my age, I'd have danced through the waves with a man like you.'

Lachlan smiled and bowed his head to her. 'And I'd have been honoured to do so.'

Alice reached her hand towards Effie. 'Come here, my girl. I have words for you.'

Lachlan moved back to stand near Walter, and Effie took his place. She knelt and Alice put her mouth close to Effie's ear.

'Your choices are your own to make, my girl. Make them

wisely. You are stronger than you were and you will be stronger still.'

She closed her eyes, then they flickered open again, and she looked towards the end of the bed where the two men stood side by side, heads bowed.

'Look after her,' she said. She gave a soft sigh and closed her eyes.

She never opened them again and died a short while later, just as Doctor Douglas knocked on the front door.

Effie held Alice's hand while Doctor Douglas confirmed what Effie already knew, then Walter took her gently by the elbow and guided her into the front room. Lachlan followed a few steps behind. Doctor Douglas came out of the bedroom a minute or two later and spoke briefly to Walter. Despite her grief, Effie's heart found space for mild irritation. Alice was her relative, not Walter's, and yet the two men were assuming responsibility.

'I'll lay her out,' Effie said.

Walter came to her side. 'There is no need. I can take care of all arrangements.'

'Alice would have wanted me to do it.'

Saying those words, it was as if the trigger on a rifle had been pulled and the full reality of Alice's death hit Effie. She began to weep violently. However tightly she wrapped her arms around herself she could not stop her frame from shaking.

'Leave everything to me.'

'What can I do for you?'

Lachlan and Walter had spoken at the same time. Effie looked at them both. Walter with his practical nature who only wished to smooth Effie's path through life. Lachlan who had sung so beautifully to ease Alice's cares. She wanted one of them to hold her. She wanted both. But how could she ever make that choice?

The answer was, she couldn't.

'I have to go.' She choked out the words and ran out of the door, blindly making her way through the streets to the harbour. The tide was out and the beach stretched endlessly away to the distant sea. The rain had started again, slow and fine, hanging like mist in the air. Even so, Effie walked onto the shingle and sat down. What did it matter if she got wet when Alice was growing cold on her bed? She pulled her knees up to her chest, bowing her head to bury her tears.

Presently, she became aware that someone approached her, footsteps crunching on the shingle. One of the men had followed her but she didn't know which one until she looked up and twisted round to see who.

Lachlan.

He stood a few paces away. Effie knew with certainty that if she did not speak to him now, the rift would never be mended.

'I'm very sorry for your loss,' he murmured.

'Thank you for your song. And for coming to see Alice.'

He nodded his head in acknowledgement without speaking.

Her grief for Alice was too big to contain alone and she knew Lachlan shared a portion of it. If she reached out to him, would he come to her and hold her as she needed to be held? She was unsure, and the prospect of his rejection was more than she could face. She didn't ask him, and after a few moments of standing silently at her side, he left.

~

Alice was buried in the churchyard beside St Stephen and All Saints. It was considered bad luck to keep mourning garments but Effie had not yet taken hers to Mr Harrelsen the pawnbroker in Whitby. Once again she found herself dressed in black crape.

Walter appointed himself Effie's aide, and in the end she was thankful that he took care of the mundane arrangements. Alice wouldn't have cared for ceremony and would have been happy going to her grave in a simple winding sheet. Leaving Walter to make decisions left Effie free to mourn and help the children with their grief.

Walter's mother had kindly agreed to take Jack and Morna into her care while the funeral took place. Walter offered Effie an arm as they left the churchyard. She expected him to escort her to the Danby home at the top of the village, but instead he walked her back to her cottage. When she opened the door and turned to thank him, Walter was standing with his hands clasped together and an odd expression on his face.

'Effie, there is something we must discuss. Now your grandmother has gone to a better place I am conscious that you are all alone.'

Effie's eyes prickled. She no longer cried at every mention, but the sadness was never far away.

'No, I'm not. I have my children. I have friends. I have you.'

A brief frown crossed Walter's face. 'Mary is an excellent friend to you but she is going to be absent for a month. I believe Morna's father does the best he can by his daughter. As for myself, we are indeed friends and have been for many years, but I want to be so much more.'

He took her by the hands and led her inside.

'For years I have loved you and held my tongue while you mourned for your lost husband. I can be silent no more.'

He held her hands tightly. 'Effie Cropton, will you become Mrs Walter Danby? I know you care for me and if your feelings are not yet love, I am confident that within time they will soften and alter favourably.'

Effie was struck dumb. The only reason she had to object was one she could not admit to. Her love for Lachlan and the nights she had spent in his arms. But those were ended now and although her love was fierce, it was tarnished by their estrangement. She could see no prospect of reconciliation and wasn't sure if she even wanted one.

'You are overcome, I can see,' Walter murmured. 'Perhaps I can tip the balance in my favour slightly.'

Before Effie could ask what he meant, he pulled her into his arms and kissed her. Whether or not Walter had romanced opera girls whilst in Europe, he had grown better at kissing since his previous slightly clumsy effort. The kiss was slow and with just enough pressure in his lips to demonstrate his mastery of the moment. Despite her surprise, Effie had to admit it was a very good kiss.

Dimly, she became aware of the door creaking. Effie opened her eyes and looked up. Lachlan was standing in the doorway. His face was like stone.

'This is a bad time. I'll come back.'

'Not a bad time at all for your intrusion,' Walter said, releasing Effie and linking his arm through hers. 'You can be the first to hear our joyful news, Lachlan. Mrs Cropton is soon to become my wife.'

'But I haven't...' Effie began, but Walter was already reaching for her hand and explaining loudly to Lachlan how long he had waited for Effie's natural womanly reservations to ease. She doubted either man had heard her speak.

Lachlan's eyes bored into Effie and his smile was fixed. 'My congratulations, Mrs Cropton. I hope you will be very happy.'

'Of course we will be happy. Mrs Cropton and I have always understood each other perfectly. Oh,' Walter said, as if just recalling something. 'There must be a purpose to your visit. Would you care to tell us what it is?'

'Nothing that can't wait for another time,' Lachlan muttered. He turned and walked out of the cottage without another word.

Chapter Twenty-Six

As soon as Lachlan had gone Effie rounded on Walter.

'Walter, why did you tell Lachlan we were to be married? I haven't accepted your proposal.'

Walter looked aggrieved. 'In that case it's a poor way you are treating me by kissing me in such a manner. Why, the touch of your lips made me almost unman myself, I don't mind admitting.' His eyes brightened. 'If that is how you kiss me before accepting, I shall anticipate our wedding day with delight!'

Effie couldn't, if her life had depended on it, decide whether he was the biggest innocent in England or the most manipulative swine.

'But why tell Lachlan?' she asked.

Walter looked genuinely bemused. 'What else could I say after he found us in such a compromising position? You would have been ruined if he told anyone what had passed between us.'

'That was hardly compromising,' she said.

Walter just looked confused. An innocent, Effie decided. No

one could be so wilfully cunning as to imply their kiss would ruin anyone, especially not Effie with a child conceived before marriage. On consideration, perhaps it was his own reputation he feared for.

'Walter, I must go,' Effie said. 'There are things I need to do.'

'Any matters you have, I can assist you with. Your burdens will soon become my burdens and in doing so I hope they will cease to be burdens.'

Effie shook her head. Walter's generosity of spirit put her to shame, but she had no intention of revealing her task to him.

'Will you at least tell me if you accept,' he entreated.

'I...'

Walter was looking at her with such hope. That such a man wanted her was overwhelming. She should accept. It would be the sensible thing to do. She would never want for comfort or love and would be redeemed in the eyes of the village. But Lachlan still filled her heart. Until she had spoken to him, she could not plan with a clear head.

'I will come to your house and collect the children as soon as I am done. I promise I will give you my answer then.'

She hurried out of the cottage, not bothering to gather her hat or a shawl. She ran down the path and spotted a small figure almost at the turn of the beach before Boggle Cove.

She found Lachlan sitting by his fire carving a large piece of driftwood. The wind was blowing in from the sea, biting and violent, and causing smoke to surge around him. He put the wood down as she approached, and Effie saw the subject was a woman like a ship's figurehead.

'What are you doing here? Have you come seeking further congratulations?'

'I don't want congratulations. Walter shouldn't have said what he did. I hadn't said I would marry him.'

'So you kissed him without accepting?' Lachlan's eyebrows rose.

'He kissed me,' Effie corrected. 'He assumed that because I didn't push him away I was consenting.'

'Most men would assume that if you were kissing them it was because you liked them. They might be fools, of course.'

His voice was bitter.

'Why did you come to the cottage?' Effie asked.

Lachlan indicated a bunch of wild flowers beside him. 'I was bringing these to ask if you would permit me to lay them on Alice's grave.'

Effie's eyes filled with tears. She didn't have money to spare for flowers and the only bouquet at the funeral had been six lilies given by Walter. This small offering would look meagre beside them but Effie had no doubt they had been offered with as much sincerity, if not more.

'Of course you may. You don't need to ask my permission.'

'I thought it best. I'll go this evening. Is there anything else you need to say to me?'

'I… I'm sorry you saw Walter and me.'

Lachlan's lip twitched. 'Sorry I saw, but not that you did it.'

He stood but remained at the other side of the fire. 'You should marry Mr Danby. Your life with him will be what every woman craves. He's intelligent, well respected and he loves you. He'll be wealthy one day. He's a gentleman. A gentle *man.*'

These were all the reasons Effie had given herself but the inflection in Lachlan's voice was more wounding than if he had struck her. A clear jibe at her calling him a monster. Who was he really? The dizzyingly skilful lover? The perplexing stranger who filled her life with wonder? The remorseless creature who exacted vengeance without mercy? All of them at once?

Lachlan stared out to sea.

'Goodbye, Mrs Cropton. I have to get on now.'

It was a blatant dismissal. Effie turned and walked away. After a couple of paces she heard a splash and twisted round to see what had caused it. Lachlan was standing by the shore and ripples of something were settling on the sea. The carved woman was no longer by the fire.

Effie made her way up the hill and along the cliff road to the Danbys' house and knocked on the door. It was opened by a young woman in a white cap and ribbons who greeted Effie unsmilingly. It felt to Effie that even though the young woman was in service, she considered herself superior to Effie.

'I am here to collect my children and to see Mr Danby,' Effie told her.

She was led through the entrance hall and into a pretty sitting room, full of feminine touches; a basket with sewing threads, an easel set at the window, fashion periodicals scattered on a small table. This must be Mrs Danby's room. Effie stood nervously in the centre. She had memories of a room like this before her parents died and she began her life with Alice but the idea of trying to fit into this environment now seemed impossible.

Presently, Walter appeared, followed by Jack and Morna who were covered in flour.

'They were helping Cook make a pie,' Walter said.

The children ran to hug her. Walter went to the fireplace

and fiddled with a small arrangement of flowers on the mantelpiece.

'Did you finish your errands?'

'Yes, I did everything that I needed to,' Effie answered.

Walter turned the vase around. Appeared to change his mind and turned it back again. Adjusted a couple of leaves. Effie could practically feel the restlessness flowing from him.

She looked at him closely. He was the familiar friend she had known for years but she tried to look on him with the eyes of a lover. The slightly full mouth that she knew was adept at kissing. A pleasing form: not too tall or too short. An elegant line from chest to waist accentuated by a well-cut suit. The hair that flopped over his forehead in a manner that still made him look boyishly enthusiastic. There was nothing unpleasant in him to offend a wife. Most importantly of all, he wanted to marry her.

'Walter,' she said, stepping slowly towards him.

'Yes, Effie?'

His face took on an eagerness and Effie grew warm inside. It wasn't the breath-taking, violent throb through her entire body that she felt when she saw Lachlan, but Walter was right: she could learn to love him and was already very fond of him.

'Walter, you made a presumption earlier regarding my answer to your proposal. I wish you had not done that, however, if my hand is still what you wish I would be happy to accept.'

Walter's face took on an aspect of ecstasy Effie had rarely seen. He stepped towards her and clasped her hands.

'Do you mean it?'

'Yes, I do. I would be happy to be your wife.'

It sounded like she was trying to convince herself.

She was.

She could be happy married to Walter if she set her mind to it. She would, of course, have to bury the memory of her brief time spent with Lachlan.

Walter leaned forward and kissed her cheek. Morna squealed with interest in this unexpected development, and he jumped back as if he had been bitten. He looked at Effie and grinned. She smiled back.

'Come with me now. We must find my father and mother. They will be overjoyed for us. Morna, stay here and mind Jack does not break anything or come to harm.'

Effie took his hand and he led her at a great pace through the house. He was like a boy with a new toy. They found Mrs Danby in the library where she was writing letters. Walter asked her to lay down her pen and come and find her husband with them. Her smile was perhaps slightly less warm for Effie's liking than it could have been as she glanced at the pair of them, but she obliged her son. Mr Danby was in his own office, in the act of poring over a large plan of something or other drawn out in neat black lines.

Walter made his announcement and Effie was relieved that both his parents received the news warmly. They had always been kind to her, even after the days of her scandalously hasty marriage. Mrs Danby rang for coffee and they all returned to the sitting room where Effie had originally waited. While Walter and Mr Danby stood together talking about Walter's plans for the house he was intending to renovate, Mrs Danby tried to draw Effie into a conversation about her wedding plans.

'I'm afraid I cannot answer any of your questions,' Effie admitted. 'Obviously I am still in mourning for my grandmother so the date cannot be too soon.'

'That is very true of course.' Mrs Danby glanced at Effie's

black clothes. 'You have been in crape for so long, poor dear. You will not wear white in any case.'

Walter looked over. 'Mother, Effie can wear whatever colour she chooses. And now I have secured her promise, I am content to wait as long as necessary for the appropriate moment. There is no cause to rush.'

He probably did not mean to imply what he did, but Mrs Danby's eyes fell on Effie's belly. Effie's cheeks grew warm. To her immense relief, Morna spoke up.

'Mama should wear blue like the sea. That's what Dada says.'

Mrs Danby raised an eyebrow. 'The child is very forward to speak in front of adults without being addressed.'

'In my house we have little cause for formality,' Effie said.

Effie drew Morna onto her lap. Often when Effie tried this Morna wriggled free, to suggest she was too old for public embraces. Now, however, she sat and gazed at Mrs Danby intently.

'Mrs Danby is correct, Morna. It isn't polite to interrupt.'

'And what of your boy?' Mr Danby interjected. 'He doesn't speak much, but I believe he is watching everything we are doing here.'

Jack was sitting on the rug beside the fireplace staring into the flames with rapt attention. He had taken five pieces of coal from the scuttle and lined them up from smallest to largest.

Effie smiled. 'I believe so too. He speaks little but he watches and when he's given a task he learns it quickly. He is obedient as much as his understanding permits him to be.'

Mr Danby eyed him. 'Perhaps we can find a position for your son in the alum works. Many young boys are employed gainfully at his age.'

Effie tensed. 'And many are not, sir, if their families are in the fortunate position not to need their financial contribution. I have no need for Jack to provide for me; I have always managed that myself.'

Walter took her hand. 'I think my father was just thinking aloud. There will be no question of Jack working in the quarry.'

'I don't want to either,' Morna said firmly.

Once again, Mrs Danby raised her eyebrows.

'And you won't have to,' Effie assured her.

An awkward silence settled on the room. Walter cleared his throat.

'Effie, I have a hankering for a teacake. Will you walk down the hill to the bakery with me?'

Dearest Walter, for seeing her discomfort and freeing her from it. She bade her farewells to his parents, gathered the children and they left.

As soon as they had left the house, Walter gave a heavy sigh. 'I can only apologise for my father suggesting Jack works in the quarry. I doubt he meant we should set the boy to labouring in the mine. More likely an office role where he could fulfil repetitive tasks. But don't fear that, my dear. I have no intention of Jack needing to do that. We will make our plans for him in other ways.'

Effie squeezed his hand. Her marriage would not only be good for herself but for her son, who would now become the son of a gentleman. Really, she had been quite selfish to only consider her own desires for as long as she had.

'And Morna too,' she said. She felt her brow crease and did her best to dismiss her frown. There were more difficulties regarding Morna than Walter could ever begin to suspect.

'Ah yes. Morna.' Walter pursed his lips. 'I am a fair man and, I hope, a generous one and any fears you have that I should not welcome the son of your former marriage into my life are unfounded. Morna has a father of her own, however. I have made my feelings clear before regarding Lachlan's responsibilities and now we are to be wed I am sure that he will no longer expect you to care for her.'

Effie concentrated on walking, staring at her feet as they moved before her. She should have considered this, but Morna's future had not occurred to her any more than Jack's had.

Walter coughed discreetly. 'I see you have doubts. Would you like me to speak to Morna's father on your behalf? A man-to-man discussion might be the most effective way of making him see his responsibilities.'

'No! No, there is no need. When the time is right I shall speak to Lachlan myself,' Effie said.

They had arrived at the bakery. Walter tilted his head towards the tempting display of teacakes and iced fancies. 'I suppose now I am here I should avail myself of a teacake.'

He leaned forward to Effie, then pulled back. He ran his hand through his hair and shook his head with a slight laugh.

'I hope it shall not be too long before I am able to kiss your cheek in public. When shall we announce our happy news?'

Her heart was so heavy with grief for Alice and the loss of Lachlan's friendship that happiness seemed out of her grasp. That wasn't something to trouble Walter with, however.

'Not until the first month has passed, at least. Before then it seems indelicate to be thinking of happy events.'

Walter nodded. 'Of course. In public we shall merely be the good friends we always have been. Only in private shall we reveal our true relationship to one another.'

He lifted her hand to his lips.

'Good day to you, Mrs Cropton.'

He walked to join the group of matrons at the bakery door, tipping his hat and greeting them heartily. Effie took the children by the hand and walked home. She did not regret her decision but couldn't help but feel relief that by not announcing her engagement, she would be able to delay the difficult conversation with Lachlan about Morna's future.

The storms that had threatened Allendale Head in November arrived in earnest in December. By the second week, the fishermen were used to battling against the waves that drove them back into the harbour whenever they tried to embark on a trip.

Effie and the children bundled into thick coats and woollen hats whenever they left the cottage. Morna did not seem to mind it as much as Effie and Jack, though she had taken to wearing her seal skin around her neck beneath her muffler. She still skipped off happily with Lachlan each day and told Effie on her return of how much further she had swum than the previous day. Effie found herself more and more having to feign excitement at Morna's achievements. Lachlan seemed to be preparing his daughter for longer trips, which filled Effie with a sense of foreboding.

The relationship between them was aloofly polite. Although Lachlan had told Effie she should accept Walter, Effie did not confirm to Lachlan that she had followed his advice. That conversation would have to happen eventually, with whatever repercussions would follow.

Effie often lay in her bed at night – now achingly alone – and imagined these conversations playing out in different forms where Lachlan was coolly indifferent, angry or wounded. She could not decide which would be worse. It meant that she was often restless and weary the next morning. Walter commented more than once about her shadowed eyes with concern. Fortunately she was able to pass it off as grief for Alice's passing. This was not entirely a lie as the hole her grandmother had left felt too large to fill. More than ever, Effie craved her grandmother's advice to reassure her that she was making the right decision.

Chapter Twenty-Seven

Two weeks after her engagement, the sound of the harbour bell cut into Effie's troubled sleep. At first, the frantic clanging, accompanied by shouting, made no sense but when she understood what she was hearing her blood froze.

The bell was only rung in times of great need. It must mean a shipwreck. Every able-bodied man in the village would be scrambling to dress and come to the harbour to see what was occurring. Effie hurriedly pulled her clothes on.

'Mama is going to help,' she told Jack and Morna as she buttoned her skirt. 'Stay in your beds until I come back and go to sleep. Do not leave the house.'

Morna nodded seriously. 'Yes, Mama.'

She felt a slight misgiving, but the fire in the stove was damped down to a glow and there was no danger as long as the children stayed in bed. Rain was hammering on the roof. Effie pulled on John's overcoat and set out. By the time she reached the harbour, oil lamp in hand, a crowd was gathering.

'What's happening?' she asked the nearest man.

'We heard distress whistles out by the Brigg and saw lights.'

Effie stared out to sea where a flicker of light appeared and vanished. It was too low to be a star. Someone was indeed out on the Brigg.

A cry from the harbour made her turn. The small lifeboat was trying to leave the harbour but was being pushed back time and time again. Men dressed in oilskin coats and hats were fighting to keep their positions at the oars. The sky exploded with thunder, and cracks of lightning speared the horizon almost simultaneously. The storm was directly upon them. The rain increased in ferocity and began to hammer down.

The man Effie had spoken to had started to move away and was now grabbing ropes to help manually haul the lifeboat out beyond the wall. The previously tense, almost silent atmosphere became a swirling mass of bodies and voices as the ship was pushed further out into the water. The men sang as they rowed to keep the rhythm and to raise their spirits. Effie peered into the darkness towards the Brigg where a tiny light bobbed up and down. Did the voices stretch over the way that far, and could any men hear their rescuers approaching? All the women could do was wait, hoping and praying that the men in the lifeboat would return safely bearing survivors. They were wives and mothers of seafaring men and would never return home until they knew the fate of the vessel.

One woman lit a fire and another brought a cauldron. The innkeeper sent down a bottle of brandy and a cask of wine to prepare a hot, blood-warming drink in anticipation of the return.

The light from the lifeboat crew grew smaller and fainter

and the women stood along the shore with lanterns raised to light the way. One gave a sudden cry.

'There is somebody in the water, look!'

She swung her lantern wide, illuminating a circle of beach. She was right; someone was in the sea – a darker, opaque shape against the translucent grey sea. It was not a survivor, however, but appeared to be someone attempting to swim out.

Other women rushed to look, also holding their lanterns aloft.

'There is no one there. You must have imagined it,' one said.

'No one could survive this sea, it would be madness to try,' agreed another.

The first woman lowered her lantern. 'I'm sure,' she muttered.

'Bring your lantern over here where it's needed.'

An older woman gripped her by the hand and led her away.

Effie knew without a second glance who it had been. No man but Lachlan would dare to attempt something so dangerous, but no man other than Lachlan was as skilled at swimming. She stood alone after the other women had gone. Without a lantern she would never see out to the sea but when the next bolt of lightning split the sky she was certain she spotted a small figure disappearing beneath the crest of a wave.

Effie would never be sure how long the wait lasted. On some rememberings it felt compressed into mere minutes, on others it stretched for hours. What she knew was that at some point the women began to grow weary and cold. They took turns standing with the lanterns on the harbour wall or standing by the fires which had been lit and singing a mixture

319

of hymns and shanties. It was an oddly companionable way to spend the night given how grave the situation was. Effie was keeping watch on the harbour when the faint lights from the lifeboat began to grow closer. The boat was returning.

The atmosphere grew tense once more as the women waited to discover if there had been any success. The waves were crashing and it took three attempts for the boat to safely make harbour. As soon as it did a cry went up.

'Three survivors. Three here.' The captain of the lifeboat was jubilant. Women rushed forwards with blankets and mugs of hot toddy ready to welcome the survivors and the rescuers.

The priority was to get the survivors warm and dry, but as they huddled around the brazier sipping from their mugs, the story emerged. The vessel had been dashed close to the Brigg and capsized, trapping the men underneath.

'I thought I was done for,' said one of the men, shivering at the memory. 'I couldn't feel my hands or feet to grip any longer and I knew I had only seconds left before I had to breathe in, even though I knew it would mean filling my lungs with seawater. I am fortunate that one of my companions pulled me free and breathed into my mouth with his own to give me air. He towed me to the rocks where I could clamber up.'

He looked at his companions who were huddled together listening with rapt expressions.

'Whichever one of you it was, I owe you my life.'

'Not me.'

'Nor I,' said the third. 'Matter of fact, something similar happened to me. I'd just given up hope and my hands slipped free when it was as though I was floating on a solid shape up until I could grasp the prow of the ship. I thought it was one of you two. Was one of you fine men from the lifeboat our rescuer?'

The men and bystanders looked around in puzzlement.

'Not any of us,' said the captain of the lifeboat. 'We found all three of you clinging to the rocks or driftwood.'

'Well somebody must have done it,' insisted the first man brusquely. 'If you're ashamed of having put your lips to another man's, there's no need to be. I'll not hold it against you.'

But still no one admitted to being the mysterious rescuer. It would for ever remain a mystery and most of the villagers were inclined to believe that in their desperation and confusion the men had imagined it.

Only Effie, standing slightly back from the fire, suspected there was truth in their words. No longer needed, she slipped away unnoticed.

The children were asleep when she tiptoed back inside the bedroom. She stood over them and stared down, caught by indecision. She had told them she would be back soon, but from experience she knew they would stay asleep until morning.

She had to know the answer to the burning question inside her. She crept out again and pulled the door to.

The winds were still fierce but the clouds were parting and a sliver of moon gave her just enough light to see her way along the beach. There was a light in Lachlan's hut and his silhouette passed in front of the window.

Effie's stomach writhed with nervousness. He might not welcome her here, but nevertheless she had to see him. She tapped softly on the door, then lifted the latch and went in.

Lachlan stood in front of the grate where a small fire was

beginning to catch. He was naked, save for his skin which was draped around his shoulders.

'I'm sorry! I didn't realise!' Effie quickly averted her eyes. Even though she had seen his naked form time after time, the sight took her by surprise.

Lachlan adjusted his skin into a more modest arrangement around his lower body, then took a step towards her, coming into the firelight. Shadows played over his face and body, flickering on and off, making it seem as though the spirals and whorls etched into his flesh and skin were dancing.

'Why have you come here?'

His voice was tinged with suspicion. Effie raised her eyes to meet his.

'The men say unseen hands lifted them from the wreckage and someone breathed air into their lungs. It was you, wasn't it?'

He held her gaze for a long time. Effie looked back undaunted, trying to read the emotion on his face. There was the customary wariness that she had come to expect since their estrangement, but also something that might have been pride. Eventually he nodded.

'Aye.'

'They are confused and each viewing another as his saviour. Why don't you come forward and tell them it was you?'

'What does it matter who saved them? The fact is they are safe.'

'But you are a hero and nobody knows,' Effie protested.

Lachlan folded his arms. 'Nobody needs to know. I didn't do it for recognition. I did it because those lives needed saving.' A shadow fell across his face. 'My kind have always helped seafaring folk in times of need.'

'Thank you,' Effie said.

Lachlan raised an eyebrow. 'Do you know these men?'

Effie shook her head. 'No. But I thank you all the same.'

He cocked his head to one side. 'What for?'

'For saving them and for proving me wrong.'

She walked closer to him. The harsh words of their argument still hung between them but Effie was finding it increasingly hard to keep her resentment alive.

'I owe you an apology, Lachlan. The things I said were terrible and unfounded. I beg your forgiveness.'

He didn't try to brush off her apology or dismiss the hurt she had caused him and for that she was thankful. Tears welled in her eyes.

'They weren't unfounded. What we did was monstrous. I allowed my grief and anger to take control of my sense. You accused me of having no remorse but I do. There is no justification for what we did.'

'Would you have done it if you had been alone?' Effie asked.

Lachlan dropped his head. 'I don't think so. It was our combined grief that spurred us on. I would not think to slaughter a ship full of men when I am in human form and I should not have done it in my other. I can never make recompense for the lives that were lost.'

'But the lives you saved tonight…' Effie said.

He shook his head. 'They still don't bring back the dead. I cannot return your husband to you.'

Effie felt the bite of hypocrisy: sharp teeth tearing into her with the knowledge that she did not want John back even if she could have had him. They had been brought together by their attraction but bound together by the consequences.

Everything that had taken place since would not have happened if that double tragedy had not occurred.

'I'm so sorry for what John's ship did to Lileas. When I think what she must have suffered I can't bear it. The sailors were wrong to hunt her.'

Lachlan inclined his head. 'Aye. But it is the way of the world.'

'It shouldn't be,' Effie insisted.

Lachlan stood a little way from her, and through her tear-blurred eyes Effie could tell he was tense; his frame rigid and ready to move. Whether towards her or away, she could not tell. Their bodies weren't touching, but still Effie imagined she could feel heat spreading from his body to hers. She wiped the back of her hand across her face, smearing tears down her cheek. She had not fully appreciated until this moment how much she had missed him. How much she cared for him.

'I can go if you like.'

'No, stay please.' Lachlan reached out a hand then lowered it. He rubbed his eyes with his fingertips. He must be exhausted after what he had done.

'What do you want from me?' he asked.

At last she knew the answer to that.

'Just hold me.'

'I can do that, lass.'

He put his arm around her shoulders and drew her to his side. Effie leaned in, letting her body melt against him. The curvature of his body was instantly familiar. Comforting and at the same time arousing. She rested her head against the hollow of his shoulder and cried. How many of her tears were for Alice, how many for John, and how many for the conflict that had torn her and Lachlan asunder, she wasn't sure.

Lachlan didn't speak. He simply held her tightly and let her spend her sorrow on his chest.

'Thank you,' she mumbled eventually.

'It's nothing, lass,' Lachlan said.

'It's everything,' Effie replied.

Lachlan took her face between his hands and wiped her tears away with his thumbs. 'You are stronger than you think, just as Alice told you.'

Effie blinked in surprise. Alice's words had been whispered. Lachlan's hearing was much sharper than she had realised.

'I'm truly sorry for your loss, Effie. Your grandmother was a rare woman. Her kind is vanishing.'

'Thank you for the song you sang,' Effie said. 'It was beautiful. It made Alice very happy.'

For a moment they held each other and said nothing. She studied him out of the corner of her eye. He had not needed to come and find her on the beach after Alice's passing. He had said goodbye to Alice, and done it in the gentlest, kindest way possible. He had owed Effie nothing. And yet he had come. That was the true nature of the man she had grown to love.

He ran his hands over her arms and shoulders, down her back then held her away from him and looked her up and down. He wound a tendril of her hair around his fingers.

'You're soaking wet.'

She glanced down at herself. The rain had penetrated the thick coat and now that she gave it her attention, she could feel her skirts heavy with water that had soaked in.

'You're dry,' she answered, lifting her hand and brushing her fingertips over his dark locks.

'Aye. And warmer than you, I'll wager. We can change that easily enough, though.'

He slipped his arms inside her coat and eased it off her, letting it drop to the floor. He pulled her back into his arms, enfolding her in his embrace. Effie caught the scent of the ocean on his body, mingling with the warm muskiness of the skin that was wrapped about his waist. She lifted her face and kissed the soft hollow above his collarbone. His arms tightened and his frame grew rigid. The spot was one she knew drove him wild when she applied the slightest pressure. She kissed him again, more firmly, allowing her front teeth to scrape against the bone.

A growl erupted from Lachlan's throat and before Effie could take a breath he had bent forward and found her mouth. He kissed her fiercely. She seized the back of his neck and head, pulling him closer, hungrily pushing her tongue against his. His hands went to her waist and she felt the tugging as he loosened the ties of her skirt, which joined the coat in a heap. Effie let her hands glide down the smoothness of his back until they met the luxuriant richness of the skin at his waist.

Still with his mouth on hers, Lachlan lifted her off her feet and carried her to the narrow bed. He laid her down, never taking his eyes from hers, and removed the last remaining items of her clothing. When she was as naked as he was, he stretched out atop her and wrapped his arms and legs around her. He pulled his skin from around his waist and threw it over the top of them both.

Effie wound her arms around his neck and dragged him down until his lips met hers once again, holding him with the same urgency with which the drowning fisherman would have clung onto the wreckage. Her need was just as desperate as theirs had been. She raked her hands down his back, fingernails teasingly scraping his flesh and causing him to moan. He buried his head against her throat. Effie's head swam as his mouth teased her senses awake, hot and hard against the tender flesh of her earlobe.

She bucked as his hand closed over the fullness of her breast. She felt ready to burst. Fruit ready for devouring.

Their coupling was urgent. Frantic with the need to bury the pain of their quarrel forever. Afterwards they lay in a tangled knot beneath Lachlan's skin while the tide of ecstasy that had washed over Effie diminished into smaller ripples until finally her senses were calm once again.

'The children,' she murmured.

'They're safely sleeping,' Lachlan answered, nuzzling his lips against her shoulder. 'I'll know if that changes.'

Effie closed her eyes, content that his connection to Morna would alert him to anything amiss.

They made love again but this time it was different; slow and intense. Lachlan took his time, worshipping every part of Effie's body with a thoroughness that left her weak and passive.

Afterwards, Lachlan wrapped himself around Effie from behind, fitting around the shape of her and pressing his head into the nape of her neck. He held her tightly while they slept.

It was only later, when Effie awoke from a deep dreamless slumber, that she came to understand Lachlan's intensity.

It was still dark outside but there was a faint mauve tinge to the edge of the blackness which suggested dawn was not far off. Lachlan was sitting on the edge of the bed. He was already dressed.

'Good morning,' Effie sighed, stretching her arms out and giving him a lazy smile.

'Good morning. Effie, you need to go now.'

He sounded grave. She sat up and clutched the bedsheet.

'Is something the matter? The children?'

'The children are fine.' Lachlan gave Effie a sidelong look. 'What's wrong is that you're engaged to another man yet you spent last night in my bed.'

Walter! Effie had completely forgotten his existence in her passion. She cringed inside.

'You know? But I asked Walter to keep it a secret.'

'Morna told me. She is so excited at the thought she might be a flower girl.'

'I'm sorry. I wanted to tell you myself when the time was right.' Effie covered her face with her hands and gave a loud groan. 'How could I have done something so dishonourable? Lachlan, what must you think of me?'

'It doesna' matter, lass. We did what we did, and there were good reasons for it. But it cannot happen again. It won't happen again.' Lachlan leaned over and pried her hands from her face. His eyes were bleak. 'I had a long time to think while you slept and I've made a decision. When the year changes on Midwinter's Day I am returning home, and I'm not coming back.'

Chapter Twenty-Eight

Effie knelt up. The hut was cold now the fire had died to embers overnight and her skin prickled with raised bumps, but she ignored them.

'Don't go!'

Lachlan narrowed his eyes. 'You would have me stay?' He gestured at the bed. 'What sort of marriage vows do you intend to make?'

'I won't marry him.' Effie blurted out her reply without even considering it. Losing Lachlan now they had reunited was more than she could bear to contemplate.

Lachlan dropped his head. 'I think you should.'

Effie slumped back, shocked beyond belief.

'You want me to marry Walter?'

Lachlan's expression was tragic. 'I didna' say I want it. But it makes sense. As I said before, he'll offer you a good life. A respectable life.'

He'd called Walter a man, too, she remembered. She flushed at the memory of the taunt he was aiming at himself as much as at her.

'But you said those things when we were fighting. You didn't mean them,' Effie answered.

'Perhaps I didn't, but they're true. He's wealthy and ambitious and intelligent. Not as intelligent as you, but that's probably no bad thing for a husband to be. With you at his side he'll accomplish more than he would without.'

'Is that a reason to marry him?'

Lachlan shrugged. 'Only you can answer that. You must have had your reasons for accepting.'

Effie's heart plummeted. She wanted him to fight for her. To tell her not to marry Walter. To be angry or hurt. But he wasn't going to do any of those things and it broke her heart to realise it.

'Walter will give you the life you deserve. A life I couldna' give you.'

'Do you even want to give me a life?' Effie asked bitterly. 'You've never said so. You never asked me to live with you or marry you.'

'How could I?' Lachlan spread his arms wide and looked around. 'What could I offer you? A cottage on a remote island with barely any company of your own kind. A half-life here waiting for me to come and go when the year turns? You deserve more than that!'

'But what about what I want? I'm used to waiting.'

'You say that now, but what about if things changed between us?' His eyes flashed black. 'Effie, you know I want you. If you don't know I want to be with you, that is my fault. But what would be the point of telling you that and making us both dream of the impossible? Would you give up your life here to live amongst my people?' Effie shook her head dumbly. She had thought about it time after time but Lachlan had never spoken of it. Oh, he'd mentioned travelling or visiting, but only in passing.

'I don't know. Perhaps I would. Or you could stay.'

He shook his head. 'I don't belong here.'

'I often think I don't either,' Effie replied. 'I don't fit into the top of the village nor the bottom.'

'But you could. If you marry Walter, you will. I'm not strong enough to bear witness to that though, so I must leave.'

He stood and walked to the hearth, head bowed. Effie reached down the side of the bed and found her discarded shift and drawers and pulled them on. She crossed the room, but, as she drew near, Lachlan turned and held out a hand in warning. She stopped abruptly.

'Lachlan, it can't be like this.'

Her voice was thin and high. She could hear tears in the tone, swimming to the surface, and wondered if Lachlan could too. He reached out and put a finger to her lips. The touch made her quiver.

'It can't be any other way. Not really. I never meant to stay and I didn't intend for this – for us – to happen.' He gave a sad smile. 'It doesn't matter. You've accepted Walter and that is as it should be. You'll be happy with him. He's a good man and he cares for you.'

Effie bit back a sob. Walter did care for her and she cared for him, but the strength of her feelings would forever be the moon's reflection to the adoration of Lachlan's sun.

Her clothes were hanging on a wooden rail with her clogs neatly beneath. Lachlan must have put them there after she had fallen asleep. She took them down and dressed. She didn't bother to fix her hair up, but let it hang loose.

She opened her arms to caress Lachlan. He stepped away, holding her at arm's length and fixed her with a stern gaze.

'No,' he said firmly. 'I canna do that. You're to be another man's wife and I have more honour than to give in to that temptation again. I think you have more honour too, Effie.'

She swallowed the lump that was filling her throat.

'Then this is how it must be,' she whispered.

'Aye. This is how it must be.'

There was a catch to his voice and his expression was of pure misery.

Effie bunched her hands in her skirts to stop them trembling.

'I'm sorry.'

'Don't be.' Lachlan took her by the arm and escorted her to the door. Icy air stung her throat and skin.

'Don't be sorry. Be happy. And knowing that you are, I can be also.'

She nodded and walked home.

Effie managed to regain her composure by the time she reached her cottage. She crept into the bedroom. Jack and Morna were still asleep. Jack lay on his back, legs and arms sprawled out and his mouth open. Morna was curled around her ragdoll. Her hair stuck out around her like a shadow dandelion clock. At the sight of her, Effie's knees went weak. Walter had already said he would expect Lachlan to take responsibility for Morna, but whenever Effie had thought of it, she had envisioned the two of them living in Allendale Head, either in Lachlan's hut or in Effie's cottage. Lachlan hadn't mentioned Morna when he had told her of his intention to go. It was devastating enough to think of him leaving, but would he want to take Morna with him?

She crept out of the room and built up the fire for the day ahead. The pan of water she had placed on the top of the stove the night before was lukewarm so she loosened her clothing and washed. When the sky grew light she returned to the bedroom and gently shook the children awake. Jack clung to her neck, pulling her down towards him in a hearty hug. He was getting heavier, but any sign of affection was welcome. She held his face firmly between her hands and peered into his eyes.

'Good morning, Jack.'

He mouthed a babbling greeting. Morna sat up and rubbed her eyes.

'Mama, are the men safe?'

Effie brushed Morna's hair back from her cheeks. 'From last night? Yes, they are.'

Morna considered it, which involved pouting and looking down her nose at her lips. 'Dada saved them, didn't he?'

'Yes, he did.' Effie squatted down beside Morna's bed. 'You're clever to know that.'

'I'm very clever.' Morna grinned. She peered at Effie. 'You and Dada are friends again, aren't you?'

Effie blinked, wondering if Morna had smelled the traces of Lachlan on her skin. The quick wash hadn't been as thorough as she would usually manage. The thought that a child might be able to sense the lingering scent of Lachlan's lovemaking was unsettling to say the least. She decided not to ask how Morna knew this and just gave Morna a hug.

'Yes we are. Now, we need to get dressed. It's time for breakfast.'

333

Lachlan appeared at the cottage at midday. He stood on the doorstep and, though he greeted Effie by wishing her a good day, his eyes spoke elegies; telling of the closeness they had shared the night before. Hot pitch filled Effie's veins. Whatever else happened in the future, she would never lose those precious memories. She was determined that they would part as friends.

For the first time in weeks, Effie invited him in. He came, though he refused the offer of a drink despite Effie's assurances there would be no obligation asked of him. Morna had been sitting by the fire, dressing her doll in the outfits Effie had sewn. When Lachlan arrived, she abandoned Lucy-May in a state of indecent undress and rushed up to Lachlan. She clung to his leg.

'I missed you.'

Lachlan prised her hands free. 'I missed you too, even though I only saw you yesterday. Why did you miss me?'

She gazed up at him solemnly. 'Because the waves were too big and loud last night. You went a long way.'

Lachlan looked at Effie over the top of Morna's head. For a moment his eyes welled with desire; the pupils black and larger than seemed natural. He blinked and the fleeting lust was gone.

'Did you tell her?'

'No. She knew by herself. Is that something you can do?'

'Aye, at times. With family or those we're very close to we have intuition. She often knows when you are almost at the hut to collect her.'

Effie's eyes pricked. Morna was not her daughter. She had no claim of birth or legality. Only of love.

'Can you do it over a long distance?' Her voice was gruff with sorrow.

He nodded and pressed his lips tightly together. 'Aye. I'm not sure how far. Why do you ask?'

Effie dropped beside Morna. 'Go and find your skin and wrap up warmly.'

She waited until Morna raced off into the bedroom, then stood and faced Lachlan once more.

'This morning when you told me you were leaving you didn't mention Morna. But you're going to…' Effie tailed off, the lump in her throat too big to allow her to finish.

Lachlan's mouth twisted downwards and his brow creased. 'I have always been planning to take her to see where she is from.'

'But now you will both go and neither of you will come back.'

Lachlan's expression answered her. At first she thought he was just going to avoid answering, but, unexpectedly, he went over to Effie and held her hand tightly.

'I have taken Effie Cropton's time and effort for long enough. I have no claim on the time or goodwill of Mrs Walter Danby, and certainly not of her husband.'

'Did Walter speak to you?' Effie asked.

'No. The decision is mine, though that suggests your future husband is in agreement with me. He doesna' want to be rearing another man's child.'

Effie shook her head. There was no reason why Walter should, but it felt unjust, and in turn she felt unkindly towards him.

'When will you tell her?'

It was already December and there was barely any time left before Lachlan was planning to leave.

'I think today would be best. As soon as possible. I want to give her time to get used to the idea.'

'Please let me be there when you do,' Effie said. She gave a sudden sob that came out of nowhere and covered her mouth with the back of her hand. She raised her eyes to see nothing but sympathy in Lachlan's eyes.

'I knew she would leave at some point but I didn't expect it to be so soon or this way. I'm going to miss her so much. Both of you.'

Lachlan turned his head away from her. His jaw tightened.

'I know. It willna' be easy for any of us but this is how it has to be.'

'What willna be easy?'

Both Effie and Lachlan started at the sound of Morna's voice. She was standing in the doorway to the bedroom, clutching her skin in front of her. Her eyes were wide. Effie and Lachlan exchanged a glance of dismay. She had appeared so quietly without them noticing. Lachlan raised a questioning eyebrow. Effie replied with the tiniest nod of her head. Nausea filled her throat and belly, constricted her chest.

Lachlan pulled out a chair and sat down. He beckoned Morna over and drew her onto his knee. He looked at Effie over her head and his eyes grew bright. He turned Morna round to face him.

'I am going to go back to Scotland on Midwinter's Day and I want to take you with me.'

Morna wrinkled her brow. 'But I don't want to. I live here. You come and go. I stay here and wait for you. That's what happens. I want to swim now.'

She wriggled free and jumped off Lachlan's knee, as if that was the end of it. Lachlan caught hold of her pinafore ribbon and held her back.

'Morna, you know that your mama is going to marry Mr Danby?'

Morna nodded. 'I want her to wear blue. He thinks she will look better in yellow. He's wrong.'

'Aye, he's wrong,' Lachlan agreed, casting a sideways look at Effie, who frowned. 'Your mama looks much better in blue. Her hair is yellow enough to cause a cornfield envy. But the fact is, your mama is marrying him.'

Morna looked confused. Lachlan raised his eyes to Effie. She sat on the chair beside Lachlan.

'Morna, your dada is being very thoughtful. I will be very busy arranging my marriage and it will be very dull for you, so he… we thought you might like to go to where he is from. You can see what the sea looks like there and meet other people like you.'

'There are more people like me? Like Dada?'

Morna's eyes grew wide. Effie took her hand. 'Of course. And you should know who they are.'

'Then yes, I will. We'll be back by Midsummer's Day. Promise me you won't get married sooner or Dada and me will miss it.'

'I promise.'

Effie gave Morna a hug, then released her. Morna skipped happily to the bedroom.

'Jack, Jack! I'm going to go and see the Selkies with Dada.'

Effie put her head in her hands. She felt Lachlan's hand on her shoulder and raised her head. He was wearing a sad smile.

'I fear that I will never be as skilled at understanding her as you. She's happy now, even if she does think she's coming back.'

Effie frowned. 'She's happy *because* she thinks she's coming back. When she learns the truth she might change her feelings.'

'She might, but that's a worry for another time. I'll take her out now.'

He called Morna, who came running out of the bedroom with Jack following her as usual. She kissed Effie and grabbed her skin then went outside, followed by Lachlan. A moment later the door slammed open and she reappeared. She ran up to Effie and clutched her tightly.

'I love you, Mama.'

She lifted her head and kissed Effie's waist, then ran off again.

Effie sat back down and wept.

Chapter Twenty-Nine

T he weather for the next week was much more settled. The sea still raged, but the wind stopped pushing the biting chill in towards land, and the sky was often vivid blue and cloudless. On the afternoon of the nineteenth, Effie accepted an invitation to join Walter on a walk. Lachlan took both Jack and Morna to play, leaving her free.

She felt his eyes on her as she left the cottage and wondered whether he had noticed how carefully she had bound up her hair in a fashionable knot and how she wore her good coat instead of her usual cloak. Walter was so well dressed that Effie had begun to feel self-conscious of her habitual low-plaited knot.

She met Walter at the top of Harbour Hill and walked beside him along the path from the top of the village along the cliff, but as soon as they left Allendale Head behind them he linked his arm through hers and kissed her cheek. If Lachlan had not noticed Effie's new style, Walter did at least. He beamed with approval.

'You need earrings to show off your neck if you are going to wear your hair high more often. I should buy you a pair when next I am in Whitby.'

'Thank you, but I don't have the occasion to wear them.'

'You will. Besides, it will give me pleasure to buy things for you now you're my fiancée. You wouldn't deny me that, would you?'

'Of course not,' Effie agreed, somewhat reluctantly. Aside from her thin gold wedding band from John, she had never owned jewellery. Earrings were not the only thing she had been promised. Mrs Danby had talked of a trousseau over morning coffee and when Effie had looked worried, Walter had told her privately that a trip to the dressmaker's in York would be a gift from him to her.

'You will see I have already begun to make improvements to Beacon House.'

Effie had not been alone with Walter since the night of the shipwreck. They had either been accompanied by the children or sitting with Walter's parents taking afternoon tea. Now she had the opportunity to speak with him privately, she could no longer put off the matter of Morna. She took a couple of deep breaths before beginning.

'I have spoken to Lachlan about our engagement. He intends to leave on Midwinter's Day.'

'So soon? That's only two days away.'

Effie bit her lip, acutely aware of how soon Lachlan and Morna's departure was. She tried to ignore the joy in Walter's voice, but it struck her deeply. The two men had never liked each other and now Walter had won Effie.

'And what of his daughter?' Walter asked, completely unaware of Effie's annoyance.

'She will go with him. For a visit at first.'

'But he might return her here?' Walter asked.

'I don't know,' Effie snapped. Walter raised his brows. She rubbed her eyes.

'I don't know if he will bring her back. Walter, can't you see this is upsetting for me? I have cared for Morna for years and now I'm losing her.'

Walter put his arms round her. 'I'm sorry, my dearest. I wasn't considering your sentimental feelings. Come, let me show you the progress on our home. That will cheer your spirits.'

He tucked Effie's arm under his and walked at a brisk pace to the iron gates, talking all the time of what he intended to do. Effie only half listened as she concentrated on gaining command of her emotions. It wasn't Walter's fault that he had no understanding of what Morna's departure would mean to her, nor that he treated Effie like a child he hoped to distract with the promise of a new toy to replace the one she had lost.

Most of the work on Beacon House seemed to have been carried out on the gardens. Where previously there had been tangles of brambles and bracken, a path had now been revealed, leading down to a newly scrubbed stone fountain. It could almost merit the description of being a lawn.

'I thought we might be able to have parties here in spring. You could sit here and paint.'

'That would be lovely,' Effie agreed. 'I have finished all my seaweeds for your friend in Manchester. I wonder if he would be interested in native garden flowers?'

Walter waved a hand airily. 'You may paint as many flowers as you like without troubling yourself over that. I don't expect my wife to work.'

'But really, it is hardly work. I enjoy it.'

Walter took her hand and patted it. 'That isn't the point. I won't ever have it said my wife needed to bring a single shilling to our marriage. I mean to support you entirely.'

'That's very kind,' Effie replied. She kept to herself the thought that not having to paint would give her more time to prepare the ointment and tinctures Alice had taught her. She suspected that if Walter did not approve of his wife earning a living, he would be doubly unhappy with the thought of her working as a part-time wisewoman!

Walter walked her towards the house. 'My grandmother had her rooms in the left wing, but I always thought the aspect from the right one was more favourable. The corner windows mean that on a clear day you can see the coast bending around over the Brigg. I would suggest our bedrooms are on that side.'

He actually blushed as he mentioned bedrooms. Effie wondered whether he intended for them to have one each or share. She and John had never had the luxury of separate rooms and when Lachlan had shared her bed she had wanted him close by.

'I think that sounds lovely. Jack could have his bedroom in the left wing where he would be able to overlook the garden. He loves birds so we could set up feeding tables on the lawn for him to look at and draw.'

'Hmm.' Walter sounded non-committal.

'If you don't want bird tables perhaps a fountain,' Effie said. 'Or do you mean you would prefer Jack's room to be in another area?'

Walter faced her and took both her hands. 'Effie, as you know, I have concerns about Jack's capacity. I asked my father to make enquiries on our behalf and he has found a most excellent institution where he believes your son will be very happy.'

'I didn't ask for you to do anything on my behalf. And

what sort of institution?' Effie pulled her hands free. She clenched her fists, feeling anxiety pushing up inside her. 'Why would Jack need to live in an institution? We will be perfectly capable of looking after him here. He really is no trouble.'

'He's no trouble now.' Walter reached for Effie's hands again but she folded her arms firmly across her chest. A flicker of annoyance crossed Walter's face.

'As he grows older he may become volatile or more unmanageable. Yes, he is happy now weaving nets and scrawling birds but with proper care and treatment he might become someone who does not depend on others for his every need.'

'What sort of treatment?' Effie asked. She shuddered, recalling descriptions of the poor souls in asylums subjected to iced-water baths or restrained in buckled garments. The very thought made her want to run to Jack and hug him tightly. 'I won't let anyone lock him up or hose him down.'

'Of course not; those methods are barbaric. There are much more scientific treatments now. Application of electricity to the skull, for example, has been proved highly effective in regulating fits in patients.'

'No!' Effie swept away down the path in horror. 'I will not let that happen to Jack. How can you even suggest such a thing? He doesn't have fits.'

Walter followed her. 'It is just one suggestion to consider. You are becoming overwrought.'

'Perhaps you should apply voltage to my head and see if that helps!' Effie exclaimed.

Walter jumped back as if she had done that very thing to him.

'I... but... The science is very clear.'

'I do not care about the science. I will not discuss this any further. I'm going home.'

She headed for the gate. Walter ran around and stopped in front of her, blocking her exit.

'No, we will not part with an argument. If my words or suggestions distressed you, I must apologise. This is not a decision which needs to be agreed upon now. Come, let us be friends.'

He stepped to Effie and engulfed her in his arms, holding her head to his shoulder with one hand while stroking her hair. She allowed herself to be held until her trembling ceased, taking deep breaths and inhaling the scent of Walter's cologne; floral with a touch of spice that made her think of exotic bazaars and *Arabian Nights*. Walter loosened his embrace and held her back at arm's length.

'Now that's better. You are happy again. I shall stay here a little longer as I wish to make some notes of the rooms. Will you be safe going along the coast path alone?'

Effie assured him that no harm would come to her in the short walk back. He kissed her and allowed her to leave. Around the bend in the path, out of view of the garden she sat on a rock and put her head in her hands. The shock of Walter's suggestion had completely upset her equilibrium. Not only for the suggestion itself but that Walter even considered it a possibility. It was so out of character for him to be in favour of anything violent. Surely if electricity could power lights, it must be harmful to the human body. If this was modern medicine, she was right to put her trust in Alice's remedies.

She started shaking again. Walter had said there was no need for an agreement at present, which suggested he hoped Effie would reach his way of thinking eventually. She never would. Though the sky was clear, it was too cold to be sitting on an exposed clifftop. Glancing back, she noticed the chimneys of Beacon House over the treetops and for the first time she considered whether Jack would like to live there. He loved the sea and beach. Morna had told Effie and Lachlan she did not want to live in the house, but Jack could not express his desires.

She should end the engagement right now. Then there would be no danger of Jack being forced into an institution or being subjected to medical procedures. She was halfway to her feet when she thought again. If she broke off the engagement then she would remain living in the cottage, sharing her bedroom with a growing boy who would become a man. He would become harder to manage – Walter was correct about that – but there would be no one to help her. Both their lives would be difficult and miserable. That was no solution.

A pair of gulls circled overhead, screeching, before flying out over the sea and along the coast. The solution came to her instantly. Morna had been granted her wish not to live in Beacon House, albeit in a way that devastated Effie. She knew now how to ensure Jack would have a future of happiness and freedom. She clambered to her feet and made her way straight down through the village and along the beach to Boggle Cove.

Jack was sitting on the shore outside Lachlan's hut when Effie arrived, snugly wrapped in a blanket. Lachlan and Morna were nowhere to be seen. Jack acknowledged her arrival with a beaming smile, showing the gap in his front teeth. He had made a collection of pebbles and rocks and lined them up in an order that made sense only to him. Effie sat beside him and hugged him tightly. He tolerated her for a short while then wriggled free and returned to his collection, getting up to potter about the shore in search of more exhibits for his collection. Effie closed her eyes. She had sat in this place so many times and felt her heart was overflowing with joy. Now it was tinged with sadness and foreshadowed loss. Once Lachlan and Morna left she vowed she would never return to Boggle Cove.

Effie was consumed by these dark thoughts and Jack was throwing his pebbles into the sea when he gave a loud squeal of glee. Effie jerked her head up in time to see two dark shapes rolling through the waves in the distance. She scrambled to her feet and ran to his side just in time to see the seals resurface and dive down again. Her heart leaped.

Lachlan and Morna.

Instantly she was transported back to the balmy evening in late summer when she had swum with Lachlan in his human form. She screamed his name before she could stop herself, rushing to the edge of the water so the foam lapped at her feet. She didn't imagine he could have heard her over the waves, but the two creatures rose up again and bobbed, heads out of the water, looking towards the shore. They disappeared from view before resurfacing further from shore, the larger seal in front and the smaller following. Tears sprang to her eyes as she watched father and daughter swimming together. Effie hugged Jack who pointed and gave a high-pitched laugh of pleasure. At that moment, Effie knew that what she had been considering was the only possible solution to the problem of Jack.

Before too much longer had passed, Lachlan and Morna appeared from around the curve of the beach, walking hand in hand. They were both dressed in their skins alone. Morna ran up to Effie and hugged her.

'We saw you, Mama. Did you see me?'

'I did, chick.' Effie bent to tuck the skin snugly around Morna. She wanted to bury her head in it and hold the child close. 'Go inside and get dressed before you catch your death of cold.'

She sent the girl off with a gentle push in the small of her back. Morna was all legs and arms as she raced barefoot across the beach. Lachlan strode over to Effie. He took her by the shoulders and started to pull her closer as if he was going to embrace her, clearly thought better and pulled away.

'I heard you calling my name. What's wrong?'

He was damp, hair slicked against his head, giving him a sleek profile. Droplets of seawater glistened on his naked chest, but Effie would gladly have buried her face against it, however damp she might become as a result.

'I want you to take Jack when you leave.'

'To visit?'

She shook her head and swallowed.

'To stay.'

Lachlan looked astonished.

'You want to send your son away?'

'No!' Effie's eyes welled up as the recollection of the horrible conversation with Walter reared up again. 'I don't want him to go, but this is no place for him. He doesn't belong in this world. He doesn't understand it and I won't have him put into an institution.'

Now Lachlan did embrace her. Wrapping his arms securely about her and pressing his head against hers, he held her close. He was a rock, steadfast and safe. She breathed in the scent of the sea and his warm, clean skin.

'You don't have to put him in an institution,' he murmured. 'Who on earth said you do?'

Effie buried her head against his neck.

'Walter,' Lachlan muttered, his voice thick with contempt.

He released Effie from his arms, as if the mention of her fiancé reminded him of the barrier that should be between them.

Effie nodded. 'He says we can't look after Jack as well as he deserves. That there are places where people like him belong, which are better for him to live in.'

'And do you agree?' Lachlan asked quietly.

'Of course I don't!' Effie whipped her head up, furious until she recognised it was not Lachlan who deserved her anger. 'Not about the institution, but perhaps I can't take care of his needs when he grows. That's why I want you to take him. He trusts you and he knows you. Moreover, Morna brings something out in him that no one else does.'

She glanced over to where Jack was sitting by the door of the hut, waiting for Morna to reappear. He had picked up a piece of wood and was scratching it smooth with his thumbnail with a look of intense concentration on his face. She thought of all the arguments she had conceived as she had been waiting and coming to the decision.

'He's learned to do so much already since you've been here. He needs a father who will understand him. He will be useful, I promise. Besides, to tear him from Morna would be simply cruel. You told me that when you were trying to persuade me to keep looking after her years ago.'

Lachlan looked wary. 'I did, that's true.'

Effie sensed he was growing convinced. She reached for his hands. He resisted for only the briefest moment before his touch became warm. Her skin fluttered and danced. She was making a mistake by letting him leave.

'Please,' she entreated. 'In all the years we've known each other I have asked very little of you. Now I am asking you to care for my son as I have cared for your daughter. You owe me that.'

348

'I owe you nothing. We agreed and I paid you with a pearl every six months,' Lachlan reminded her.

'And I can return all but one to you. I've kept them all safe.' Effie pulled her coat tighter around her. The sun was sinking and the air was growing colder. 'It is the only obligation I will ever put you under.'

Lachlan's fingers tightened around Effie's hands and his eyes narrowed.

'The only obligation you ask of me.' He bowed his head. 'Very well. I see the wisdom in your words. I will care for your son as you have cared for my daughter, if that is truly what you desire.'

'Thank you.' Impulsively Effie rose up on her tiptoes to kiss his cheek but he backed away.

'I don't allow other men's wives to kiss me.'

'I'm not yet his wife and I only meant it as a sign of friendship and gratitude.'

'You're as good as,' Lachlan said. He called Morna and she came out of the hut, fully dressed, with her hair combed and as tangle-free as it ever was.

'The tide will be coming in soon and the light is fading. You should go. Morna and I will leave at dusk two days from now. If you still want Jack to go with us, bring him when you bring Morna here.'

He went inside the hut and closed the door. Effie leaned against the rocks. Her heart had never been so heavy.

She was making the right decision for Jack and Morna. The right decision for Walter, even. But what if the decision was wrong for herself?

Chapter Thirty

Midwinter's Day arrived cold and overcast. Wind rushed along the length of the beach, tearing at the piles of seaweed that littered the foam-flecked shingle, creating white horses that leaped out to sea. Colder and rougher than the day six years previously when Effie heard a cry, saw a basket, and stepped into the water, changing her life forever.

What would her life have been like had she not pulled the basket and babe from the water? Would Lachlan or his folk have found Morna themselves? What if she had not refused to surrender the child when Lachlan appeared at her door a year later? She could drive herself insane by imagining the different possibilities.

Morna and Jack ran around the cottage in excitement for the duration of the morning while Effie packed a case with clothes and favourite toys for the two children. She had not changed her mind and was determined that Jack would have his carefree life beside the sister he loved.

It was only when Morna ceased her game and investigated the pile that Effie was gathering that a problem arose.

'That's for summer,' she remarked, pulling a green dress out of the pile. 'I won't need that. And you've packed all my books and Jack's straw hat.'

She looked at Effie suspiciously. 'Mama, how long am I going for?'

'I don't know,' Effie admitted. 'But your dada will take care of you and Jack and we both love you very much.'

The answer was clearly not to Morna's satisfaction because tears welled in her eyes and she stamped her foot. 'I don't want to go. I won't leave you. I don't want Dada to leave you. You belong to us.'

She was still inconsolable by mid-afternoon when someone knocked on the door. Effie opened it quickly, hoping to see Lachlan but it was Walter. He was bundled up in a heavy coat with a silk scarf knotted at his throat. Morna ran off into the bedroom and slammed the door, which Effie considered a blessing.

'I know your foster child is leaving today. I imagine you will be sad to see her go, so I would like to invite you and Jack to walk with me once you have said your goodbyes. What time are they departing? I would like to come and bid them farewell myself.'

Effie smiled at him. He had been instrumental in making it possible for Morna to live with Effie. His kindness was touching, but the things she wanted to say to Lachlan on their parting were not for the ears of her fiancé. She had not told him about Jack and that news could wait until after the deed was done.

'Thank you, Walter, that's very kind. I would rather say goodbye alone, but I will join you for a walk. I shall meet you at the top of the hill at the crossroads just after dusk.'

He agreed and bade Morna farewell.

By the time Effie and the children set off along the beach to Boggle Cove, Morna was inconsolable again. Lachlan greeted her arrival and the floods of tears with astonishment.

'She has realised we were not truthful about how long she would be gone,' Effie whispered to him.

He winced. 'I'm sorry, that must have been trying for you.' He took the case from Effie and put it in front of the hut beside a wooden crate. He came back to Effie and held his hand out. 'Morna, you need to be sensible. You can't stay with Effie any longer. Her life will be different and yours will too. Jack is coming with us.'

Morna just shook her head and thrust her hands behind her back. Effie knelt down.

'Morna, you have to go with Dada. It's very important. Would you like me to tell you a story?'

Morna stopped crying and nodded reluctantly. Effie cleared her throat.

There was once a seal child who became lost at sea. Her mother and father and all the people of her clan searched everywhere, for they feared she had been taken. The whole clan grieved for their loss. But the child had not been taken. She had been found by a woman whose heart had room to spare for her.

She stopped and blinked furiously to clear her eyes that were brimming with tears of her own. Lachlan stepped to Effie's side and rested his hand lightly on her shoulder. His touch gave her the strength she needed to continue her tale.

The woman took the seal child's skin and kept it safe, not knowing how powerful it was. One night a stranger appeared who claimed the child as his own, but the woman did not wish to lose the girl she had come to think of as her daughter. The stranger knew the child was safe with the woman and he agreed because the bond between mother and foster-daughter was too strong to ever break.

'You may keep my child for now, but when she's grown I will return for her, for she is a daughter of my clan and that is her rightful place.'

One day the seal child's father returned and showed his daughter the power of her skin. The child knew straight away that was where she belonged, so like many seal maidens before and many that would come after, she took the cloak of her own skin and returned to where she belonged.

Morna sniffed and stroked her skin, which was wrapped snugly around her shoulders. Lachlan's hand tightened on Effie's shoulder, a reassuring pressure that made her body quiver. Effie kissed Morna's forehead.

'That's not the end of the story because the seal child had a life to live, but you'll have to discover the rest for yourself. Now it's time for you to go with Dada.'

Lachlan took Morna by the hand. 'Let me show you the boat while Effie talks to Jack.'

He led her away to the shore. His boat was ready on the shingle for the tide to catch it and now had a tarpaulin stretched over a frame to give protection from the elements. Effie drew Jack to her and held him tight, pressing her whole body against his.

'Jack, you will be happy with Morna and Lachlan. There will be birds and fish to draw. I love you so dearly, my darling boy.'

She had no idea if Jack comprehended what she was doing or why. He wrapped his arms around her and rubbed his face briefly against her skirts, then he wriggled free and ambled to where Morna was inspecting the boat. There would be no electricity to heal or hurt him, on Skailwick. No institutions to hold him. Her heart was shielded from the sorrow she felt by the sense of relief.

Lachlan walked back to Effie. As always he moved with grace, his long limbs and slender frame in harmony with his surroundings.

'When will you leave?' she asked.

He stared out to sea, studying the waves or the wind.

'Another half hour, perhaps. The tide will be right. I think the water is calmer further out than it is close to the shore. We'll be safe from the rocks.'

'Good.' Effie shifted her weight from foot to foot, unsure of what to say or do. There was a gap of a foot or two between them, but it might as well have been an ocean. Lachlan took Effie's hands and pressed them to his heart. He looked deep into her eyes. The black depths surrounded her, obliterating the world.

'You have raised my daughter to be strong and kind, and you have given me some of the greatest joy I have ever known. I wish our time together didn't have to come to an end but I will always treasure the memories I have of you.'

He ran his fingers through her hair. 'Gold and sunlight. I'll see it when I dream.'

Effie put her hand to his cheek. 'I wish...' she began.

He covered her hand, clasping it tightly for a minute, then removed it and placed it by her side.

'Don't wish. Don't give me any reason to carry you away with me now.'

He turned away and put his hands to his face. When he turned back his eyes were sparkling bright and black.

'Let this be another story like the ones I've told you before. A tale of the seal man who loved a human woman but couldn't keep her. Not all stories have a happy ending.'

'You love me?'

Lachlan raised his brows in astonishment. 'Aye, I do. Did you doubt it?'

'You've never said it.'

He reached out a hand and brushed her cheek with his fingertips.

'I thought I had shown it.'

Then they were kissing. It was not a kiss of passion or lust, but a slow, measured acknowledgement that the love they felt for each other ran deeper than any sea. Their lips moved in farewells that could never be spoken with words alone.

She savoured the taste of him, the scent, the hot, sweet softness of his mouth with the pressure of his lips on hers and committed it to memory. A gleaming moment in the darkness she could take out whenever she wanted. His hand found hers and their fingers intertwined. He clenched it tightly as if he intended never to let go. His lips grew still, pressing into Effie's until she felt that her own would always bear the imprint of his touch. It didn't matter that she was engaged to someone else, or that their children were standing observing what they did. This lingering goodbye was for them alone.

Effie tasted salt and realised she was crying. When finally they drew apart and she opened her eyes, she saw that Lachlan's eyes were rimmed with red, lashes glistening and the pupils black. The saltwater had not been from her eyes alone.

Stumbling slightly over the uneven rocks, she gave the children a final, brave smile then turned and walked away.

Walter was waiting at the top of the hill, pacing back and forth in a slightly agitated manner. Effie had returned to the cottage and washed her face, dressed her hair in a high knot and applied a dab of rosemary and lavender water to her temples before joining him. She was able to summon a smile for him.

'My mother has invited you to call on her. I know the hour is late, but will you come?'

He did not mention Morna's departure or ask where Jack was, and Effie was glad of it. If she had to speak of what had passed, she would crumble and weep. She agreed and Walter linked her arm through his. They walked along the path towards Walter's home. It was colder up on the cliff top than in the shelter of Boggle Cove and Effie wished he would perhaps put his arm around her to warm her, but it didn't seem to occur to him.

'You are very indifferent this evening, Effie.'

'I'm sorry, Walter, for not being more animated. I'm just still sad about Morna leaving and I am being self-indulgent.'

Walter wrinkled his brow.

'Morna is going with her father to where she belongs. And from what I gather, her father has given his assurance that he will bring her once a year so that you might see her. She isn't your flesh and blood so the loss cannot be too great.'

'Flesh and blood are not everything,' Effie whispered.

But Walter was not a father and could not possibly comprehend the attachment.

'Jack is my flesh and blood,' Effie murmured. 'I've sent him away with Lachlan to live.'

'Why? Effie, you had no need to do that. I would have found him the best asylum with fine wardens. There are many fine institutions within a day or two's travel.'

Effie's skin prickled. The wind whipped around her, clutching at her hat and the hem of her skirt.

'Because I don't want him in an asylum, no matter how

fine. I would rather he was free and wild than enclosed and guarded. I would rather he had stayed with me.' She turned to him and lifted her eyes in entreaty. It might not be too late to change his mind. 'Walter, are you sure there would not be the space for him and a nursemaid in Beacon House? There are so many rooms. If Jack needs care why should it not be given in my home as I always have done?'

Walter sighed and there was a note of exasperation that the wind carried away from him. It made Effie start in surprise.

'Your time will be busy enough. We have great plans to expand the village, don't we?' He stopped walking, taking her hands between his and pressing them tightly.

'I hope one of our plans involves populating those empty rooms with children of our own. Your grief will diminish as we welcome our own family. And with all God's blessings on our side our children will not be afflicted as Jack has been. I trust that when you are my wife you will have no need to exert yourself to the extent you did which brought on his premature birth.'

Effie looked at him in surprise. He did not know the truth. Or he had ignored it. If he truly believed Jack was a seven-month baby, he was attributing Jack's affliction to his gestation. Whereas Effie could not rightly say that any future children would not also carry those traits which made her son such an oddity.

Walter rummaged in his coat pocket and faced Effie.

'I know we are not announcing our engagement for the time being, however I have something I would like to give you.'

He pulled out a small box and pressed it into Effie's hands.

'I was going to wait until we were in the company of my

parents but I can see you need something to distract your thoughts. Open it,' he said eagerly.

Effie obeyed. Her breath caught in her throat. Nestled in claret-coloured silk was a ring: a thin band of gold with a square diamond clutched in the clawed setting. She looked up at Walter. He smiled widely.

'Even if you don't want to wear it in public I thought you could wear it when we are together or you are at home. I would like to show it to my mother and father this evening. Here, let me help you.'

He plucked the ring from the box, took Effie's left hand and slid it onto her third finger. It was a perfect fit.

'Do you like it?' Walter asked.

'It's beautiful.' John had never given her an engagement ring. They had barely had an engagement worth speaking of before they hastily took their marriage vows.

She lifted her hand. The sharp edges of the diamond glinted in the last rays of sunlight. It looked wrong on her hand though. Her fingers were too rough and raw. This was a ring for a lady who had never worked, not a woman who scrubbed her own floors and wrung out linens weekly. Walter did not truly understand who Effie was and never would.

The veil that she had woven to cover her true emotions ripped, leaving her sight free, and in that moment three things became abundantly clear.

Firstly, she did not want any more children beyond the two she had just sent away. Secondly, she did not want rings or elaborate houses, not even with Walter. Thirdly, and most crucially, the man she loved was preparing to sail away without her. Might have left already.

She lifted her chin. 'Walter, Jack was not an early baby. John and I made him before we were married. He's why we got married.'

She watched as her words sank in and Walter's face changed to an expression of dismay.

'Did you really not know that?' she asked. He really was such an innocent.

'I knew the rumours, but I didn't believe them. I have always been your staunchest defender.' He gripped her hands, uncomfortably tightly. 'Are you telling me those rumours are true? That I have defended your scandal and called others out for slandering you?'

His expression was disapproving.

'I never asked you to,' Effie protested. 'I thought you knew.'

He dropped his head. 'I am a fool.'

Effie wriggled her fingers to loosen Walter's grip and pressed his hands. 'You're not a fool. You are a good man, honourable and upright. That you believed me to be better than I was is the greatest compliment you could pay me. But I am not the innocent woman you believe me to be. And I realise now what I have known for a long time. I should not be your wife. I am too forthright. Too passionate. Too wild. I would make you unhappy.'

'But I love you,' Walter said.

Effie slipped her hands free from his grip and put one to his cheek. 'You do now, but how long before I disappoint you or embarrass you and your love turns to misery? When I continue to walk along the shore in clogs with my hair loose? When I teach our children to swim, or tell them tales of wild sea creatures? When I stare at the sea and yearn for something I can't name?'

'I can name it. The thing you yearn for,' Walter said quietly.

'It's him, isn't it? Lachlan. You look at him in a way you never have looked at me. I've tried to pretend I was imagining it, but I wasn't.'

His words stuck a knife in her breast. His expression twisted it. She couldn't deny it when faced with such honesty. She slipped the ring from her finger and put it into his palm. He closed his fingers over it.

'I release you from our engagement and I truly hope one day you find a woman worthy enough to be your wife and give you the happiness you deserve.'

She turned away.

'Where are you going?' Walter asked. He caught her by the wrist.

'They are leaving soon. I have to go with them.'

'To live on an island in the wilds? That's really the life you would prefer?' he asked incredulously.

Effie nodded. She looked at his hand. 'Please. Let me go.'

For one awful moment she didn't think he was going to, and that she would have to physically pull herself free, but Walter slowly unclenched his fingers and stepped back.

'Thank you,' Effie murmured. 'Thank you, my dear, dear friend.'

Without any further hesitation and without looking back, she picked up her skirts and began to run towards the village.

Chapter Thirty-One

E ffie didn't pause to catch her breath until the cliff path met the road at the top of the village. Dusk had crept up stealthily and the sea was dark. In the shadows of clouds she could see a glow on the water and the triangle of a sail, pitching over the shallows from Boggle Cove.

Lachlan had already left. She was too late.

She drew a breath and screamed his name, even though she knew he would never hear it. A group of men who were heading to the Whaler's Arms pub turned at the sound of her scream. She ignored them all and ran down Harbour Hill, through the village.

She reached the harbour-front in time to see Lachlan's boat dipping up and down on the water with a small lantern rising and falling. He was following the line of the beach and would become parallel with the harbour soon. She yelled again, hoping that from this close he would hear but the wind swept inland, buffeting her and throwing her voice back at her.

As she stood in despair, fortune favoured her. The wind gusted then fell still and Lachlan's sail hung loosely. The gentle breeze would not be enough to carry him far out. He could row, but that gave her a wild idea. She ran down to the wooden jetty where rowing boats were neatly tied up along the front. Within the curved harbour wall the sea was calm, but beyond its treacherous waters foamed white and grey.

Effie untied the nearest boat and clambered in. There was a cry of indignation from the owner. Desperation made a thief of her.

'I'll bring it back, Edgar,' she shouted to the owner. 'I have to reach Lachlan.'

If she was lucky she would be able to intercept Lachlan beyond the harbour. She scrambled for the oars and began to heave on them, out of time at first but then she got the rhythm. She could hear people on the harbour calling her name; crying that she was mad or a fool. That it was certain death. She didn't care.

Outside the harbour wall the waves grew immediately fierce, forcing her small craft backwards. She feared she would be crushed against the stones designed to protect the town from the sea's ferocity, but, little by little, she managed to pull further out. The wind was picking up and her fingers burned with cold, making holding onto the oars an endurance of agony, but she could see Lachlan's boat making its steady way along the line of the coast.

At any moment the wind could pick up and catch the sail and they would be lost to her. She pulled on the oars once, twice, three times. On the fourth stroke she drew a breath and screamed his name. His hearing was better than anyone she knew. Surely some faint trace of her voice might reach him. She had no light to signal him by, not even the smallest lantern.

Again, she pulled three more strokes and cried his name on the fourth. The wind circled out from the harbour to the sea, as an outgoing wave pushed her further away from safety with a dizzying lurch. It carried her cry on the wind towards him but it also caught his sail.

The small lantern on Lachlan's boat dipped up and down and gave a sudden turn as it gained momentum. Effie's eyes blurred and she howled in frustration. She was losing him.

Then a sound reached her ears that gave her hope. Not Lachlan's voice but Morna's, calling to her mama. She pulled the oars in and knelt up, waving her arms. She screamed Morna's name, then Jack's and then Lachlan's until her throat was raw.

The clouds parted for just a moment and the quarter moon illuminated the sea and the figures on it. The tallest figure was standing at the prow of the boat. Effie called his name with all the volume she could muster and scrambled upright. Her small vessel tipped precariously and she spread her feet wide to balance as she waved her arms.

She heard a cry that might have been her name. He knew she was there. She gave a sob of relief and in her triumph she never saw the wave that caught her boat. Never felt the gust of wind that dragged at her skirt. She was barely aware of the violent tilting that sent her lurching forward, tumbling with her arms flailing and plunging into the sea.

The water closed over her. So cold. Her limbs stiffened and her chest tightened so violently she was unable to fight her way upwards. Her skirts had become tangled around her legs and it was almost impossible to kick effectively.

This was not like swimming with Lachlan where her lightweight shift had floated and sunlight had made the water clear. The wool skirt was her enemy and she was in a world of ink. She thrashed her arms and felt pain as she knocked against something hard. The boat was above her. She had the notion that if she could grasp it she might be able to pull herself up to the surface, but as her fingers scrabbled all she felt was smooth wood with no chance of gaining purchase.

Her lungs were screaming for air and before too long she would have to obey their command to open her mouth and admit water and death.

She gave a kick and her foot collided with something. Had she somehow turned upside down and was now kicking against the boat, sending herself further into the depths?

Whatever it was brushed against her leg, then she felt herself lifted, suspended on a pillow of sorts and carried to the surface. Her head emerged and she opened her mouth to gasp in the life-giving air. Something – some*one* – was beneath her, conveying her to safety. Her strength ebbed away and she closed her eyes, knowing that whatever happened now was out of her control.

When she next opened her eyes she was lying in the bottom of a boat. Morna was kneeling at her side, holding her hand. Jack sat beside her. Someone had removed her wet skirt and covered her with something warm and soft. She was wrapped in fur.

Lachlan's fur.

'Dada, she's awake.'

Lachlan appeared at Effie's other side. His shirt was open, and his chest and hair were wet. His face creased with relief. He pulled Effie into his arms, burying his face against her neck. She tried to wrap her arms around him but she felt weak from her ordeal and had to be content with clinging to his collar.

'You saved me.'

'Despite your best efforts to drown yourself! What were you thinking?'

'That I had to reach you. I have broken off my engagement

to Walter. I should never have accepted him. I want to come with you. I want you. All of you.'

She pushed herself upright and gazed around at the boat's three occupants. Lachlan held her at arm's length and gave her a serious look. 'D'you mean that?'

'I do. I choose a happy ending.'

Lachlan's face broke into a smile. He reached a hand to her face and caressed her cheek. Effie leaned into his open palm. She reached for his skin, which was still around her shoulders, to hand it to him, but he stayed her hand.

'I give it to you for keeping, Effie. My whole self. Will you accept it, and all that goes with it?'

Effie knelt up and put her arms around him. No diamonds could compare to the euphoria she felt at what he was giving her. Morna wriggled between them into the embrace, pulling Jack with her until all four of them were holding each other and laughing through tears.

Her family.

'We should go back to shore before the waves become too fierce,' Lachlan decided. 'I'm guessing you didn't think to pack before you hurled yourself into the sea?'

'There's nothing I want besides what is in this boat,' Effie declared, squeezing his hand tightly.

Lachlan's eyes crinkled. 'That's not quite true, I suspect, romantic as it sounds.'

'A few things perhaps,' Effie agreed. 'But we've left now.'

Lachlan put his arms around her and turned her to face the shore. The lights of Allendale Head glinted in clusters around the harbour and further up the winding hill. Somewhere on the top of the cliff Walter would be breaking the news to his parents. They would console him and assure him that being jilted by the scandalous, strange widow was a lucky escape.

'We're not too far away. Setting out in this weather and at this time of night was foolhardy, but I couldna' bear to stay any longer knowing you were going to Walter. We'll return to your cottage for tonight. If you truly want to come with me we'll leave at first light.'

'I will,' Effie assured him. 'I know what I want and what I should have recognised a long time ago.'

Lachlan grinned. 'In that case, Mrs Cropton, pick up that lantern and guide us to shore.'

Dawn had barely broken when four figures, warmly wrapped in cloaks and coats, stood in the doorway of Effie's cottage. Effie had decided she needed a few things after all: her paints and brushes, the clothes that were not mourning wear, the patchwork bedspread, two favourite knives and Alice's books.

And safely stowed inside a folded handkerchief embroidered with John Cropton's initials, Lachlan's pearls.

She locked the front door and left the key in the lock. Someone would discover it eventually. She wondered fleetingly who the next occupants would be. Whether their lives there would be as eventful as hers had been.

'Are you sure you don't want to leave a note?' Lachlan asked.

'No. I'll write to Mary at her aunt's address at some point. I said everything I wanted to Walter last night. There's no one else here I want to tell.'

She picked up one bag, Lachlan took the other and, side by side, with their children following, they walked to the waiting boat, leaving Allendale Head for the last time.

Epilogue

I n the far north, where the daylight lasts until the evening is old, Jack and Effie waited at the sea's edge. The tide swelled as the moon grew large, and presently two lithe figures slid from the waves onto the land. They gave a shrug and a shiver, and between two heartbeats, a man and a young woman stood there.

Even though she had seen it a hundred times, Effie had never grown tired of watching her lover and daughter transform between states.

Jack pulled free from his mother's hand and ran, squealing and waving, to greet his sister. Together they ran along the shingle, chasing and racing, skipping through the foam. He was tall now at twenty, yet still retained his childlike manner. He could easily outrun Morna if he chose to, but he never did.

Further along the beach, three more figures were walking from the water, throwing their skins about their naked forms. Effie waved to them as she waited for Lachlan to reach her, his lean frame stepping lightly across the white sand. With open arms she received the two skins he offered and stowed them in a basket at her side, exchanging them for a cloak of heavy wool.

'Your skin is starting to show grey,' she teased, reaching up to brush a hand across the side of his temple where a trace had begun to show in his hair too.

'Aye, but I'm still handsome,' he said.

He threw the woollen cloak over his shoulders, and before the cloth had settled around him, he drew Effie under the cloak, into his arms and into a kiss, deep and true and passionate enough to bridge worlds.

The seal folk gathered together that night under the New Year's Eve stars to celebrate the turning of the century, members of the clan coming from all over Skailwick and beyond. Morna sat with a lad her own age who was visiting from across the sea. They had their heads together as they whispered. Effie wondered if there would be a handfasting in the not-too-distant future.

Firtha called for a story and hush settled over the gathering.

'Lachlan, let's hear one of yours,' called Seathan, a broad-shouldered man with grey hair who resembled his brother enough for the relationship to be apparent.

After a pause to look at Effie, nestled beside him against the cold, Lachlan cleared his throat and began to speak his tale.

There was once a seal man who loved a human woman. He thought for a time he had lost her, but she chose to leave her life among her own folk and go with him. He gave her his skin as a sign of his love and faithfulness, and she displayed it openly in their bedroom, as a sign of hers.

He broke off to kiss Effie before continuing.

Not all stories have a happy ending, but this one does.

Author's Note

This story began life as a writing contest prompt of 'The Girl from the Sea' for the Romantic Novelist's Association annual conference in 2018. It is a measure of how little I expected to win that I didn't even have my shoes on under the table when they announced my name!

Thank you to the judges involved in choosing it as the winner of the Elizabeth Goudge Trophy, and everyone who encouraged me to take the story further, and especially my brilliant editor Julia at Harlequin Mills & Boon who put me in touch with the equally brilliant Charlotte at One More Chapter.

Allendale Head is based on Robin Hood's Bay and Runswick Bay on the North Yorkshire coast. These are some of the places from my childhood beach trips, along with Whitby, which gets a mention and is home to the best fish and chips bar none. I strongly encourage everyone to visit if you get the chance. At low tide you can walk along the beach from Robin Hood's bay, past Boggle Hole to Ravenscar. There you will find a clifftop hotel that was once a private residence, along with a layout of roads, sewers and foundations for a town that was never developed, and which gave me the inspiration for Walter's grand scheme.

As a Yorkshire lass now uprooted to Cheshire it was wonderful to have an excuse to visit the area again to soak up the atmosphere (and the rain). Apologies to my kids for dragging them out in torrential rain over a late September weekend while we grabbed a non-Lockdown trip, but everyone must suffer for my art!

I did buy them chips afterwards.

YOUR NUMBER ONE STOP

ONE MORE CHAPTER

FOR PAGETURNING BOOKS

One More Chapter is an
award-winning global
division of HarperCollins.

Sign up to our newsletter to get our
latest eBook deals and stay up to date
with our weekly Book Club!
<u>Subscribe here.</u>

Meet the team at
<u>www.onemorechapter.com</u>

Follow us!

 <u>@OneMoreChapter_</u>
 <u>@OneMoreChapter</u>
 <u>@onemorechapterhc</u>

Do you write unputdownable fiction?
We love to hear from new voices.
Find out how to submit your novel at
<u>www.onemorechapter.com/submissions</u>